.I 368
F7

The idea of the company was a source of strength but as people started falling away one by one, the idea seemed increasingly fragile. Of course we were always picking up strays, new faces, but at the cost of someone familiar and therefore precious. With each such loss, we lost a little more of our will for anything but release from the endlessly benign violence. (Benign? After all, we weren't being hurt.)

The only consistent thing that year, the only truth about that place, was change. The rest—our desire for predictability, stability—was illusion, dream.

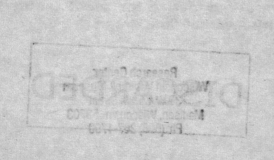

ROB RIGGAN

FREE FIRE ZONE

FAWCETT CREST • NEW YORK

For Margalee

Only when the milkrun passed,
*   moaning high,*
did I flee on that
*   loon cry:*
far up the river,
far away in time where
silent woodlands, dark beneath the moon,
tore my heart with
*   brittle fingers.*

When we leave to go home, we receive a memento, a yearbook entitled *TOUR 365*.

There's a letter at the beginning of the yearbook telling us what a good job we've done, wishing us luck in the future. It's signed by our principal, Creighton W. Abrams.

The book contains a history and loads of color photographs. Little cartoon-like cherubim wearing Army helmets dot the pages, adding humor and a sense of youthful nostalgia. There's a map showing the big operation of our year, and a scoreboard listing our victories as measured by the annual statistics:

ENEMY KILLED—152,387
HOI CHANHS—9,272
VIETNAMESE ABDUCTED—6,672
VIETNAMESE REFUGEES—1,180,491
CIVILIANS ASSASSINATED—4,234
TERRORIST INCIDENTS—7,387
ARVN CASUALTIES:
    Killed—18,230
    Wounded—43,081
U.S. MILITARY CASUALTIES:
    Killed—Army 6,607, U.S. 10,503
    Wounded—Army 49,202, U.S. 78,493

Frank T. Mildren, Lieutenant General, U.S. Army, tells us in the afterword that our families and friends are proud of us and that with us "goes a world of knowledge and impressions based on the experiences you have had in Vietnam."

ONE

I met Casey in a bar in the town downriver where I live. She was with some guy in bib overalls with long hair and a deep tan, as though he seldom wore clothes at all. She was bored so I picked her up.

Casey's nineteen, almost four years younger than I am, and she works as a clerk typist somewhere across the river in New Jersey. She's a small person. Her head reaches only to my chin. Light brown hair hangs loosely to her shoulders. She's only just pretty; her hips are too low-slung, her face is almost nondescript.

But her eyes are blue, her lips full and a bit sullen, her mouth vibrant, incredibly supple. Her legs are pretty and her breasts are large, the nipples and rosettes very large and I find this exciting. They remind me of the breasts of the women in the soft porn magazines where the photographs are black and white, nonglossy.

I knelt on this bed with her and sweated gently, not violently the way I did for an entire year. Drops of sweat rolled off my forehead and moustache, slid through the hairs on my chest and down my belly. The sides of her calves pressed against my neck. I leaned forward in the semidarkness, pushed her legs toward her face with my shoulders. The lips of her mouth were soft, but I couldn't smell her; there wasn't time.

Only once before had I set out without pretense to seduce a woman, to touch someone this way out of sheer desperation, to feel life this way whether the person wanted to be touched or not. There's nothing irresistible about me, but determination has its own attraction. That first time was utterly spontaneous and uncontrived. Tonight, it was remarkably easy but not unpremeditated.

And only once during the past year was my physical need so great that an erection was painful; this was another such time. I became so large my skin was stretched almost beyond endurance. Casey's fluid heat was only a surface balm around a deeper pain that radiated from my groin and made me dizzy. If at first I tried to please her, I quickly became overwhelmed by my own sensations and needs, by the sounds and smells, the wet nakedness, my vision of myself: a ghostly figure on a moonlit bed, every muscle and tendon pulled from my extremities into her. At the same time I seemed to be watching myself as in a movie. I was remote from and disdainful of what I was doing.

Then Casey reached around herself and rammed her fingertips into my inner thighs, making me moan, forcing me higher on my knees. I cried and spewed into her.

"I have to go to sleep now," she said, four or five minutes later—no longer. "I have to get up at 6:30 and go to work." Her voice was flat. There had been only perfunctory endearments.

Her hand rested across my body, fondled my limp though still swollen penis. All my body was drenched with heat. I could see the vague whiteness of her skin and mine. A breeze rustled the trees beyond the single window of this attic room. Below, the river washed gently against its bank. There was a shrill bird-cry somewhere across the road, somewhere in the nearby woods that climb the steep cliffs out of the river valley. I scarcely heard the sounds of birds for an entire year.

"Listen," she said. "I really have to get up in a few hours and go to work."

"Sure, I understand." I felt as though I were speaking with my hands pressed against my ears.

"So why don't you go, now? It's been nice." She tapped my belly with her fingers, a gesture I found intensely annoying.

Then my words came, were out before I could call them back. "No, I can't go! I have to stay here tonight."

She sighed heavily. "Lookit. My supervisor's been on my ass all week. If I'm tired and screw up, I could lose my job."

"I won't bother you." It was a lie, but I didn't care. All that mattered tonight was this need to be where I am, beside her in this house along the river. How do you tell someone you need their privacy?

I can hear diesels whining through the woods, northward, black like the night. For almost six months, I've lived across the river from these same tracks, but until tonight, I never knew the trains were so frequent. I didn't hear them. In the daytime, one doesn't hear sounds so much. It's easier to hide in the day. The train whistles, a drawn-out sound this time, more of a wail. The last train tooted in a conversational manner. Each one's been different, every driver making his own appeal to the darkness.

Casey put her back to me, but soon her abrupt silence became the deeper rhythms of sleep. I lay thinking of nothing but the empty space between us. Then, still in her sleep, she rolled onto her back, up beside me, just touching me, and I haven't moved for the longest time since.

She begins to snore and that's making me tense, but I don't want to touch her and tell her so. Pleasure is a cautious breath. There's terrible pain if you breathe too deeply. At least now I can feel the heat of her body. Later, I want to put myself back inside her. I wish I could sleep, but the trains keep coming with their questions and answers that echo up and down the river.

I used to lie awake like this in the plantation, only I wore undershorts then—I didn't dare sleep naked. Self-arousal can be an obsessive and terrifying experience when there's nothing else. The darkness wasn't fragrant like the June night here. Nor were the night sounds gentle: they were deafening. Screeches, chirps, whines I couldn't identify even after many months. There were all kinds of bugs. There were three-inch crickets, huge rhinoceros beetles . . . and centipedes.

One of the doctors had a pair of centipedes that a patient brought him. They lived in a six-foot glass case with a screen top. Inside there was a large branch of a tree. The centipedes lay in semidarkness among the leaves and debris on the floor —one was over a foot long and about three inches wide, the other slightly smaller. Despite their size, I had to strain to see them. I was astonished by their beauty, the blues and yellows, and multitude of shadings. I was terrified by them, by their huge fangs. The doctor delighted in their predaceous habits, feeding them live insects that he gathered at night.

The centipedes seldom seemed to move: they just lay on the floor of the case. The doctor loved to watch them react when he put other creatures in with them. He would say "interact." He also kept and fed giant praying mantises that moved to kill

3

*with astonishing speed. He loved to see if the males would
escape their coital peril as well as the centipedes. The doctor's
name was Shelby and he called his glass case The Circus
Maximus. He would talk about taking his specimens home
with him. He'd explain how he'd first inject them with zylo-
caine, then preserve them. "Painless," he'd always say.*

*One of the men transferred to us from the Demilitarized
Zone told me about treating a marine whose helmet had
struck the roof of a Viet Cong tunnel and torn open a nest of
centipedes. More than a dozen of them poured out of the
ceiling, over his face and body, stung him again and again in
that close, scrabbling darkness. Afterward, he went mad.*

*In all those miles, in all that torn, beautiful land, there was
no place to go. You didn't go into dark places. You just didn't
go into dark places if it could be avoided. And yet I arrived in
the darkness, over 30,000 feet in the air . . .* Lights like
fires glowed out of the night below us and vanished. We
might have been over Gary, Indiana, if the plane's captain
hadn't insisted otherwise in a flat, indisputable tone. Stewardesses with polished legs and miniskirts took our pillows away
from us. As we trooped out the door into a vast, bearingless
darkness, the stewardesses said, "Good luck! See you in 365
days." We had a bearing then.

Suddenly we're running through a maze of stacked fifty-five
gallon drums, NCOs shouting at us to "Run, run, run!" The
tail of the DC-8 that brought us glows a soft, eerie white as it
towers above us.

We burst into a huge, steel shed with glaring lights. A
mass of soldiers, homeward-bound on our plane, mill around
in a roped-off area grinning at us. I have no sense of how I
got from the plane to the shed.

We're ordered to take seats in rows of hard chairs so a
Puerto Rican staff sergeant with a whisper-thin lifer's moustache and a huge barrel chest can harangue us about the bad
things we better not have brought into the country, such as
hunting knives, switchblades, brass knuckles, U.S. currency,
drugs. They're going to let us voluntarily surrender these
items without "fear of recrimination" even though they seem
to know the offer will be refused.

"What are they going to do if we don't?" someone murmurs. "Send us to Vietnam?" I laugh with everyone else, a
bitter edge to the sound.

The veterans with their one year of war disappear in the

night, into that expanse from which they will suddenly awaken and find themselves home. There are no bridges between this place and The World. *I said "The World." Those words, capitalized, mean Home, the USA, as though there, where we were, was something unreal. "I'm going back to The World, man!" Like everything's going to be alright.*

They load us onto buses. The windows are covered with wire mesh to protect us from hurled objects. Beyond the diamond screening I watch the first day break. Dawn silhouettes a ruined stone observation tower and the broken shafts of concrete utility poles. The landscape that unfolds with the rising sun is a snarl of barbed wire and shattered trees.

We roar through a large town. Among the buildings of substance are hovels of plywood and tin. There's a freshness and vibrancy to the early morning streets with their crammed stalls and shops. People have begun to appear, to zap by on scooters and pile into curious three-wheeled minibuses called lambros that bob in and out of the burgeoning traffic. Everything's diminutive: the people, their transportation, their soldiers. We bump over a railroad track and I glance down its narrow, littered length. In the shadows, an old man sleeps in a chrome and vinyl chair inches from the track where a baby crawls between the rails.

We swing briefly onto a four lane paved highway, then into the replacement center—exposed, wooden, barrackslike buildings that cling behind barbed wire to stripped hills where a jungle once flourished. I'm reminded of a concentration camp although the land's been peeled, the fences built to keep away the enemy: rationally, I know this. I just can't feel it.

. . . *and even days later, many miles from the replacement center, when I boarded a small air force transport that would lift me out of a parched base camp in a remote plain, headquarters for my new battalion, to carry me up country another forty or fifty miles to my company, the feeling of oppression remained. I stood at the end of a long, empty runway, the glare burning my eyes, surrounded by dust, miles of barbed wire, acres of single-storey, dirt-colored buildings with metal roofs that gleamed in the sun, and nowhere in sight within the protective confines was there a tree.*

In the plane, my cheek pressed to the glass of one of the few windows, I gaze through an empty, bright sea toward red gashes in a landscape that is at one moment lush, then inexplicably barren. Tiny dark objects scuttle over these red tears, casting small clouds. Overhead, the port wing dips and the window falls away disclosing a verdant circle surrounded by acres of raw earth. A wide swath, consisting of a landing strip and highway, splits this green island. The highway vanishes into the hazy jungle in one direction, transverses acres of rice paddies toward a distant village in the other.

The wing rises and I shield my eyes from the sun. We sit webbed to the fuselage, facing each other across the aisle, about forty of us within the shadowy compartment. Our glances meet and avert as we watch the dusty light roll across the floor.

I find myself staring across the aisle at a heavy face with two thick eyebrows and a tangled shock of hair. There's something inherently agreeable about the burly, coarse features, a gruff kindness. On one lapel of the man's fatigues is a caduceus, on the other, captain's bars. The name "Brock" is printed in black letters above the right-hand pocket.

Beside him, looking out my window, sits a master sergeant, "Smith" on his nametag. He's dark-haired and strikingly clean-shaven and neat. He catches my eye, nods and smiles as though confirming Brock's appeal, not his own. We start to drift downward, the wing dipping again as we circle lower toward the plantation. I watch the mass of green become individual trees, and then I see tents and buildings, roads, vehicles, people, barbed wire. High wooden towers rise along the perimeter of what is evidently a hill. Despite the vastness of this place, the telltale machinery of an industrial world, I'm reminded of illustrations of Caesar's camps from my high school Latin books. There's that kind of rawness, a quality augmented by the ubiquitous concertina wire, its razored strands spiralling convulsively along the outer defenses.

We streak through the trees, sunlight and dust, thump and bob. The thunder of our landing fills the compartment and then the rear of the plane falls away into the lime haze of a rubber grove. I walk down the ramp behind Brock and Smith into stultifying heat. Soldiers bound for bases farther up country file out of the trees, a stream of helmets, tanned faces, clinking automatic rifles.

A line of Huey slicks shimmer down the runway, almost touching the steel surface, noses toward the ground, tails canted skyward like scorpions. The helicopters rise and curl over the treetops leaving me with an image of white faces and my own clouded fears.

A jeep arrives to collect me, Brock and Smith.

I never saw a good map there, never understood the totality even after a year. I knew Highway 10, knew that it ran, vaguely, north from Long Binh, but I'm still surprised when I locate it on a real map. It never seems to be in the right place, never conforms to where I think it was. A paper map is worthless!

. . . there's this island lodged in my memory, and a highway leading to it. The world might as well have been flat two or three miles in any direction beyond the highway, have ceased abruptly for all I knew. The helicopters that rose suddenly on the horizon were from alien worlds, shuttling back and forth from me to nowhere.

I'm at the end of a cul de sac formed on three sides by tall, columnar rubber trees and opening eastward upon the perimeter of the plantation and a guard tower, a skeletal structure with a sloping, shed-style metal roof. I can just see two men standing in the tower. The air is motionless beneath the sun, and the heat of the pavement on which I'm standing—a small square about forty feet on a side surrounded by dirt and weeds—penetrates the bottoms of my boots.

Morrisey's beside me. I've been assigned to his hooch, a large tent stretched over a wooden frame that serves as sleeping quarters. The only permanent structures in the company are the mess hall and latrines. I'm struck by his bunk area: three ammunition boxes nailed to the wall are filled with books. Gittoni and Dunn, both radio operators, also live in my hooch. It's considered a quiet tent, there are no stereo sets or televisions in it, no refrigerators.

Morrisey's about my height and weight, but he's three or four years older than I am, almost twenty-five I think, making him one of the oldest men in the company except for the doctors and NCOs. He has striking angular features and thick, curly black hair that hangs in ringlets over his brow. His skin's very fair but he doesn't look fragile. There's a strong suggestion of aloofness, even contemptuousness in his bearing. Morrisey's a college graduate, one of only two enlisted men in the company who are. The other is Jenkins, a black man and psychologist, or, as the army terms it, psychological technician—psych tech. They are friends.

The sun glints on the stainless handles of a pair of bandage scissors that protrude from Morrisey's left chest pocket. A rubber tourniquet tied through one of the loops of the handles dangles down over the bleached green material of his fatigues. My own new, dark olive fatigues still smell of the factory and I feel very self-conscious.

I hear a faint throbbing sound. The men stop talking and those who have been smoking grind out their cigarettes with their boots. Black patches of sweat have already spread across Morrisey's back and under his arms.

Major Mendez, a surgeon and our commanding officer, stands with his hands on his hips in front of the treatment tent, an imperious tilt to his chin. Beside him is Captain Brock, dressed in a sweaty green T-shirt and fatigue pants. Brock's chewing a dead cigar while he alternately scratches his belly and the bramble on his head. A white and tan dog, one of six mutts in the company, sleeps in the sun at the major's feet, its chin resting askew over an outstretched front leg.

There's a reddish hue to this world, the color of the dry earth that rises with the slightest pressure. The land reeks of oil, of burned fuel, pesticides, feces. Human waste is burned. There's another smell, one that I recognize instinctively without having encountered it before. It emanates from the hot canvas litters held by the men around me and from a large litter storage rack a few yards away.

As the throbbing intensifies, I spot two specks skimming the ground below the roof of the guard tower. The noise becomes a pounding that shatters the air. The specks turn into pinwheeling insects hurtling toward us at incredible speed. The first helicopter clatters over the wire and descends upon us, rearing back and flashing a red cross on its belly. I duck into the crook of my arm as debris blasts up against me. Then, bent over with the others, I rush the descending ship.

A door slides open. Two men, dazed, shirtless, filthy with dust, oil, and blood sit in the side compartment. To their left are three stretchers stacked one upon the other, and beside the bottom one, a fourth now being dragged into the sunshine. A medic moves me aside with a curse. The din of the helicopter's tremendous, yet I'm rooted to the pavement. The medic grabs the rear handles of the litter. It bumps against my leg. I stare down at a blackened face, the rims of the blue eyes white like a minstrel man, the eyes staring without comprehension at the blur of the rotor. A second litter is taken out and still I remain frozen in front of that door.

Someone yanks my sleeve. I turn and see Morrisey move away to help the crewchief lift the third litter off its hooks. He nods at me. When the litter's securely on the floor, he grabs the handles and starts to pull it out of the ship. I reach in, clutch the rear handles and find myself drawn away. The wash tugs at my clothing and hair, whips the loose corners of the blanket that covers the wounded man.

I see the second ship now, a gunship that has landed in the scrub and squats menacingly in a haze of dust. A machinegunner vibrates idly behind his weapon in the open doorway, watching the wounded as they're lifted down from his ship onto litters. I'm aware of harsh light as we move along the road toward the trees and the treatment tent. Morrisey's shirt is black with sweat, his neck red from the sun, the fringes of his hair dripping. I feel my own shirt slapped against my skin as though I've stepped from a downpour into a furnace. I'm in a pocket of solitude that contains only the sun, myself, the silent medic in front, and a grimy face peering over a blanket, saliva trickling from a corner of its mouth.

We lift the stretcher onto a table. There are eight tables in the treatment tent. Across the aisle from us, Major Mendez straddles the soldier with the minstrel face, pumping at his chest. The major's black hair flies, sweat streams down his cheeks. The violence is magnificent but what *good did it ever do? We were a fucking medical clearing company, twenty minutes by air from the nearest surgical hospital. Who was going to do CPR on a crammed helicopter? All we did were tracheotomies and cutdowns. We stabilized or watched them die. The major's efforts were absurd . . . only that didn't occur to me then. It seemed proper then.* The smells and heat of the tent are stifling. I feel nauseous. Morrisey gently lifts the blanket, pulls it back to reveal stumps truncated just below the knees and a mass of bloody gauze. A length of saffron bone protrudes from one of the wrappings and ends in jagged suspension above the glistening canvas. Captain Brock moves in beside me.

"Driver," Morrisey says. He explains that the engine compartment door of an armored personnel carrier is located inside the cockpit next to the driver's legs and opens against them. It blows in the same direction when a mine is struck.

Morrisey's very efficient, more so than Brock, but then

Brock is as new to this place as I am. Morrisey's been here for almost four months. He swabs for an I.V., tells me to do the same. My performance is awful. I still can't comprehend what's happening.

The major's shouting at someone holding the receiver of a field phone. "Tell commo to hold one of those ships, Davies!" He has to shout because the thunder of the idling ships has suddenly risen to a crescendo. Dust bursts through the screens of the treatment tent. Our own bedlam suddenly becomes depthless, flat, as the helicopters clatter away.

I can't find any vein! I can barely see with the sweat pouring in my eyes. The room's jammed and I can't . . . "Give me a hand, someone! I'm blowing this!"

Brock nudges me aside and tries.

Morrisey curses, then glances at me with exasperation. "I can't raise shit, either!" His eyes are like hematite, virtually black and of astonishing depth and variation. They look utterly candid. I don't believe any emotion could pass unrevealed by them.

We do a cut-down. Under the surgical light, I watch the vein appear, transformed now into an object with its own fascination, unrelated to a living creature. My absorption blots out all feeling of where I am, of time, protecting me for a moment. Brock's incredibly swift at tying it off, despite his thick hands. I'm reminded of raw chicken with the veins still there among sallow fat and flesh.

"ETA ten minutes!" somebody screams.

I hear the rising howl of a turbine, then the first chops of a rotor as it begins to spin; another ship's lifting out of the revetments. I look back. Brock's gone, moved to another table.

We're in the sunshine picking our way through stretchers on the ground where men lie waiting, silently staring into the treetops. A third medic walks with us and holds a bag of blood aloft. Another bag rests on the blanket beside the wounded man's arm. It is momentarily frosty in the heat. The rate of drip over the little blue wheel and down the translucent tube is very fast.

I remain with several others on the pad after the patients are loaded. The Huey rises a few feet, swivels one hundred and eighty degrees, lifts its tail skyward and flies away. As it hammers around the distant edge of the plantation, it rolls upward on its axis and presents its back and the full gyre of its rotor.

A stretcher is taken out of the treatment tent. I watch its passage across the yard before a crowd of spectators. Someone leans out and snaps a picture. The stretcher's carried behind the sickcall tent to a small tent in the deeper foliage of the plantation. A blanket's been pulled over the head. Mendez, Brock, and our third doctor, Captain Shelby, are all out in the yard now, moving in pantomime among those who have yet to be treated, selecting the most needy, forgetting struggles as fast as they fail or fly away. Everything seems to be forgotten the moment after its occurrence. Time is not linear but fragmented, episodic.

It's evening. The shadows are long in the mess hall but no lights are on. Beyond the screen doors and the high windows, the sun still casts its heat on the earth. There's a peculiar feeling of seclusion in the vast room with its fans vibrating overhead, the subdued murmurs of the less than half-filled hall, the clatter of dishes and babble of the Vietnamese civilians in the nearby wash house. Our mess sergeant stands at one end of the steam tables talking in a low rumble to one of the paper-hatted cooks. A second cook seems asleep on his feet. The food line is vacant. At the far end of the hall, farthest from the steam tables, laughter erupts from the officers' section, separated from the rest of the room by movable partitions. The NCOs are seated on the near side of the partitions. At the moment, there's little conversation from them; they're absorbed in eating.

I'm at a table with five other men, only one of whom I've met: Gittoni, the radio operator who sleeps in my tent. He laughs a lot and seems very much at ease in our surroundings. Two of the other men are medics from Dust-Off, the air ambulance helicopter unit with whom we share these facilities. With the exception of these two men and three crewchiefs at a nearby table, everyone else looks grubby. We're eating an hour later than usual because of the casualties. This morning, that moment of helplessness when I confronted my first shipload of wounded men, happened years ago. Everyone's clothes are soaked and stinking. We simply splashed our faces and hands at the fifty-five gallon drums in the treatment area, removed the worst of the filth. I've been told things aren't usually quite this bad, the hours, the endless sickcall and mass casualties, but even with my arrival, the company's still way under strength—sixteen men short.

On my tray there's some stringy beef, mashed potatoes, waxed beans, and lots of gravy. There's a large piece of bread and some butter, a glass of milk, a dish of cherry jello. The bread's leaden, the milk has a burned taste, the jello's rubbery. Somehow, I'm managing to eat. I'm telling myself I need it. I won't complain.

Morrisey's at the next table, behind Gittoni. There are other people with him whose faces are familiar now. Conversations and easy banter flow around me but I don't feel comfortable enough to join in. I listen and am surprised when someone addresses me. Everyone seems friendly, even solicitous, but this only makes me feel more conspicuous. There's a terrible unreality about this meal after the work I've been doing all day.

A phone rings faintly in the distance, from the direction of Dust-Off's company area. Chairs scrape behind the partition and I glimpse two officers heading for the back door. One of the medics at my table and a crewchief sitting across from Morrisey rush out, leaving their unfinished meals. Another crew left some time ago.

The whine of a jet pierces the hall as a helicopter starts to crank up. Imperceptibly, people have begun to shovel their food. Some shove their trays away and light cigarettes. A couple of men head for the coffee urn to fill their cups. I watch Morrisey check the time, then stand up and walk toward the back door to the wash house with his tray. My tray's still half-full. I try to eat faster.

A field phone on the wall behind the steam table buzzes. The mess sergeant steps back and answers it. He's an obtuse-looking person, named Milliken. "Fourteen litterbearers!" he calls out. "Three minutes out!" There's a moment of silence, then the roar of chairs.

"Fuck!" someone shouts as we run out on the road. I hear a high, shrill sound. A helicopter's just crossing the perimeter wire.

It's all in my throat and chest, the winded pain and excitement, the mass sense of desperation as my legs propel me past other men in a race for the litter racks. One part of me wants to laugh at the futility of this apprehension that drives us to our work. The meal, the relative calm of only moments ago seems like a dream.

12

A line stretches from ship to treatment tent. We're sweating freely and our stink has risen again. A GI hangs on a medic in front of me, his arm draped around the medic's neck. His T-shirt's torn. Blood dribbles from his ear. He was face down in the dirt somewhere while I was eating. His head lolls back, drops forward. The medic tightens his grasp around the man's waist. There are four of us carrying my litter. Over the rhythmic clump of boots I can hear the canvas creak.

Nothing's changed. Mendez is slicing the shirt off a man on one table, Brock's calling for an I.V., the phone's ringing. Someone hollers for twelve litterbearers—the second ship's arriving. We hoist our load onto a table. I start to run for the front door but the major shouts for two units of blood and points at me. I turn back toward the ice chest, fighting the surge of men heading outside.

"For Christ's sake!" someone cries. "Hurry the hell up!"

I yank back the lid of the chest and reach for a bag of blood. An arm thrusts in beside me, snatches a bag and disappears. I glimpse glasses and a scowling face.

"Four more litterbearers! Hurry!" a voice yells outside the tent. I drop the bags on the table and start for the door.

"You there! Start an I.V.!" the major orders. When I turn he's assumed my compliance and has become absorbed by a huge hole in the man's belly. I look around wildly for a canister of swabs. A medic on the other side of the table quietly indicates a stainless steel container, then returns to his work. I open the lid and, calmed for the moment, feel the cool, moist cotton. An I.V. kit hangs from a hook overhead, awaiting a bag of blood.

Mendez moves on to another patient. "Six priority, Davies!" he calls.

At the telephone, Davies replies, "Eight ambulatory still out there, sir. They'll be taking another ship. ETA maybe thirty minutes." Mendez does not acknowledge the report.

I've done my third I.V. for the day, the hole's been wrapped, the sleek intestines have vanished, and how the hell can he live with that? I'm wiped out, but all I can think is how will we get through this? There just aren't enough of us.

How many days was it before things finally sorted out? I suppose it wasn't really that long. Often during those first weeks, I'd only get two or three hours sleep a night, but still I wouldn't be wiped out the next day. It was not as though there was a choice. When the cries for litterbearers came, there was no taking turns. Everybody went; even the off-duty radio operators got out of bed with the rest of us. The NCOs were the only ones who didn't. It was an unwritten code: the NCOs didn't carry litters and Major Mendez didn't challenge that privilege. I suspect he might have created it. After all, he was career army and he believed in rank.

The NCOs were rarely in the treatment area except when supervising sandbag details and other maintenance jobs, with the exception of Smith. He was made the NCO in charge of treatment, and from the outset seemed to be everywhere trying to learn the operation. He spent a lot of time with Morrisey picking up the routines, and Morrisey said he was quick. He also figured out how the unit ran on paper, as well as in fact. That galled Navarra, our company clerk, who had been running the orderly room, mostly by default of the NCOs. Smith never struck me as the kind of person who would be impressed by that arrangement, and in no time, Navarra hated him. Smith and Morrisey, however, seemed to get along very well.

Morrisey was a medic like most of the rest of us, 91 B 2O: the recipient of simple combat medic training, glorified first aid. But he was the only other enlisted man, besides Owen and Newell who had had special training in the States, to be assigned full time to the treatment room. Newell taught him the extra he needed, with support from Mendez, Shelby, and even Owen, the company prima donna. They were right. Morrisey assumed responsibility the way most of us put on clothes every morning.

Smith was the enigma, though. With his square jaw and smooth-skinned good looks, his way of watching, he conveyed a sense of alertness and intelligence that was unusual for lifers like our other noncommissioned officers. The amazing thing was that even in the sodden, tropical heat, his fatigues always looked starched and trim. Brock became Smith's champion . . . the first I heard say that Smith was an outstanding NCO, soldier and person, and would to God we had five or six more like him. Smith, he said, was officer material.

Major Mendez and Smith had problems from the beginning. Nothing about Smith's behavior was less than correct, but he managed to convey disapproval of the major simply by his presence. Mendez dressed up only to exercise his authority in the orderly room, for formations and inspections, and to leave the company area. Usually, he wore a smock and fatigue pants, and he sweated and got dirty and bloody like the rest of us. Off-duty, he performed as a doctor in whatever clothes he happened to be wearing when the call came. Smith, however, never stepped outside the NCO hooch in anything more informal than his fatigues, unless he was going to the showers. There was an immediate sense that Smith had been leashed, that Mendez was deliberately keeping him in control.

I was a little wary of Mendez. He believed that sports reinforce teamwork, provide relief from daily tensions. There was a combined volleyball-basketball court in the motor pool area and a baseball diamond out in the scrub beyond the helicopter revetments. I hate organized sports, but I was warned that the major got upset if we didn't show up to play. To my surprise, I came to enjoy the raucous sandlot quality of the games. All the officers generally showed up, along with the personnel from Dust-Off, so there were about thirty people on any given evening. Brock was a regular, a standout with his cigar, and even Shelby appeared now and then, after a fashion. Major Hargos, Dust-Off's commander, was pretty incredible, with his madras shorts and his fifty-dollar sandals from which he was forever wiping mould. (It was rumored that he had a python under his cot.) Hargos and Mendez always pitched—that was the only rank they pulled.

Mendez was Morrisey's hero, but it was Morrisey himself who said that Mendez only bought us time, that's all Mendez ever could have done. Mendez didn't play favorites. He was the best commanding officer I've ever known . . . and we would have been better off without him, without the memory of him, his standards and his brash dedication. Morrisey, Brock, Shelby, me, the others like Davies, Jenkins, and Smith, that immaculate sonuvabitch—Mendez kept it all together, and even made it work. He haunted us all right to the end.

TWO

Navarra, our company clerk, is driving the commanding officer's jeep, one hand on the steering wheel, his left foot suspended by the heel over the edge of the open door. His blonde hair whips in the wind. He's laughing.

Morrisey's beside him, a can of pretzels and a carton of cigarettes on his lap, watching a spotter plane race us along the runway. We've just been to the PX. I'm in the back, my hand pressed to the top of my cap to keep it from blowing away. A post regulation states that headgear must be worn at all times outside company areas, and I'm not inclined to defy it. Navarra and Morrisey don't seem to give it a second thought.

The three of us are heading north along the airstrip, approaching the air control tower that juts above the treetops. Running parallel to us across the airstrip are rows upon rows of revetments, walls of sandbags for the protection of aircraft. The airships, fixed-wing planes, Huey slicks and gunships, Cobras with their rocket and minigun pods bulging from tiny wings like egg sacs, bask in the hazy afternoon, undulating gently through the waves of heat rising from the steel runway.

Highway 10 is not very crowded at the moment. At this time of day, to avoid the inspections by the military police at the North and South gates or checkpoints, most of the through traffic circumvents the plantation on crude bypasses. There's a steady stream of scooters, trucks, and gaudy buses bouncing through the holes and ruts, churning billows of dust that stretch far away across the butchered land. In the mornings and late afternoons the flow of traffic is very heavy within the base.

"Smith has been on my case all week!" Navarra shouts to Morrisey, becoming serious after several minutes of mirth prompted by a remark Morrisey made about the lifers.

Morrisey looks at him.

"Yeah, really! He's been double-checking everything I do, making sure I don't know anything more than he does."

"But he still doesn't know the half of what I do in there," he continues when Morrisey doesn't respond. "It's all a matter of timing." Navarra grins savagely.

We pass the Vietnamese-manned firestation that serves the entire plantation, a metal building with two bays and two converted army trucks, painted red. Several of the firemen are leaning back in chairs against the front wall, sunning themselves as they monitor the desultory activities along the highway and airstrip. Because of its location, the hundreds of Vietnamese civilians who pass along Highway 10 can watch the firemen scrub their trucks and lean back in their chairs the way firemen do at home. I suppose it's a symbol of our willingness to help the natives help themselves.

"I hear Smith fucked you over, too."

It's a moment before I realize Navarra's talking to me. "How do you mean?"

"Assigning you to A&D with Davies. You know there was a lot of talk about your being trained for treatment. It's true, isn't it, Morrisey?"

"Navarra, you're a fucking shit stirrer! Leave the guy alone. Do something constructive like getting laid." Morrisey looks away in disgust.

"Hey, I just didn't want O'Neill to have any illusions about that prick Smith's gladhanding. What did he tell you, O'Neill? He needed your experience, those two years of college and typing skills? Good records are top priority!"

There's no need for me to answer and Navarra knows it. He laughs.

And I should have known something was up when Smith stopped me the other day and casually asked, "How's it going?" I'd scarcely talked to him since we arrived—I didn't have any occasion to. He's a big man and has a way of projecting himself when he's talking that makes me very conscious of his size and appearance. His cap was off, a singular experience, and his hair had fallen across his forehead, an indication he'd been working. I can't fault Smith for laziness. And he didn't bullshit me—he came right to the point. "I wanted to know if you'd mind working in Admissions and Dispositions with Davies?"

I didn't try to hide my disappointment. I'd been working in treatment since I arrived and had begun to feel I needed that kind of work. But his features seemed to freeze and I decided I should answer carefully. "I suppose, if you haven't got anyone else, Sergeant. I was hoping for treatment."

His face relaxed. "You've got the training—two years of college, typing. I think you'd be good. Davies gets a little high-handed, especially with the Vietnamese. And I'll tell you something else: that job in treatment is pretty vulnerable. I mean, suppose there's a levy for field medics—you've got a whole year ahead of you."

It was the first time I'd thought about that possibility. We're so shorthanded, it never occurred to me, but he was right: nothing's ever guaranteed in the army.

Smith seemed to expect a prompt acceptance, but I couldn't answer.

He smiled. "I'll plan on it, O'Neill."

Our jeep gains on a lambro, one of the ubiquitous three-wheeled minibuses. Several women face each other on the little benches in the crowded, open-sided conveyance. Navarra glances over his shoulder. "Hey, man, I didn't mean to get you upset," he says to me.

"Forget it," I reply. Navarra's OK—we tolerate each other. He runs our NCO-EM club, as well as the orderly room. He created it, in fact, with the major's blessing, and he's pleasant when he's tending bar. He's also informative as well as efficient in the orderly room. There's nothing the lifers plan to do that we don't know about well in advance. Why they remain puzzled about this defies comprehension.

I feel very young when I'm with Morrisey and Navarra. With Morrisey, it's not an unpleasant sensation; he's older, conveys more experience, but he isn't condescending. Navarra's often patronizing, and there's a ruthlessness about him I distrust.

The lambro's scooter motor pops and whines. The jeep creeps up alongside. There are no doors on the tiny cab. The driver looks surprisingly cool and neat in a clean white shirt with a pack of cigarettes and a ballpoint pen in the breast pocket. He's wearing aviator-style sunglasses.

Morrisey peers in among the women. He's in easy reach of the sleek black hair flowing out the sides. The occupants seem oblivious of us, and the intimacy of their nearness is disconcerting. Suddenly, a young, pretty girl looks at Morrisey, stares with such candor that he blushes and turns away.

Navarra guides the jeep back into its lane just as a truck crashes past in the opposite direction. For a moment we're enveloped in a cloud of dust and black exhaust, then we're back in the relative peace of the hot sun. Navarra taps Morrisey on the arm. "Over there!"

Ahead of us, two MP jeeps have pulled a commercial truck off the road. One of the MPs is examining the Vietnamese driver's papers while another has lifted the canvas flap to check the cargo. Two other MPs are standing together, ignoring their partners' check of the truck, their attention focused instead on a second truck parked a short distance down the road, under the shade of some trees. It's not difficult to understand their apparent agitation. The truck, an American three-quarter ton vehicle, is an outrage by any military standard. Plastered to its sides are a profusion of STP, Hurst Shifter, Holley, and Champion decals. Two small South Vietnamese flags droop from chrome rods fastened above the headlights.

Even more outrageous than the truck is the man standing beside it. With one foot on the running board and a hand gripping the top of the door, he's having a casual conversation with several Vietnamese civilians. It isn't the camouflage fatigues, or the bandoliers across his chest, or the fact that he's hatless that makes him stand out: it's the shaggy, reddish hair that obviously hasn't been cut in weeks, the rimless eyeglasses, and the full beard. "My God," I say, "he's an American!"

Morrisey and Navarra laugh.

"It's Eddie Mathias," Morrisey explains, "our local legend."

"So what's the legend?" I ask when Navarra brings the jeep to a halt in front of our orderly room.

Navarra already has a hand on top of the windshield, ready to pull himself up and out of the jeep. "You're not going into this bullshit again, are you Morrisey?"

"He asked."

"Aaagh!" Navarra shakes his head and climbs out. "You're going to wish you hadn't, O'Neill."

The screen door shuts behind the clerk. Morrisey and I start for the hooch. "No one really knows much about Mathias except rumor,'' Morrisey says. "One version I heard: he was a draftee who did a tour here a few years ago when it was still voluntary, then got discharged and went home to knock up the daughter of a Mafia don in Kansas City. He had to come back here because there was no place else in the world he'd be safe.''

I laugh. Morrisey shrugs. "Now he's an advisor for the Military Assistance Command, MACV. He has his own company of ARVNs. Everybody, our own guys included, says it's the toughest outfit around. I heard one story about him jumping off a moving armored personnel carrier during a sweep just south of here. He saw a clump of grass move and he went over to it and yanked it up, and there was the entrance to a tunnel. He didn't hesitate—jumped right in. When he came out a few minutes later, about a quarter mile away, there were twenty bodies in that tunnel. And there was another story about him and four of his ARVNs taking on a whole company of North Vietnamese regulars, blew an ambush on them.''

"Tough," the term Morrisey applies to this American and his South Vietnamese soldiers, is not a common assessment of any native troops except the ROKs, and they're Korean. The idea that Mathias is a source of wonder among our own troops seems utterly implausible. As I listen to further exploits of the legendary Mathias, I can't keep a straight face. But Morrisey's wound up and seems to relish the chance to talk about this man, his flamboyant truck and blatant disregard for convention. He tells me about midnight rides to Saigon on a black Triumph motorcycle in defiance of both curfews and common sense—conveys a vision of Mathias blasting along a deserted, presumably mined, Highway 10 through silent hamlets at speeds approaching a hundred miles per hour with an audacity so compelling that not even the enemy with their virtual control of the dark countryside can bring him screaming to a stop. And all this for the sake of a woman.

"A gorgeous half-caste," Morrisey says, "the Dragon Lady incarnate of Southeast Asia. I've even heard she was educated in Paris.''

"As a whore?" I can't resist the question.

For a moment he looks profoundly disturbed, even hurt by my comment, but lets it pass with a curt, "You have no respect for myths.''

"You actually believe all of this!" I cry, amazed, then laugh again.

He becomes evasive, saying only that he can understand why people want to believe these things, just as we believe in the Israeli Army—if not its war—because we envy dash and success born of a sense of purpose, of survival. "There's no way we can show the Viet Cong the same respect, though. They don't dress like soldiers; you know they're sneaky and they don't come out in the open and present themselves like men, bullshit like that. Our rules have a lot more to do with how we dress for war than fight it, but you'll understand what I mean soon enough."

He's at the foot of the steps leading to our hooch, one hand on the door. "I've seen it, seen women like that, half-French, half-Vietnamese. I couldn't believe how beautiful they were. We had one here, in the treatment room, one night. She was a Viet Cong soldier, in shreds from a Claymore. The American sergeant who blew that ambush flew in with her. He was totally unhinged. Can you imagine groping through the wreckage of an ambush in a jungle in the middle of the night and suddenly coming across a beautiful woman who starts to curse you in flawless English—calls you fascist pig and shit like that?

"She was still at it on the table, cursing him and vowing revenge from the grave. I mean, she was literally torn to pieces and doing that! That sergeant kept saying 'Jesus Christ!' over and over until we just ignored him."

I'm silent.

"Really, O'Neill, can you imagine that?"

He's become so worked up telling this story that I can't answer.

"We took her to the morgue, the rest of them to a chopper, then went back to clean up. The sergeant was there in the middle of the room, tears pouring down his cheeks, his AK-47 dangling by his side the way a kid would hold a ragdoll. Just like that—sobbing and moaning, 'Jesus Christ! Oh, Jesus Christ!' over and over."

My amusement has vanished, if not my skepticism. Those black eyes pour into me, silence me.

"What does it do to one of our guys when he shoots a six- or seven-year-old child because he's stealing grenades? I've seen the results of that, too . . . and what's it doing to you and me to be looking at this shit day in and out?"

"I don't know . . . it's like meat. I have no feelings."

"You're right, you don't know. I don't either. Maybe you believe we should be here . . ." He searches my face for a reaction. When I lower my eyes, he says, "Yeah, well if you ever decide you *don't*, it could get a lot worse."

"It's not as simple as just deciding you don't believe in it!" I reply, piqued, *but it's true: I don't believe in myths anymore—at least certain ones*.

He goes into the tent. "You want to go to the club?" he calls over his shoulder.

I check my watch. "It's too damn early. It won't be open for another hour and a half." For the moment, the last place I want to be is in the club with Morrisey, drinking and listening to more of this.

"The window's open. Annie will pour a shot in a can of Coke for you."

"No, thanks."

"I didn't mean to piss you off."

"Yeah, well you and Navarra are gifted."

Finally, I do go to the club, only much later, after supper and a game of volleyball, and after I've simmered down a bit. Maybe I don't disagree with Morrisey as much as he thinks, but I don't like him cramming stuff down my throat.

Annie, our Vietnamese barmaid, waves when I enter, then turns back to Morrisey who's sitting on a stool talking to her. She leans close in order to hear him and I feel a pang as I think of her being that close to me, smelling her hint of delicate flowers.

There's a deep pleasure in being alive that finds expression in Annie's every gesture, so unlike the other civilians who work in the company. I find it hard to believe that she's an ARVN who disappears three or four days a month on some obscure military business. It's just as difficult to imagine her travelling south in one of the large, incandescent buses with ladders leading to a rooftop full of luggage and people, and rock hard wooden seats down below packed with peasants and livestock. The stink in one of those things would be unbearable.

But Annie's extreme femininity is without pretense, and she conveys an almost paradoxical toughness with it.

When I first arrived in the company, I thought she and Navarra were lovers, so unconscious and complete is their communication when they're working together at the bar, but

22

in time I realized that Navarra's role is protective, like the rest of us. It's Morrisey who can induce an anxious glance or a sudden bellylaugh—as incongruously deep and rich as any I've ever heard. I don't think they see each other outside the club. There's no opportunity. Navarra or the first sergeant take her home.

If Morrisey's in the club, he's usually on the same stool next to the wall with an open book in front of him—he always has a book with him wherever he is. She often stands in close proximity; the two of them talk or simply watch the rest of us. Unlike her relation with Navarra, with Morrisey there are moments of almost tangible intensity, or harmony or strain.

When Morrisey returns from his R&R he brings her a set of antique jade earrings. I'm in the club with Buster Wilbur, one of the NCOs. It's late afternoon when Morrisey walks in and instead of taking his usual place, leans against the bar and hands her a small box. Her reaction is laughter, but it's strained for there is a quizzical look in her eyes as she tries to calculate the meaning of the gift. In the abrupt silence, Morrisey seems totally unaware of Wilbur's and my presence.

Reluctantly, she lifts the lid and withdraws the jewelry. He has become exceedingly uncomfortable, almost shy, and seems impatient to leave. Her thanks are perfunctory. I can feel her withdraw from him, but then he's gone and the box and its contents have vanished somewhere behind the bar. Annie's being her old self again with her customers. I must confess to a certain satisfaction.

Morrisey does not return to the club for several days. One evening he arrives, takes his usual stool, and it's as though nothing ever happened between them. The next night she's wearing the earrings. Her long, black hair is drawn behind her ears and the gold spangles gloriously in the multicolored lights of the room.

Where is she now? Where will she be ten years from now? Some questions shouldn't be asked. I can't even look beyond tomorrow and this bed where I'm lying with a woman who doesn't want me here.

But Annie could. She had hope and it wasn't just Morrisey. It was more consuming than that. Her father and mother were killed in a rocket attack long before she went to work for the Americans. Her twelve-year-old sister was maimed, lost an arm and leg, in another rocket attack while we were there, and lived with Annie in a crammed apartment building. Morrisey described it to me, but I still can't visualize it because it didn't seem to fit her. Her hatred of the VC, her commitment to the ARVN were born of this personal violence, not politics. Hatred wasn't a response I recognized as hope.

The field phone behind the bar buzzes and Navarra, who has elected to remain on the customer side for the evening, goes behind and answers it. He tells the radio operator to repeat himself, then points at Morrisey, who makes a face. "Two litterbearers!" he shouts.

I join Morrisey at the door and we make our way through the darkening shadows. With obvious delight, Morrisey recounts the latest rumor that First Sergeant Buelen wants all NCOs to be addressed as "sir," to be shown respect the way they are in the marines. Rumors like that are endemic in our company.

As we enter the motor pool area, I hear the faint drumming of a helicopter. Morrisey runs toward the treatment tent to turn on the lights and almost collides with Captain Brock, who's stumping up the road from the officers' quarters. I grab a litter from the rack near the front road and continue my dash toward the landing pad.

Out across the berm, beyond the tower, a white eye floats out of the last vestiges of twilight, searching for the entrance to the plantation. There is no flashing red light. "Must be a gunship!" I shout as Morrisey runs up beside me.

Like a huge, armed dragon fly, the ship alights only for a moment, scarcely touching the pavement. I glimpse a helmeted figure behind a machinegun. Someone jumps down out of the ship then reaches back inside. The crewchief guides another man out of the ship. "There's a litter!" the crewchief shouts at us. We've scarcely cleared the blades with the litter when the helicopter begins to hammer again, to rise and turn.

That last of daylight has faded. There's only darkness and the noise of the departed ship and then quiet, the sounds of our boots and those of the soldier the crewchief helped down, trotting beside us.

"A fucking dog!" Davies, my supervisor, says, pen and tags in hand. He scowls at the huge German shepherd when we place him on the treatment table. The soldier who ran in with us, the dog's handler, doesn't seem to have heard anything Davies said. It's hard for me to contain my amazement when Brock calls for a saline I.V. The dog dies of heat exhaustion. "Twenty thousand bucks, or something like that, for this mutt," Brock growls in an effort to explain the absurdity of it all.

Morrisey and I clean up while Davies chuckles with puerile anticipation at the surprise awaiting the men from Graves Registration. "A fucking dog!" he repeats for the third or fourth time. The only other sounds are the sobs of the dog's handler from the bench in front of the tent.

Then Morrisey, Davies, and the handler are gone. I've turned out the lights and opened the back door when I hear a jeep stop. I wait, my hand on the door. There are voices. From the front porch I hear someone walk down the road. The sickcall tent a few yards away is dark and there's no sign of the charge of quarters. I tell myself to call commo about that later. Someone coughs in the ward nearby.

An orange flare pops beyond the perimeter wire, followed by another. I wait on the edge of the porch, leaning against the door frame, and try to quell a faint uneasiness as two men appear. One is tall and wearing a helmet, the other's a little shorter and wearing a cap.

"Hello?"

"Can I help you?"

The shorter man speaks with a soft, pleasant voice. "Did you receive any casualties from the Dong Ha Bridge this afternoon?"

"Yes." I can't see the rank of the men I'm addressing and choose to ignore the problem.

"What units?"

"We had a few from the Tenth Air Cav."

The man speaks haltingly. "How about the Third and . . . Two thirty-second Infantry . . . Battalion?" He seems to be having trouble forming the numbers, or remembering their sequence.

I step off the porch. "Let's go check it out." Despite the dark, I move easily across the yard to the sickcall tent. I ask them to wait, then feel my way down the short hall to the curtain that serves as a door to the A&D office. Inside, I grope for the light, yank the chain and immediately shield my eyes from the glare. There's no one else in the tent and I remember again that the CQ should be on duty by now. I reach for the field phone on Davies's desk just as the two men push their way into the tiny office behind me.

Gittoni answers the phone in the small, sandbagged cube with all the radios in it about a hundred feet away. "Yeah?"

"How about a CQ?"

"Who is it?"

"Ask Top."

"Roger."

The phone goes dead. The log for American casualties and sickcall lies open on a counter to my right. The counter gives out into a long hall where a bench runs the length of the tent. The hall is dark except for the light shining over the counter onto the white bench and a copy of the *Berkeley Barb*. I smile and wonder who in the company distributes the underground paper. It always appears mysteriously after dark.

One of the men behind me clears his throat.

I flip the pages of the log until I come to the day's entries. There are thirty entries to the page. I run my finger down one page and am halfway down the next column when I find the men of the Tenth Air Cavalry. There are eleven entries. All the men were shipped south to evacuation hospitals. I let my finger roam to the bottom of the column, then over the next two pages until the entries cease.

Turning, I face the two men. The short one is a captain, about my own age. The other is a first sergeant, heavyset and flabby at the jowls. He glares at me with bloodshot eyes.

"There's one more possibility." I reach for a wooden box nailed to the wall above the desk, pull out a stack of field medical tags and start thumbing through them. "Here's one! James Murphy, Spec Four, Company A . . ."

"Wait a sec." The captain has pulled a spiral notebook from his shirt pocket and is trying to write down the information. He seems to have difficulty focusing on the page, first moving the pad closer, then farther away.

" . . . gunshot wound, fracture left femur, Evac Twenty-fifth." I look up. The captain continues to write. A huge moth thuds against the screen beside my head.

"What's that mean?" It's the first sergeant.

"That means we got one of your men through here, First Sergeant, and that he was sent south to the Twenty-fifth Evacuation Hospital. Someone slipped over the card when he was entering the information in the book, that's all."

"Why south?" the first sergeant demands.

"We don't keep anyone with a major wound, Top. All we

do is stabilize them and ship them out. We haven't got the facilities for anything more than minor wounds and illnesses.''

"Well, where are the rest of them, goddammit? We've driven almost forty miles to get here, it's dark and we got to spend the fucking night in this hole.''

"Can't help you, Top. We haven't got any record of them. They probably got shipped directly south—it happens all the time.''

"Are you trying to tell me I got to go another seventy or eighty goddam miles to find these guys?''

"That's up to you, First Sergeant!'' I'm surprised at my audacity.

"What?'' The NCO shoves between me and the captain. I can smell liquor.

"It's up to you, First Sergeant,'' I manage to repeat.

"No, soldier! It's up to you! I've gone just as far as I'm going. Now suppose you get on that horn and find those men.''

I sidestep the first sergeant and appeal to the captain. "Sir, it's virtually impossible to get any kind of information at this time of . . .''

But the captain's transfixed by a praying mantis that has alighted on the coffee urn in the corner.

"Sir!''

The captain turns slowly. There's something funny about his eyes—as though he's looking through me. "Yeah . . .''

"Sir, why don't I call the man who was on duty when these casualties came in and you can work all this out with him?''

"Yeah, that's great . . .'' He picks absently at the notebook.

I crank the field phone, dreading that for some ghastly reason, no one's going to answer. Gittoni finally comes on the line.

"Get Davies, will you?''

"I'll see what I can do. CQ show up?''

"No.'' The first sergeant has crowded me against the desk. I can't bear the feeling of those eyes burning into the back of my neck. I turn around. The first sergeant sways ever so slightly.

"You people don't wear hats around here?''

I force myself to look directly at him. "It's not required in the treatment area, First Sergeant.''

"I see. You guys aren't part of the army.''

I hold my breath. I don't want to answer. For once I want Davies to appear.

"Well?"

"Did you ever try to carry a litter under a helicopter with your cap on, Top?"

"Don't give me your lip, PFC! Why didn't you salute the captain here? That not required for your work?"

"That's correct."

"That's correct," he mimics. "You look pretty ragged for a rear echelon type."

I sense that he desperately wants to hit me.

"You going to find those men?"

"Sergeant, I . . ."

"Your moustache is too long, or have you been in the field so you haven't had time to trim it?"

Suddenly there are footsteps coming down the hall from the back of the tent. Davies stops at the counter, flops his elbows on the open log and blinks his eyes. "What is it, O'Neill?" he asks with surprising mildness.

He's popped a couple of librium, I think. "These men are looking for information and I've done all I can do. Maybe you can help them."

Davies peers over the top of his glasses—a habit I ordinarily find annoying—at the two men as though they are bugs. What a gift! I step around the first sergeant and start for the door.

"Boy! I am not used to some REMF motherfucker walking out on me!"

I step to the ground and turn to face the silhouette of the NCO. "Why don't we go see the major, Top?"

"The who?"

"My CO, First Sergeant. He can explain these things to you."

"Yeah?" He hesitates. "Yeah, OK, goddammit!"

At the officers' club, I look through the screen and see Mendez studying his cards. Hargos and the major are partners against Brock. They're so quiet in their concentration that I can hear the heavy breathing of the sergeant as he lumbers up behind me. I tap on the door.

"Come in!" Brock calls out.

Mendez looks up. "What is it, O'Neill?"

"Sir, I have a first sergeant out here who needs to see you."

"What about?"

"We've got a problem, sir."

The major looks past me, then glances at the floor where my foot is jammed against the door. The door shakes. Mendez lays his cards face down on the table and excuses himself.

The major opens the door on the sergeant who looks down with consternation upon the dark-haired officer who's wearing nothing but shorts and thongs, his usual apparel after the last meal of the day. Sweat gleams on the bare, brown skin. "What seems to be the problem, First Sergeant?"

"What happened to the lady with the worms, O'Neill?" It's Brock. A large puff of smoke billows above his head as he speaks.

"Village nurse told Morrisey she died, sir."

"Yeah? I didn't think it'd take long. Jesus, Pat," Brock turns to Hargos. "You should have seen this woman. Goddam worms coming right out of her nose. Her lungs were crammed. Not a thing to do about it but send her back to the village dispensary."

Hargos shakes his head slowly, then looks at me. "Taking over for Davies?"

"I guess so, sir." I feel tense and excited, even servile when talking to Hargos.

"But you're a medic . . ." There's a slight suggestion of a smile, then he bows his head and studies his cards.

"Yes, sir," I reply, more quietly, but I think he's forgotten me. I wonder why he'd know that.

"You did the right thing, O'Neill," Mendez says on his return. He's standing inside, holding the door open for me. "The sergeant's very drunk." He stares at me for a moment. "Your moustache is too long. I want it trimmed by noon tomorrow."

THREE

There's no birdsong in the plantation. It's rare when the specks flying across the torn horizon aren't mechanical. Sometimes the war seems very far away from this our unnatural island, although rockets land within the perimeter with some regularity. Within the native hamlet—for propaganda purposes—they come even more frequently. The number of persons injured or killed as a result of these arbitrary intrusions, native and American, is statistically insignificant, as I'm in a position to know.

Our hilltop base is unique for having a native hamlet within its confines. No civilians enter or leave the hamlet after curfew except by special permission of the provost marshall, and no Americans enter it at all except on an emergency or other official basis. I hear there are ways to breach the fence and bypass the American guards, but the risks seem too great to me.

The residents of the hamlet who don't work in civilian jobs for the Americans are permitted to operate a number of bars and retail shops for the benefit and relaxation of American troops within still another enclosure next to the hamlet. The girls who work in these bars are more often known by number than by name: "Number Six at the Blue Baby Bar" refers to a specific girl. (The numbers one through ten are also used by the natives as a scale of worth: number one being the best and number ten, the worst.)

A few of the men in my company are regulars in what is euphemistically known as "the village," not to be confused with a real village that lies a few miles south of the plantation. Newell from treatment is one, Stevens, our company freak is another, and Dunn, one of the two radio operators from my hooch. These three often return giggly and loaded down with trinkets and other junk from the legitimate native market.

The place is like a circus with flimsy, false-fronted buildings painted bright blues, pinks, purples, greens, and yellows. Abrasive rock music explodes from open windows and doors into the crammed streets where soldiers rummage for souvenirs and vendors hawk their goods. At the arched wooden gate with its gaudy red letters, MPs scrutinize all visitors and cruise the crowd in pairs. Native men are seldom in sight, just old women, young women, children, and the club girls in silk *ao dais* and miniskirts glimpsed as they emerge like huge painted insects from the shadows of their working places. I have visions of a violent wind descending on this place and twirling it away in splinters: soldiers, girls, glitter vanishing like a dream. When the dust has settled there's nothing left, no trace except for an old woman, draped in black, crouching in the dust.

We've pushed our way through the bamboo beads that constitute the entrance to The Yellow Peril and are sitting at one of the many rickety tables scattered throughout an enormous room. The furniture is imitation Gay Nineties, flimsy round chairs with heart-shaped backs. Ceiling fans twirl and colored lights drift across the dance floor and stage where a rock band of local teenagers in mod clothing strives irreparably to give a professional rendering of American music. The looks, the atmosphere are all wrong—it's depressing to watch someone try to imitate something that's yours when you can't have it yourself. Any comfort provided by the barroom dusk is destroyed by the too brilliant sunshine beyond the doors and louvered windows, and the alien clamor of the streets. (I remember going to bars or movies at home in the afternoon—that sense of waste I invariably feel when I come out and the sun is still shining, the feeling of having lost control of the day.)

Newell has already dropped more than ten dollars, that's a thousand piasters, on Number Three (or Suzy Dong, as he calls her) who is sitting on his knee. She's a skinny girl wearing a purple miniskirt and spike heels, and except for the color of her dress, she looks like every other girl in the place. Newell's persistence and money have resulted in one very

31

brief feel, but he seems delighted. Prostitution's illegal here. His ardor increases as the girl wiggles around avoiding his assaults, the two of them conversing in English at the level of retarded five year olds. Newell and Stevens are both stoned; they got that way in the back of the ambulance that brought us here. Dunn is chugging so-called screwdrivers—atrocious drinks made of cheap vodka and orange soda—and waving a handful of money at Number Sixteen, his regular. Number Sixteen's cadging drinks from a brutal-looking infantryman who acts as though he'd like to break her in two. Frightened by this, she flees across the room to Dunn's lap and unleashes her fury on him. Dunn wallows in it.

Morrisey's with us, the only time I've known him to come to the village. It's only because of my insistence that he came at all. He looks bored.

"Morrisey, you're giving me bad vibes," Stevens says. He's been watching Morrisey closely for several minutes, the look on his face gradually changing from one of vacuous merriment to hostility. Stevens isn't very big and I get the feeling this is a problem. I have little contact with him except when we occasionally carry litters together, and during evening sports. I don't know much about him. His impertinence with the lifers is legendary, however, and he's the most sought-after driver in the motor pool.

"How's that, Stevens?"

"You're not enjoying yourself. You're uptight, Morrisey. You haven't got it together."

Morrisey smiles. "Got what together?"

"Not letting things get to you. Enjoying the girls here—I get the feeling they offend you. They're doing a job like everyone else, and we're helping support them."

"That's a nice sentiment. I've had my share of blueballs for this lifetime, thanks, Stevens."

"You're conceited, Morrisey."

"Relax. I don't give a shit what you do."

"You know, I didn't even want you to come . . . I told them you'd be a drag."

"Hey!" I interject. Newell's still wrestling with Number Three but Dunn and his girl have stopped their antics to watch. "For Chrissakes, Stevens! No one tells you how to enjoy yourself."

"To hell with you, O'Neill! You're not having a good high ruined."

32

Newell peeks around Number Three's tits. "I want some french fries!"

We get up and leave the girls to their business.

"God, she gives me a hard-on!" Newell groans and scratches his balls with both hands while we stand outside The Yellow Peril trying to get our bearings in the bright, searing heat. He removes his glasses, rubs his reddened eyes, then lunges into the stream of Vietnamese and GIs.

There's a lot of yelling ahead of us, then the crowd presses together, turns sullen as we push through. "You fucking guys are the goddamn Gestapo!" a voice screams, a howl of rage verging on hysteria. Suddenly there's nothing in front of us except a dusty patch of street and the pink corrugated wall of a building. I stop short as though I've touched an invisible fence.

A soldier's been slammed against the wall, his legs spreadeagled. He is looking over his shoulder as two MPs rip through a cloth bag. His hat is on the ground, his hair is mussed. He looks terribly young. There is just the hugeness of his mouth, the yelling and rage and panic. "Kiss my fucking ass! A guy can't even relax without you fuckers butting in!"

One of the MPs, a beefy-looking corporal with his helmet raked forward to his nose, suddenly turns the bag upside down. Mirrored sunglasses peer from the shadow of the helmet as a stream of trinkets, small toys, and a colored, silk pillow plop to the dust, followed by a clear plastic sandwich bag filled with a brownish green substance. The two MPs stare at the soldier, then the MP with the mirrored glasses moves toward him. The soldier turns and buries his head in his arm. He looks naked. I hear him moan "my God" as the MP grabs his wrist and slams a cuff against it.

"That poor bastard's looking right into Long Binh Jail," Morrisey says.

"Fuck you, Mirrors!" someone shouts.

"Yeah, I thought you were OK, Johnny, you fucking Nazi!"

Mirrors slowly looks back at us. "I'll see you later."

"Ohhhhhhh," the crowd goes, and then everyone breaks into laughter.

"Big man! Go get your ass shot instead of hassling us, shithead!"

"A couple of weeks out there and maybe you'll want some of that stuff, too! My God, a man's stash isn't sacred anymore!"

The Vietnamese in the crowd watch without speaking. Many smile nervously.

The other MP squats down and scoops the souvenirs into the bag, quickly, carelessly.

"I was going to send those home," the handcuffed soldier pleads, his voice shaky.

The MP ignores him. He scrunches the bag closed with one hand, keeps the marijuana in the other. "Let's get going, Johnny."

Mirrors clamps a hand on the GI's shoulder and pushes him through the crowd. The MP isn't as big as he looks, I realize; it's the way he carries himself, immutable, mythic.

"Oh, O'Neill, I don't need this," Stevens says, giving my sleeve a tug. "Fucking pig looked like a bruiser. That's heavy."

I laugh at Stevens's blatant paranoia. "The guy was an asshole carrying that stuff around here."

"You ever seen LBJ?"

"No."

"It's a hellhole. It makes any stockade in the States look like paradise."

Newell leads off and we follow him to a three-sided shanty buried in the maze of streets and pathways about twenty feet from the hamlet fence. There's a certain wildness about the place with its tufts of high, coarse grass protruding through the dirt and scraping against the plywood walls. We sit down at a table just under the roof and order "33" beer. "Gives you a hangover before a buzz," Morrisey remarks.

Stevens laughs, a little too loudly. He seems to have forgotten the recent tension and is smiling at everyone. Dunn has become giggly.

Behind a white counter made of boards nailed on top of ammunition crates and covered with oil cloth, a young, fairly pretty girl perfunctorily slices potatoes and drops them in a wire basket. There's an overpowering smell of grease that I associate more with her than the premises. When the basket is filled, she sets it gurgling into the vat, then disappears through a door in the middle of the back wall. When she comes back from what appears to be a storage room, she's carrying our second round of beer.

Stevens grabs her wrist as she puts her hand out for payment. "You number one boom boom?" I'm startled. He seems too intense to be joking.

She shrugs, stashes our money in an apron pocket, and starts for the door to the back room. Stevens stands up. "Back in a while, you guys." He disappears behind the thin, plywood door.

The rest of us exchange awkward glances, then stare at our beer, and then look anywhere but at each other. Trying not to hear, dreading any noise from that back room, I examine some ragged bushes growing along the base of the cyclone fence. Beyond the steel mesh capped with three strands of barbed wire, a decrepit wooden wall meanders through the scrub. A cluster of gritty-looking palms shimmers from somewhere within the protected hamlet.

The door opens and the girl emerges, stares at us with an inexorably bland expression while she wipes her hands on her apron, then turns to the counter and lifts the basket from the vat.

After a few moments, Stevens appears, hiking his pants. He looks disgusted. "Exactly two and a half minutes," Newell announces, glancing at his watch. "Must have been a number one boom boom!" We all laugh while Stevens flops into his chair and slams his elbows on the table making the bottles clink.

"Shit! And she charged me the full twenty dollars for it! Military Payment Currency!" He's playing to an audience. He's good at it.

The girl sets the cardboard containers of potatoes down on the table. "That's OK, Stevens," Morrisey quips, examining the contents of one of the containers, "looks like you'll get some of your investment back on your french fries."

Stevens glares at Morrisey who's laughing with the rest of us. The girl wipes her hands on her apron and waits for our money.

It was Stevens who, on his return from a week in Vung Tau, raved about the first unshaved pussy he'd fucked in Vietnam, a gorgeous black flowering, while I listened with a mixture of curiosity and revulsion. The idea of a shaved pussy was weird enough to me—I could only imagine screwing some little girl—but with all the venereal disease I encountered daily, the idea became revolting. I did think about it—no, more than think. It was haunting. You can't help getting horny, but shit, to get it that way! To look so smooth and hairless, unsullied—it wasn't natural. I suppose the women did it to control lice. The hooch girls used to sit around picking nits out of each other's hair when they weren't working—a regular social event, only those were head lice. They had them all.

"Small, hard tomboy bodies," Stevens said, still relishing the memory of that luxuriant growth. "No hair on pussies like brown apricots. Can you imagine screwing that day in and out for your whole life? No wonder the gooks can't win this war by themselves. Give me American pussy and big tits, white and smooth, a little flabby."

It's true. I don't know the woman I'm with now at all, but we're not aliens. Casey's milky softness is familiar. I can cling to it. Not all the women there had to be whores, either. Even Stevens agreed Annie was special.

Once the war got you, all you could do was ride it out, although someone like Stevens seemed better adapted to do it than most. The war got me because I thought I believed in something. I didn't believe in school anymore so I dropped out, but because I wasn't playing games—I was very serious about my capacity to make moral decisions—I had to choose between the army and prison. The distinction seems a little vague now, but I was trying to pay tribute to the rule of law, a social contract. I was big on that. How irrelevant it all seems now. My ideals floundered on the realization, no, the admission I'd go nuts inside a cell. I doubt I could ever believe in any of that again.

My assignment to A&D didn't help. There was no escaping a new sense of being trivial. I couldn't escape it in The Yellow Peril, or anywhere else for that matter. Wars aren't made to be reduced to numbers. Morrisey told Smith that one time while trying to explain my lack of enthusiasm. (I did the job well, but that wasn't enough for Smith. His saving grace was that he was good about standing behind me when I had problems with that job.) Only Morrisey said, "I think if I had to reduce this fucking war to paper, I'd go absolutely crazy." Smith became stone-faced, so I later heard. Those two could never avoid for long their difference in priorities.

I'm doing my first monthly report with Davies who hates this ritual and has caused me to dread it. Actually, I think his ability to do the report gives him a sense of superiority. But I'm beginning to understand why he hates it: not because we must make statistics out of virtually everything, but because it must be done in precise order, and written in precise order with no visible erasures and many copies. Otherwise, the report will be rejected by battalion headquarters, specifically the colonel, our battalion commander, who values a neat report above everything. Both Davies and Smith have repeatedly advised me of this.

Davies has very long fingers. He points over my shoulder at the next step outlined in an old copy of the monthly report: "Civilians wounded."

I open the separate log we keep for Vietnamese. It scarcely looks used in contrast to the battered condition of the American log. The entries are scanty, only a fractional representation of the actual number we've treated during the past month, but no one, except Thieu, our interpreter, speaks the language and the civilians always seem to arrive in hordes so there's never time for name gathering. I'm not sure anyone gives a shit anyhow. All Vietnamese casualties, military and civilian, are sent on to Tainan, a native hospital farther south, because they're not permitted to stay here. Under any circumstances.

I look up at Davies, who's scowling. "I count fifteen."

He peers over the top of his glasses. "Three hundred," he says.

I dutifully note the figure on my worksheet.

By the time he snatches the last page of the rough copy off the desk and staples the pile together, I'm exhausted. "I'll copy it over tomorrow," he says. "I'll be taking it to battalion the day after tomorrow, so you'll have to run sickcall."

I nod wearily. "Why don't you type it, Davies? It's just as fast."

"You type it once and you'll be typing it forever!" he snaps. "And all these goddamn cards, too!" He drops the huge stack of field medical tags in front of me. "By the way, you got to write neater."

"Neater!" I sneer, and immediately feel like a jerk, but that's the petty way it's gone all night. Most of the problem isn't the report, it's the emotional level of this whole exercise. "Good night, Davies."

"You remember, I'm senior man in this office . . ."

"Good night."

Davies stamps out of the office leaving me in peace, of sorts. I'm upset. I can't deal with a person like Davies without getting that way, feeling afterward that maybe I went too far, or that someday I will and I'll find myself alone, completely at the mercy of an imperious turd like him. I should accommodate him.

The field phone rings. "Dust-Off will be going out in a few minutes—a malaria case. No rush. I'll call you."

"Thanks, Dunn."

Someone dashes past the tent and disappears in the dark. I replace the receiver and swivel my chair so I'm facing the screen wall and the lights of the treatment area beyond. This is nothing new: it is one of the few fascinations of A&D, the opportunity to see Captain Shelby hunt. On several nights I've watched him flow here and there, in and out of the lights, his movements languid as if he's dancing. Shelby may be a good surgeon, but he's some kind of junkie, too, with all the skill and finesse of a professional chemist. No one moves like that normally, even if he is feeding centipedes.

One night, though, he suddenly zipped out of the shadows like an overwound mechanical man bent over ninety degrees at the waist, the spaghetti strainer he used to capture his prey held in front of his face like an inverted catcher's mask. He vanished behind the tents and trees, then whizzed into the incandescent pools, scooted back and forth, faster and faster, while I waited, awestruck, for the spring to snap, for Shelby to fly to pieces . . .

He darted behind the treatment tent one last time and I didn't see him again until the following morning when he was his old, serene self once more. It didn't occur again, so he must have considered the experiment a failure. The Physician's Desk Reference *missed a good one: I never found any counter-indications to explain it.*

He discouraged fraternization, although not because of any military code—he was a loner. His performance in the treatment tent was always flawless, occasionally callous. He was nonchalant with patients, particularly with the men who were brought in on helicopters, torn to pieces. His hands never quivered and his level of concentration was enormous. Not a facial muscle moved, not a hair on that marvelous, bushy, illegal moustache of his, not a drooping eyelid twitched! I can't remember that he ever left the company; he was a self-proclaimed recluse in Vietnam, but only the first I'd know. If I'd been asked early on, I'd have said he was slipping, falling behind . . . but he was really miles ahead.

I'm returning from a late shower, whistling, feeling pleasantly cool for a minute, wearing only my towel and thongs. The sound of acid rock permeates the darkness, mingles with the pandemonium of the insects, lizards, and other creatures that whisk out of sight and mind at dawn.

Suddenly I'm assaulted by the reek of English Leather, of dormitory shower rooms and crammed vehicles groaning toward the nearest girl's school, and Stevens falls into step beside me. He's outrageously buoyant and garbled and I have to smile at his intermittent stabs at profundity and bursts of private amusement. "What do you think?" he demands, lifting an elbow and thrusting an exposed armpit at my nose. I turn my face and exhale noisily.

"You put aftershave on your armpits?"

"Hee, hee," he says. "You wanna see my hemorrhoids?" He howls with laughter at the memory of a tentative diagnosis I made of hemorrhoids for a bartender from the base NCO Club. They turned out to be venereal warts. When he calms down, we stop to light cigarettes. The NCO hooch is nearby, and Smith's voice is urging someone "to keep up the good work. You're one of the best I've seen." Chairs scrape, beads rattle, and Morrisey appears silhouetted at the back door.

"Thanks for the drink, Sarge."

"It was good to talk, Morrisey." Beneath a bare bulb, Smith looks incongruously soft and untanned without his shirt. The door squeaks open and Morrisey feels his way onto the steps through a cloud of insects.

I feel naked standing there in the shadows clutching my soap dish and towel. The tobacco of the cigarette locked between my moist fingers begins to come through the paper. Stevens tenses up and pulls violently on his cigarette. "Sucking ass, huh, Morrisey?"

Morrisey stops. I can't see his face, only the rumpled outlines of his fatigues and an occasional wild curl fleeing his head. I can't sense his reaction, either: his voice is calm, good-natured in a cautious way. "Sure, man, like I need to."

Even the insects seem to be listening.

"Hey, Richie," I mumble. I'm much too awkward, much too late to disassociate myself from Stevens who's searching for a reply, the slow workings of his mind forced from the peculiar reality and flow to which it's become chemically accustomed. The process, almost audible, takes far too long, then grinds into futility. "I can't remember what you said," he manages, then after another long pause, "It was heavy, but . . ." He falters again. In an almost apologetic tone, he completes his thought. "I know . . . I know you were in there sucking Smith's ass."

Morrisey hasn't moved, not a muscle, but now I can feel something else although his voice is unchanged. "He wanted to know about drugs, Stevens. Maybe you can tell him." Morrisey disdains drugs, even grass. He told me once that he had to face his tour clearheaded, without any artificial supports or hindrances that might victimize him at some critical moment, that might offer him an excuse. But he usually isn't arrogant about it.

I was torn. What difference did it make two days later, much less two years, what Vietnamese were wounded, or even killed? For that matter, what difference did it make what names and dates and statistics were recorded for anyone once they were dead? But I saw that one coming and I really can't blame Morrisey: he escorted the Vietnamese officer from the treatment tent to the A&D office and didn't escape in time. It was nothing new to me.

"Even if they told me their names, I couldn't spell them!" Davies snapped at the ARVN officer who had come seeking the names and whereabouts of some of his men wounded a few days earlier. Davies had the log open to the date of their supposed arrival and the terse, and at the time, funny notation: "16 wogs." I watched him write it down after they'd gone and laughed. We both laughed—one of our rare instances of harmony.

"Can I see the book, please, sir, to read it—maybe I understand names . . ." the officer said.

"Fuck no! It's written in code and I can't read it myself— top secret!"

At that moment, Morrisey baked out of the office, profoundly embarrassed. Later I saw him standing at the door to the treatment tent as the ARVN walked, defeated, toward his jeep.

Morrisey'd had a bellyful when the night disgorged the group of sailors, USN printed in neat letters on their field medical tags, with one exception—a Vietnamese sailor. It was shortly after three and I felt totally disoriented as though I hadn't really awakened, but was groping in a turbulent dream of flashing red light. We were over fifty miles from the sea, so why sailors?

It will be daybreak in less than two hours, I've been up for almost a half hour, but I still feel forsaken in this velvet oppressiveness where insects tap on the screens and men who appeared from nowhere lie in waxen agony. The Vietnamese sailor's eyes are shut. He's handsome and surprisingly tall. The one American who is still conscious lifts himself up on his elbows with great difficulty, then twists his head to look at the Vietnamese.

"River patrol?" Brock asks, but the American ignores him and asks about his comrade.

"Don't worry about him now."

Morrisey and Newell, Newell with his perpetually ferocious appearance—I have yet to see him smile—are working together. Only a few men have lingered to help carry the litters to the helicopter. Morrisey carefully lifts the conscious sailor's leg so Newell can wrap the foot-long rent in the flesh.

The Vietnamese sailor dies before he can be carried back to the helicopter; the two units of whole blood, only partially used, lie unhooked on the stretcher beside the body, glisten in the pale light of the surgical lamp. The other sailors are carried off in a throbbing, wind-strewn darkness. Everything is still now. Once more, the treatment tent manifests itself as a surreal place of deadened tone and livid colors.

"Why did you give this guy whole blood, Morrisey?" Davies demands when he returns to retag the dead man. He rips away the card he filled out only ten minutes ago. "Well?"

Morrisey's wiping sweat from his face with a towel. "He was with the Americans, Tim." He sounds exhausted and the clerk's innate prissiness grates.

"It's not done, you know that! Look at the waste!"

Brock, who is unwrapping a cigar, looks up. "Is that right?"

Davies checks his anger. "Well, sir, we don't usually give them . . ."

"This guy was pretty bad, so why don't you worry about getting his full name, and maybe even his unit instead of that diddleyshit you got there, and let me worry about the blood." He lights his cigar. "Goodnight Newell, Morrisey."

The rear door slams behind Brock. "Get that thing to the morgue!" Davies orders.

Morrisey grins.

"Can he do that?" I ask after Davies goes back to the A&D office.

"I wouldn't carry it. I'd leave it here to rot," Morrisey says, but Newell comes over, grabs the rear handles of the litter, and motions toward the door.

As is his habit, Morrisey goes out and sits on the bench in front of the treatment tent to stare into the darkness, listen to its sounds, watch the occasional bursts of flares and tracers, eruptions of brilliant color, until he can scarcely keep his eyes open. Then he knows he'll be able to sleep. Newell and I return from the morgue and sit down with him, saying nothing.

Smells are like a map in the darkness. I can visualize the pad, the litter racks, the helicopters nesting in their revetments, excreting their stench of fuel, metals, and blood, can pinpoint it all even though I can't see it. It becomes a game: the sudden burst of a flare furnishes my proof, my reward. To our left, the single light of the A&D office casts a dim glow among the trees. We hear the hearse grind its way along the back road to the morgue, hear the twin thunks of closing doors. Swarms of bugs press against the screen, clamber over each other in their obsession with the wan light in the office where Davies is standing at the counter, his back to us, all T-shirt, elbows, and shoulder blades. It's his night on duty in there.

Lattimore and Hueme, the men from Graves, make their belated appearance in the office. Hueme is exceedingly tall and gangly, has straw-colored hair and a cowlick. Lattimore, the short, cocky spokesman, has his hands forever in his pockets in an effort to control his impulse to toy with nearby objects. "Hey, Davies!" Lattimore says, one hand now out of its pocket and playing with the stapler on the counter. "Who is this guy? You didn't tell us he was a gook." The stapler's on its side now, and Lattimore's examining the bottom.

Davies reaches over, snatches the stapler and plunks it upright, far away from Lattimore's grasp. "So he's a gook! You made me lose my count!" He starts to recount a pile of used field medical tags.

"Hey, man! It's almost four-thirty in the fucking morning! You got any certificates on this guy? Identification? What do you want us to do, rush it to Saigon?"

Davies slaps the cards on the counter, one by one, and doesn't reply.

"Hey!" Lattimore pinches a bit of Davies' sleeve and yanks. "What's got your ass? Where's Thieu?"

Davies turns, pulls his glasses down and stares over them. "Thieu can't come out at night—you know that! And I don't know what the fuck you're going to do with it, because we don't do certificates on Vietnamese, and you know that, too! I'll send Thieu down in the morning."

"Hey, ain't you got a name or unit on this guy? We might have problems."

"Here." He hands Lattimore a tag.

"What's this shit? First name and rank—that's all?"

"You want to do this job?"

"Aw, fuck you, Davies! Say, you got them Preludins?"

"In my tent. I'll send them down with Thieu."

"Twenty bucks, right?"

. . . but it was Morrisey who anticipated the helicopter, as though by sitting and staring into the darkness that night, he foresaw the events, the words, signals, the ringing phones that started it clattering northward. So when, at last, it hammered over the perimeter wire in the morning sunshine, he was not puzzled, or awestruck, or panicked like Owen.

Owen's shouting into the field phone at the front of the treatment tent, demanding that someone in commo tell him what the ship is doing here. "I hate phones!" Owen shouts and slams the receiver into its cradle. "Those snotnose sonsuvbitches won't tell me shit!"

Morrisey, standing nearby, ignores the outburst. He's as transfixed as the rest of us by the ominous, anthropodic beauty of the white UH-1 helicopter that has pounded within a hundred yards or so of our landing pad. It swivels broadside to us and hovers while it flaunts its gleaming figure and the florid, blue medallions on its doors.

Turning again, it floats toward us and settles to the pavement, tipping forward slightly on its skids, then rocking back as the engine dies. The only sound is the rotor slicing the heat.

The side door rumbles open, and a heavy man in a brilliant white uniform emblazoned with gold braid steps down to the tarmac, contrives despite his bulk to make the drop a fluid, even graceful motion. Three other men in only slightly less extraordinary blue uniforms tumble out and group behind the official in white as he starts to walk toward the treeline, no, float, for there is not a trace of physical exertion about him.

"Find the major!" Owen hisses but Morrisey continues to ignore him as though he already knows the reason for the helicopter's arrival. The look on his face is one of intense anticipation, even satisfaction.

I see anew what a striking person Morrisey is, the white, untanned skin of his neck rising from the open collar, concluding with that chiseled face. Suddenly, I'm afraid as he stands in the sunlight and waits, already, even ruthlessly satisfied. I realize he is experiencing some kind of obscure fulfillment.

Morrisey disappears. When he comes back, Major Mendez is with him, the blue smock he ordinarily wears during duty hours replaced by a full fatigue uniform, including a cap. Mendez salutes the man in the white uniform waiting in front of the treatment tent, the only one of us to have done so, then introduces himself.

The man in white returns the salute while his small eyes carefully study the major. When he makes his own introduction, it is in flawless English. He is an admiral, he explains, and is seeking the body of his son, reportedly killed the night before on a river patrol. "He was with American sailors," he adds.

"Sailors?" The major looks at Morrisey. "Did we get sailors?"

"Yes, sir. Captain Brock was on duty . . . should I get Davies?"

"Please."

. . . and there it is. Now I know what's going on, although there's nothing on Morrisey's face to betray it.

Davies is standing on the step to the sickcall tent, has been since the arrival of the white helicopter. Before Morrisey reaches him, he ducks inside and immediately reappears holding what I presume by its pristine condition is the Vietnamese log. He marches right by Morrisey without a glance.

But Davies looks increasingly upset as he approaches the major. He shows Mendez the entry, the first name and rank, explains with much urgency that that's all the information he had time to obtain. The major takes the book, hands it to the admiral and asks if that is the first name of his son. The admiral doesn't move. The major turns the log around and holds it out.

The naval officer looks down at the book, then at the

major, his face still expressionless. "That is what the American sailors call him."

"That's right, sir! I got the name from one . . ."

"Where's the body, Davies?"

"I don't know, sir."

"You don't know?"

"It was at Graves, sir, but Thieu was here a little while ago and said he'd made arrangements to take care of it. I don't know what they were. Graves and Thieu have their own system, sir."

"And this is all the information you could get?"

Davies looks at the ground. "That's all the American sailor I spoke to knew. He was the only one conscious."

"No tags or wallet?"

"I didn't look, sir. Graves would probably know."

"Why didn't you check with them this morning?"

"I don't know, sir . . . I was busy."

Mendez looks at the admiral. "Did you understand that, sir?"

"Yes." There's a long silence. "Can you bring this Thieu to me?"

The major looks at his clerk.

"I doubt it, sir. You know Thieu." Davies stares right at Mendez, his eyes wide, face flushed and sweaty. He's to one side of the admiral and cannot bring himself to turn and face the Vietnamese officer.

"Do you under . . ."

"Yes, Major. I understand." The admiral turns and starts back toward the helicopter pad.

"Admiral! Can we make arrangements to take you to Graves Registration?"

The admiral stops and halfway turns toward the major, twists his head on its thick neck slightly and speaks over his shoulder. "That won't be necessary."

"I'm sorry, sir," Mendez calls.

We watch the whiteness fade like a mirage in the shimmering blue day until there is nothing but the distant echo of its passing. A skycrane flies overhead with a huge, netted cargo, punctuates the hush that has descended on us.

The major looks at Davies.

Morrisey watches this encounter for a moment, then goes inside the treatment room. If in the time before he turns away he knows anything but pleasure, I don't see it.

"Why don't you know what happens to Vietnamese soldiers?" Mendez asks in low, clipped tones.

"I'll find out, sir."

"I've talked to you about this before. So did Sergeant Smith—just the other day! You screwed up on me, Davies." He turns around and, with his head lowered, pushes through us toward his quarters. Davies stands motionless, devastated.

FOUR

Two miles across the plantation from the medical company, ninety-six other men and I police the compound at the division's jungle training school. It's been almost two months since my arrival in Vietnam, fully six weeks after the time when I was to take this orientation course, and except for the fact that I've enjoyed some uninterrupted sleep, the school has been an exercise in convention. Smith made me attend because of his inflexibility about rules: there was no mark on my records signifying I'd attended the school. In no way could he have foreseen a lesson in guilt.

"Fire!"

Flames leap above the roof of the shanty we used less than an hour ago for the tear gas exercise.

Master Sergeant Pinedo, who's in charge of the five day course, stands between us and the road to the shanty. He's a huge, neckless, red-haired man with skin like ivory and a swath of freckles arching over his nose. He raises his hand in a listless gesture to indicate that we should remain where we are. He makes no motion toward the building. The gas-permeated wood crackles with the cheeriness of a winter blaze.

We watch the fire with curiosity, welcome the diversion. Pinedo makes it plain that not only are we not to do anything, there's nothing to do. I wouldn't exactly say he's been nice during this week, but he's been exceedingly patient, disavowing the usual harassing training methods. More important than that, however, is the fluid, almost feline spareness of his words and gestures, his compelling sense of selfcontrol.

The orange and yellow flames roll upward in a dense cloud that vanishes in the green canopy of trees, then reappears to coil lazily high into the empty afternoon. Somewhere in the distance a siren wails, its urgency muffled by the tropical heat.

Near the end of the road that tunnels through the foliage toward division headquarters a fire engine, resplendent with flashing lights, growls through an intersection and disappears. There's a stunned silence among us. Pinedo bends down slightly and peers up the road. I can almost feel the beginning of a smile on his face.

The fire engine backs cautiously into view. As it turns and begins to barrel triumphantly down the road toward our compound, spewing huge clouds of dust and black exhaust, we burst into cheers. We applaud it right through the gates to its screeching stop near the burning building.

The fire pops merrily.

Hanging to the truck, dressed in American firefighting equipment many sizes too large, are the plantation's Vietnamese firemen. As they jump from the vehicle, the rolled cuffs of their boots cause them to hop and hobble like stricken fowl. An occasional grin flashes among the bobbings of the enormous rubber helmets.

Our cheers become peals of laughter.

Under the raging supervision of an American civilian, the lead fireman gallops toward the collapsing frame of the shack. To the applause of the crowd, a stream of water gushes forth, describes a lovely arc over the fire, then subsides to a few drops.

I sink down on a bench; the pain in my sides is excruciating. I can't stop laughing. All around me my classmates wipe tears from their eyes, shake their heads in disbelief, or simply seek physical support from each other. I have scarcely regained control of myself when, as though by prearranged signal, the firemen turn toward us in unison and smile.

The ovation is thunderous.

The American civilian looks up from the broken pump and casts a bleary glance over his shoulder, first at his firemen standing in a row holding the limp hose, then at us, then at Pinedo, who has leaned against a tree and buried his head in his arms. "Sergeant! Get control of these men!" the American screams.

Pinedo raises his head and studies the civilian while we break up once more. He gives us rein for several moments, his eyes locked with those of the civilian, then glances at his watch. "OK, gentlemen," he says, scarcely raising his voice.

Amid quiet murmuring and occasional ripples of mirth, we casually resume our police call.

A sultry post-noon silence descends on the compound. We're in the bleachers now, in a large, open-sided shed. Struggling to keep awake, the undertones of conversation soothe me until, with a snort, I jerk my head up from a feverish sleep. It's Texas all over again, thirteen weeks earlier and thousands of miles and lightyears away.

Unidentified objects from the trees drop onto the tin roof of the shed with the softness of rain. We are waiting for a representative of the judge advocate general's office to talk to us about the Geneva Conventions. We've already spent interminable hours firing weapons from the sun-blasted perimeter of the base, reviewed the uses of a compass and maps, and learned the use of plastic explosives. I'm one of only three men in the class not destined for the infantry, and the only one who has already been introduced to his permanent assignment. Everyone else is still in transit, although this class is the last phase.

On one hand, it's hard not to feel smug about my assignment. I'm lucky that the course is only an exercise for me, a fulfillment of protocol, and I do very well in these exercises. Maybe I'm a natural leader, or would be except for one thing: I'm beginning to be afraid that I'm a coward because I'm not going to combat. This hasn't been a serious problem until now. I try to tell myself that the others are simply unlucky. At one point I even tried to imagine the landscape as my classmates might, as a foretaste of a coming ordeal. Suddenly, I became humiliated by this childish indulgence. I haven't done it since.

At night in the school's screened hooch, I invariably awoke to the pounding of approaching helicopters, and in their wake, heard the breathing of the men around me. I wondered if they had any intimation of the meaning of that vibrato, if they, too, were dragged from a warm sleep to listen with a tightness in the stomach. Here, I could go back to sleep: only my mind raced toward blasting lights, watched other men abducted from their dreams. I realize from the soundness of my sleep here, the relief, that I'm exhausted at some gut level after only two months.

"TENSHUP!"

A sunny world . . . activity around me . . . a clatter that swells carrying me with it, causes me to rise before I'm even sure where I am.

"ALL AWAKE NOW? YOU THERE, YOU AWAKE?" Pinedo, down in front of the bleachers, smiles over his huge chest.

I blush. "Yes, Sergeant!"

"GOOD! Now . . . SEATS!"

Once again I'm moved by sound, this time downward as scores of men take their seats on the wooden bleachers. I note the muffled thuds, the erratic quality of sound that five months ago in the cinderblocked classrooms at Fort Dix would not have been tolerated. In one class at Dix we were forced alternately to sit and stand for an hour until the desired "thump" of perfect unison was achieved. By that time the class was over—I haven't the faintest idea what it was originally intended to be about.

"OK, you guys, listen up! Last class! Stay awake!"

I stare numbly at the lush surroundings, at a swarm of insects spinning upward beyond the shed.

"A Captain Marchel is going to speak to you about treatment of enemy captives, but he isn't here yet and I've got a few final announcements, so listen up . . ."

It seems so civil, so normal. "A few final announcements" and we'll go back to our barracks or home on pass for the weekend. Take a bus, a train. How has anything this absurd become so tolerable in so short a time? I contemplate the world beyond the confines of the shed: the scenery's all wrong.

The announcements completed, the shed once again fills with idle chatter. Pinedo's talking to a recruit; my eyelids begin to sag. The Geneva Conventions are only dimly comprehensible, like World War II movies and huge city theaters with uniformed ushers . . . from another time. There's a screech of brakes, and drops of perspiration fall from my armpits, glide down my skin.

"TEE-IN-SHUP!"

I'm on my feet again. A slight man wearing captain's bars stands beside Pinedo holding a cap in one hand, a black portfolio in the other. His hair is neatly combed and parted and his dark eyes sweep the audience from behind a pair of black-framed glasses. All that's missing is a leather chair and walnut panelling. Maybe he has the trappings, too, in one of those mobile homes the Judge Advocate General Corps uses for its offices.

"At ease, gentlemen. Take your seats." The voice is not loud but piercing. "I know some of you are going to think this little talk is so much crap, but while I'm here you will pay attention." He holds up a small, folded card with the Military Assistance Command, Vietnam, or MACV, emblem on the cover. "Have you all been issued this?"

He's answered by sporadic grunts of assent.

"OK, how many have read it?" Several hands float up. "Not bad—about half. For the benefit of those who didn't, we're going to read it again." He starts to read the abbreviated Geneva code, emphasizing certain parts in a manner that defies my dozing. Suddenly, very loudly, he repeats, " *'Mistreatment of any captive is a criminal offense. Every soldier is personally responsible for the enemy in his hands.'* And that, gentlemen, does not mean your CO or platoon sergeant." He glances around. "OK? Now, let's go back and look at this card again, only I'm going to read you a few of the related articles of the Conventions as well. Then I want you to tell me what you think they mean."

My first impulse is to laugh at the idea of a seminar, but gradually I become vaguely bothered, then fascinated by these questions of law. Soon, I begin to raise my hand and before much longer everyone except Sergeant Pinedo is doing the same, hotly discussing and arguing the "issues." But I'm also angry because I've been stimulated this way. It's stupid in a place like this.

The discussion roars on for several minutes before Marchel holds his hands up. He waits a few seconds, then starts to speak. "Not bad. I think you have a pretty good idea of what those words are trying to convey. Now who's going to be the *Argosy* hero who is going to ask why we honor accords the enemy hasn't even signed? Who's going to ask why there have to be rules and laws about fighting a war, particularly one as thoroughly screwed up as this one is?"

"Right here, sir!" someone behind me shouts, "but it's not *Argosy,* it's the New York *Daily News!*" Marchel laughs

51

with the rest of us. When he stops, a few lingering, self-satisfied chortles echo from the top of the bleachers.

"You know and I know that when you get out in the field, particularly you infantrymen, you're going to be able to do just about anything you damn well please without fear of legal reprisal, at least in regard to the enemy. No cops. Let's face it—you got permission to kill people. Some of you are going to take advantage of it and what I want you all to understand is no matter what you think about applying rules to war, if you throw them away things will only get worse.

"As long as you have laws that point toward some recognizable sense of justice and order, some carry-over from your so-called civilian lives, you've got a handle on brutality. You close the channels those laws provide, you lose that handle —it's as simple as that. I doubt that you'll ever be more susceptible to barbarity than right now, right here in Vietnam, particularly when your life is threatened or one of your friends is maimed and you begin to get angry about it.

"I bet most of you feel you've been sent from a great civilization to a backward land to help some poor, downtrodden gooks win a war they couldn't win otherwise. On the other hand, maybe a lot of you wonder why Uncle Sam couldn't have left you alone?" This observation is met with a roar of applause.

Marchel sweeps an arm in a gesture that encompasses the entire outdoors. "Look at them . . . they still use water buffalo and think they're really hot shit if they own a Honda 90." He ignores the scattered snickers. "War's uncivilizing as well as uncivilized. Individuals become uncivilized. This country isn't. These are good-hearted, intelligent people, and the fact that it's still apparent after almost three decades of continuous war is a tribute to the greatness of their civilization.

"I've spoken about the Geneva Conventions—by extension, there's even a good reason for Army Regulations . . ." Marchel pauses and smiles in the face of wild boos and hisses. " . . . a rationale for the Army Regs, the chain of command. These are vestiges of law, of order and predictability—a little crude, I admit, but they're intended to help keep you guys together so you can help one another and get out of here in one piece, not only physically, but mentally. I believe all laws are based on the fact that every man is capable of doing terrible things. No one here's an exception.

Being civilized is not an automatic provision of American citizenship.

"Some of you are going to chuck the rules. I don't care what your reason is—and there are some pretty powerful ones floating around—you'll forfeit your claim to being civilized, and you'll be screwing up your buddies' chances of maintaining theirs. I don't give a shit if you rip the card up when you leave here, there's still wisdom there that could have a lot of bearing on how you make it out of here one year from now."

The audience is hushed; a year, suddenly, is a very long time.

"Put a different way, just recently the war's become especially ugly in this division. Many Vietnamese, including the enemy, have a strong belief in what's called 'transmigration.' They're ancestor worshippers. They believe that when they die as humans their souls assume other living forms—animal, whatever."

"Captain! I bet they're glad they got that transmigration what with the pee we're raining on them!"

"Yeah, they're all going to the dogs!"

The assembly roars.

Pinedo looks up and lets his gaze wander toward the top of the bleachers. The beginning of a frown wrinkles his brow.

"To a Vietnamese who believes in transmigration, if he's physically mutilated in this life, he'll suffer a similar disfigurement in the next."

"My God! I bet they got steel jockstraps!"

"ALRIGHT BACK THERE!" Pinedo jumps to his feet and points past my head. I feel mortified despite my laughter.

The man sitting next to me buries his face in his hand. "Christ! I wish they'd just let the poor sonuvabitch finish," he murmurs.

Marchel suddenly looks tired. Our initial absorption, the vestiges of seminarial discussion and comprehension have vanished. He doesn't look surprised. He lowers his voice, causing us to strain to hear him. "So it's funny . . . Well, for a long time this was a fairly clean sector of the war. Men died, them and us and a lot of civilians, but no one seemed to relish the job, no one did any more than might be expected. Then some wiseass started cutting off ears for trophies to show Sarge—body count and all that, and maybe to have something to take home to show the guys on the block what a tough man he was. He had the ears strung like a necklace. POK—proof of kill. You'll find out about it soon enough. It's very seductive.

"It spread. More ears got cut off and a lot of guys got into stuffing the division patch in the mouths of the enemy dead. It was real macho to go around with a few threads dangling and a dark place on your fatigue shirt where your patch had been. Then one day one of our own men was found dead, and where his tongue had been was his division patch. Big outcry! Goddam gooks are perpetrating war crimes! It got a hell of a lot worse around here until we managed to catch up with a few of the guys. A couple got sent to LBJ, a few more home, and things began to settle down a bit . . . but it's really hard to stop once something like that gets started. After it's been done once, once soldiers are made conscious of the possibility, it's much easier to cross that line into brutality. The enemy's no different than you in that regard—he's tough and he doesn't want to see his buddies maimed any more than you do. That's what the Geneva Conventions are about."

For an instant, that white face beneath its crisply parted hair knows us in a terrible way. The eyes encompass us in one brief sweep, then drop, and Marchel begins to put his papers back in the portfolio.

He seems surprised when he raises his head and finds us still in front of him, motionless and silent. "That's all I have to say, fellas." He flips his hand in a gesture of dismissal and starts to walk out of the shed.

The applause is spontaneous, tumultuous. I slam the palms of my hands together with as much fervor as the rest of my classmates. I can scarcely distinguish my own sounds through the roar of stomping feet, whistles, clapping—I can't understand the emotions that besiege me.

Pinedo shouts for quiet. Beyond the shed the captain's jeep roars out the compound gate. Whorls of dust churn through the trees.

I want to talk to Marchel again, to field ideas about law and war, magnificent thoughts! Maybe I can find out where his office is . . .

"Hey, Sarge!" It's one of the men from the top of the bleachers. "Hey, Sergeant Pinedo! You never cut no ears off, did you?"

Pinedo smiles broadly. The tension in the bleachers snaps

with thunderous guffaws. The laughter devastates me, obliterates any illusions. For the first time I sense just how far I really am from home.

After that school, that afternoon in particular, I had a feeling of relief and familiarity, a perverse security as I heard a helicopter begin to crank up, the jet rising to a high scream before succumbing to the chop of the rotor. Vanishing into the azure furnace, it would return like some blinded creature to alight on the tarmac and disgorge its load: one man strapped to a litter who's shouting obscenities at the crew, the medics who carry him in, and Brock until all Brock wants to do is punch him in the mouth. Instead, he sends someone looking for Jenkins, our psychological technician, and reaches for the thorazine.

"These goddam anxiety reactions—I've had them up to here!" Brock draws a hand across his throat.

"You sonuvabitch! I ain't gettin' no shot!" The soldier, his eyes squeezed shut, tears oozing through his long lashes, thrashes and jerks against the straps like a trash fish some fisherman has thrown on the shore.

And maybe that's the way he feels, I think without sympathy. Once begun, something like this develops its own momentum and has to be played out—the humiliation must be incredible. This guy isn't nuts. But by now I've seen this sort of thing far too often to muster the angry resentment that many others express. Brock, though, is in an exceptional mood: he usually reserves his fury for stimuli outside the patient category. He's not having any success administering the thorazine. He even bends the needle when the soldier yanks his arm away at the moment of impact, producing a tiny spurt of blood.

Suddenly Jenkins is standing at the foot of the litter. He's well over six feet tall and black. His gaze is fixed on the soldier. The rounded cheekbones, large brown eyes and slightly flattened nose suggest a gentleness that belies his dispassionate scrutiny of the patient.

"I've been trying to give him thorazine," Brock says with a note of defensiveness. "He's hyperactive." He glances at the psych tech to register his reaction. He knows Jenkins doesn't like the administration of thorazine before he's had a chance to evaluate a patient. This is a running conflict between Jenkins and Major Mendez and Newell, both of whom have no tolerance for psychic ills.

"Give it to him if it makes you feel better, sir," Jenkins says.

Brock looks at the hypodermic in the open palm of his hand, then at the soldier who's watching both men, wide-eyed. "Jenks . . ."

"Sir?"

Brock flaps his elbows downward in a gesture of defeat, then rams his hand through his hair. "I'll get back at you on the basketball court."

A huge grin spreads over Jenkin's face. Brock places the hypodermic gently on the table and walks out of the tent.

A few minutes later Jenkins leaves with the soldier beside him, unstrapped, walking. They go to the psych tech's office at the back of the sickcall tent where they are able to ignore the next helicopter that arrives carrying another soldier from the same platoon. When that man dies of fragment wounds, a large crowd begins to gather outside the sickcall tent to watch the body's removal to the morgue.

Morrisey forces his way into the sickcall tent. Several men are casting angry looks toward the back, toward Jenkins and his patient. There's a pungent smell of hot canvas and moist wood, and a constant murmur of voices in the yard.

Morrisey and I start down the long hallway, leaving Davies at the counter diligently writing the dead man's name in the log, acting as though nothing unusual's happening. Morrisey knocks on the partition.

"What's going on?" Jenkins asks. There are two chairs at a desk. Jenkins is in one, the soldier in the other wiping reddened eyes. He looks sheepish and very young.

"Can you come up front for a minute, Jenks?"

Reluctantly, Jenkins pushes himself away from the desk.

Morrisey speaks in a loud whisper. "Some of our men, some of the dead guy's, some of the patients don't like your patient. They think he should have been out there when his buddies got hit—that maybe the first dust-off generated the second."

Jenkins listens with his head bowed slightly, then walks past us to the front doorway. I stop beside the counter, across from Davies; my eyes are fixed on the back of Jenkins's shirt.

"You think he's nuts, don't you?" Jenkins jerks a thumb in the direction of his office. "Well, *he* thinks *that* guy was crazy!" He thrusts his arm out and points toward the morgue.

The men turn away in embarrassed silence.

My vision blurs and I can hear Jenkins's footsteps pass behind me, down the hall.

When they died on the treatment table or came in DOA, the body was exposed to view, to light, a logical, comprehensible phase in passage. A bag was different. Unzipping a bodybag's like turning over a rock.

Patients are staring at me as I duck into the small tent we call the morgue. Wearing blue pajamas and white slippers, the patients are gaudy, intense-looking creatures who forever hover with their anxieties around the perimeters of our work. There's a CONNEX a few feet away, a steel box about seven feet square, its contents, if any, a mystery. I find myself imagining the heat inside.

I glance at the patients craning in my direction, bite my lip and yank the tent flaps down. The interior is cast in the murky, brownish gold light of the translucent canvas. The bag's on a litter against one wall. A zipper runs its length, dividing the top. I study the shape, the rise for the feet at one end, the more gentle mound for the head.

Brock pushes through the tent flaps, out of the steaming brilliance of the day; the canvas makes a soft scraping sound as it drags over his clothing. "What a fucking day! This is the fourth, isn't it?"

"Fifth."

"That guy with the trach's going to live, I think. Murphy said he'd find out."

Murphy's a warrant officer, a pilot for Dust-Off. He's younger than I am, and a little crazy, but we all are. The heat alone would be sufficient.

Flies buzz in the tent. I realize that Brock's waiting for me to open the bag. I kneel on the ground beside the litter, pinch the large zipper between my thumb and index finger, and pull downward toward the feet. The zipper moves stiffly, grates and jerks on invisible grime.

The tent is low, forcing Brock to stoop. He gazes at the contents as I spread the bag open. "Worse than the last." He bends over, places his hands on his knees and studies the remains more carefully. The torso's virtually in two pieces, the head canted to one side, mouth open, skin saffron. The man's shirt is unbuttoned, disclosing a splattered chest, the dog tags flopped to one side. Brock reaches down and picks up the tags. The chain is still around the neck. "Private First Class. Probably not here very long. Want these?"

"No, sir. Leave them for Graves. I'll just take down the name and serial number."

He drops the tags back onto the body; they make a flat, metallic clatter. I twist them so I can read the information stamped on the surface. Then I glimpse what looks like a piece of copper wire sticking out where the dead man's shirt has fallen aside. I reach into the bag and lift the body slightly, feeling the dampness. I think of unimaginable horrors thriving in the gloom where my hand is groping. Dropping the tags and pen, I pull the shirt out from under the soldier's back. There's a second piece of wire and I unwind the two of them. The mangled field tag I withdraw bears the man's name, rank, unit, and race, "Cau," all hastily printed, the shaky letters protruding from the alloted spaces, the ink smeared.

Brock backs up against the center pole of the tent while I zip the bag.

"Diagnosis?" I ask.

"What was the last one?"

"Massive fragment wound to the stomach."

"What hit these guys?" Brock pushes his hand through his hair. It's prematurely grey. He looks in his midforties but is only thirty-two. His burliness is reminiscent of an old family physician.

"Hate to use the same diagnosis twice in succession. This guy was worse off." He ponders the situation for a moment, scratches his head furiously, then pushes out through the flaps. "Come with me."

I squint as I step into the light; a sense of intimacy, of solitude melts away as I stand erect and take notice of the world I left. The patients are looking at me now as though I've somehow changed.

We walk down the road behind the treatment area to Brock's hooch. Inside, a small fan whirrs beneath the mosquito netting draped over his cot. A book lies open on the poncho liner that also serves as a spread; its pages flutter in the breeze. Five packs of White Owls are piled on the desk. Brock walks over to an ammunition crate nailed to the wall and pulls out a paperback thesaurus; its cover is missing and the pages are tattered. "I rescued this from a trash barrel outside the orderly room the other day. Lifers probably didn't know what it was, except confusing. Here's the word: evisceration.'' He closes the thesaurus and holds it up with both hands as a preacher might a prayer book, then turns to me with a faint smile. "Put down 'traumatic evisceration.' Yeah, I gotta remember that. Sounds pretty good.''

"Yes, sir.''

I grinned at his professional satisfaction although I'm not grinning now. I didn't change last year. The World changed. The day-to-day assimilation of minute, even microscopic change was so completely disrupted that I was forced to confront the sum of 365 days. I'm now abhorrent of this place that wears the guise of home as I once knew it.

FIVE

Due south of the plantation a few miles away, there's a large village. I saw it from the plane the day I arrived from battalion. On the west side of the village is a military compound that once housed a French garrison but which is now occupied by the ARVN. A large stone tower looms above the compound where, beneath a limp, canvas roof, guards stand silhouetted against the sun. At the base of the tower, claymore mines peep toylike through the coils of wire at the crowds on Highway 10 and its intersection with the main street of the village.

Stalls line this intersection, primitive fast-food operations that provide—in addition to food and drink—pornography, dope, women, in fact everything that is sold in the village proper, only at higher convenience prices.

The main street leads away from Highway 10 and the compound into a large square with a fountain that has been defunct since the time of the French. The square serves as the village's open-air market, a raucous place where, among live and slaughtered fowl and other animals, vegetables and rice, stalls display an abundance of electronic equipment: transistor radios, television sets, cheap household utensils, furniture, and the gaudy bric-a-brac that marks a healthy tourist trade and black market.

Beyond the market, the main street winds among a maze of shops and houses. During the colonial era, the village was of some bureaucratic importance, a fact attested to by the number of substantial buildings and imposing residences. But the village ceases abruptly at the edge of a destroyed jungle, a landscape of ruptured trees. Here the main street splits and trickles east and south out into the hinterland to the American firebases.

Most of the residents of the village travel the few miles to the hilltop to work for us. The acres of rice paddies along the highway have been abandoned like the crumbling ancestral graves that protrude from the dust left by hundreds of passing vehicles.

It begins with a mortar barrage on the village square, the market place with the fountain that doesn't work. For more than two hours the helicopters arrive and depart constantly, ferrying civilian and American casualties from the village and its immediate environs. There are even occasional ARVNs, someone says from Mathias's unit, but all except two arrive in rubber bags.

The treatment area is choked with dust and litters. Davies and I move among the wounded in the yard, among the silences and beseeching groans of persons lying down, sitting up, of old women in black and babies. These are considered less urgent than the ones we've already tagged in the treatment tent. I'm sweating profusely as I kneel here and there and try to communicate with torn, unintelligible creatures; the moisture pours off my face onto the book of field medical tags and renders my pen useless. Davies, a few feet away, is standing up. Pen and tag book hang limply at his side. His T-shirt is plastered to his body. He shakes his head. I hear the swelling clatter of still another inbound helicopter and glance toward the tower, wiping my face with my arm. Two helicopters are approaching and suddenly the phone's ringing on the tent porch behind me and men are dashing toward the landing pad.

Thieu, our interpreter, arrives on his Honda, pulls the small bike up on its stand and walks over to Davies, who's desperately trying to control his anger. He's furious with Morrisey for what he considers a waste of time, is seething because he's been ordered by Mendez to waste time, to get the names of Vietnamese casualties when it's all he can do to keep up with what he considers essential—what we've been told is essential—all because Morrisey told Smith about the sixteen wogs and that business with the admiral.

I can hear the rage in Davies's curt greeting to Thieu, but Thieu kneels to talk to the wounded who can talk with a look of smooth-skinned, childish abhorrence, the restrained horror he invariably displays in such situations despite his repeated acquaintance with suffering, despite the fact that he's seen it for longer than any of us and will undoubtedly see it long after we're gone. He gives Davies each name, spells each one carefully; his dark eyes study the clerk as he presses his pen to the book of tags and scribbles with a ferocity that conveys itself in every muscle of his body.

Another helicopter arrives, then another.

"Awww, shit!" someone groans.

But the ships are empty. They've refueled and now squat down to wait for more litters to carry south.

"Close the fucking door!" Newell screams from inside the tent as the wave of dust swirls through the trees.

And then the worst cases are gone.

The tables in the tent are still occupied but the remaining patients are mostly ambulatory and will be treated and allowed to return to the village, or their units, or wherever they came from. I'm beside one of the wounded ARVNs watching Morrisey debride shrapnel from the man's right arm and belly. Smith and Buelen recently arrived and are a short distance away, near the back door, talking quietly to each other.

Brock's working on another ARVN at the table next to ours.

Irritated, Morrisey turns to find a short American soldier in camouflage fatigues peering over his shoulder. "What do you want?"

Smith stares in our direction. A puzzled, almost belligerent look appears on his face.

"I want to see my man," the soldier, a sergeant E-6, says. He's wearing a battered jungle hat and rimless glasses. With his full, reddish beard, he looks like a Mennonite farmer. A belt of cartridges is slung over his right shoulder, a grease gun hangs loosely in his hand.

Morrisey spots the submachine gun. "Hey! First put that thing out on the porch!"

Startled, the sergeant looks at Morrisey, then at the gun. "Oh," he says and walks up the aisle to lean the gun against the door jamb.

Smith has started toward us but hesitates at a motion from Morrisey. He shakes his head with an expression of disgust. Buelen's disapproval is equally apparent.

"It took me a moment, but that's Eddie Mathias," Morrisey murmurs as he turns back to the ARVN and pulls the surgical light over the arm.

"I know," I say. "No one else can look like that around here and get away with it."

The ARVN lifts his head and watches the bushy American sergeant, now back at Morrisey's side. He asks Mathias something in Vietnamese. The sergeant replies quietly in the soldier's language.

"How bad is he hurt?"

Morrisey's located another small piece of shrapnel; he pushes the tissue aside so he can extract it with a pair of forceps. "He'll be OK when we get through here if he keeps the wounds clean. X rays showed nothing serious."

Mathias relays this to the ARVN, who relaxes and lies back. He doesn't look soft and fearful the way so many ARVNs do.

"Doesn't have to be hospitalized?"

Morrisey lets the bloody bit of steel drop in the pan beside him. He shakes his head.

"My weapon was empty. Sorry. I should have left it out there in the first place. I forgot I even had it in my hand."

"No problem, Sergeant Mathias." Morrisey pronounces the name carefully as though to confirm the reality of the man beside him.

And he's not the only one. I'm having a terrible time relating this short, casual person to the figure I first saw beside a flamboyant truck in front of the hamlet gates. He seems much smaller now, as diminutive as the natives he leads. I glance out the front of the tent. The outrageous machine with its flags and decals is just in sight beyond the corner of the ward.

Mathias moves on to the next table and starts talking to Brock just as Major Mendez comes down the aisle, observing each patient in turn. He watches Morrisey for a moment, then goes to the next table where he immediately becomes embroiled in a lively conversation with Brock and Mathias.

I hear a commotion in the yard between the treatment tent and the back of commo. Smith is trying to collect the men who formed his sandbag detail before the cry came for litter-bearers, but Stevens is complaining, insisting one of the helicopters is still out. Smith smiles. "Stevens, you never want to work."

"That isn't true, Sarge!" but the others laugh and he's defeated.

Smith removes his shirt to begin work, an effective measure for silencing complainers.

Thieu has vanished.

Mathias leaves with his two ARVNs, heading for Graves Registration to reclaim the rest of his men. The only clue to the distress he might feel is the extreme gentleness he displays to the survivors.

Three patients remain: two GIs and an enemy soldier. All are to be sent south but they aren't priority and nothing has been heard from the helicopter that's still out. Davies, who has made a valiant effort to obtain information about the Vietnamese wounded, makes no attempt to learn the name of the Viet Cong soldier. That is work for the MI, the Military Intelligence team.

Only moments after Mathias's departure, they arrive. In the front of a jeep are two hatless ARVN officers with their sleeves rolled up and their watches gleaming from their wrists. A tall, bulky, and uncoordinated looking American captain clings to his cap in the rear seat. They bounce right into the yard and stop with a brief screech a few feet from the bench at the front of the treatment tent. The American, still grasping his cap, seizes the driver's seat with his free hand as he's propelled backward. A cloud of dust overtakes and swamps the vehicle. All three clamber out of the jeep and scramble toward the major, who watches them with an obvious mixture of curiosity and distaste.

By some unseen signal, the captain's suddenly launched to the front of the trio to present their request.

"No, Captain," Mendez replies. "You know my policy." There's no emotion on either side.

"But we might save American lives, sir."

The major smiles briefly, ironically. "This is a medical facility, Captain. The man's a patient and in no condition to be interrogated, not here."

And that's all. The jeep with its three officers and two wristwatches bangs out of the yard and away down the road. "Juan," Brock says, ambling up beside Mendez, "you know those shitheads are just going to go on down the line and do their thing."

"Let 'em! I'm not running this war."

Soon there's nothing but the drone of fans in the treatment

tent, brief snatches of conversation, the clanging of a tire iron in the motor pool. The yard is empty; the landing pad ripples in the heat. A faint breeze rustles the trees that tower above us, causes leaves to fall in slow gyrations.

The two GIs and the enemy soldier lie quietly on their stretchers, secure in the knowledge they are still alive and will probably remain so. The doctors have retreated to their quarters leaving a group of us on the bench, smoking and idly watching the horizon.

Gittoni, the radio operator, suddenly appears at the front door. He gazes toward the tower for a moment, then smiles, remembering the reason for his visit. He slaps Morrisey on the shoulder. "Twenty ARVNs, inbound."

Morrisey stares at the grinning radio operator. "You want to know what I think?"

"Nope. Murphy says his ship's like a bucketful of night-crawlers. His crewchiefs threatening to bail out and he hasn't heard from his medic in ten minutes."

The shadows of the trees have crept out to the edge of the tarmac. The air is hazy with the blue-black smoke of rubbish burning down the road at the engineers; the eternal dust drifts in the wake of a passing convoy. We all stare at the horizon.

"If Gittoni left his radio to tell us, it can't be that urgent," I say. To a man we're skeptical, we wonder how there can be twenty of anybody on a Huey when the usual complement, excluding the crew, is four to seven.

The distant vibrations begin to roll in. We wait, motionless, constrained by the interminable protraction of that sound. At last the ship appears. It seems to float sideways out from behind the rubber trees, then hangs for an instant against the sky, the flashing red light fighting that moment of perilous stasis.

Suddenly it's upon us, hammering down the alley scarcely inches off the ground, losing its battle for altitude. The skids slam the pavement, the ship rocks, and we remain frozen by the spectacle in front of us.

Both sliding doors are open. ARVNs literally jam the ship; their legs dangle from the doors, their arms are in constant motion as they struggle to maintain any handhold against the mounting pressure from within; their faces form a mawkish wall of pain. And over the roar of the ship itself another sound rises like the ululations of hell. Stuffed against the rear wall of the side compartment facing us is the crewchief, his face burning with rage. I can't see the ship's medic.

"Oh, mother!" someone screams behind me. We hesitate one last instant, then rush under the blades. The surge throws me up against the ship where I seize an ARVN by the arm. The soldier leaps past me and crashes on the tarmac with a howl.

"He's a fucking faker!" the crewchief bellows, whipping his mouthpiece aside. He shoves himself down out of the helicopter and jams a boot under the soldier's ass. The soldier screams again but refuses to stand. A medic beside me drops a litter and starts to kick it open, but ARVNs are dropping to the ground everywhere and he's inundated.

Hobbling beyond the blades, clutching arms, heads, bellies, any area of their bodies they believe injured, the ARVNs form a gyrating morass led by a shirtless soldier hopping on one foot. Gradually they move down the road toward the treatment tent; discarded ammunition belts, grenades, weapons, helmets, canteens, packs, litter their wake.

"Is that sonuvabitch hopping on his left foot?" the crewchief hollers.

"What?" I shout.

"That sonuvabitch in front there! Is he hopping on his left foot?"

"Yes!"

"That fuckhead was hopping on his right foot when we picked him up!" Having said this, the crewchief whirls, reaches into the compartment with maniacal fury, grabs any extremity—arm, leg, foot, finger—that avails itself, and begins to yank startled men from the ship faster than they can tumble out on their own accord. Fallen ARVNs scrabble over the pavement on their hands and knees and in among our legs as they try to avoid colliding with their companions crashing to the ground behind them.

I'm immobilized again, this time by laughter. All I can think of as I watch these soldiers with their silk kerchiefs draped over their collars, the number of their infantry unit embossed in a red circle in the middle of the kerchiefs and on the brass slides at their throats, all I can visualize is a terrorized troop of boy scouts—which undoubtedly, until a few months ago, they were.

There's only one more litter patient. Hanging from the top rung, he peeps over the edge of the canvas at the ferment below; his kerchief, supporting his jaw, is knotted like rabbit ears on top of his head. I reach up and grab the litter handles while the exhausted crewchief unhooks the stretcher at the other end. When our eyes come level the ARVN crinkles his face and squawls.

We pass the two Americans and the Viet Cong soldier being carried to the waiting helicopter when we cross the road into the grove.

The treatment tent is absolute chaos. ARVNs sit, lie, stand in every conceivable position on the floor, benches, and tables. Laughter and stacatto snatches of blithe conversations in Vietnamese mingle with the moans and wails of those who have yet to be convinced they're not dying. And all of these sounds are accompanied by a steady stream of curses—in English.

Brock arrives fresh from a short nap. His hair is frazzled and the butt of a cold White Owl snatched from the ashtray wags at the corner of his mouth. He stops just inside the back door. "What the fuck is this?" he demands with a look of mounting consternation, "Headstart?"

One soldier has a bullet wound in his leg. Fifteen minutes later, he's the only patient remaining inside the tent. The others have received tetanus shots and bandaids and have been herded out into the yard, where they limp here and there, far fewer limping than before, and gather their very lethal manhood with profound delicacy.

Brock joins Morrisey and me just as a South Vietnamese Army truck arrives. "Who the hell do we think we're kidding?" Brock asks.

Two ARVN officers have climbed out of the cab and are threading their way toward us among the anxious looks of their soldiers. They salute Morrisey, presumably because he's wearing full fatigues and is propped against the doorway in such a manner as to convey a casual sense of authority. Brock's decked out in his usual soiled T-shirt.

"How many hurt?" one of the officers asks Morrisey, who jerks a thumb in Brock's direction.

Brock holds up an index finger to the astounded officers. "One." They quickly salute him.

"That all? These can go?" the other officer asks, amazed, as he surveys the men in front of the tent.

"Yeah. Get them out of here."

It wasn't the weapons they used, or the uniforms they

wore, or even how they wore them—pants tapered to such absurd extremes that they hopped around like bandy-legged chickens. It was simply the people themselves, their naive antics and damn puerile charm.

Now the Viet Cong, the NVA, they were their own soldiers, were themselves. You had to respect them even if they were gooks. None of this ARVN, Regional Forces, Popular Forces, Regular Forces chickenshit dreamed up in some corporate general's office in the Pentagon. Berets, kerchiefs, patches, medals, Weblos.

Monthly reports . . . this is my second monthly report and Davies's last if he has anything to say about it. Captain Shelby enters the office and stares over my shoulder.

"Number of civilians seen, Davies?" It's the second time I've asked the question. "How the hell am I supposed to compute it?"

"What do you think, sir?" Davies asks, the inflection in his voice changing—I wouldn't exactly call it simpering.

"Hah!" Shelby retorts. He's unusually animated tonight, a fact I have corroborated by the size of his pupils. "How many girl scouts came here on that tour last week?"

"About thirty, sir." Davies beams with anticipation.

"OK. That means we saw thirty civilians in the treatment room, thirty in the lab, thirty in X ray, thirty in the dental tent, thirty in sickcall, and thirty on the ward making a grand total of . . ." He rolls his eyes up in their sockets while he does the calculation, "one hundred and eighty civilians seen at this location!" He promptly departs, waving his spaghetti strainer in little circles and chuckling grandly to himself; his rubber sandals slap on the tent platform.

"Alright, Davies. How many Medcaps were there?" Medcaps are our service to civilians, bringing medicine into the countryside and villages. It stands for "medical capitulation" or some such bureaucratic nonsense. I ceased deciphering all the abbreviated military terminology about two hours after my induction. "Well? Three? Four? Should I put down ten?"

He glares at me over the rims of his glasses. "The major has to sign this report, O'Neill. Look it up!"

"Where, Davies?" I'm tired of being a yo-yo for his emotions—Morrisey would have told him to fuck off a long time ago. He should have taken this job, I conclude as Davies shoves past me and snatches a small, bound volume from a shelf above the desk. It's the first I've known of its existence. Another secret revealed.

Medcaps are important because they're part of the pacification program. To be able to record several of them on the monthly report is a measure of accomplishment, verifiable progress toward peace. You can make almost anything look good on paper, even death. It becomes a measure, and to measure is to know you're civilized.

The number of Medcaps performed and their success is contingent upon the attitude of the commanding officer of the medical unit performing the service and the war's caprice. Mendez is almost a believer, particularly because he thinks it's good for us to get out of the plantation. He tries to organize at least one Medcap a week, two if possible, but all arrangements must be cleared through PIO, the Public Information Office. PIO invariably milks these events for their propaganda value. They prefer Medcaps under trees in thatched hamlets to the clinic variety that is likely in the large villages, but they settle for anything.

Our local PIO is headed by Captain Donald Sylvester, a pejorative name in our company, especially among the officers. Sylvester believes in numbers. The more people seen, the greater the pacification. He continually thwarts the major's efforts to establish a regular schedule with follow-up medicine, and if for some unlikely reason he's not being an obstacle, the war often is. Military exigencies take priority. If a village or hamlet is declared unsafe, we can't return.

For the enlisted men in our company, Medcaps have become the reward Mendez probably intended. It's great to get out of the plantation. And despite certain dog-and-pony characteristics to many of these trips, working with the natives offers a much more interesting and positive sense of usefulness.

As good a medic as Morrisey is, he's almost too good. No one wants to let him out of the treatment room to go on Medcaps until Smith arrives. Although he frequently grouses about this prohibition, I suspect he's never tried very hard to overcome it because he's pleased to be considered indispensable. One evening, however, he takes Smith aside to launch the obligatory request to go on the next day's journey.

"You mean you haven't been on a Medcap before?"

"No, Sergeant. Because of sickcall."

"That's ridiculous! You'd be excellent. We can always get

someone to fill in for you. We should be training others anyhow.''

Morrisey looks crushed.

Later, Jenkins and I go looking for him and find him in his lawn chair in his hooch, feet on his cot, reading a book.

"Let's go to the club."

"I'm busy reading."

"Going tomorrow?"

To the club? I wonder, but Morrisey's not that naive.

"Didn't take long for that to get around."

Jenkins grins.

"I'll believe it when it happens. I don't trust Smith."

"Sounds like he's doing you a favor."

"I don't trust favors, especially not from lifers."

"C'mon, you're paranoid—you're not indispensable anymore."

"Fuck you, Jenkins!" Morrisey's savage. He buries his head in the book and tries to ignore us. Jenkins just stands there, a hand lightly on my forearm.

"I'll even buy the first round, Morrisey."

When we arrive in the village the next morning, the clinic seems vacant. "I wonder what the hell this was?" Brock asks as we pull into the courtyard and he views the three-storey structure. The steel gates to the courtyard, capped with iron bars like prison windows, are fastened open and streaks of rust are eating through the soft, blue paint. From the thick, cream-colored walls and interior shutters to the grates over the main-floor windows, the building's entirely French. The clamor of the market place with its defunct fountain a short distance up the street seems remote from the walled pocket in which we find ourselves, creates a disconcerting feeling of solitude. No one awaits us on the high steps.

Brock climbs out of the jeep and starts up the steps toward a covered porch and open doorway. With reluctance born of a sense of invading someone's privacy, or of an impending, dire mistake, Morrisey and I drag the wooden box of medical supplies out of the back of the vehicle. Nothing of value can be left behind, even for a moment.

Brock waits for us at the doorway. Together we step into the cool building onto a clean tile floor. Directly in front of us, midway across a room with lofty ceilings, is a small table and two chairs. The walls are bare, their length broken on both sides by pairs of panelled doors. The doors on the right are shut; those on the left, open, disclose a lone, glass-fronted steel cabinet painted white. Sunlight streams through the courtyard windows casting barred shadows across the floor to the base of the cabinet.

An archway in the middle of the far wall opens onto another room and a short flight of stairs. The stairs descend into a tiny court where the sun pours in among the shadows and accentuates a single, green plant.

Brock resolutely starts to comment on the architecture, his voice vaulting through the silent chamber. He has just commenced a discourse about the failings of French colonialism when one of the doors on the right opens and a woman glides into our presence. Suddenly the building seems vast and secretive, full of distant, empty rooms.

"Doctor Brock?" the woman inquires in a soft voice.

"Miss Lahn?"

The woman is young. I contemplate the spotless white dress, the cascade of black hair, the way she moves like a shadow, and find her both appealing and absolutely unapproachable. From the doorway to the sun-striped room with its steel cabinet Morrisey scrutinizes her, striking as he does so an unconscious pose as a classical god; the chiseled features and flying curls, cast half in shadow, intensify the sense of keen observation and a somewhat cynical amusement.

"Sergeant Thieu no come?" Miss Lahn asks.

"No. He had to go to Saigon."

"That OK. I speak English."

"Good." Brock lets his gaze drift around the premises while he struggles with mounting incredulity.

Thieu, with his Honda 90, Seiko watch, and pair of Bausch and Lomb sunglasses, is some kind of power in the hamlet inside the plantation. He's a medic in the ARVNs, too, which accounts for his assignment to us as interpreter. Brock says he's good. I've never seen him in anything but the custom-tapered fatigues that are all the rage among the ARVNs and make them look like storks. Like a lot of people here, they are probably the best, if not the only, clothes Thieu owns.

Morrisey claims Thieu runs the hamlet—calls him Wyatt Thieu. The problem with Thieu is he's never around when we need him, like today. Supposedly he's in Saigon on military business, but we all know that's bullshit.

Something in the room changes. I turn quickly to find an emaciated old man hobbling through the door on crutches.

He's wearing nothing but a pair of dirty shorts and a pith helmet. His skin is stretched tightly over his ribs. A bloody handkerchief flops from one hand. He stops and coughs violently into the rag; the effort causes his knees to collapse against each other, his entire body to shake.

Women press in behind the old man, some holding babies, others the hands of small childen. They stand in silence staring out of flat, broad faces, waiting at the edge of some imaginary line while the sun blazes peacefully behind them.

"My God!" Brock exclaims. "Where did they come from?"

"Ahhh! They know! I send word yesterday. You use table, Doctor." Miss Lahn turns and speaks to the patients. The clipped sounds of her native tongue and an added tone of severity contrast sharply with the gentleness of her English.

The old man has tuberculosis. Brock asks Miss Lahn about getting him to Saigon for further tests. She replies "Yes," or "Of course, Doctor," to everything he asks. Brock winces. "We could send him to the States. Might even cure him," he mutters, "so the folks at home can feel a nice, warm glow all over. Hell, Morrisey! Give him some sedatives. He's an old man and doesn't deserve such an ordeal."

Brock's lancing a large boil on the arm of a two-year-old boy who watches in silence from his mother's arms. Occasionally he raises his large, brown eyes to stare at the doctor, then lowers them again with the increasing pain. "In the States," Brock remarks as he pushes gently on the lance, "a kid would be screaming bloody murder if I were doing this . . . and the mother, too."

An American officer, a captain, bursts through the door, dwarfing the villagers who scramble to make way for him. "Captain Brock!"

"Captain Sylvester," Brock replies without moving his eyes from the lance.

"You were supposed to wait for my team!"

Brock contemplates Sylvester's crisp, starched uniform as he approaches the table. "It's the purpose of my organization, Captain Brock, to arrange these visits. We have reports to file, pictures to take. I realize you're new."

Sylvester towers over the table, over the mother and her son, over the frowzy-headed doctor. For an instant I feel sorry for Brock, for his sweat-soaked fatigues . . . he'll never be able to wear a three-piece suit, I think. I take an intense dislike to Sylvester.

"And you are late, Captain," Brock says, resting his chin in his palm, "and I have a lot of work to do here. Also, I believe the word for what you do is 'publicity,' isn't it?"

Miss Lahn clasps her hands together and presses them to her stomach.

"OK," Brock continues. "There's an old man on crutches out there somewhere. Just left. He's wearing shorts and a pith helmet. We successfully treated him—a good example for the folks back home. They'll know that their tax dollars are being . . ."

"Thank you, Captain!" Sylvester interrupts. "In the future, I hope you won't try to make my job any more difficult than it already is." He turns toward the door just as shouts explode in the courtyard.

"What the hell's that?"

Sylvester stops, places his hands on his hips. "One of my men, Doctor, giving candy to the kids."

"You little shit!" a voice shrieks. "You already got one!"

"You're right, Captain. You're indispensable."

Sylvester glares at Brock, then lunges through the door.

Brock returns to the child, who is staring, like his mother, after the retreating PIO officer. "Pompous ass," he grumbles, and the child slowly turns his head and bathes him with his eyes. Brock winks.

"Miss Lahn."

"Yes, Doctor?"

"Until this boil is completely drained, the dressing should be changed daily."

"Of course, Doctor."

"You'll do it?"

"Yes, Doctor."

"You have bandages?"

"Of course, Doctor."

Brock looks thoughtfully down the line of villagers. The faces, the bodies are motionless, projecting a burden of expectant silence. "May I see them?"

"Bandaids? Of course we have them!" Miss Lahn exclaims, more loudly than at first. She starts for the room with the cabinet, then stops just inside the doorway, her shadow hesitating on the floor while she reaches into the pocket of her dress. I can feel the starch rip as she pushes her hand down and retrieves a small key.

Painstakingly, she unlocks the cabinet, swings the door open and withdraws a small, cardboard box. At this moment I see her shoes for the first time. As though the fact that she's wearing shoes, white oxfords of some sort, isn't wonder enough, as though anyone not American, or ARVN, or a whore wearing shoes in this village isn't a matter of some surprise, there's a chunk missing from the ankle of the left shoe, a ragged U-shaped piece as though a dog, or some toothed animal—maybe Miss Lahn herself in one of those empty rooms—simply took a bite out of it. It's only with the greatest effort that I'm able to remove my astonished gaze from her foot as she closes and relocks the door. She puts the key back into her pocket, watching her own movements intently, then briskly marches back to the table and presents the box.

Brock stares at the inscriptions on the sides. "You read French, Morrisey?"

"A little, sir."

"Yeah." Brock turns the box over and scratches at some mildew.

"I forget brush it off!" Miss Lahn reaches for the box but Brock tears it open and withdraws a gauze pad. When he pulls gently, it shreds.

"Give her what we got, Morrisey."

"Sir, these have been here for years! She'll just hoard whatever we give her!"

"Dammit, Morrisey, do what I say!" Brock drops the rest of the gauze onto the table and puts his hand out. Reluctantly, Miss Lahn reaches into her pocket for the key.

Morrisey follows Miss Lahn into the side room where Brock is rummaging through the bottles and containers in the cabinet. "Jesus, Morrisey! Some of this has been here since 1951. Lookit this!" He hands over a bottle.

"Take everything out of here and give her everything in the box!" Brock turns to Miss Lahn. "We're giving you new supplies," he says and walks back to the table and the line of villagers, the child waiting patiently in his mother's arms. Miss Lahn flutters after him, ecstatic with her new treasures.

"Make sure you empty all the containers in the wastebasket first," Morrisey cautions as we start to unload the cabinet. "Otherwise, she's just going to put it back in."

"What did you find so amusing when she first came in?" I whisper.

"Thieu warned me about her. He calls her 'Madame Schoolgirl.'"

. . . but there was really no human claim on the building with its walled courtyard, its unnatural feeling of quiet and seclusion in that raucous village. It was an artifact—it didn't belong to that time, to that particular world, or even to the men who created it. Polished, clean, it was not inhabited in the sense of being possessed—the same way a museum is not inhabited, not possessed.

I feel it even now, almost more than then . . . feel it as I see it, the unseen rooms where slitted sunshine pours over the tiles. Far, far downstairs, the green plant burgeons in the inner yard, attentive, as men in black steal through with a soft, lethal padding of bare feet. Within the sweaty walls of an upper room, Miss Lahn scrabbles about on her hands and knees, wide-eyed, munching on her shoe—that obsessive symbol of her station. My God, the horror of being alone in the top of that place and listening to a world close in.

"How do you feel about going to language school at division next week?" Smith asks. He hovers behind me while I log in sickcall, while I face the daily line of hushed resentment, of men guilty of the crime of being sick instead of shot. (I have to agree with Morrisey. It's hard to stand here and smell my juices, feel the sopping grasp of my clothing, and confront Smith, immaculately dressed, the cool eyes watching, absorbing imperturbably everything that happens.)

Of course his question's tantamount to an order—I know him that well by now, but as long as I agree, it will remain an invitation to respond. "As you know, O'Neill, we've been having a lot of trouble reporting these Vietnamese. Newell and Morrisey have agreed to go. With you in A&D and the two of them in treatment, it would form a pretty effective team, don't you think? The major thinks it's a fine idea."

"Sounds good, Sergeant," I reply and the more I think about it, the more I actually believe it is a good idea. It's an opportunity for some direct link to this country, a bond I've lately begun to need acutely. Yes, and although I dislike the colloquial use of the word "school" for a few days of classes, the idea that there might be three of us with a rudimentary understanding of Vietnamese is appealing.

At Morrisey's insistence we choose greater heat over closer obsevation, and climb the bleachers to a point several feet above the door to the auditorium that's to be our classroom. The bleachers slope down in a semicircle from the ceiling of this huge, louvered building to a raised platform with a lectern, a microphone, and three metal chairs. A four-foot reproduction of the division's insignia looms overhead.

An American major is standing beside an ARVN, the major wiping a prodigious amount of perspiration from his face with a white handkerchief while the ARVN, hands behind his back, makes polite conversation and smiles, oblivious to the heat.

I've already had indications, when we were coming over in the ambulance with Stevens, that neither Morrisey nor Newell share my enthusiasm. They claim there's no value in a class of such short duration, especially one conducted by the army. My arguments produced only silence.

Morrisey says, "If I can stay awake ten minutes in this heat, Newell, I'll buy you a beer."

There's a sprinkling of other enlisted men in the bleachers, but a far larger group are still outdoors, smoking. The major checks his watch, then fumbles with the microphone, lowering it for the ARVN. He flicks his finger against the mike and a hollow, metallic sound echoes from the loudspeakers. He leans down to announce the beginning of class.

"Christ, they look earnest!" Morrisey exclaims as the rest of the men enter the building. "Just check those uniforms! I thought we were bad."

"What in the hell are you talking about now, Morrisey?"

"Lookit 'em! They're all dressed up pretty to go to school. I wonder if someone remembered to bring a nice shiny breadfruit for the teacher."

The major begins to call the roll by name and unit. "Do you suppose they're going to do this every day?" Morrisey whispers.

"What?" Newell hisses back.

"Take attendance."

"What if they do?"

"Tell you later."

The major begins to introduce the Vietnamese instructor.

"I'll bet you another beer his first name's Nguyen or Tran, and that there's a Van in the middle."

The ARVN is introduced as Tran Van Thuong. He beams

at the class and nods his head several times as though to applause.

"See?"

"Morrisey, will you shut up? I'm here to learn something along with O'Neill, even if you're not!"

"Well, you'd best listen up, boy, and stop talking."

The room is suddenly filled with a nasal, singsong rendition of English. The instructor turns abruptly to the board and writes the word *Có*, the writing spidery and delicate like the writing we see on their medical tags and the endless notes from obscure village dispensaries. He writes the English translation, Yes, beside it.

"Incredible! They can write like that with chalk, too!"

"Shut up, Morrisey."

The ARVN points at the word, pronounces it carefully, then exhorts us to repeat it. His effort is met with silence. He repeats the request, urges us to respond in unison. A few voices chime a dubious response.

"No!" the instructor says, shaking his head vehemently. He pronounces the word again, then nods at us.

"Có!" we roar, the noise so loud and absurd that I laugh.

The ARVN beams. "Good!" He proceeds to write *'Khong* and the English translation No, then turns, pronounces the word, nods smartly toward the bleachers and waits.

Everyone resolutely shouts his own version. I've heard that in Vietnamese, one word can have dozens of meanings depending on how it's pronounced—that pronunciation is crucial, but with this bedlam, God knows what we're saying. I persist though, listening intently to the instructor, trying to echo him; the rest of the class repeatedly drowns out my voice.

"Life on the Commune," Morrisey mutters.

The major departs after turning the class over to the instructor, promising to return at the first break. Morrisey now wonders aloud if he hasn't crossed the road to the division's Officers' Club to escape our insane yelling and to get quietly plastered to the rhythm of the airconditioners. "Maybe he even sees this school as an accomplishment! I wouldn't be surprised if he's bragging to his buddies about it, code name "Project Native"—a tremendous step forward for the division, for the cause of communication with our Allies, for the promotion of World Peace!"

"Sah'woo!" the ARVN shouts, pointing to the word *Xâu*. "This means Bad!"

"Sah'woo!" we shout. The ARVN claps his hands.

After several minutes more of this, I hear a loud snort beside me. Morrisey's chin is almost touching his chest; beads of moisture drop off his face. He snorts again, lifts his head, starts to open his eyes. The whites roll upward as the lids drift down and soon his chin is on his chest again.

Newell jabs him. "Wake up, Morrisey!"

"Dau!" the instructor hollers.

Morrisey shakes his head and his eyes roll into focus. "Oh, Jesus."

"Dow!" the class bellows.

"Dau!"

"Pain!" Morrisey yells. The men in front of us promptly turn around and glare.

"No! Not by itself!" The ARVN shakes his head violently. *"Sú dau dón!* This mean pain!" He jabs his finger against the board.

"Shove it!" Morrisey says when he stands up for the break. He and Newell don't stop outside the building but keep on walking across the headquarter's baseball diamond and down the shady road in front of the Officers' Club.

"Hey! Where are you guys going?"

They stop and turn around. "C'mon, O'Neill!" Morrisey shouts, nodding his head in the direction of their travel.

"The class isn't over," I reply doubtfully.

"That's a class? C'mon!"

I shake my head and he shrugs. "You and Stevens pick us up at the EM Club, OK?"

I nod yes.

"Have fun, student!" They continue down the road with its palm and rubber trees and speckled light drifting through the dust and lush green interior of the plantation.

Two hours later Stevens and I park the ambulance and cross the expansive lawn toward the former home of the plantation manager, now the base EM Club. We climb the steps to the wide veranda and enter the cool, stuccoed building with its shutters and fans, walk through the billiard room, the reading room, on into the bar where the only bright light comes from a jukebox. We find them at a table on the rear veranda, their feet on the balustrade, guarding a pile of empty beer cans.

The next day when they discover the roll's no longer being

taken, Morrisey and Newell stand right up and start to leave the bleachers. "Coming, O'Neill?"

I shake my head.

When we climb out of the ambulance on Friday, returning from the last class, Major Mendez is waiting for us. "Learn a lot, Morrisey?"

Morrisey smiles. "Yes, sir."

"Yeah, I bet! How do you say 'beer' in Vietnamese?"

Morrisey and Newell stand there grinning like idiots. I'm furious, about to tell the major that at least one of us made the effort! But all I can think of is me and seventy or eighty other jerks shouting a bunch of strange words. At this moment my mind goes blank; all I can remember of the past five days is that one word *dau*, and I knew that before I went. Mendez doesn't seem to give a shit the way Smith might . . . he wouldn't believe me, anyhow.

Morrisey had his own rules. I still feel embarrassed thinking about our first day in language school, about what an ass he made of himself. But then he can be so good, so gentle with the most outrageous patients, like now, when the shirt has been cut off the black GI. Bright arterial blood glistens against the purple-black of the man's skin. The forearm lies beside him on the litter, detached, packed in a plastic bag of ice. Two units of blood drip simultaneously into his body, one into the remaining arm, the other into a leg. Two extra bags lie beside the severed limb. They'll be needed before the helicopter reaches the evacuation hospital.

It's another of the endless, brilliant days when the earth puffs about your feet and the horizon is a radiating blur. The stretcher is loaded into the helicopter, the ship rises and turns, its black exhaust orifice shimmering on the dull, brown roof. It drifts away, raises its tail and blasts the powdered earth.

"How about my buddy?" another black soldier asks. He's lying on one of the tables while Morrisey debrides shrapnel from his arm.

"What was he doing, riding on a track?"

"Yeah. Shit! He should never have climbed on."

"I'm pretty sure that arm's lost, but at least he'll get home."

"Man, his mind's been all fucked up since he took that passionate leave."

"Passionate leave?"

"Yeah, you know, Doc. The dude gets his hole to write

79

him a letter sayin' she's leavin'—can't stand him bein' gone no more. So he acts all busted up, gets the Red Cross to check it out and the Man to OK it, and sure enough, she's filed some papers that don't mean shit unless she goes through with it, but it shows, uh . . . intent. That's it! In-tent. So they give the dude time to go home and patch things up with the woman. Just regular leave time, not free time like some of them others, but you get a little vacation back in the World. Anyhow, my man done it and it fucked him up good. Too much pussy. Lotta dudes doin' it, but man, if I ever got back there, no way you'd see me again.''

"That's passionate leave, huh?"

"Yeah. Ain't you ever seen it before?"

Morrisey probes with the gleaming forceps. "Yeah, I guess I did and didn't recognize it. Compassionate Leave: somehow, it doesn't sound as good."

The soldier laughs quietly. "Yeah, man. Dig."

SIX

Annie's running the bar tonight. Navarra's at a special table piled with drinks bought especially for him; he's been doing a valiant job of consuming them. There are times I can't see him because of the crowd. Even the NCOs, all of them, have arrived for the occasion and seem to be having a good time. Tomorrow, Navarra's going home.

Morrisey arrives late, a fresh bloodstain on the lower front of his shirt. Newell clumps in behind him, hurling gloomy imprecations about life in general at Morrisey's back. Navarra spots Morrisey and with a huge, besotted grin, gives him the finger. "Fuck you, Morrisey, you fucking douchebag! Have a drink!" He bangs his fist on the table and a stack of empty glasses teeters off onto the floor. A cheer bursts from the crowd.

From a chair beside the door, Smith grins with what appears to be pleasurable, and for him, magnanimous disbelief.

"What the fuck you got with Smith?" Navarra demands as Morrisey settles himself at the table. Morrisey reddens and glances over his shoulder in the sergeant's direction. Smith is no longer visible.

"Aw, for Christ's sake, you pussy! He can't hear you!" Navarra's almost shouting.

"I got nothing with Smith. You keep asking me that."

"Bet your ass I do! Dogs depend on you—fucking guys'll let 'em down, you watch. You can't let 'em down."

Morrisey laughs. "You don't know what the hell you're saying, Navarra!"

"Smith's after the dogs. Smith's after the whole fucking

company. Shit! He'll be after you before it's over . . . you two too much alike.''

"I'm not like him.''

"I know, I know!'' Navarra flaps a hand. "But you're alike.''

"Why do you say that?''

Navarra twists his head one way, then the other, and tries to focus on one of the remaining piles of glasses.

"Well?''

"Well what, Richie?''

"How are we alike?''

Navarra stares at him blankly. At this moment Newell pushes up to the table and sits down beside Morrisey. "Fuck you, Newell! I'm going home.'' Newell's mouth makes a peculiar, lopsided motion that I suddenly realize is a smile.

Navarra jumps to his feet and slaps his hands on the table. His chair crashes to the floor. "The army sucks!'' he bellows. Everyone cheers.

Buelen turns on his barstool and eyes the clerk over his glasses. His face and nose are very red. "Settle down, Navarra!''

"Yay, Top! You hot shit!'' Arms flung wide, Navarra stumbles toward the first sergeant. Buelen grins and throws an arm around him while someone else shoves a stool under the collapsing body. Navarra, his head bobbing, a smile plastered to his face, tries to focus on Buelen. "Don't let Smith push you around either, Top. Hear? You're OK for a fucking lifer!''

Soon after I arrived, two men left for home—a motor pool sergeant whose name I could never remember, and a Spec Five I never knew at all. Their departure made no impact on me. Navarra's changed everything.

For the first time I felt as though I was being left behind, abandoned in a place where I'd never belong. Navarra was only the first of a forceful group of men who'd been in the company almost since its assignment to the plantation to go home, to disappear with the finality of death itself. Once they had gone it was as though they and our friendship with them had never existed, so quickly did events—and our need to respond—pour in to fill the void. How could anything be more relevant than what was happening to us every day?

The idea of the company was a source of strength but as, one by one, people started falling away, the idea seemed increasingly fragile. Of course we were always picking up strays, new faces, but at the cost of someone familiar and therefore precious. With each such loss, we lost a little more of our will for anything but release from the endlessly benign violence. (Benign? After all, we weren't being hurt.)

The only consistent thing that year, the only truth about that place was change; the rest—our desire for predictability, stability—was illusion, dream. Isn't it the truth that everything's forever changing? So why was our yearning for home as something stable, secure, and essentially unchanging so damn intense? Why couldn't we accept the truth?

How I hate to leave anywhere now! Any departure that occurs outside my daily routine between Dix and my river town, whether it's from a friend's house, my parents' home, or, God help me, even from this girl tomorrow, are torture. For the first ten or twenty minutes I'm desolate, close to tears. This need for human contact—it scares the shit out of me. I don't want to be a clinger. I can't trust people, their concern or kindness, their desire to be with me; it must be pity they feel.

But I can't will the loneliness and sadness away either. The sound of the car, the preoccupation with driving, a road or house I recognize alleviate it eventually . . . but it always comes back.

I have a friend, Jack. We share my house in the river town. When he came home, he flew over the Aleutians to Anchorage, then on to McGuire in New Jersey where he arrived in a snowstorm still wearing his jungle fatigues. "I don't know where the nightmare began or ended, or if it did," he said. "Whether getting off that plane was the end, or arriving in the snow was the beginning. The planeload of us—it was dark when we landed and all we could see were those blue lights streaking by the windows—was up in the aisle, pushing toward the door where the stewardesses stood in their snappy winter coats wishing us goodbye; and when we stepped into the darkness, there was that white stuff floating around like confetti, tons of it all over the ground—our heroes' welcome.

"Then we were in this room in the terminal—it seemed like there was scarcely enough room for all of us—sitting on those metal chairs that creak and clank, when suddenly, like right out of basic, there's this fucking lifer in front of us wearing a baby blue ascot and all his medals and screaming for quiet. "Welcome home, boys! How many orders we got for your

free steak dinners?'' and when nobody answered, I mean that silence was awful, he shouted, ''No takers? This free steak dinner's your right and our gratitude! You gotta eat something.''

''Why don't you eat my shorts, lifer?'' someone said, and that awful silence was right back on us. The lifer just stared like he didn't believe it, as quiet as the rest of us, then nodded his head quick and walked out. When he came back a couple of minutes later he started processing us.

''And when daylight came over those ratty warehouses and barracks down there at reception, it was still spitting snow and there we stood in our dress greens with heavy overcoats watching our breath and waiting for cabs, going home, and it was suddenly like we'd never left. It was like when I walked out of that airplane the night before, someone flipped a switch and it was not only all over, it never was . . .

''But it was—dammit, I know it was! Even though my house, my family, the fucking dog, even my car were the same, they were all different.''

''Like shock therapy,'' I suggested. ''I hear you forget events surrounding it, but you can never forget that something's been done to you, changed you.''

''Maybe,'' he said. ''I don't know.''

And at that same fort where I now work, in one of those same buildings from the Second World War—once immaculate and impressive but now dilapidated relics deemed adequate for us—a sergeant, a fat fucker E-7 type stopped me yesterday. The collar on my whites was open but I wasn't aware of it. He was just suddenly shouting at me and all the people in the hallway stopped and turned around. My eyes were riveted on his fat face, piggy nose, and greasy curls rippling over his brow. I bit my lip and said, ''Yes, Sergeant!'' or ''No, Sergeant!''—whatever he needed to have me say for my humiliation.

. . . and a week ago in Trenton, some asshole came out of a side street right in front of me. I know he saw me, but I was driving a little car, not one of those big fucking boats like his. All I could do was hit the brakes and pound the rim of my steering wheel over and over. I imagined that bastard melting in a ball of fire that crackled and poured ugly smoke into the sky . . . and I shivered with pleasure.

I cried halfway across the United States for an autistic boy and a pony on a movie screen when I was going home.

My parents' home is in New England, a place where I'm plied with food and talk about neighbors, jobs, old friends, my future, and where, because I have nothing to contribute to these conversations and choose to remain silent, I must catch their eyes turning away. I don't have a fatal illness: I just have nothing to say! It doesn't mean anything . . . there's really very little that does except that I survive another seven months without a court-martial and get forever beyond the reach of barbed wire.

And there's my home down the river; sometimes Jack, my roommate, and I don't see each other for days. Our schedules at the base are different, but we're both in that house for the same reasons. Occasionally we see each other on weekends when we talk—long talks.

I'll never trust a telephone again. A lot of what Jack says is in his face, especially his eyes. He starts talking about certain things and his eyes begin to move, avoiding me and, it seems, himself. He just turned twenty—that makes him slightly more than three years younger than me. He goes home a lot, to his parents' house near the shore. They live in a development, in a house painted Tiffany Blue—the only house painted that color so you can spot it if you know what Tiffany Blue's supposed to look like. Usually there are several cars in the driveway, at least one of which will be up on blocks. His younger brother's always tinkering.

Jack was in an air rifle platoon—AARPs they called them as though they were something extraterrestrial. We were at Fort Sam together before we went to Vietnam. I will not call it "Nam!"

One event in particular causes us to talk. It's a scandal. We are watching television. Jack's sitting on the couch diagonally across the livingroom from me, his smelly feet propped on the coffee table, a can of Bud in his hand. On the screen are some palm trees, a lot of high grass, an ubiquitous blandness. The camera follows a dirt road and suddenly focuses on a large ditch.

"They can't catch the smell of the place with a camera. It's lying," Jack says.

I grunt. It's true—the smells of the land gave it special life, a reality no American television audience will ever comprehend.

A picture is superimposed over the film of the road and the ditch. It's a still of the same ditch, a photograph, but there are people lying in it, old men, women, children, a baby or two—it's hard to tell. The bodies are misshapen.

"How much did they pay some jerk with a Nikon for that one?"

Jack doesn't reply.

A photograph of an American officer fills the screen. The army's instituting court-martial proceedings against him and his superiors for having perpetrated the scene in the ditch. The Congress is upset, the anti-war groups are upset but feeling vindicated, American mothers are outraged, and of course the American Legion and VFW are upset that everyone else is.

"Jesus."

Jack's angry. "They can't pin it all on him—no way!"

"I feel like a leper . . ."

"Jesus."

(I know now what I didn't then—or wasn't sure of. But it was already that way when those wheels screeched as they touched down at Travis. Nothing was the same. Something was being held in reserve, something that would not commit itself to my living, to events. I still find myself both actor and audience, but never participant, plagued in everything I do by a desperate wish for a particular sense of freedom, a trust that produces spontaneity, that I never knew I had to lose.)

There are confessions from haunted soldiers, precipitate outpourings before the onslaught of histrionic, off-camera voices, and, of course, official denials. I don't think we . . . I know I don't know of a specific case of quite such magnitude, but Jack and I understand it; we know its truth implicitly.

Initially, I'm surprised at the public outrage, but then, as I begin to comprehend why people feel that way (and I begin to feel that way, too), I start to feel something akin to defiance, something approaching boastfulness: a "Now you see!" rub-their-faces-in-it anger . . . but the anger's invariably diminished, choked by indistinct echoes of my own confusion, and finally outrage from that distant time.

As the days go by and the accusations and denials go on and on, and the anticipation that something good, something liberating might come from all this dies, a different anger emerges—anger at people so self-righteously offended by it. How do they think I felt about it? What are they doing to me? What more are they doing to me? Outrage can be the enemy, too, like everything else over there—everything else that seems so secure, so sure here. Unless they've been there, they'll never understand . . . and I wouldn't wish that education on anyone.

"I'm not part of that!" I shout one day. The house is empty except for the sparse, used furniture and the wind moaning through the back windows on the third floor and down the narrow, steep stairwell. Jack's home at his folks', nervously giggling a lot probably, like he often does. He also stutters sometimes—something new, he claims. And it's not true, what I screamed. I'm terribly sickened by it and so much more.

In time that anger also recedes and the pictures in the news magazines disappear and everyone's cleared except Calley, who was the sole perpetrator.

"No fucking way Medina and the other assholes didn't know what was going on," Jack says. That's the last time we talk about it. To talk about it to outsiders is to cheapen it, to cheapen ourselves, debase ourselves, squander our last shred of human pride, or dignity, or whatever it is that can still allow us to look them square in the eye. Our absolution is to have no absolution at all.

When we first landed on the moon, the Stars and Stripes ran a front page picture. The paper was lying on the counter next to the log. It was late morning during a bad sickcall, because the line was still way out the door and I'd already been interrupted at least twice for casualties. One of the patients looked at the paper and said, "That's something, huh?"

I glanced at the photograph, at the white, robotlike creatures with the American flag. I had seen it an hour before and had already forgotten about it. "Hah!" a tall, black soldier snorted before I could answer. "I been on the moon ten months and they ain't takin' no pictures of me!"

. . . but the loneliness is terrible. I love my river town. It's quaint, has a feeling of history and stolidness in a flimsy way, like it all might be washed downstream, and the dark fields creep right up to within a block of the center of town. People are friendly and say "Hello," and I don't know them but they seem nice and they don't try to know me and that doesn't matter . . . but there are no people in my world now except maybe Jack, and there are certain things even we don't talk about.

I need a dog, a puppy. I could make it happy and that

would be its own reward. We could walk in the fields in the evening.

I had a dog in the plantation. I didn't want it—her—but she became mine in a peculiar way. We had several dogs in the unit, four more than the alloted two, but they were cared for and loved because they would accept a confidence when no one else would, or could, and they could be loved unequivocally for listening because they wouldn't hurt us. Probably because of what Navarra said, Morrisey claimed it was Smith who tried to get rid of the excess dogs (the first attempt occurring less than two weeks after his arrival) and who failed only because the major intervened. Mendez had a heart for such things, like leaving us alone at certain times.

The dogs were mutts; their distinct personalities became evident only after long association. They were all duly licensed, tagged and vaccinated, much to the irritation of our NCOs because it meant that the base veterinarian—the meat inspector—was not doing his job enforcing the restriction on the number of dogs, or he was being bribed. Bribery, known euphemistically as "trading," was the express preserve of the lifers, or so they thought. I think they saw the general erosion of their authority symbolized in our canine population, and that's why they were so hostile to the dogs.

Dogs had a rough life in Vietnam. Gittoni had a picture of one being boiled in a huge pot in a local hamlet.

Our dogs hated Vietnamese. They could smell them in the dark. Because of us, they tolerated the civilian employees, but even then the mutual avoidance pact was tenuous at best. Routinely, someone would stray too close to one of the dogs, or vice versa, and the resulting pandemonium, unbridled snarling and snapping, the frenzied shrieks would be absolutely chilling. One of us, or worse, one of the lifers would have to intervene and restrain the offending dog. But how could the dogs be blamed? They knew us better than we knew ourselves.

But I didn't want a dog. I didn't want anything to have to depend on me that way. *It was a short sickcall and I was filling in the disposition of the last patient of the day.* A man who arrived a while ago complaining of low back pain is being returned to full duty by the division surgeon. I feel mildly relieved when he returns to the counter to be logged out because he spares me all but a sullen silence. The set of his shoulders when he stumps out of the tent, however, attests to his intense displeasure at the outcome of his visit.

A helicopter lifts out of a revetment across the road and sails away over the wire. I ignore the dust, ignore the helicopter. Commo phoned a few minutes ago saying it was a supply run south. Some days they let me know, others I have to call to find out. At commo, they're a moody lot with everybody but the pilots—even Gittoni. Moody isn't the right term: elitist is more to the point.

An electric saw screeches from the direction of a new ward tent that Smith is building. Sounding more like Navarra, Morrisey's insisting that Smith has grandiose ideas for the company. So far the major's limited his ambitions to this one new structure, and this amuses Morrisey.

"What's wrong with fixing the place up?" I asked him.

"Wait until you take your first monthly report to battalion headquarters, O'Neill. Then you'll see where Smith's coming from."

Jenni, my dog, enters the tent through Jenkins's office and clicks down the aisle. She stops on the other side of the counter and looks up at me, her tongue hanging way out in the heat. I talk to her for a moment, then she walks behind the counter and starts drinking from a water dish in the corner. I watch her. I found her behind this same counter one morning almost two months ago, her left side slashed open. It took a hundred and fifty stitches to sew her up.

"Christ, I don't know . . ." Shelby said when I walked in with her in my arms. "I haven't touched a dog since med school," but he was already exploring the outer edges of the wound. He spent over an hour with her with that phenomenal concentration and steadiness that only he can muster. "I don't think she's going to live," he grumbled as he wiped his moustache with his wrist, then started to pull the surgical gloves off with a snap. He was only contradicting himself again, speaking feelings with which he seemed more comfortable but which were belied by the purity of his work. I didn't have a doubt.

I carried Jenni back to the office and placed her in a box where she remained semiconscious for almost a week. She would make a supreme effort to drink from the water dish if I held it for her, but that was all.

And first thing every morning before sickcall, Shelby would wander in to look at her. After a short while, he would kneel and finger the sutured wound as though confirming something. Sometimes he'd talk in subdued tones and I'd have to listen carefully because sometimes he was talking to me, making suggestions for her treatment, but more often he'd be talking to her, or simply to himself. He never came to see her at night when the bugs were out.

One morning her head was up and she was looking for me when I came on duty. I was still on the floor beside her when Shelby pushed through the curtain. "Look, Captain Shelby!" Jesus, I was close to tears. "Thanks!"

His eyes widened as he watched her, then he glanced at me, gave me a quick nod of recognition and ducked back out. That was the last time he checked up on her, but she's been my dog ever since, if only in the manner of company dogs: I'm her favorite.

She stops drinking now—only she uses this particular bowl—walks the few steps to me and stops. I kneel, stroke her head and pluck bits of debris from her coat. She looks like a miniature German shepherd whose hair is too coarse and legs too long. After a few minutes, she turns and goes out the door. Normally, I won't see her again for several hours, maybe even a day or two, but she always comes back to the water dish. On rare occasions, she comes to my tent and lies down on the floor beside my bunk.

I watch her cross the yard toward the ward and think for a terrible moment about what will happen to her when we leave, about her instinctive hatred. She and the others will be left loose on the land to be killed, eaten, or just feared, their affinity for humans soon forgotten in a ceaseless recoiling from pain, or the threat of it. Someday she'll hate all men.

That's the kind of thought you push away in a hurry.

I'm in agony from the prickly heats and there's not a damn thing I can do about it in this humidity.

"We got a body count of thirty-five in that scrap last night."

I'm bent over the log again. I look up at the man who's suddenly appeared beside me, and when I do, the pages of the book lift, then fan in the breeze, burying the entries of the preceeding evening. "You're kidding me."

Master Sergeant Rillings puts his clipboard and pad down on the counter. "Hell, no! They went out and counted at dawn. They were hanging on the wire and everything."

"Yeah, but thirty-five? C'mon, Sarge!" I like Rillings, a

soft-spoken Georgian with ten years in the service who never seems to be upset by anything. It's just as well, because his infantry battalion is taking the worst drubbing of any in our area. His job is to contact us when anything happens and assess the extent of the damage, write names and dispositions, find missing personnel. A military claims adjuster, I once called him.

"You know how it is. The CO figured there were a few who managed to crawl away into the bush before they died."

"Right! Like twenty-five?"

Rillings grins. "Hey, Jon! We got to get the pennant for Bravo Company this month."

"The what?"

"Pennant. You know, a little flag. The company with the largest confirmed body count gets it, and if you get the pennant, you get a five-day standdown. You get to take a shower and battalion gets brownie points." He's picked up his clipboard. "What was the spelling on that last guy?"

I flip the pages back to yesterday. "D'Antoni. D apostrophe capital A."

"Yeah, I remember this one—mortarman. Too bad. He had only a couple of months to go. Shit, if this keeps up, I won't have any reason to come down here."

"What makes you think battalion's going to believe that figure?"

"They won't. But five of our guys got killed, another twenty-two wounded, so they'll give us some benefit of the doubt. They automatically knock five off any estimate. They like their proofs of kill—a pocket or anything—but there's not always time. For this one we can give them about twelve POKs, and they'll let us have another eight or ten."

"They give merit badges, too?"

"Purple Heart, Arcom, Silver Star . . . what's yours? Silver Star's out because that leaves me only the Medal of Honor if I put you in for that Silver Star, and there's nothing above that for the CO, much less the battalion commander. We all got to get credit for whatever you did."

SEVEN

Everything rots in the humidity—people, buildings, food. Dry foods become limp, fresh fruits and vegetables overripe, and the ubiquitous plastic dishes develop a soft, mucouslike skin that can be peeled by running a fingernail across the surface. That gummy growth seems impervious to washing.

And I have broken a vow based on instinct: not to eat fresh, uncooked vegetables, like salads. As a result, food simply falls into my belly now, and festers in a heap. Aside from acute, body-doubling pain and burning defecation, the psychological aspect is the worst: I am forced to identify with my surroundings. My rectum becomes so painful that I dread the time following the release of my bowels more than the attacks themselves.

Brock prescribes medications, but cautions it will take two weeks, two cycles of the parasites through the digestive track into the bloodstream, then into the lungs and back to the digestive track, for the cure to take effect.

An enemy underground hospital has been discovered and the entire human contents shipped to us. The treatment tent is filled with wounded Viet Cong soldiers in various stages of dress, filth and decay. Two jeeps and several members of the MI team hover expectantly outdoors. I finish moving a surgical lamp for Captain Brock and then the pain hits me. It is a long, excruciating run to the patients' latrine and tears are flowing from my eyes by the time I swing the door open. I sit clutching my head with my hands, my head pressed almost to my knees, and piss out my asshole into the bucket below.

The door squeaks open, Owen steps in, settles himself onto

a neighboring seat and jiggles until he's comfortable. With his pants pulled carefully down to about an inch above his knees, he sits primly, his hands folded on top of his belt. There follows a long, strained silence while we are entertained by our mutual symphony. My view is generally restricted to the floor, but by peeking around my left hand, I'm able to see Owen poised with a perfectly straight back upon his throne while he stares through the screen with aristocratic disdain.

I emit an involuntary groan as I start to clean up.

Owen glances at me. "You OK, Jon?"

"Fuck, no!"

There's genuine concern in the eyes staring around the rather large, freckled beak. "You'd better tamp."

"What?"

"Tamp. Don't wipe."

"Oh . . . yeah." I tamp, and feel more of an idiot for Owen's approval.

"There's a real prize outdoors there," Brock says when I return to the treatment tent. He indicates the direction with a pair of bloody forceps. "What a joy it must be to practice medicine in a hole."

The prize is a VC soldier whose bladder has burst internally as the result of infection. I smell him before I see him. He's lying on a litter in the sun, naked except for a blanket that covers him just above his genitals. His belly swells over the edge of the blanket; his eyes are closed, his breathing irregular. Flies crawl over the eyelids and taut stomach, down under the edge of the blanket.

Two Vietnamese members of the MI team signal me frantically from their jeep. One has his foot up, about to clamber out. The American captain sitting alone in the rear passenger seat appears aloof and unseeing.

You sonuvabitch, I think as I turn my back on them, all I'd have to do is nod my head a thirty-second of an inch and you'd trample the rest of them getting here. I want to grab the captain and rub his face against a tree.

I hear a click and find Thibauld, a corpsman on the ward, taking pictures of the VC's festering mass with his new Minolta. He takes three more pictures, moving slowly around the litter, one leg bent back slightly, his face hidden behind the metal box.

"You've forgotten what the major said, Thib?" I ask.

His long, angular face pops over the top of the camera. "Shit, man. It's not one of ours."

"Mendez didn't make any distinction. No picture taking in the treatment area."

He shrugs, wags his head and grins in a breezy, lopsided way as he clasps the camera to his chest.

I'm feeling wretched again. I want to lie down. "What are you going to do with them, Thib?" My voice sounds hollow and shrill. "Going to show the folks back home what a dying man looks like, a *real* dying man? How would you feel if that was you and some asshole was snapping pictures?"

"Hey, lighten up, O'Neill! I don't mean no harm. I bet he don't even know I'm here, or you either. Just a few pictures —what the hell do you care? You're beginning to sound like Morrisey."

I go inside, out of the humid stinking heat, where I stand with my face to a wall fan.

"Pretty, huh?" says Brock.

"You're going to leave him there in the sun?"

"He was in the shade a while ago. God, I don't see how these guys do it."

I'm positive I can hear the flies buzzing around the litter.

"Oh, well, he's dying," Brock says. "The only thing we could do for him now is to ship him to Tainan where they'd leave him out anyway. They don't even have trees down there. Take this guy. He's lucky. He's going to be all right. Hey, Juan!"

I look over Brock's shoulder at a large hole about the size of a softball in the soldier's leg. It's an undulating sea of maggots.

Major Mendez shoves in beside me with Morrisey right behind. "What is it?"

Brock points at the wound. Mendez proceeds to study it with profound interest. He takes the forceps from Brock and pushes some of the maggots aside. The muscle tissue and flesh look bright and clean. Stirring the maggots with the instrument, Mendez turns to Morrisey. "Maggots eat the rotting flesh—that's a clean wound. During World War I they kept jarfuls of them just for this. Can't let them go too long, though."

Brock reaches in with a gloved hand, scoops some out and shakes them off in a wastepail. Mendez watches intently.

"Yeah, well go ahead and send that bladder case on the

next ship, O'Neill! The stink's beginning to get to me, too.'' Brock grabs another handful and flings them in the pail.

It's afternoon before one of the helicopters cranks up to fly the wounded Viet Cong to Tainan. There's much excitement among the members of the MI team. I have held them at bay during the lunch hour, at the major's request, because I don't feel like eating. When the train of litters begins to emerge from the tent, the two jeeps roar away, their passengers, I assume, bound for the Vietnamese hospital by means of another helicopter.

Then I turn and see Dunn rock the litter.

Morrisey and the radio operator are carrying the soldier with the maggots to the waiting ship. Morrisey's in the lead and is obviously having difficulty holding onto the handles; they're shaking erratically. About halfway to the pad, he shouts at Dunn, who doesn't reply. The jiggling of the litter is so violent that Morrisey almost loses his grip. ''Jesus Christ!'' he screams over his shoulder. ''What the hell are you doing?''

The shaking stops as they reach the helicopter. The crew-chief stares with obvious distaste at the contents of the litter. Morrisey points at the bladder case already suspended inside the ship. ''Don't ride downwind!''

Morrisey catches up with the radio operator. ''What were you doing out there?''

''Adding to that gook's pain a little bit.'' Dunn starts to walk on but Morrisey grabs him by the shoulder.

''Wait a minute! You mean that was deliberate?''

''Yeah. He's the fucking enemy, isn't he?''

''I almost dropped that guy!''

Dunn shrugs, a comprehensive gesture from his large, pear-shaped hips to his shoulders. His face remains impassive except for the natural hostility of his mouth. ''You in love with the VC?''

Morrisey grabs Dunn's shirt. As his fist embeds itself in the moist, soft skin of Dunn's chest, Smith suddenly appears at the entrance to the treatment tent. ''Morrisey!''

''You sonuvabitch, Dunn! When a guy gets here, he's out of the war and I don't care what side he's on,'' Morrisey yells. ''You want to fuck with the enemy, go volunteer for the field!''

''Why don't you? Maybe you wouldn't love them so much.''

Morrisey shakes him. Dunn offers no resistance as his head rocks back and forth.

"Morrisey!" Smith leaves the porch and begins to run.

"Don't you ever pull a stunt like that on me again, Dunn!" Morrisey releases the shirt, dark with sweat where it was crumpled in his hand.

Dunn looks down and smooths the cloth. "Why don't you fuck yourself!"

Before Morrisey can react, Dunn turns and walks right into the sergeant. Smith grabs him by the shoulders. "You alright?" I have seen this look, this fury before.

Dunn moves out of Smith's grasp. "Everything's fine, Sergeant." He walks away toward the commo shack.

"What's wrong with you, Morrisey?"

"Nothing, Sergeant."

"Nothing! Don't you let me see you treating anyone in this company like that again!"

"You tell him to stick to his radios and there won't be any problem." Morrisey's calm at the moment.

"I'll tell you one thing, soldier! You'd better watch that temper of yours."

Morrisey smiles.

Smith is speechless. I'm waiting for him to ask for an explanation, or for Morrisey to demand one, but it doesn't seem to occur to either man. What the hell has happened between these two? I'm asking myself, when Morrisey finally speaks, this time with anger. "You condone that kind of patient care, Sergeant?" He meets Smith's gaze, knowing, I'm sure, that the NCO can read everything he's feeling, especially the contempt.

Smith blinks several times as though he's having trouble focusing. "Don't raise your voice at me."

"I'm sorry, Sergeant." Morrisey sounds genuine.

Then Smith's in control again. He places a hand on Morrisey's shoulder. "You're doing too well to let yourself get fouled up. You got that promotion to Spec Five because all of us, NCOs and officers, agreed you deserved it, but you've got responsibility with that rank. Don't disappoint us."

Morrisey jerks away. "I don't need any favors, Sergeant," he says, and walks off.

I wanted to fly to battalion, to take a helicopter—it would have been a cinch with Dust-Off—but Smith insisted I go with Buelen, who was setting out on one of his "shopping" trips. He was borrowing the CO's jeep for the occasion, with Stevens as driver.

I arrive at the orderly room clutching the monthly report in a brown manila envelope. "Where the hell do you think you're going?" Buelen snarls.

"Battalion headquarters with you, Top. I got to deliver the monthly report."

"Not like that, buster."

My mind makes a quick check: shined boots, shave, clean fatigues, cap, insignia.

"O'Neill, you're dense! How about a helmet, and flak jacket, and maybe even a weapon."

We roar onto the jammed highway heading toward the village. Alone in the back seat, I feel idiotic with the heavy helmet jiggling on my head and an M–16 on my lap. I'm already melting in the heavy vest they call flak jackets, and I can't wear helmets—I never could. They don't fit right.

"Lock and load, O'Neill!" Buelen orders as he slams a magazine into place, turns the selector lever to automatic, and chambers a round.

Reluctantly, I insert a magazine and start to turn the selector lever, but then I discover Stevens looking at Buelen with undisguised horror. He's wearing a holstered .38 revolver that he borrowed from Owen, who in turn snatched it from a pile of ARVN weapons in front of the treatment tent. No one even knows if it works.

"Nine people got killed by a mine just east of here last week," Buelen explains.

"That was over a month ago, Top, and it was north of the plantation." Stevens peers around a Vietnamese truck, seeing if it's safe to pass.

I place my weapon back on safety.

Dust from the truck rolls up on the hood and over the windshield. Stevens drops the jeep into a lower gear, floors it, and we bounce out into the clear day. Abruptly, he reaches up, yanks his helmet off and drops it between the front seats.

"What the hell are you doing?"

"Goddam thing keeps dropping over my eyes, Top. Webbing must be loose." It's a gorgeous day, Stevens's defiance is liberating, and I remove my helmet, too. We curve around the village. Stevens beeps the horn, shifts' gears, guns the motor, shifts, slaps the horn. Brown, flat-nosed faces swarm around us, then fall behind. He beeps again as we roll past several Hondas. Cries and laughter ring from roadside stalls. A lambro wobbles out in front of us causing Stevens to jam the brakes and hit the horn once again. "Goddam gooks!" he screams. The Vietnamese stare at us; one or two smile. The jeep jerks and we roar around the minibus, swinging in suddenly to avoid an oncoming truck. Buelen seizes the handle on the dash with his free hand. His large bulk flops back and forth in the seat.

"Jesus, slow down, Stevens!"

The sun flashes on the gold rims of Stevens's sunglasses as we blaze out between the last buildings of the village onto a long causeway cutting across acres of abandoned rice paddies. An ARVN outpost squats on a distant hill, its flag lifeless on a crooked pole. Within moments, the dust of our wake boils over the concertina wire into the dreary compound.

Rice paddies rise once more to greet us with lush hues of green. The road unfolds beyond the hood, momentarily vacant. I feel surprisingly free and unconstrained—I wasn't aware of a sense of confinement before, but now we are truly going somewhere, travelling. Stevens is in his element, as is Buelen who is scrutinizing the brush and paddies for signs of the enemy.

We approach a red cloud, far ahead. Soon we're swallowed in the whine and rumble of an armored column, the drivers of the armored personnel carriers goggled and dust-covered, sitting on the edges of their open hatches, leg extensions reaching the pedals inside. Several drivers flash us the two-fingered V that is no longer a sign of victory, but of peace. Stevens returns the greetings. A tank clatters by, a yellow flag with a wolf's head logo flapping from the antenna.

Blue sky again, and palm trees with thatched huts among them, and beyond these, a gnarled, scraped earth: our repeated passage from beauty to ugliness assumes its own flow and emotional rhythm.

We arrive in a plain. In the distance a small grove of trees rises upon a knoll among soft grasses. Beyond, the sun glints harshly upon the roofs of the base camp that is our destination. *Once, flying to battalion by helicopter, I crossed over that knoll. Hidden from the nearby highway by the high grass, the antiquated star-shaped foundation of a fortress veered among the trunks of the trees that grew upon that lovely, but curiously isolated spot. It seemed totally removed from the clamor of the highway and nearby military base, but it was also a shock to confront, in such an indisputable manner, the insignificance of our presence in a place where someone had always been at war.*

Shortly past the knoll, a wide road branches from the highway directly toward the high wood-and-wire fences and wooden guard towers of the compound where battalion's located. Stevens reaches down and grabs his helmet.

"In there," Buelen says, pointing to a blue, wooden building, and then he and Stevens drive away.

"What's this?" I have just dropped my report on a desk in front of a chisel-faced clerk. He was typing when I entered and is still glowering at me because of the interruption.

"Monthly report for Bravo Company."

The clerk drops a pencil on the envelope and shoves away from the desk. "Where's Davies? He hasn't gone home yet."

"No, but he thinks he has." I manage a smile and am rewarded with a contemptuous glance as the clerk bustles across the room and disappears through a door. Those two would get along!

I'm perspiring heavily despite the fan whirring softly above my head. I'm also afraid to move. Why didn't I just toss the report on his desk and leave? The world beyond the louvered walls remains silent, frying slowly, the air rippling from the earth in that endless, barren sky. I sense the building turning to tinder around me, crackling softly, about to erupt in flame.

"Do you usually dress like a pig?"

Startled, I turn and face a colonel. He's tall and slender with dark, wiry hair streaked silver through the sideburns and over his ears. His face is finely chiseled with a suggestion of aristocratic breeding and unmitigated self-indulgence, qualities augmented by a faint petulance. A captain, an obese sergeant major, and the clerk are ranged around him like bodyguards.

"Answer me, soldier!"

"Sir?" I slam to attention and salute.

"Do you usually dress like a pig?"

I look down the front of my clothes. There are sweat stains and a fine film of dust. "Sir, I just came fifty miles in an open jeep."

But he's moved past me and picked up the envelope. He pulls the report out and starts reading. I can't look at the other men, so I stare past them. The back of my neck is burning.

The colonel moves away, around his bodyguards, toward

the inner door. With final scowls in my direction, the captain and sergeant major follow. Only the clerk is left.

"Well, what are you waiting for?"

"I don't know. You tell me."

"The Colonel has accepted your report."

"Lovely." I push through the door into the sunshine. A flag hangs from a gleaming white pole. There are stones, painted white, surrounding the yard, and marigolds growing from a huge tire, also painted white, at the base of the flagpole. The sign over the door reads "Battalion Headquarters, 41st Medical Battalion." The medallion on the sign is bright orange and yellow, the colors of the marigolds.

I set out to explore the battalion area. Everywhere are indications of order, of a fastidious attention to detail: signs in both English and Vietnamese, barrackslike precision in the ordering and maintenance of the hooches, painted butt cans, minute plots of lawn, signs of name, title, rank, that peculiar sense of refined military order that exudes a feeling of harsh but doubtful permanence.

Stepping from the shadows at one intersection, I squint as I try to gain my bearings, then plunge into a shadowed walkway where the eaves cut a path of deep blue sky. I'm reminded of bathhouses and seagrass, am disoriented by an overwhelming anticipation of passing one last building and finding myself on a vast beach, facing an ocean where not a single sail breaks the isolation.

But the boardwalk stops, the buildings cease, and I confront a coiled, evil-looking fence, barren ground, torn, uprooted vegetation: the sea is miles away, as far away, it seems, as the moon.

Life has fled indoors at this hour. Through the screens I hear undertones of conversations, bursts of male laughter, the banality of a base Dee Jay transmitting trite commentary between his selections of apocalyptic rock music. I pass an NCO billet and the strains of country and western greet me with a sense of a different and more personal impending tragedy.

Twice I pass a building painted baby-blue like the orderly room, but with a red cross over the door. I'm tired of exploring, fatigued by a fundamental sense of inertia and the sun. I'm supposed to meet Stevens at the holdover barracks because we're going to spend the night here. I would like to nap now if my anxieties about interruptions and harrassment will permit it. I climb the three steps of the blue building and pull the screen door open. A fan rumbles from the far end of a large, narrow room, casting a faint, humid breeze. Examination tables line the walls, interspersed with stainless steel cabinets.

Next to the fan, a corpsman in a blue, sleeveless smock is seated at a desk. He looks up as the door shuts. "The dispensary is closed except for emergencies," he says peevishly.

"I'm from Bravo Company. Can you tell me where the holdover barracks are?"

He stands and points down a walkway. "Down there, take your first right, go straight and in a couple of hundred feet you'll walk right into a small, brown building with a dirt floor. That's it. Make sure you salute any officers, and also watch the monkey three hooches up—cute little fucker and he'll bite if you get too close. Don't kick him. He belongs to the first sergeant."

"You're part of Headquarters Company?"

"No, this is Alpha Company—we're together. They call us 'Gay and A.'" The medic smiles.

"So what do you do here? Any casualties?"

"Not any more—not like there used to be. Occasional ambulance case, but mostly base sickcall and some Medcap problems. We've got three wards and use only part of one. But we get all kinds of battalion awards for excellence—we get inspected almost every day."

A few minutes later I leave the corpsman armed with tips on how to survive at battalion, and for the moment feeling considerably less paranoid about the surroundings. The monkey takes a violent lunge at my right calf, but runs out of chain. I leave him scrabbling on the boardwalk, teeth bared.

I find the holdover barracks and the jeep, but neither Stevens nor Buelen. I go to supper without them. The clamor of the huge mess hall is alien to me. The faces of the men behind the serving line seem hostile even though there's much jostling and laughter. The officers and NCOs routinely walk to the head of the line that extends out the door and far down along the boardwalk. Why does that seem so strange? The NCOs and officers can do the same in my company if they want. Often they don't, however, but are interspersed in groups or singly among the rest of us—either way seems natural in the plantation. Nothing seems natural here. Here I feel deeply antagonistic to the strict adherence to protocol and privilege—and inconsequential.

A furious shuffling occurs in the line behind me and suddenly the colonel, his captain and sergeant major troop by. The men in line grow noticeably quieter and move closer to the wall as the small party passes. A hand extends and gives the finger to the retreating figures. "Dinner first," a voice cautions. Several men snicker.

An intense smell of rotten garbage that followed me indoors is dispelled only at the steam tables by a wall of moist heat. A black sergeant in a white paper cap watches me take a tray. "Who are you?" he demands. His face glistens with sweat.

The line comes to a halt behind me. I can feel the anticipatory silence. "I'm from Bravo Company," then quickly add, "Sarge."

He slowly inspects my entire person. "You got a ticket?"

"I didn't know I was supposed to get one. I just came down to deliver a report."

I feel the impatience of the men behind me. The sergeant does, too. "Well, go ahead!" he snaps. "Next time, get a ticket."

"He's a first-rate shithead, man. Don't let it get you," someone murmurs in my ear.

I eat quickly and retreat to the holdover barracks. It's with tremendous relief that I watch night fall. In the morning we'll be on the road again, heading up-country. I'm lying on my back on a mouldy mattress, staring into the dark, when the screen door opens near my head. "Stevens?"

A furious groping ensues. Suddenly there's a snap and the single, bare bulb flashes on. Standing at the foot of my cot, still holding the light chain, is a gray-haired, gaunt soldier whose age might be anywhere from thirty-five to sixty. On his cap is a black, hollowed-out wedge that indicates his rank: private first class.

"Hullo," the PFC ventures as he peers at my shirt collar. "And what's your rank . . . sir?"

"Specialist."

"Oh, of course." His fears seem allayed. He even manages a limp smile as he points at my collar. "Yes, of course! They wouldn't put an officer in here . . . just that one might accidentally wind up here." He sits down on the bunk across the aisle where a duffel bag was dropped sometime earlier in the day. He pats the duffel bag. "Had quite a little beer tonight, I guess. I'm kinda dizzy. What are you doing here?"

"I had a report to deliver. I'm going back to my unit tomorrow."

"Oh? And where's that?"

I tell him, but I'm so appalled by his rank that I can't resist asking in turn how many years he has in the service.

"Nineteen, Specialist."

"Good God!"

"Oh, that's nothing, Specialist. With my time in service, I might still get a decent retirement. They should retire me at my highest achieved grade . . . only now they're trying to send me home and discharge me before I got my twenty years."

"Why? And don't call me specialist."

He looks down at his lapels, sticks his thumb under one of the insignias and pushes it out toward me. "New rules. Gotta weed us out." He grins foolishly. "I got passed over twice now for promotion."

"That's the highest rank you've ever made?"

"Hell, no! I was a first sergeant one time, but got busted down. Worked my way back up to sergeant first class after that, but . . . you know. I should have learned to keep my mouth shut. But if they discharge me now, I won't get any benefits. I was in Korea, Lebanon."

"How old are you?"

"Thirty-eight."

We both fall silent.

"You know," he says at last, "I can see the change in the army. A lot of you young fellows are tearing the place up—fuck the army and rights, and all that sort of thing. Maybe that's good, but I can tell you, the army's been a fine home to me! Three squares a day, decent living quarters. I had a real setup in Germany. That's when I was a first sergeant and had me a couple of *fräuleins* regular and all that. I've had some real decent assignments." He nods his head emphatically several times.

"What do you do now?"

He shrugs. "Not much. Like you—don't tell me it ain't true 'cause I understand. Having to deal with a PFC my age bothers people. They give me errands just to get me out of the way. I worked for a supply outfit in Long Binh for a while;

then they shipped me here. You know, here and there—wherever I can make myself useful.''

I look down at the floor, unable to face the spaniel eyes. I think if I were to move closer, I'd smell his failures.

''Rank's easy for you guys nowadays!'' He pounds his fist into the open palm of his other hand, a gesture as feeble as the sternness that enters his voice. ''Make E–6 hard stripe, some of them do, in two years! Well, it don't mean shit!'' His voice quavers. ''Used to be, a man worked a lifetime for that —worked hard, too! Why, I remember being real proud of making E–4, only it was corporal the first time—didn't have no specialist then. I bet you didn't think nothing of it.''

''I guess I didn't.''

''No. You guys don't mean any harm. It's just everything's been too easy for you, too soft. The whole country's that way now. Gone soft.''

I've heard it all before. I yawn. ''I'm kind of tired, man. I need some sleep.''

The PFC nods, resigned. He fumbles with the lock on his duffel bag, then withdraws a portable radio and a stack of tattered magazines. He switches on the radio and the room is filled with the tinny reverberations of a country dirge. Settling his head on the duffel bag, he flops his legs up on the bunk and lights a cigarette.

I hear him drop the magazine. I've been trying unsuccessfully to doze, an arm propped over my eyes. ''Hey, Specialist! You got a blanket?''

''No,'' I mutter without lifting my arm.

''Look, it'll get chilly before morning. I got a poncho liner here.''

''Hey, don't worry about it. You need it.''

''Naw, I got two! Traded with a supply sergeant down in Bien Hoa. Got them for two quarts of Johnny Walker.'' He jumps up and digs into his duffel bag. ''I hope they don't check too close when I leave . . . I wrote the sergeant major of the army in Washington D.C. and asked him to help me —the enlisted man's friend, you know. Anyhow, they're going to have some kind of hearing or something for me at Oakland . . . so I hope I don't get caught with these.''

I feel the soft, almost weightless plop of the poncho liner landing on my legs. ''Thanks.''

''Sure, sure, Specialist. Just make sure I get it back. You know, if I'm still asleep when you leave in the morning.''

"I'll do that."

He's curled up like a child, his face strangely placid and soft when I place the poncho liner on top of his boots. The boots have been shined since I fell asleep and are lined up, side by side, under his cot. "C'mon, O'Neill!" Buelen whispers from the door. "We gotta get breakfast and get outta here soon's the road's open."

Despite his impatience, Buelen feels compelled to stop at the battalion orderly room before we leave. I wait for him, hatless, in the rear seat of the jeep. Stevens appears, cocky as ever, but it's suddenly obvious he didn't anticipate this particular delay. He glances cautiously at the door of the orderly room. "What's Top doing inside Liferville? I thought he wanted to get out of here."

I shrug. "Where the hell were you last night? Got a cigarette?"

"Well, I don't like it," he says, reaching into his chest pocket. He withdraws a pack of menthol cigarettes. "Every time I come to this goddam place, I feel like a rib-eye steak, and you know what lifers think of steak. I stayed with some buddies. Hey," he cautions, his gaze riveted on the door where Buelen disappeared, "don't grab the wrong one."

I look more closely at the opening in the pack. All I can see are the tops of the filter tips. I withdraw one and examine the opposite end.

"Don't make it so fucking obvious!"

"OK, OK! This looks like an original. How can you tell without checking?"

"Life becomes a continuous surprise, O'Neill." With a flick of the thumb, he thrusts the pack back into his pocket. "Be seeing you! The fucking lifers are coming . . . tell Buelen I had to take a shit."

"Hey! Stevens!" Stevens disappears in the maze of hooches. "Sonuvabitch!" I mutter as I glance over my shoulder and see Buelen holding the door for the colonel. There's no time to run after Stevens.

"Who's this soldier, First Sergeant Buelen?" I recognize the colonel's snappishness. I salute him. The eyes that stare back at me have a capricious quality.

"Out of that jeep!" the captain beside him, his executive officer, orders. The captain reminds me of a junior executive, tight-lipped, aggressive.

"Yes, sir!"

"What have you to say for yourself, soldier?" the colonel demands.

"About what, sir?"

"Are you being insolent?"

"No, sir."

"You'd better not be with me, young man! Where's your helmet?"

"On the floor of the jeep, sir." I feel the sun-heated steel of the vehicle press against my leg. Tentatively, I start to retrieve my headgear.

"And why isn't your flak jacket fastened?"

"It's hot, sir. I was waiting until we got on the road."

"What kind of nonsense is this, First Sergeant?"

Buelen shuffles a bit, but before he can reply, the colonel discovers my M–16. "Inspect that, Sergeant Major!"

The sergeant major grabs the rifle, examines the exterior, checks the chamber, looks down the barrel. "Filthy, sir!"

"It was clean yesterday, Sergeant Major!"

"I said it's filthy, soldier!"

"This man ought to be court-martialed, sir," the captain whispers loudly to the colonel.

The sergeant major moves closer and starts slowly to circle me; he's studying the line of my hair—I can feel it. His breath is sour. "When did you have your last haircut?"

"About a week ago, Sergeant Major."

"You'll get one now—a good one. You're not going up-country shaming this battalion."

"Yes, Sergeant Major."

"I would expect a lot more from someone in your company, Sergeant Buelen," the Colonel adds. Buelen is writhing under his gaze, his flaccid face crimson. "I want this man in the orderly room for a full inspection within the hour!"

"Yes, sir!" Buelen comes to attention, his chin down, hand jerked up in salute, cap slightly cock-eyed. "Goddam you, O'Neill!" he grumbles a few moments later as he guides me toward the nearest barbershop. "I'm going to see you get one hell of a haircut!"

"Top, they didn't say shit about my hair yesterday, and my weapon's clean—look at it!"

The humiliation and anger become almost unbearable as the Vietnamese barber shears the sides of my head. I didn't even bother to open my mouth before he started to work, knowing any instructions would be ignored.

Standing in the orderly room again, with the smug, scrawny clerk at my back, I'm given a cursory inspection by the captain and allowed to depart. Buelen's slumped in cold fury in the front seat beside a virtuous Stevens sitting bolt upright, his helmet on his head, flak jacket fastened.

I climb into the back beside a huge carton of steaks, a case of whiskey, and numerous cases of C-rations: black market currency—the fruit of Buelen's shopping trip. Stevens flashes me the peace sign. "Thanks for the warning, buddy," I respond as he starts the jeep.

EIGHT

"You awake, O'Neill?"

Someone is shaking me, rolling me gently, whispering my name. "They need you in treatment," the guard whispers. I can see the dim outlines of his body through the mosquito netting.

"Yeah."

He flashes a light across my face, forces me to cover my eyes with my hands. "Christ! Turn that thing off!"

"Shh. You're awake." I hear him creak across the floor, the soft clink of his rifle.

Peals of laughter greet me as I approach the tent. Light streams through the screens. I find Brock, Morrisey, and Owen in various positions of repose as they confront a hatless American soldier holding a bandaged hand level in front of him. The bandage looks pristine beneath the blue glint of a surgical lamp. They're all smiling, something extraordinary for this time of night. "Sorry to bother you, O'Neill," Brock says, "but we have to evac the lieutenant here and we thought you'd better write it up."

I yawn in response. The lieutenant has a MACV patch on his shoulder. He's probably an advisor.

"He's going to the Ninety-sixth, Jon. Gunshot wound to right hand—traumatic damage to metacarpals."

"That's what you were laughing at, sir?" I'm bent over the table beside the lieutenant, filling in the little spaces on the medical tag. The lieutenant grins. He has an infectious smile. He's short, his hair is a bit too long, he's wearing gorgeous mother-of-pearl beads. They've been talking about Mathias.

"Connelly, James C.," the lieutenant tells me. "Did you hear about Mathias and the President?"

"No," Morrisey says. He's perched on a table across the aisle. Brock's beside him, tapping cigar ashes onto the floor. Owen's putting sterilized instruments in the cabinet.

"Mathias shaved his beard off, found a man lying half-dead of malaria at one of the evacuation hospitals, and conned his way into the front row of the formation to greet the president on his 'historic trip to the combat zone,' wearing, of course, the sick man's uniform. You know, I heard from some other guys that they spent days getting ready for that. They polished all the jeeps and helicopters on base, made the guys get haircuts, wear pressed uniforms, and issued new helmet covers with none of that FTA stuff written in ballpoint pen on them. They even set up a little demonstration: helicopters, a mock landing zone, and a few guys running around with rifles pursuing imaginary gooks.

"The President comes down the line shaking hands and asking little questions like, 'Catch the Red Sox game the other night? What did you think of that score?' What does he ask Mathias?" The lieutenant can barely contain himself. " 'How's the food?' That's right! 'How's the food?' Mathias didn't comprehend at first, and then it dawned on him: the food! This dink thinks this is some kind of picnic . . . and so he said, real loud, 'It sucks!' And here the President was shaking his hand real firm, like Dale Carnegie, you know, one of the boys. That shake just kind of wilted while he considered that answer.

"In the meantime, he'd already moved on with the momentum and was shaking hands with the next guy and asking him if he caught the game with the Senators and what did he think of that score?"

We're all in convulsions.

"Wait a minute!" the lieutenant says, holding up his good hand. "All the birds and generals and secret service men in the president's entourage swooped down on Mathias and wrote down his name—from the nametag on his shirt! They'd get him—they had a name and unit!"

"Did that really happen, Lieutenant?" Brock asks, smiling still, but in a more patronizing fashion.

The lieutenant returns the smile. "How the fuck do I know, Doc? You can't be sure of anything you hear about Mathias. Anyway, what difference does it make?"

Bits and pieces of the night thrash against the treatment tent, burst through the screens as bright red trunks of rubber trees flash into view for an instant, then vanish, then flash again in the roaring darkness. The noise abates, becomes a steady purr.

"That's your ship," Brock says, sliding down off the table.

The lieutenant looks at his injured hand. "Hey, Doc, am I really going to lose the use of it?"

"I'm not sure," Brock replies irritably. He puts his arm around the lieutenant's shoulder. "At least you're alive."

"That reminds me of the Indian chief with the good news and bad news for his tribe . . ."

We stop at the door and stare at this remarkable man with the purely ingenuous look on his face.

"The bad news was that they were out of corn and would have to live on buffalo shit for the rest of the winter, but the good news . . ."

"Yeah," Brock interrupts, "there was plenty of buffalo shit."

And I'm laughing again, the tears streaming down my face, and I don't know if it's the chagrin on Brock's face, the lieutenant's grin, or just a hell of a lot of other things blowing off. With a growl like an old bear, Brock claps his arm around the lieutenant once again, and the five of us start through the trees toward the waiting helicopter.

My eyelids begin to feel heavy. Sleep is difficult despite the lack of it. There are still far too few men in the company to meet the war's demands. I reach out and drop a cigarette butt into the tin can beside my cot. There's a brief hiss as it strikes the water at the bottom.

I have no memory of dreams, of ever dreaming since my arrival. A cannon booms near by, and moments later, booms again. I lie with my eyes pressed closed, thinking that if I open them, I'll lose my grasp on sleep forever, that if I can only relax, release the tension throughout my body, the intrusion will go away. My eyes ache now. I become giddy and the cannon booms again. My eyes are wide open.

I lie still, listening to the cannon, the boom raising the dead, all the cannon in this country booming and raising the dead, a wide, red river where carrion repeatedly sink and float again *but the cannon were nothing except absurd steel tubes hurling projectiles into the vast emptiness of the night, into the harsh, splintered wreckage that was once jungle: that was the essence of that sound.*

And like the jungle, our essence would have been the sum of coincidence, the random and contradictory projectiles of that war, like the lieutenant with the back of his head blown away, or the arrival of Smith, the maiming of my dog Jenni, the departures from the company that would always leave things altered slightly, a little less secure—or a great deal so. It's the same now—it's got to be. I can feel it despite the soft sounds of leaves and the river beyond this room. The only way you can keep from being destroyed by coincidence is by having something at the center of your life to bind you, to give you something to hold on to. I should have understood it better then.

It was Morrisey who said, sometime toward the end, that Mendez had been an anomaly, that he only postponed the inevitable.

I have no patience with the cannon, now. Whenever I think that at last it has fallen silent, it fires. When the insect shrieking finally takes over, I remain poised for an explosion that won't occur.

As I drift away, somewhere there's a whine. The pitch rises. I'm awake, listening to the ship throb away into the dark. I wait, tensed, for the cry. I'm still waiting when Morrisey shakes me.

"Litterbearers, Jon."

"No cry . . ."

He shakes me again, infinitely patient and gentle. There's activity around me, shuffling sounds, men dressing. Gittoni says something about a light and I hear a soft, metallic snap.

I cover my eyes. "Ohhh, Christ . . ."

I stumble on the hummocks as I run through the trees toward the motor pool. Once I land on my knees, pick myself up, brush furiously at my pants and feel the unseen grit fall away. It's early morning and there's a chill in the air. I shiver slightly as I stand in the darkness with the others.

There are three litter patients with gunshot wounds. Gunshot wounds, I long ago concluded, usually represent passive misery; there's little of the stark horror associated with grenades, mines, and fire. Persons shot seem quiet, their fear more internalized.

Before he dies, the face of one soldier is the color of the dead. When Morrisey and Newell roll him over, the tiny entry hole to the left of his heart at the front has mushroomed into a massive wad of pulp. The helicopter crewchief who walked in to determine the cause of the delay watches the quiet conclusion while the other two patients hang cradled in the vortex of his ship.

And what did that have to do with where I am now, and Dix, and everywhere I've been, before and since? Everything's in such disarray: I can't tell where one dream ends and another begins because they're all dreams now and I move through them, from one to the next, back and forth. The plantation's lost now, relegated to some dominion beyond the realm of dreams.

I landed at Wake Island on my way to Vietnam, a measure of distance but not in terms of miles or maps. It was me as a very young child growing up in a deluge of glorious, obscure places, remote battles, victories and immeasurable expectations. The smoke-filled cabin in which I'd been floating for hours alighted somewhere momentarily so I could look out at the lights of a small, nondescript terminal that bore a compelling name from a time I could never recapture. It vanished behind us in the darkness, as elusive again as the memory of the war that propelled it into history.

I arrived at Dix at night, too, the same day I was inducted. I was immediately, totally lost. We marched endlessly in a freezing mist among ghostly buildings that beckoned us.

And we waited in lines for well over five hours, shivering, unable to understand the endless delays. It took three hours to get pillows and another hour to discover they'd run out of sheets and we would have to return and stand in line after daybreak. It was hard to know what the pillows were for: their use that night seemed increasingly remote, sadistic. They continued to march and run us, pillows in hand, through strange streets, across acres of slick railroad tracks that gleamed faintly in the glow of a switch or signal light, past miles of sealed warehouses, while road guards in luminescent orange vests wagged flashlights as though a sane creature would be about in that forsaken world.

Just before dawn, we were forced to run one last time, the icy water from the puddles sloshing on our civilian pants and shoes. All we had been issued in the way of military clothing were World War II and Korea vintage overcoats and fatigue caps that made us look like the refugees we felt we were.

First light threw me out of kilter again. Roads that had seemed interminable in the darkness, trees, barracks, warehouses, railroad tracks, all became finite, but still, I'd never seen anything like it. The heart of the maze through which we'd been marched was a wooden behemoth of interconnected buildings. Long halls joined chapels and hospitals to mess halls, aid stations, orderly rooms, and more and more halls climbed and descended small hills, followed streets, enclosed patches of earth and trees, formed arches that spanned roads and alleys.

Our first meal was in a vast mess hall, a part of the behemoth. The hall listed a few degrees to port on crumbling pilings. The clatter, shouts, and clangs of a mass-produced military meal issued from steamed-up windows, yellow with incandescent light. I shivered with everyone else while we inched our way up the street into a wobbly corridor, and from there, around a corner into the oppressive warmth of the mess hall. Myriad windows wet with the grey, early spring rains, much of that huge complex surrounding us lay empty, rotting under the New Jersey sky, its silence disturbed only by clanking radiators and the hiss of steam.

We didn't belong to those echoes from another time, to that perverse nostalgia. But I could almost feel the brown uniforms, the bustle of the now idle railroad yards with their passenger platforms still intact, the disgorging and loading point of hundreds of troop trains, thousands upon thousands of men.

Who saw troop trains in 1968, or girls wearing lipstick and waving goodbye, or running along the platforms of small towns and cities to be lifted off their feet for a final kiss as cars squeaked into life and rumbled away toward that rail yard with its waiting, bleak-faced sergeants?

I looked across the tracks that first morning and saw the new base with its brick, sterile buildings like public schools, or prisons.

And I had to come back there and work—I work there now, inside the behemoth. But by degrees, it's slowly disappearing, being mysteriously demolished, eaten away. The mess hall is long gone, just like the events of that first morning.

Despite two straps, one buckled across his chest, the other

across his abdomen, the lieutenant is trying to roll off the litter.

The wash of the helicopter tugs as we carry the litter away and plunge into the night toward the dim light of the treatment tent. There are four of us, one to each handle, and we're running.

The lieutenant has a large hole in the back of his head and three more in his chest. Small chunks of grey matter have spilled onto the canvas under his head and are dropping like bits of sponge. He groans, strains violently at the straps. The litter creaks with his efforts. A syrupy, scarlet puddle has formed on the canvas.

His back is bared as he wrenches part way up onto his side, the pale, yellowish skin streaked with mud. A swatch of blood stands in hideous relief across the flesh and soggy green cotton. The lieutenant grunts and collapses on his back.

Brock is actually swearing because the guy won't stay still. "Jesus Christ!" he says. "Morrisey, Owen! Wrap those chest wounds!"

The lieutenant yells when his shirt is cut open. I reach over his torso and pull the field tag from the buttonhole of his collar. "Enemy action" has been hastily scribbled with a pencil across the tag. That's all.

The field phone rings behind me. Someone yells to Brock that a ship will be on the pad in five minutes to take the lieutenant south. Brock doesn't reply. He's trying to put an intravenous in one of the lieutenant's arms. "Two more units of blood!" he shouts. Sweat pours down his face.

"Hwannnnnnnm! Hwannnnnuhh!" the lieutenant cries and lifts his head.

"Relax!" Brock shouts into his ear. "We're trying to help you."

With a ponderous, robotlike motion, the lieutenant pulls his arm up, tearing out the I.V. Again, he lifts his head.

"He's acting like we're trying to kill him! Hold his goddam arms down!"

The lieutenant's feet start jumping. They thrash off the litter.

"Holy Jesus, get his legs! We're trying to help you!"

"Hunnnnnnnnnhh!" he gargles, jerking his shattered head from side to side.

The helicopter begins to crank up. "More blood! Get some extra blood on this guy!"

There are four medics sprawled across the litter now, fighting to hold the lieutenant still. Two other men are buckling more straps across his legs. The lieutenant yanks an arm free once again. Blood from the dangling tube starts to drip on the floor.

The helicopter lifts out of its revetment. I watch the flashing red light float down to the pad. "They're ready!"

"Call 'em, O'Neill! Give us a couple of minutes . . ."

It's only twenty or thirty feet to the commo shack, but Dunn's voice at the other end of the line sounds miles away, utterly detached. "Roger that. I'll see what I can do."

I glance at the table as the receiver slips out of my hand into its cradle. The lieutenant is staring at me. His head has flopped backwards and is partially off the end of the litter. He is still while Brock pulls out the I.V.s. "Tell Dust-Off to go back to bed."

I reach for the receiver. "Dunn, you got any unit on that guy?"

"Negative, but you got more coming."

A few minutes later, another helicopter hammers across the perimeter, its landing light slashing through the darkness, roaming the torn earth until it finds our little square of pavement. The men on board are from the lieutenant's platoon, but they're all ambulatory.

Morissey's examining shrapnel in the arm of a sandy-haired PFC. There's a rough handsomeness about this soldier, a sense of belligerent self-assurance. He looks both old and very young. Dirt streaks his face and covers the front of his shirt and pants as though he's been lying on his stomach. His fatigues are sopping, just like the lieutenant's were. Bandoliers, loaded with .30 caliber ammunition, crisscross his chest. More than belligerence, I sense something contemptuous in his attitude when I begin to ask him the routine questions for my records.

"Let's get this crap out of here," Morrisey says, and starts to lift the bandoliers over the PFC's head. He takes them outside.

I ask the PFC the lieutenant's name while we wait for Morrisey to return.

"Marshall, Everett C.," he says, watching intently as I write the name in the alloted space.

"Bravo Company, too?"

"Right."

Morrisey's back, cutting the shirt off the PFC. "It'll be a lot easier," he explains.

"I don't give a shit. Need a clean shirt anyway."

Morrisey swabs at the right arm, then pulls the surgical light closer. Brock stops and pokes his head under the light. "Just superficial wounds, huh?"

"That's all I see, sir."

Brock lifts the PFC's forearm and turns it slowly, examining the skin. He picks up the other arm and does likewise, then presses his thumb to the soldier's forehead, next to a spot of dried blood. "That hurt?"

"No, sir."

"Must be someone elses blood." He moves on down the aisle.

"Superficial!" the PFC snorts. "This is the third fucking time I've been superficially wounded."

"You should be about ready to go home," Morrisey says conversationally. He's bent over the arm, pulling a small fragment out with a pair of forceps. "This may need a suture." The empty hole slowly fills with blood.

"One month and days," the PFC replies. "The lieutenant didn't make it, huh?"

"No, but I never saw a guy fight so hard to live."

"Yeah?" The PFC scrutinizes Morrisey's face.

"Half his head was blown away." On impulse, Morrisey looks up and meets his gaze.

"That green dumb fuck tried to order our medic to fetch a wounded gook—in the middle of the firefight! Someone had to stop him . . ." The scrutiny continues, the soldier's gaze appallingly direct.

Morrisey betrays no emotion. "Why don't you lie down—it'll be easier."

"You're not going to report it?" I ask. Morrisey and I are somewhere in the motor pool, heading toward our tent.

"Why don't you?"

"But it's wrong!" My protest is empty. He knows I can't do what I'm demanding of him. I can feel the anger in my face.

"Given a little time at home, a change of scenery, and, unfortunately, it's likely to begin to seem that way to him, too."

116

"Huh! I thought if anyone would do anything about it, it would be you."

Morrisey ignores the vindictiveness, his voice remaining reflective. "If I thought I should . . . ." but whatever he's going to say, he lets drop.

We never spoke of it again. I wouldn't have broached the subject with anyone else. But he wasn't really inconsistent. I just couldn't understand, and I don't think that sonuvabitch gave a damn if anyone understood him or not! He rarely explained anything. He should have.

"Where are you headed, Captain?" A ruddy, cracked-faced MP sergeant squints inside the ambulance. It's almost eight in the morning and vehicles are backed up from the south check-point almost halfway across the plantation.

"The village dispensary, Sergeant, then Dong Nai hamlet later this morning," Brock replies.

The sergeant's long head seems swallowed by his helmet. He lifts the helmet off and scratches his thin, sandy hair. The skin at the front of his neck hangs loose in two large flaps. He pulls unconsciously at one of these as he looks down along the line of vehicles toward the gate. He sighs. "They found some mines in the road near Binh Lu. It'll probably be another thirty minutes before they're here. Why don't you pull on ahead, park behind that lead jeep. Tell the corporal at the gate I sent you down. We'll let you get going soon as the highway's cleared."

"Thank you, Sergeant."

"That's OK, Captain." He ambles across the road in front of us toward a disabled truck with its hood open.

"Shit!" Stevens mutters as he shuts off the engine and slumps down in the seat. He had insisted we leave late for the Medcaps to avoid the morning traffic at the gate. There is one vehicle in front of us now, an MP jeep with a radio mounted on it. Beyond the gate are several coils of concertina wire and the dirt road rambling toward the village and Saigon far to the south. To our right, beyond the perimeter zone of the plantation, a quilt of abandoned rice paddies sprawls toward a line of jungle. A bluish mist rises from the lush greens of the diked earth. As late as it is, the morning still feels clean. I remember other early mornings in other places, like riding the train from Chicago to Denver, seeing the first automobiles of the day shining in the sun as they rolled away behind while I sat mesmerized by the prairies that sailed by, the telegraph wire that swooped up and down, mile after mile.

"Hey guys, check this out!" Stevens says, pulling himself to an upright position. Morrisey and I crowd the door that separates us from the cab. On the left side of the road, about half a mile beyond the farthest coil of wire, several shrines in various phases of ruin rise from the ragged earth. Beyond these, a cloud of dust approaches. Beneath it I can discern a cluster of small vehicles.

Doors start to slam. Men walk past us toward the gate, coming from farther back in the convoy. "What's this, Sarge?" someone passing beneath Brock's window shouts, the sound strangely muffled yet intimate as though I'm locked up someplace listening to the noise of the outside world. "Gook minesweepers?" The men at the gate laugh. I grin. The day begins to assume a festive, if unsettling atmosphere.

The vehicles are closer now. They're lambros. Bright bits of color flutter from the passenger compartments behind the tiny cabs. The MP sergeant emerges from his hut beside the gates and shades his eyes in the brilliant sunshine; he's clearly agitated. "Shit, didn't someone tell them dinks we ain't cleared the road yet?"

The dozen or so lambros start to round a bend. We can hear the whine of the tiny motors now, the infuriated insectile snarl of the miniature buses. Silky colors spill out behind like loads of disintegrating butterflies.

Someone else notices the colors. "Hey! Them are the PX girls!"

The MP sergeant stares bleakly down the road. "Heinz! Jackson! Open them fucking gates! Step on it! Goddam dinks!" The two subordinates trot toward the center where the two halves of the gate meet. Under the intense, static watchfulness of their sergeant, they drop the chain and push against the gates; the halves part like a curtain upon the brilliant spectacle churning toward us.

A blue lambro breaks ahead of the rest of the group. "Hot damn!" someone screams. "Two to one on the blue lambro!"

"You're on!"

The blue lambro, now several lengths ahead of the others, is so close that I think I can see the driver bent over the handles, can fancy him grinning behind the plexiglass windshield. The passenger box sways from side to side as the tiny wheels bounce over the rough surface; the front wheel rises and falls like a jackhammer. I also imagine the chatter, the nasal cries and laughter in the packed passenger compartment.

"C'mon, Blue!" an infantryman bellows and shakes his fist.

The two MPs begin to unhook the second coil of concertina wire. They still have two to go. Their activity is disconnected, even peaceful.

The sergeant's forehead crinkles into a frown as he continues to watch the road over the remaining coils of wire, oblivious of his two men. The blue lambro is less than a hundred yards from the last coil. "Isn't that dumbshit going to slow down?"

Suddenly, the driver hits the brakes. The back of the vehicle begins to catch up with the front; chunks of dirt fly from the skidding wheels. The other lambros start to crisscross the road like frightened chickens. The MPs jump out of the way with the remaining coil of wire. The blue lambro putt-putts up beside the sergeant and stops. The driver, a big smile on his face, salutes. "Morning, Sahgint!" The other lambros file in neatly behind the blue vehicle. We can hear muted laughter from the backs of the conveyances.

"It's a wonder the MP sergeant didn't kill that little fucker," Stevens remarks. It is almost eleven. We still have five or six miles to go to Dong Nai, and aren't moving at all. Traffic is backed up on Highway 10 as far as we can see; we're stalled among the fumes, dust, and incessant racket about fifteen miles from the plantation.

Brock suddenly grins. "Yeah, isn't it wonderful! The marvels of American civilization bestowed upon these poor unfortunates . . . The Rubber Tree Speedway!"

We all laugh, as much from relief as anything else. Brock hadn't said a word to anyone since we left Miss Lahn's in the village, except once to whisper to Morrisey, "That goddam bitch wanted me to give her all our supplies again! Did you see her hanging around that cabinet making a big fuss about wiping the dust off? Not to mention the fucking regulars she pulled in on us."

The "regulars" included the old man in the shorts and pith helmet. She had requested us to stop by to look at three or four difficult cases, according to Brock. There was a line of at least thirty when we got there. "We got to be in Dong Nai this morning, too, Miss Lahn!" Brock said.

"They can wait another day," she had insisted. "Many patient here you can see."

"Get out the hydrogen peroxide, O'Neill," Brock ordered after making a cursory examination of the people in the line. Most of the patients had common skin ailments for which there was no cure except nonexistent soap and clean water, and regular medical follow-through, equally nonexistent. Peroxide foams and makes for a wonderful magic show.

"Want to hand out a bar of soap, too?" Morrisey had asked.

"Sure, why the hell not? They can trade it on the black market for something they really want. Who gives a damn for health around here?"

A scant forty-five minutes later, an enraged Brock had followed the last patient, happily clinging to his bar of soap, out of the infirmary and waited in the ambulance for us to pack up and to cope with Miss Lahn's astonishment.

Now Stevens is slumped in his seat again, smoking a cigarette, trying unsuccessfully to disguise his agitation. On each side of the highway, the embankment drops several feet into drainage ditches for the rice paddies. Some naked, young boys are jumping off a culvert pipe into the scummy water. The water splashes over the open spillway of a small irrigation dam above the hole where the boys are rollicking like children are supposed to, except that the calendar backdrop, the sylvan forests and rolling fields surrounding the waterhole are missing.

Brock belches a huge cloud of cigar smoke out the passenger window. "Go around them, Stevens."

Morrisey presses his hand against the rear door to keep from falling when the vehicle lurches into the oncoming lane. Pulling himself up to the cab, he squats in the door, clutching the jamb on either side for support. He's passed the halfway point of his tour, making the chances of a change in duty or transfer to a field unit negligible. But he's spending more time by himself, and seldom ventures from the company except on Medcaps. He's superb on Medcaps—Smith was right. He and Brock work together on an almost one-to-one basis in the villages. Despite their profound skepticism about the value of their work, there are often moments of special satisfaction, as transitory as they might be. But the frustration is far more prevalent. Morrisey and Brock have probably become as close as they can be, allowing for the difference in rank.

It's curious to me, but I'm not as cynical as they are. I look forward to Medcaps, to helping, too, and I'm a little surprised by my missionary zeal. That's something I've never experienced before, but then I'm being momentarily relieved of my paper war and can afford a little extra good will.

"Goddam, lookit that!" Stevens exclaims. We're creeping along, halfway onto the far shoulder while oncoming traffic skims off one side and pedestrians jump away on the other as our horn blares. Amidst the military and commercial vehicles, a pink and black 1956 Ford Sunliner rumbles by, its top down, driven by a Vietnamese civilian in sunglasses and silk ascot. The car threatens to engulf the Renaults and motorscooters jamming the highway. Stevens shakes his head. "Lookit that fucking wog! He thinks he's king—like a nigger! I used to have a car like that . . ." He jams the heel of his hand onto the horn causing a flurry of activity beyond the hood.

We enter a small hamlet, a poor place of wood huts, thatched and tin roofs. Several armored personnel carriers are parked along the highway and in among the palm and rubber trees; a couple of American drivers are propped on their hatches sucking on cans of beer. There's no other activity in the hamlet, no other sign of life except for a single Vietnamese militiaman sporting a black beret.

A Huey skims over the hamlet, its wash whipping the trees, churning dust and bits of trash among the huts. We watch it hover, then sink below the treeline.

The ambulance stops behind a parked tank that is taking up an entire lane of the highway, creating the bottleneck. Traffic crawls bumper to bumper in the other lane, amid a chorus of beeps and clouds of bluish exhaust. Scooters dart in and out among the larger vehicles. The entire scene shimmers in the heat. No one's directing traffic.

"We got a Dust-Off, sir. We don't need you," the tank commander, a sergeant, says. His goggles clapped to the crown of his head, he climbs on the running board of the ambulance.

"We weren't planning to stop," Brock replies.

The sergeant's face is caked with dust. He grins, a sudden pristine flash. "Got a gook bullfight going! A platoon of

ARVNs decided to take on that water buffalo. Right now looks like the buffalo's winning. It's killed one already, and just gored another.''

Brock yanks the door open. He and the sergeant walk to the edge of the highway. Morrisey, Stevens and I follow. In front of the tank the causeway narrows where the highway crosses a small, wooden bridge. There's a sandbag pillbox at one end of the bridge, a Vietnamese flag rising above it. The railing of the bridge is lined with American soldiers, Vietnamese civilians, and a smattering of ARVNs. More people are sitting along the edge of the highway while children scoot among them hawking Coca Cola and Carlings.

A short distance beyond the bridge, the Huey has settled down in the middle of the road, momentarily halting all traffic. The copilot stands beside his door looking out into the rice paddies where a platoon of ARVNs have a water buffalo surrounded. Two soldiers, bearing a litter, have slogged their way out of the paddy and are threading along the top of the dikes toward the helicopter.

Even from where I stand, I can see the torn shirt, thick blood and entrails of the ARVN on the litter.

''That's a live one,'' the sergeant says.

''Not for long,'' Brock replies.

Automatic rifles chatter. Blood spurts from the buffalo's side. The soldiers splashing around the animal cheer. Again there's gunfire across the paddies, the sound strangely innocuous and remote.

The animal swings its enormous head from side to side, then lunges at one of the Vietnamese. The soldier jumps back. I can see a smile on his face.

''Why didn't you break it up, Sergeant?'' Brock asks.

''Shit, sir! These dinks aren't any good at fighting—might as well provide us with a little entertainment. And, hey, I haven't got any authority with them, anyhow. Hell, they got one of their own officers out there with them!'' Brock and the sergeant stare in renewed silence. ''And, sir, they're helping the economy. Why these little bastards are selling Coke like it was the Fourth at Coney Island.''

I've been watching the assortment of onlookers, specifically four whores who moments ago alighted from a bus and are already hanging on the arms of four grinning GIs. With the nocturnal softness of their tumbling, dark hair and silk dresses, I'm reminded of four elegant moths.

The crowd roars and one of the soldiers falls face down in the water, trying to dodge the buffalo's horns. The tip of one horn plunges into the man's back and there's a wild scream as the animal yanks its head up, trying to pull free. The torso of the man on the end of the horn lifts out of the weeds, the arms flailing savagely. The animal shakes his head. The other ARVNs shout. One soldier strikes the animal's rump with the butt of his rifle, then sloshes out of the way. Suddenly, the flesh rips and the wounded man plops back into the water.

Another soldier, this one on the side of the beast away from us, starts shooting at the animal. The barrel flicks up with the burst of fire. Something pings off the turret of the tank behind us.

"Goddam! JONES!"

A corporal leaning on the railing of the bridge turns and looks at the sergeant. "Yeah, Sarge?"

"Jones, go tell them fuckheads to aim the other way or we'll blow them outta this goddam swamp!" The tank commander's livid. He yanks his goggles from his head and crushing them furiously, shakes them at the Vietnamese

Across the bridge, the Huey starts to lift, rising from its dust in defiance of visual logic. It clatters away toward the plantation. No attempt is made to retrieve the man just gored.

"Can you get us out of here, Sergeant?" Brock asks. "We have to go to the next village." He turns to Morrisey and says, "Mendez has a better chance with them than we do," as though trying to excuse what we all feel.

The late sunny morning haze produces a dreamlike quality as the ARVNs dance and the buffalo plunges in semiblind fury, blood pouring down its face and muddy sides. "OK, Doc. I'll get you going."

"Someone got the time? My watch has stopped," Brock grumbles as the ambulance starts across the bridge past the sergeant and two other soldiers directing traffic for us.

"Just about noon," Morrisey says. It's the last thing anyone says for a couple of miles as we breathe the air and purge ourselves of a numbing oppressiveness.

On the way back we see a helicopter rising from the area of the bridge. Once again, Stevens plunges into oncoming traffic and follows the shoulder of the highway, and once again, the sergeant helps us across the bridge. The crowd has noticeably diminished.

"That's eleven been evacuated, sir. Three dead so far: the two you saw and another one over there." The tank commander points to a dike where a heap of pale skin, olive cloth, and scarlet cook in the sun. "I don't see any reason to recall Dust-Off for him. He was killed before I got here this morning, but they just dragged him out a while ago. Probably stinks like hell." He wags his head. "That ol' cow's done a number on them, but I'm afraid she's done for."

Out in the paddy, the water buffalo's on its knees, its hide caked with blood, dry and fresh. The blood sparkles in the afternoon light and the creature's head sinks lower and lower. From time to time, it bellows and tries to rise, or thrusts its horns at one of the soldiers, but the motions are feeble. The ARVNs are idly emptying their rifles into the animal's sides.

"I feel sick," Morrisey says.

"That's two of us." Brock says. "Well, at least Mendez got stuck with these stupid bastards. Next time, maybe he'll volunteer for a Medcap."

Stevens threads the ambulance through the parked and moving vehicles in the middle of the hamlet. Members of the armored unit, wearing only open flak jackets over their tanned torsos, pants and boots, lounge on their vehicles and against the walls of the huts. Painted on the side of one of the vehicles is a wolf's head. A yellow flag bearing the same emblem droops from the antenna of one of the armored personnel carriers.

A girl, about fourteen or fifteen years old—maybe younger—sits on a soldier's lap. He has an arm around her waist and is holding a can of American beer.

"These guys look like they swung out of the treetops," Stevens says.

The soldier with the girl spots the red cross on the side of the ambulance. "Hey, Doc!" he shouts.

Stevens slows the vehicle and Brock, his arm hanging out the window, nods at the soldier.

"Hey, Doc! I think I got the crud from babysan here. You wanta treat my dick?"

Brock yanks the bandage scissors from his chest pocket and waves them out the window. "Sure! Bring it here."

The men start to laugh. The soldier with the girl smiles, then the smile freezes. All at once, before me is a daguerreotype of quiet men standing in front of hovels and steel gears, wheels, tracks, all signs of humor erased as they encircle the girl on the soldier's knee. The girl snaps into focus, almost consciously takes possession of the scene. Her straight, black hair falls on each side of her gaunt face. Her dark eyes stare balefully at us.

Morrisey touches Stevens on the shoulder. "Get going, Stevens. Move."

NINE

"Just listen, will you?" Morrisey demands, his head bowed as he strives to gather the thrust of his argument. He's very excited.

It's late afternoon, I'm on my way out the back door of the sickcall tent, and I've obviously interrupted some sort of impassioned appeal to Jenkins, who's sitting imperturbably at his desk, feet up, listening with a silence as intense as Morrisey's agitation. Jenks even seems profoundly, subtly amused, but that's Jenkins: he has a wonderful sense of limitation and folly, especially his own, but there's no cynicism attached to it. He's acknowledged me, although his eyes haven't left Morrisey. His face has a peaceful, fixed quality.

"O'Neill?" Morrisey says. "Do you remember that night I came out of the NCO hooch and ran into you and Stevens?"

I blush.

"Yeah, you remember. That wasn't the only time I was in there," he continues, directing his argument towards Jenkins again, "but it was the last. I never saw a guy with such a need to talk—not to converse, but to assert, to vocalize all his frustrations. I couldn't take it anymore. There's nobody in the NCO hooch who likes Smith. They might respect him, but they hate him. They're scared of him. Talk to him for a while, and it's obvious he's got nothing but contempt for them."

"So what, Richie? He's more intelligent than all of them put together."

"Jenks, they hate him because he's a hypocrite! He wants the same damn things they do, but he puts on this other face

126

and shows them up all the time. He told me himself he thought discipline in the company's terrible. You know that's a crock. But he thinks we've got it soft and don't know it. He even gave me that shit about if we'd been to the field, we'd have a deeper appreciation of how well off we really are. That sonuvabitch was never in the field!"

Jenkins laughs. "Why are you all upset?"

"Man, the guy really bothers me! He thinks battalion's a model facility. He feels he should be allowed to build all kinds of bunkers, wards, all sorts of fancy buildings. Yeah, and he thinks the major covers for us too much. He's bullshit about the fraternization in evening games. 'Bad for morale,' he says. 'Too much free time. The major's a good CO, especially in treatment, *but* . . .' and off he went about how much better we'd be doing if there were better physical facilities, a little less fraternization, and if people showed more respect for the NCOs and the army regulations. But he's really big on battalion. You know about battalion, O'Neill."

Jenkins turns on me. "That was a slick haircut."

Thibauld marches past the tent with two cameras dangling around his neck, scores of film cases attached to the straps. "Hey, Thib!" I call. "I heard *Jack and Jill* hired you as their war correspondent!" He whirls and glares, then storms away toward the motor pool.

"What's that all about?" Morrisey asks.

"Nothing." I wish I'd never opened my mouth. There was much more emotion in that remark than I intended. Who needs the aggravation?

"Morrisey," Jenks continues. "Smith's just another lifer. You got to tell yourself that. I thought for sure you'd be moving in the NCO hooch once you got Spec Five. I mean, you're invaluable . . ."

There's not a trace of amusement on Morrisey's face while Jenkins hee-hees behind the desk, thoroughly tickled. "Smith did come to me, Jenkins, and said maybe that Spec Five could become hard five and I *could* move into the NCO hooch." He bursts into an involuntary grin and waits for Jenkins and me to quiet down.

"Go ahead, man," Jenks says at last, his forehead cradled in his hand.

"While he was congratulating me on my promotion, he told me how soft we have it—easy rank. It took him years to earn hard five back in the old army."

I remember the old PFC who slept in the holdover barracks with me, the gleaming polished boots placed neatly beside the cot, face like a little boy's. That's a fact about the military: you got to love having a stern daddy.

"He's married," Morrisey says. "Married for twelve years and no kids. His wife's a schoolteacher in Ohio. She's pretty —he showed me a picture. He inherited the family farm and talks a lot about getting his twenty in and going back to farming."

"Every lifer's dream, Morrisey. A cabin in the mountains, a small farm, beautiful sunsets . . ."

"OK, OK, but with him it's different. He once thought about getting his BA and going to OCS. You see he believes those compliments from Brock and Shelby, and all the others who say he's 'officer material.' His wife believed him, too. She helped him with his courses until he got transferred to Germany. She went over with him and taught school in Heidelberg, but didn't fit in with the other NCOs' wives. He didn't say it in so many words, but I bet he didn't fit in either. Probably the other lifers felt the same way then as they do now."

"Like you feel."

"That's right, Jenks. I think he'd make a lousy officer." Morrisey's sudden irritability is startling. He turns away from us and stares out into the yard. He suddenly seems very frustrated with Jenkins, and angry. Jenkins's amusement isn't helping. I don't think I count.

"So what happened in Germany, Richie?" Jenkins sounds apologetic.

"He got promoted to staff sergeant and decided to forget college," Morrisey yields, reluctantly.

"And . . ."

"I don't think he liked school that much. Now he says there was a real need for good NCOs. His wife lives on the farm and teaches school. He says he's going to get his twenty in at the end of this tour and then he'll retire to the farm. But I think he wants to make first sergeant, and will re-up and extend to get it.

"And I also think he really enjoys the independence of his own little shitass room and meals in a mess hall. Obligated to no one. A real lifer."

"Just what I've been saying."

"With this difference. That bastard finds leverage, Jenkins, and he uses it. He's got the frustration of ten lifers. Don't ever trust him. He's out to change things."

Jenkins pushes himself away from the desk and stands up. "Still sounds like an ordinary lifer to me, but man, you sound just as bad as Navarra did. What did he do, ordain you before he left?"

I laugh. "C'mon, you guys, the club's open in ten minutes."

"Never trust anybody who won't look at himself, Jenkins. That's where all that frustration comes from."

"I trust a lot of people who don't look at themselves."

"Yes, but they want to."

Jenkins checks his watch. "I got to go down to division before chow." Suddenly the warmth of Jenkins's interest vanishes. He walks right out of the office without a word of farewell. I feel absolutely disconcerted—it's hard not to take that kind of exit personally.

"Aw, that's just Jenkins," Morrisey says. "I won't see him for three or four days and then it will be like he never left the room—like he can focus on only one thing at a time. Really singleminded. It's probably healthy."

At the club, Annie's laughing, and blushing, too. Milliken, the mess sergeant, is ribbing her about being an ARVN. "Tell me, Annie! What's it like marching around with all them men?"

She laughs and shakes her head. "I not march with men." She's wearing a brilliant red robe slit to her waist on both sides, and white silk pants. A kerchief, the same color as the *ao dai*, holds her hair in place. Her eyes sparkle. She bends over to put some glasses on a shelf, then looks up, the color still high in her cheeks and glances at Morrisey.

"You don't march, then what do you do?" Milliken sniggers. "What do you think of that, O'Neill? Goddam ARVNs got a better thing going than we do."

"You kill lots of VC, Annie?" Milliken goes on.

She shakes her head violently, then confronts the sergeant who's sitting on my right at the far end of the bar. "You acting number ten today, Sahgint. I not kill anybody."

Milliken makes a long face. He's big and stupid looking with a large angular nose and hair matted across his brow. He's probably thirty-four or thirty-five, but he looks fifteen years older. He's already slightly inebriated, his pale cheeks tinged pink. "Awww, c'mon girl! What do you do every month when you go to Saigon?"

She notices his glass is empty and snatching a bottle off the shelf, fills it until it overflows. Her wooden sandals give her gait a slight rocking motion. "There, Sahgint! You keep asking question, I get you smashed!" She takes the cost of the drink from the pile of flimsy paper currency that Milliken slapped on the bar when he first arrived, puts the bottle back and grabs another. Milliken's wiping whiskey off his hands with a handkerchief.

Annie holds the bottle up and waves it at Morrisey who's buried in a book. She clops down the bar and gives his sleeve a tug. "Hey!"

Morrisey looks up. "Thanks, Annie." She bends her head slightly to pour the scotch, then rewards him with a smile. Morrisey goes back to his book and she turns to me.

It's just past five and the bar's been open for about a half hour. A pair of ceiling fans fluff the parachutes suspended from one end of the open tent to the other. Two patients in blue pajamas are sitting at a table across the room, playing cards.

"He reads too goddam much, Annie! Doesn't appreciate you! Now take me—I can look at those pictures and be happy." Milliken indicates the Playmates stapled to the wooden marquee above the bar. "That's all a man needs, ain't it, Morrisey?"

Slowly, Morrisey says, "If you say so, Sarge."

"Yeah, well I do! Why don't you put that book down for a change and pay attention to that woman."

"Sergeant, why don't you mind your own business?"

The patients turn and watch us but the moment passes.

"Hey, Annie! How 'bout another . . . there's a good girl."

She shrugs and reaches for the bottle.

Stevens bounces in, slaps me on the shoulder and passes under the counter. As he rises behind the bar, he switches on the stereo. "How about some Beatles, Sergeant Milliken?"

"You and your goddam Beatles! Why don't you play some good music for a change. Something Country."

"Right, Sarge! How's this?" He pulls a record out of its jacket, blows on it, and drops it on the turntable. The first strains of "Sergeant Pepper" burst upon the room.

"Stevens, you're not authorized behind the bar!"

"Sarge, I'm the new night bartender."

"This ain't night. And you know, this is supposed to be an *NCO*-EM club."

"Right, Sergeant! I tell you what . . ." The smile vanishes. "You let us keep liquor in our hooches and you can listen to any damn music you want in here."

"It's against the army regulations. You're not an NCO."

"No shit, Sergeant. Thank God for small favors. How are you doing, O'Neill? Need a refill?" He winks at Annie, ducks back under the counter and plops on a stool beside me. "Morrisey, would you please get your face out of that fucking book?"

Without raising his eyes, Morrisey gives Stevens the finger. I think they're beginning to like each other.

"Seriously, Sergeant!" Stevens leans forward and looks around me at Milliken. "You guys couldn't function without the ARs, could you?"

Milliken starts to reply, hesitates, then scowls.

"Look! What I mean is, it's the basis of your authority— all those rules, right?"

"Right . . ."

"So without them, you couldn't, command jack shit for respect, right?"

Milliken chews his lower lip. "Boy, you're playing with insubordination . . ."

Six hours later, I leave a very drunken Stevens at his hooch and stumble on through the trees to the sanctuary of the bench in front of the treatment tent. Morrisey disappeared hours ago, but I find him here. I slump onto the bench and together we watch a flare float down the sky. Another flare goes up and pops. "It's so quiet . . . is there a war going on here?" I giggle softly, feeling my head swim round and round as it tries to overtake my eyes floating down the sky with the flares.

"Oh, yes." I can almost hear him smile in the darkness.

"You never get drunk . . . or stoned . . . or anything like that! You afraid?"

"Not of getting drunk or stoned."

"Well, I think you're afraid. I don't think you want anyone to get a fucking handle on you. Like Stevens says, Morrisey, you're too uptight. You let things get to you." I mutter on, uninvited, feeling very wise and righteous and concerned and open and honest. *And like a horse's ass the next day, although he never appeared to mind at all. I started to apolo-*

gize when I saw him that morning, but something made me hold back—something he conveyed. As someone said, you shouldn't drink if you're going to apologize for it.

I'm fumbling toward my hooch through the rubber trees and screeches of the invisible night world. There are no lights anywhere, just smells. Morrisey left some time ago. I must have slept. I found myself lying on the bench, chilled.

Odors of oils, grease, moist steel fill the air when I enter the motorpool. In the distance I hear the drone of a propellor plane and stop to listen. It's an intrusion upon the heat and sublime resurgence of insects, almost as though it's approaching out of the past, from a more tranquil time. Like a wave, the sound grows until there's only that rhythmic thunder rolling over the plantation, then over me . . . even the insects seem to be listening. It feels as though the sky's about to fall. I hear a new sound in the treetops, a hiss and rustle. I stand like a blindman, frozen by the sound while I fight panic at thoughts of misplaced defoliants. Something flutters past my head, touches my sleeve. Expecting to look up and see the skeletal ravaged arms of trees silhouetted against the sky by some horrible light, I run, stumble toward the refuge of my tent.

Morning reveals thousands of little slips of paper, a plane's bellyful from an abortive psychological operations mission. We have to pick them up. There's writing on both sides of these leaflets, and photographs, although the quality of the printing and photo reproduction is crude. One picture shows a very unhappy Viet Cong captive, but turn the paper over and there, beneath the caption "Chieu Hoi!" are two more photographs of the same captive; in one he's holding a white flag, and in the other, he's happily working a rice paddy behind a water buffalo.

"I suppose 'Chieu Hoi!' means 'I give up,' " I say.

Jenkins chuckles. "Yeah, and look at all the bennies you get—farmland, tools. I've heard of more than one Charlie jumping out in the middle of a firefight with his hands in the air, shouting 'Chieu Hoi!' They didn't get any rice paddy and buffalo."

Buelen blows the whistle behind us and men start filtering through the trees toward formation, depositing handfuls of paper in the trash barrels.

"Hey, Jenks," Morrisey says. "Try forty acres and a mule."

Jenkins stops dead, then explodes with laughter. I'm surprised by the depth and spontaneity of his reaction, and find myself laughing, too. He always seems so self-possessed; I've never even heard him raise his voice.

"Morrisey! Jenkins!" Buelen shouts. His whistle shrieks impatiently. "We ain't got all day!" I start to walk more rapidly, but as neither of my companions changes his pace to accommodate the first sergeant, I feel compelled to slow down again.

"Holding everybody up as usual," Buelen storms as we slip into the back line of the formation.

"Must have been pretty funny, Morrisey," Smith says, smiling and trying to be agreeable.

Morrisey doesn't answer, just stares.

Smith's smile vanishes. For a few dreadful moments we watch him contrive to become businesslike, to make that change appear natural.

Sometimes I don't go to bed, no matter how tired I am, because I need the solitude. Sometimes. Tonight it's because my mind won't stop running and give me peace. I could take the solitude. Gittoni's asleep in his bunk at the far end of the tent. The only light in the room comes from beneath my mosquito netting, a pale greenness that heightens my sense of isolation. It would be peaceful except for the blank stationery lying under the light and the unused pen in my hand. I hear a helicopter approaching in the distance, over the airstrip toward us; nothing we should be concerned about. The white paper is like a huge wall, is in fact keeping me from sleep. The noise of the helicopter grows louder. I lay down my pen to listen.

"Get a flashlight!" someone screams as the ship hovers directly overhead, thunderous, drumming. I run for the door, past Gittoni fumbling with his mosquito netting. Bits of leaves and trash fly by through the darkness. I can see streaks of red on the rotor above me, then it's gone and in the abrupt silence, someone's hollering wildly inside the NCO hooch.

A light stabs in the direction of the noise but I can only see huge, boiling clouds of green, purple, and red smoke. The lights inside the NCO tent cast a dim, lurid glow.

All feelings of urgency cease with the realization that only the NCO hooch is involved. Gittoni and I sit down on our tent steps and are soon joined by Morrisey. Lovely whorls of light snake among the trees.

A purple silhouette floats out of the depths of the smoke and emerges as Buelen, wide-eyed, pale, his hair frazzled, a hand to his face in the glare of several flashlights. "Turn them fucking things off!" He's wearing the bottoms of a pair of red striped pajamas, the strings dangling to his knees. The lights die and the first sergeant fades back into the dreamlike mist.

"Had to be Murphy," Gittoni says. "His ass will be grass for this," but he laughs with pleasure and admiration at the scene before us.

"Hargos will chew them up one side and down the other," Morrisey says.

"Yes, but he'll love Murph for getting the 'fat jackals' even if he won't admit it."

"Can't, not 'won't.' "

Gittoni chuckles in reply, his delight as keen as ever.

The smoke slowly dissipates. A crowd gathers outside the main door of the NCO hooch. Buelen and the other noncommissioned officers have dressed and gathered behind a table in the center area, facing the door and the crowd beyond. Murphy and his copilot suddenly appear, still in their flight suits, holding their helmets by the straps, and escorted by Major Mendez.

"Lifers!" someone shouts as Mendez and the two flyers go inside the tent.

The three of us leave our step and move closer to the far end of the NCO hooch, near the door where Buelen first appeared. From here we can look down a long hall and see them at the table.

"Why did you drop those smoke grenades?" Buelen demands.

The two flyers look at the floor and don't respond. They're not grown men anymore, but little boys, red and sullen. No, I decide, Hargos won't love them for it.

"Well, are you big enough to answer the first sergeant's question?" Mendez asks, his words clipped and nasal with his anger.

Murphy slowly meets Buelen's gaze. He looks humiliated but not repentant; I feel embarrassed just watching him.

"It's like he got caught screwing the head cheerleader in the locker room," Gittoni says.

134

"Just responding to natural urges," Morrisey says.

"No, the crime was getting caught. They have to be punished."

"That's a surprise coming from you, O'Neill," but he laughs.

". . . and you may not like us," Buelen is saying, "but aside from maybe burning down our tent, you have an example to set. You're officers!"

"What did Murphy tell him?"

"He said he didn't know why he did it."

Smith is standing just behind Buelen, grim-faced, a familiar, taut fury to the set of his mouth. "What are we going to do about it, First Sergeant Buelen?"

Buelen glances at Smith, then considers the two flyers. Mendez remains silent and watchful behind them. Buelen mumbles something over his shoulder at Smith, then, with a lopsided smile, waves the aviators away, suggesting that the incident is already forgotten. The two fliers are twenty one and twenty respectively. Something in Buelen's manner acknowledges this. He shakes his head, loudly suggests they use more sense in the future.

Murphy thanks him and apologizes again with obvious sincerity, but he doesn't look at Smith.

Buelen goes down the hall in the direction of his room and shattered sleep.

"If you men ever do a thing like that again," Mendez says, "I'll have you court-martialed."

Visibly relieved, the two pilots turn toward the door.

Only Smith hasn't moved. His anger's been unyielding except for a moment when he looked at Buelen with surprised contempt for the first sergeant's capitulation.

There's tension in the crowd waiting at the bottom of the steps for Murphy and his copilot. We can feel it from our vantage point. "They'd applaud," Morrisey whispers, "if the major wasn't here."

"They're fools," Gittoni says.

The major appears at the top of the steps. The crowd is already breaking up before he can reach the boardwalk.

Now the company is silent again and I'm confronted with that blank page. I'm trying to write a letter home. I have written weekly since my arrival, but it's becoming difficult. How can I respond in any meaningful way to the claims of family, the almost whimsical accounts of the activities of friends and neighbors thousands of miles away? Why should I be expected to? I've told them about the sun and heat: the nonessential matters that don't make me feel cheap to communicate, that aren't cheapened by my efforts.

Last week was the first time I didn't write and it's just as hard to write now. The question, "We didn't hear from you. Is everything all right?" is infuriating.

So I'm immersed in a sea of insects that screech and clatter in the darkness; their cousins on the light in front of me are tame by contrast, as they flutter softly and pat against the metal shade. To stop writing would cause terrible anxiety at home, even hurt: I don't think I could bring myself to that, to be as blunt as Morrisey was with his family. More frequently now, the most petty activities seem incredibly compounded, enmeshed in irrelevant matters I can't fathom and have no desire to.

Morrisey stopped writing home regularly within weeks of his arrival. He told his family that correspondence would be intermittent because he found it difficult, but if something was not alright, they would surely hear about it: silence could be solace.

Gittoni wrote to his girl every day, his parents every other day, and taped conversation on his portable recorder and told them everything that was happening . . . and really nothing, but he didn't know that then.

I don't have to feel ashamed, not about that or anything else. So why do my feelings about one thing feed my feelings here and now? This room's getting claustrophobic. I don't have to feel ashamed. The equation was there the moment the guy in the bib overalls and I saw each other: whoever took Casey home was going to get laid, one equaled the other. It was no big macho thing. Casey was no such conquest. Everything in her looks, her bearing said that—she knew that about herself. She was indifferent. She had to have known the equation.

I've never been comfortable with competition, organized sports or anything else, but especially when another person was involved: when a woman was the goal. All my life, I've hated that sort of thing: maybe because I'm afraid of it, afraid of losing. But tonight there was no question. I've carried these feelings a long time—I mean, I've been without a woman. So there wasn't really any contest. Casey and the guy in the overalls didn't act like strangers so he'd probably been in her pants before—no surprise in store for him.

Not that he liked my moving in. There was one moment when he and I first saw each other when, without realizing it myself yet, I'd decided to pick Casey up. He must have sensed it because as soon as we looked at each other, all the stallion stuff was there. I could feel the adrenalin—even a slight smile as though I were truly enjoying it. There was no stopping me. He just walked away.

But there's always the question of what you've won: no one ever talks about that. And she knew the equation, she was up for grabs. She didn't give a damn who took her home as long as she got fucked. But it's not that simple either.

It wasn't bad in bed—she knows all kinds of tricks. She's no stranger to men. And she's not stupid. I don't think so. And I'm sure it's not drugs, although she uses them, too. I've just never tried to talk with anyone with less enthusiasm for conversation, as though she knew it was all bullshit anyway. So even if it was, she made it worse.

When I first went up to her at the bar, I wasn't even choked up like I usually am. I knew I was going to get what I wanted. I introduced myself and after a few moments, I asked her what she did.

"I'm a tramp," she said, and smiled. She looked really pretty when she did that. I was startled. That wasn't what I'd been watching from across the room.

"Wonderful!" I grinned and lifted my glass to her. "How do you live on that?"

"I don't." She smiled again but it seemed automatic. I'd only been kidding along with her. "Don't you think I'm a tramp?"

"No." I could feel her watch me lie. "Of course not."

She simply nodded.

"Why do you think you're a tramp?" I tried to make it light again. I was already thinking I'd made a mistake. I didn't want to hear anyone's troubles.

"Because when he's not calling me a split-tail slut, my father says I'm a tramp. He says that about my mother, and all the other women he's balled, too, I guess. But they have a nice new house and two Buicks in the driveway."

By this time I was wondering if I should even bother to be polite when I left. But then her hand took my arm very gently. "I'm sorry. It's been a long day. I'm not really a tramp. I work for an insurance company as a typist. What do you do?"

"I'm in the army."

Her hand didn't move, the pressure on my arm didn't vary, but I felt something go out of her touch. "That's a bummer."

"Yeah, that's kind of how I feel about it. I just got back from 'Nam." I let that one fall, settle between us to emphasize my reply. I felt cheap instantly, physically sick for doing it. I had betrayed myself. I've always hated that word.

"I'm nineteen," she said after an awkward pause during which I agonized that she'd sensed my betrayal. "You seem older," she urged, bringing me back to the bar and her.

I didn't answer that, although it was true. Changing the subject, I asked if she lived nearby.

Whatever spontaneity or real interest there'd been in her voice faded. "A few miles away."

"With your parents?"

"No way. I've got a place."

"You need a ride?"

She reached down for her purse perched on the rail of the bar. "I came with that other guy."

"So?"

She shrugged, then walked to the back door, turned and watched me. Her face was blank and not pretty.

There were long silences after that. I tried to draw her out, her interests, movies, whatever. She seemed indifferent, but that in no way diminished the sense that everything was waiting for me. After a while, I didn't even try. We just drove on, up the river. I think if I hadn't needed her so much, I would have let her off at her house and driven back. I don't like to fake it. I used to be quite capable of leaving girls off like that . . . my pride can get in the way and I start feeling ambivalent. But how the hell was this girl going to hurt me?

We went through one village, then another, the headlights rushing along picket fences. Old white frame houses, stone houses with white trim, inns with long, roofed verandas sailed out of the gloom. I thought, why do colonial structures here (and in Vietnam) exude such loveliness and feelings of permanence?

The smells of June, of river, fields, woods poured in through the car windows, lush and clean—not overripe, not laced with fuel and the sweet stench of the litter racks. Suddenly I felt exhilarated, physically, even erotically happy. All the anticipation, all that special freedom to move at will in the darkness again without fear, and to know with reasonable certainty that soon I would be lying with the person beside me without any clothes on—that freedom, too—all churned with the smells and warm night air.

"God, I love this valley," I blurted out. "Just smell everything!"

She laughed, a pure, gut laugh, and pleasing. "I've always wanted to live along the river. I looked for months to find a place."

"You live next to it?"

"Oh yes, with a backyard that borders the canal. Rhododendron everywhere. I'm useless in the spring—all I want to do is sit at home and watch things grow. I want to be kind of a hermit then—people are hassles."

I could easily relate to that. I glanced at her. She had been flopped against the door, but now she was sitting upright staring through the windshield with the peculiar intensity of a child attempting to express something.

"I've lived near Doylestown all my life," she said. "All the housing developments—everything's new. I feel sheltered here. They can't build. They'll fall right over the cliffs into the river."

"I envy you." I meant it. I was beginning to enjoy her. I told her how much I liked living in my river town, the town where I picked her up.

"Don't you find the crowds, you know, the tourists kind of hokey?"

"I don't mind so much, now. You get used to it." But I was thinking how wonderful a place this far up, this secluded would be. It was still some way from Easton, from the edge of the coal country and the Water Gap and the sense that things were much more ordinary, like New Jersey across the river, more used and abused by people.

She fumbled in her pocketbook. I heard a match strike, then smelled marijuana. She sucked on the joint a couple of times and offered it to me, a tender gesture for her, the back of her hand gliding lightly over my arm.

I didn't know it mattered that much; it never had before. It was all up and out before I could stop it. "I've had more of that shit than I'll ever need, thanks!" Why the hell did people have to fucking light up whenever they felt good?

It died after that, the feelings I'd been having, that for a moment we'd both had. I heard her take a couple of more hits, then saw her snub it out in the ashtray with her fingertips. She put the joint back in her pocketbook, reminding me how precious grass is at home.

The small house stood by itself in the woods, on the side of a hill. We went in from the back, which was really the front. I could hear the river sliding along the bank below. I didn't ask if I could come in—I walked in with her. She shrugged, dropped her pocketbook on the dining table and turned to me. I bent down and kissed her. Mechanically, she stroked my pants. Her lips were incredibly soft. She twisted her head away and whispered, "My roommate may come in." Even then, even as she led me through the kitchen and up the steep stairway into the attic, I felt I'd disappointed her. What did I expect? Maybe the guy in the overalls could have turned her on—knew some tricks. Then she might really have given something back.

For a year I yearned to be home where things could be in proportion again, the rain, the sun, insects, smells . . . where things could mean something without risk. I'm still waiting for the magic. There are a few things, sounds for instance, that mean something different. I hear things differently.

Two weeks ago, Jack brought his brother's motorcycle from home and let me take it out. The sun was beginning to slide down over the bluffs, drawing its light in behind it. I rumbled along a dirt road that led off the river road not far from this room, casting a cloud of dust behind me, but the dust was beige, almost white in color. There were fields on either side, a stone farmhouse partly surrounded by a hedge. The handlebars jiggled as the front wheel bumped and skipped over the rough surface. I was being careful—it had been two years since I'd been on a bike and I knew, better than I ever had, what could happen if something went wrong.

At a covered bridge, I yanked the motorcycle back on its stand and left it tinking in the soft evening air to go and sit beside the canal. Away, up river, the sky began to vibrate. Gradually the noise filled the valley, became louder and louder, hammered at me. I turned and saw a woman hanging out clothes behind the farm house. I wanted to reach for her. My hand slid through the grass.. She didn't seem to hear anything.

God help me! My eyes welled up. I looked across the canal, toward the trees above the towpath, and waited as the *noise crashed around me, up against the hill. For a year I'd heard that sound, been thrilled by it. Now the land was quiet and it brought terror.*

It passed. The propellor sound of its wake, the steadier drumming faded into a soft chop as the Huey vanished over the trees where the river road wound up into the escarpment. The woman was watching me, puzzled. How long had she been watching me? She smiled tentatively. She had never looked up, never heard it!

I rode upriver after that, under the trestle where the tracks cross the Delaware into the station at Easton. The dampness of the stone abutment chilled me as I passed under the bridge and into darkness farther north. My white shirt fluttered and billowed softly. Through the sudden coolness of the low places and soggy warmth of the rises, I followed my headlight, flowed as one instrument into the winding darkness, still sedate, controlled.

When I turned for home, I waited on the shoulder for several minutes while the engine idled. Headlights bloomed out of the night, swept over me, whizzed away, became little darts of red. I lifted my hand from the throttle, reached around the grip, closed my grasp and twisted the rubber all the way toward me.

I sailed off the Easton highway onto the river road, felt myself coming parallel with the pavement, glistening adhesive that would rip my limbs away in one screaming instant. I tore at the throttle—the blast echoed among dismal little houses that flashed by. As I streaked through the lower valley, fireflies drifted upwards from the fields.

In the parking lot of an all-night diner, I climbed off, held my sides, and shook. My teeth rattled as I repeated, over and over, "I'm free, I'm free, I'm free . . ."

The diner was a creaking, wooden building with a screen door that discharged its load of insects into the night behind me. The donuts were slightly stale and the coffee was good. I watched a tall, gawky boy lean over a pinball machine, clutch the sides of the box with his huge hands, and start jerking his body while the machine dinged and hooted its pleasure. Beyond a grimy window, the moon rose.

Back in the softness of the night—sedate, controlled once more—I swung across the river into New Jersey, into a small town cupped against the hills, the houses old and neat, buried under trees. At the grade crossing the signal lights were flashing back and forth, the bell ringing. I waited for twenty minutes, but no train came. There was no distant whine or rumble, no brightness creeping along the steep hillsides. Nothing was moving in the streets—the town seemed empty, dead. For a moment I felt in my guts where I was, I felt myself.

Then I fled, roared downriver.

TEN

A Vietnamese woman sits on the bench in front of the sickcall tent waiting for assistance from us, the Americans, and Davies in particular, although she doesn't know this. Her face shows lines of age despite the fact that she's holding a little boy no more than two years old on her lap. The child is mute in the strange surroundings that are making his mother anxious under a mask of placid endurance.

Several times the woman looks directly at me. I'm sitting on the other bench, the one in front of treatment, with Morrisey and Newell, eating oranges. Every time I glance in her direction, I swear she's watching me. I'm becoming paranoid about her, resentful of that expectant look and the guilt she's making me feel because I have food in my hand. I refuse to be Davies's conscience! I've called him twice; I even asked the woman what she wanted and she handed me some scribbles on a scrap of paper. She speaks no English, of course.

No, and when I checked the Vietnamese log, there was no entry in it from last night, although Dunn swore there were a couple of ARVNs that came in around 2 A.M., so it's Davies's problem.

I pointed toward the office and repeated, "Man come! Man come soon!" Her incomprehension was silent, blank, and I simply walked away. I feel just great.

Davies is becoming more and more unreliable as I assume more responsibilities and his day of departure comes closer. He's also getting more callous.

A low rumble surges across the berm. Newell points to the left of the tower. Far away, two columns of black smoke drift into the sky. The sound of a second explosion reaches us before I see the plane; wings and fuselage plunge toward the earth, then soar again. The canopy glints briefly in the sun. A third column of smoke floats upward from the hazy terrain and moments later the sound arrives. The plane circles, almost thoughtfully, before it swoops once more.

There's a disconcerting lack of menace, even of reality, as though I'm watching the news on television. Behind me, the whistle blows for afternoon formation.

When I return, the plane has gone. A pall hangs over the bombed area, but low on the horizon something new has intruded: a solid bank of silver-gray clouds. They've rolled into view and paused, like a powerful invader on the threshold of battle. Overhead, the sun blazes with ferocious disregard in an otherwise empty blue sky.

The yard's empty and the landing pad shimmers in the heat. I'm sitting on the bench again, staring with awe at the clouds I first saw almost two hours ago. They seem not to have advanced, but have risen ominously in a vertical plane until now they form a solid wall thousands of feet high. The silver that laces the bellies of these monsters becomes black in the higher altitudes. If I crane my neck, I can see white and yellow streaks at the very top.

Brock joins me and the two of us sit in silence. The breeze is stiffer now; gusts wave the trees and cause the thick leaves to spin to the ground. Gittoni announces that a ship's five minutes out and he has no idea what's aboard.

Morrisey, an arm wrapped around the poles of a litter, stands on the tarmac beside me. The Huey's far beyond the perimeter when we spot it, suspended in the sun, its red light flashing against the dark sky. Moments later it floats in and we start to run. A few feet off the ground, it swivels and heads into a revetment. The crewchief, perched on a side seat in the open door, shakes his head at me. The ship settles to the ground, the front door opens and Murphy casts a questioning look in our direction.

I hear a snarl like a model airplane and I turn to find a tiny observer helicopter hovering a few yards off the pad. There are two men aboard, the pilot and a lieutenant colonel in fatigues and camouflage helmet. The colonel has a .45 strapped to his side. He waves Morrisey and the litter away. The rotor feels uncomfortably close as I run, hunched over, to the side of the ship.

The colonel lifts a small cardboard carton, about six inches square, from his lap and hands it to me. "Take care of this, son." He seems distracted. His face is gaunt, without the usual Hollywood bravado.

I give a small wave with the box and dash out from beneath the blade. The helicopter zaps away. The box bumps lightly against my leg as we walk back to treatment. "Wonder what this is all about?"

Morrisey shrugs.

I examine the box more closely and notice a field medical tag, a name and unit scrawled on it.

"What's the matter?"

"Christ, this pisses me off!" I flip the box to Brock who's standing in the door. "I guess we're running a delivery service around here now."

Brock twists the box around, studies it from all sides. It makes soft, thudding sounds as he turns it, as though something's loose inside. "Never heard of this guy. I don't think he's on the ward. It isn't sealed. Maybe I'll just take a look."

The clouds are moving in. I hear the first drops of rain splat in the trees overhead. Raindrops speckle the soft, sandy surface of the ground as Brock walks into the tent and carefully places the package on the nearest table. He goes on down the aisle then out the back door, ignoring a shaky greeting from Shelby.

Morrisey and I are in a forbidding isolation, with Shelby at the back door, Brock disappearing beyond the lab, and the box with its flaps lifted and beckoning. Slowly, we look inside.

The contents are confusing, disjointing. But the parts, separate from the whole, are only a momentary puzzle: the few scraps of flesh, some teeth, part of a jawbone.

Someone in the distance is shouting to lower the tent flaps. Suddenly the tent is enveloped by a loud roar as the sky opens. "I'm running for it!" Shelby hollers. He plunges into the rain and out of sight, his clothing soaked, his hair draped over his ears and face.

Morrisey stares into the deluge. "That's yours, I guess," he says, indicating the box.

"Yeah." He watches with curiosity, and I suppose surprise, as, almost lightheartedly, I close the flaps. I walk the fifty-odd feet to the sickcall tent, ignoring the rain pouring down my face. "Hey, Davies. Present for you." I toss the box onto the clean white pages of the open log book, right under Davies's suspicious stare. "Have a body, ace. My appreciation for your promptness with that Vietnamese woman."

So I really got to tuck it to Davies just that once. It's all I needed. It didn't seem at all peculiar then. He didn't speak to me for days after that!

In the ensuing weeks, the sun would appear, a huge flaming ball that silhouetted the stubbled horizon, the tower, the barbed wire, the helicopter blades. Its heat permeated the world below, creating mists and fogs that lifted from myriad pools and puddles and vanished by midmorning. As the sun battled for ascendancy, smells rose from the sodden ground, putrid smells of decay and human waste—alleviated only by breezes that could become gales and tear savagely at the plantation. Trees would swirl in huge, supple circles until they came crashing down. The breezes came before the daily rains.

Nothing was ever dry anymore: my cot was damp, the canvas tents mildewed along with clothing. And there was the red, adhesive muck that clung to boots and fell off in gobs.

It isn't simply raining; it's roaring so loud that I have to shout to be heard. The floor fan makes swooshing sounds when a gust of wind tears through the screens. From the treatment tent, I look out toward where the helicopters would be in their revetments if I could see them. It's four o'clock in the afternoon and so dark that a few minutes ago I switched on the lights. Overhead, a deep bulge has formed in the canvas roof. The excess water cascades over the eaves and splashes in the mud by the outer screen door.

"O'Neill, this equipment's got to go." It's Sergeant Smith. He's wearing a poncho, something only the NCOs do. For the rest of us, a poncho's useless. It gets in the way. I look at the pile of weapons and ammunition accumulating on the porch.

"We've called the units several times to come get this stuff, Sarge," I say. "As far as I'm concerned, the first person who wants it can have it all."

Even with water streaming off his face, Smith manages to look neat. I feel grubby in his presence and automatically begin to catalogue my faults: the smelly shirt that was clean nine hours ago, my muddy boots, my own smell and stickiness. I wonder for the first time if Smith doesn't deliberately foster this discomfort.

"Plastic works pretty good, doesn't it?"

I nod. He enclosed the porch with plastic recently and is now talking about a solid inside door. He still has to convince Mendez, however.

"You ever seen rain like this?"

"No, Sergeant, or muck." I lift a boot and point at it.

"Yes, there should be some way of dealing with that."

God! How can you respond to that? It grows darker and the rain gets worse. We stand in the doorway and watch the water sweep the road. Smith clears his throat. I try to think of something to say.

"How are things going?" he manages at last, but at that moment, out of the rain comes a faint whine. With immense relief, I excuse myself and retreat into the tent where Morrisey's spreading a blanket over an ARVN. He lifts a bottle of saline off the hook and lays it on the blanket beside the arm to which it's attached by a tube. I grab the front handles of the litter and lift.

Smith holds the door and stares dispassionately at the wounded man. Then we're in the downpour, instantly drenched. My hair slops into my eyes and I can taste salt on my face. The soldier's not heavy—one good thing about the Vietnamese.

But not all of them were like that. I saw a wounded Montagnard chief, a tall, beautiful man wearing a brilliantly colored loincloth crafted from thousands of tiny beads. He wore jewelry around his neck, a large medallion and several gold necklaces. He seemed a glimpse of vanished splendor and primitive power, a magnificence greater than any thousand war machines . . . or any dream by men in three-piece suits.

It took four of us to carry him and even then it was work —not unlike some GIs. The bullet had penetrated his chest and lung, a neat, small hole, harmless looking. The white bandage was in striking contrast to the dark, hairless skin: he could have been Aztec or Incan, his eyes as black as the hair on his head, his gaze intelligent and penetrating, empty of fear or personal affliction.

Seeing him, I learned the meaning of the word "king," a word as well as a concept lost to the past, glimpsed by me and lost again as the helicopter swept him away.

My boots slide in the mud. The helicopter's red light streaks through the rain, the draft tugs at us and we push the litter across the floor. The crewchief reaches for the sliding door as we turn and run for the plantation.

Smith has gone.

"What was on Smith's mind?" Morrisey asks.

"I guess he wants us to get rid of that stuff on the porch."

"He made a special trip to tell you that?"

"I doubt it. I don't know what was on his mind. He's shy, isn't he?"

"I hadn't thought about that."

By evening, the storm has gone, leaving a golden glow that tinges the treetops and bathes the distant tower. Mist rises from the puddles lacing the ragged growth. I'm sweating profusely, simply exchanging moisture for moisture, smell for smell, like the land around me.

"They're sending some kind of kiddie slide out to the orphanage, sir. That candy-striped thing over there." The infantryman languidly points in the direction of the helicopter. "Some kind of PIO thing, I reckon."

"Publicity stunt for the good folk back home," Brock replies. Dressed for once in full fatigues, cap included, he has an elbow propped on a fender of the ambulance we procured for a PX run. We brought several patients, their blue pajamas a colorful contrast in the crowd that's gathered in the PX parking lot, not a couple of hundred feet from the division commander's helicopter pad.

The commanding general's sending one of his personal helicopters, the kind painted with high gloss enamel instead of the dull, nonreflecting paint used on the combat ships. The division insignia's emblazoned in bright colors on the nose and side doors. The ship gleams like a Packard. Twenty or thirty officers stand nearby. The general's waiting impatiently beside the copilot's door.

There's a flurry among the officers and Captain Sylvester, the PIO officer I saw at Miss Lahn's, struts into view with a Catholic priest in tow. The priest is the director of the orphanage, located a couple of miles south of the plantation on the outskirts of the village. A gawky specialist with a camera and assorted photographic paraphernalia around his neck dashes up, contriving to keep his cap on his head and equipment under control at the same time.

"I wonder if they've charged extra admission to see Sylvester in action," Brock quips.

The crewchief squats in the open door of the helicopter and studies a cable that trails out from the belly of the ship to a brightly painted slide that's to be a gift from the division. He looks up and watches Sylvester arrange the priest and the general in a suitable pose. The PIO officer bustles here and there, his face flushed with exertion as he tentatively indicates his wishes to the commander and more abruptly seizes the priest by the arms and hustles him to the desired location.

"I'm surprised he doesn't give the priest a piece of candy."

Sylvester wipes his face with a handkerchief, then shuffles in behind the general and the cleric who are shaking hands and looking at the camera. The priest smiles, the general endeavors to appear stern but manages to look even more impatient.

Brock lights a cigar, shakes the match, and crushes it with his boot. "He'll never make chief-of-staff with that kind of facial control."

Sylvester and the priest clamber aboard the helicopter, followed by the photographer after he finishes a number of long shots that catch the slide and helicopter in their vibrant splendor. The copilot looks over his shoulder with the studied disdain of professionals for publicity stunts.

"I wonder if Eisenstein there is going to double as candy-man at the orphanage," I say.

"Hah!" Brock scratches the top of his head furiously. "With any luck, Sylvester will meet a nun and we'll never see him again."

The jet turbine whines into life and the general quickly shakes hands with the priest one last time. The priest, dressed in a black cassock, beams from his perch between the two Americans. Sylvester talks across him to the photographer, gesticulating in the priest's face with his large hands. The rotor begins to revolve . . . once . . . twice. The crewchief snaps his microphone across his mouth. His eyes are on the cable and slide.

"That's not just PR for the folks back home, sir. That's in-service stuff," I clarify.

"Yeah?"

"Sure. Lifers in the navy and air force are supposed to turn green. Military cheesecake."

One of the patients is beside me, intent on the proceedings. His face is deeply tanned, his hair bleached by the sun. He's a mortarman with one of the local infantry units. "You guys are being kinda rough. That's a nice thing they're doing."

Brock looks thoughtfully at the patient, then at the helicopter and nods his head. The air is beginning to vibrate. "Yeah!" he shouts. "I'm not saying it's a bad idea, only it's a hell of a waste ferrying a slide a couple of miles by helicopter when they could take it out there by truck in almost the same time and at a fraction of the cost."

"C'mon, sir! When you were a kid, you would have gotten your jollies if someone had done this for you! I've been in some of those orphanages. Those kids have nothing. It's really pathetic."

Slowly the helicopter begins to rise from the pavement, hurling grit and sand. The spectators back away and clutch their caps.

"Hey!" Brock yells, his head turned from the downdraft. "Isn't someone going to guide that thing so it doesn't get to swinging? That cable's too goddam long!"

The general appears to have the same idea, for suddenly he's pushing three men in the direction of the gaudy steel frame with its heavy ladder and glistening chute. They've barely reached the tarmac when the cable goes taut.

The crewchief has a troubled look on his face, and I see his lips move. In response, the pilot tries to maneuver the helicopter over the slide but it's too late. The slide is already high in the air and swinging like a pendulum; the pilot's efforts only aggravate the motion.

"Sweet Jesus!" Brock roars. "Land the thing!"

The mortarman beside me is frozen, openmouthed.

The helicopter's above the trees, the pilot by now desperate in his attempts to control the swing, but the arcs of the heavy slide are widening, climbing higher and higher.

The general, red-faced, screams at the pilot, the crewchief, anyone up there who might possibly hear. He shakes his fist above his head. All I can think of is Sylvester, his stooge, the grinning priest . . .

All around me people are beginning to run. I look one way, then the other. Only Brock's still with me—the others have disappeared. I spot them. They're crawling away on their bellies; they jerk, wrench, claw like serpents with arms over their heads. My legs won't move, won't even collapse. I watch the slide swing up into the tail rotor.

I exhale but it's a cry of pain. I can hear myself cry, far away. Brock's trying to pull me down.

There's a pause, arrested time, motion . . . then the sound comes; the helicopter jerks, spins howling out of the sky.

And there we were with an ambulance. It seemed like hours before the heat went away enough so we could retrieve the remains. There was a second ambulance by then, and several more medics and all kinds of brass poking around but our feelings were pretty well closed off. The worst moment came when I started filling out a field tag on Donald Sylvester, talking to a short, barrel-chested major from PIO who clipped his words as he rattled off the information from memory and let his gaze rove the smoking debris. I placed this tag on a green rubber bag that contained a blackened, legless lump. Such things simply can't be reduced to paper, but they were, and I did. By the time I got around to doing the death certificates—there were six sets of six pages each to do, thirty-six signatures for Brock—everything was OK again. It was a matter of careful typing, making no errors.

The daily rains came just as we loaded the last body in the ambulance. The sun still shone as sheets of water tore across the perimeter almost two miles away and marched up to inundate us and the steaming, hissing wreck.

ELEVEN

It's Saturday evening and the club is crowded. A short, solid figure appears at the door. He's wearing a clean set of fatigues; a pair of scissors glistens from his left pocket. His black hair is plastered neatly across his forehead, probably the way it's always been on important occasions since he started worshipping God and the Holy Mother thirty-three years ago. The thick, black frames of his glasses look cumbersome. There's a hesitant, almost shy smile on his lips.

The sudden silence in the club is electric.

"Newell," Mendez says quietly, "you are buying, aren't you?"

"I am?"

"I'll have scotch."

Newell goes over to the bar and orders the drink. Mendez follows, accepts the glass from Stevens, then turns around and surveys the room with keen interest. I can remember a half dozen times, perhaps, when he's been in the club, but never for long, always for a reason, and never by himself. He raises the glass to us, then takes a sip.

"Shit! I'd forgotten!" someone whispers behind me. "He's going home tomorrow." In the hush, everybody hears him.

"You always had a lousy memory, Gittoni. Always thinking about that girl of yours, or helicopters. I don't know which you love more," Mendez says.

Gittoni grins and stands up, holding a can of beer aloft. "To the best commander I've ever had."

A yell bursts from the back of the room followed by an explosion of laughter and scraping of chairs as we rise, *en*

152

masse, and mob the major. I've never experienced such a spontaneous venting of group emotion. I've never been aware of my own feelings about the major until now: emotionally, the major's been unapproachable. You didn't have to think of your feelings for him.

"Whoa!" Mendez raises a hand to hold us back.

"Drinks, Stevens!" Gittoni roars, slamming his fist on the bar, completely ignoring the major who's reduced to helpless laughter.

I make it through three rounds before the phone rings. Within minutes the room's become jammed and the door is still creaking open with monotonous frequency. A Dust-Off contingent's arrived led by Major Hargos himself. Mendez has disappeared in the crowd, moving and being moved from person to person. Jubilation follows him like a wake throughout the room. Newell's shouting in my ear about having met our new CO, a captain by the name of Howard, a righteous turd in his estimation, when the phone buzzes.

Stevens, sweating profusely from his exertions behind the bar, grabs the receiver and shouts, "Yeah?"

"Ten beers over here, Stevens!" Gerty, our lab tech, hollers. He's an Irishman from Boston, tow-headed, skinny, with intense nervous gestures, incredible rages, and a sleazy smile. He's scarcely been with us long enough to say goodbye to anyone.

"Wait a fucking minute, will you?" Stevens calls, cupping his hand over the receiver. He lifts his hand. "What? Yeah, OK!"

I've become a fatalist. When he hollers for an A&D man, I'm already waving "so long" and starting to push through the crowd at the bar. No one would dream of bothering Davies on such an occasion.

Owen's waiting for me in the treatment room. "I started to do this but I thought I might screw it up," he says, handing me a book of tags.

"Thanks." I mean it. Owen's good about helping when he's in the mood. "Is that a party I hear?" he asks and starts for the rear door without waiting for my confirmation.

There are two malaria patients bound for an evacuation hospital. Both are conscious, but terribly uncomfortable. I have to lean close to hear their responses to my questions. At these times, I feel superfluous, an intruder.

Brock and Morrisey are sitting on a table toward the front

of the tent, talking. We grab an orderly from the ward to make a fourth litter bearer, load the men in the ship and watch it spin away.

"I was telling you about my old man," Brock says as we reenter the tent and Morrisey flicks on the lights. The music and yelling from the club is quite audible, the urge to return to the party overpowering. Brock has begun to pull a wrapper off a cigar with the infuriating slowness of someone who's settling down for a long chat about matters that excite only him.

"My father never said a goddam thing about the war until the night before I left. We were eating dinner—I can remember everything in that room. My wife was wearing a pink blouse and flowered skirt—the skirt was white. Did I ever show you a picture of my wife and kids, Morrisey?"

"No, sir." Morrisey's smiling at me, sensing my impatience.

"Next time you're down in the hooch, I'll show you some pictures. My kids are three and five. The older one's a boy." He explains this to me. Apparently, Morrisey's already shared this momentous information. "Yeah, and we were having steak that night—filet mignon and french fries and peas. The old man was going to take the kids for a walk after dinner so Meg and I could have a little time together."

I've never seen Brock open up like this. I don't know what's triggered his mood. Maybe it's the major's departure, but that thought makes me restless all over again. I lean against a table, not wanting to be impolite but not wanting to encourage him either.

"You're not in a hurry are you, O'Neill?" Brock says.

"No, sir."

"Yeah, well this is really interesting. For the first time I can remember, the old man brought up the war. We were eating, well, he was slurping. He always slurps his food and makes a lot of noise. Drives Meg batty thinking what kind of impression it must be making on the kids." Brock smiles at the memory.

My insides churn. I'm sure that whatever's going on in the club is going to be over before I get back there . . . and that sonuvabitch Morrisey wouldn't be so smug if he had an inkling of the party that was brewing when I left.

"My father was in the First World War, the infantry. I was the youngest of seven kids—he was forty when I was born —and I'd never heard him talk about it. But right out of the blue he says to me something like, 'You've never been the humble type. Remember that over there.' I ask you guys, what would you do if your old man threw a curve like that the night you were leaving for a war?"

This is an honor, I keep telling myself. Brock doesn't do this with just anybody.

"I didn't know what to do. I kind of half-ass asked him what he was talking about, but he had his head buried in his plate, pushing in another shovelful."

An enormous moth crawls shakily up the screen. We remain silent. A faint, rhythmic percussion heralds the approach of a helicopter. The sound grows louder, blasting the air around the tent. "That us?" Brock asks.

I leap for the phone with almost embarrassing haste. "That's a negative," Dunn says before I can even ask the question. "It'll be shutting down."

"Where was I? Oh, yeah. So he didn't answer me and I began to get pissed off because the wife and kids were fidgety. It was my last night home for a year! 'What do you think I'm going to do?' I asked him. 'Mutilate people? I'm a doctor!'

"He looked up quick then, but there was something in his eyes I'd never seen before: not quite what you'd call sad, but something like it. Boy, I was bullshit by then, and he just kept sitting there.

" 'Who's talking about your being a doctor,' he said. 'That's irrelevant. I don't care if you watch a thousand men die, you'll be damn lucky to see one man really die . . . to realize what it means.' He sounded bitter.

"Christ! Meg's eyes filled with tears—I'd worked so hard to become a doctor. The kids looked confused and began sniffling, and I couldn't say shit! The old man apologized later when things quieted down. I suppose it was his way of showing how upset he was about my going.

"I've thought about it a lot, Morrisey," and it's as though Brock's completely forgotten I'm in the room, "and I still don't know what he was talking about, and I've seen God knows how many men die."

He glances up suddenly. He's been studying the stub of his cigar. "Got you thinking?"

"Yeah," Morrisey says.

A long silence follows.

"Excuse me, sir," I venture at last.

"What is it, O'Neill?" He looks surprised by my presence, and then he hears the noise from the club. "What's happening down there?"

"A farewell party for the major, sir."

"Oh, Jesus, why didn't you say so sooner?" He looks mortified. "I didn't mean to keep you from that."

"No, no, sir, it was interesting." How can a person you like so much be so tedious? You could never tell him that, I tell myself, so don't be embarrassed by bullshitting him.

At the club, I'm totally unprepared for what I find. The place is mobbed. Stevens keeps wiping his face with his forearm while he fights to keep abreast of the orders. Annie's gone home, leaving him with a mob with an unquenchable thirst. But despite everything, he's laughing, not at all disgruntled.

"Hooray!" everyone shouts when I open the door. I'm flooded with free drinks. Brock and his morbid ruminations are instantly eons away. The major's going home!

"Hooray, O'Neill," Anderson, the new and notoriously unobtrusive company clerk, mutters as he slowly turns two drinks over on top of his head. Anderson's shirt has been mysteriously slit up the back and the two pieces are held together only by the front buttons.

Someone with a large towel draped over his head and his hands held up monster-fashion is jumping up and down to the stereo while many hands empty beer cans over the towel. Everyone's laughing; tears run freely. The towel continues its ponderous jumping. Three or four tables are overturned, their legs in the air.

A sharp clatter echoes from the back of the room as another table falls. A roar of applause greets this latest catastrophe and the room again sinks into teary laughter as Gerty rolls the table out the back door.

Major Hargos, in jersey and shorts, sprawls on a stool at the bar, Murphy and Gittoni on either side. His blondness and tan suggest blue uniforms and stewardesses, a slick sensuality. My mouth goes dry as I momentarily imagine tearing one of those broads out of her uniform, any uniform as long as it's tight and full.

"Something, isn't it, O'Neill?" Buelen raises his drink to me.

"Yeah, I guess so, Top."

Sitting against the front wall, isolated in an intense and

vaguely hostile way, Smith is speaking fervently with a strange officer, a captain. The captain's legs are crossed and he's tapping his knee with the bill of his cap while he listens and nods his head from time to time. He's not very tall and has almost delicate facial features. Smith looks older without a cap—some grey hairs are more prominent. There's something terribly intimate about this, as though by simply removing the cap, he's shown me his mortality.

The captain's face suddenly becomes clouded with a devastating contempt. There's such arrogance in the look that I turn quickly to discover the cause. All I can see is the back end of someone crawling away on the floor on his hands and knees. Given the circumstances, this doesn't seem particularly outrageous.

But something in the room has changed. Many persons are searching the floor around them and I detect several wary looks. There's a sense of anticipation, even of the hunt, but I can't fathom the source of it. I push through to the bar. Stevens is bent over examining a slit the length of his left pantleg. He looks at me in confusion, "What the fuck's going on?"

"I don't know," I reply. "All I want's another drink."

"Yeah, well fuck! Some sonuvabitch slit my pants! What's so funny, O'Neill?"

I shake my head.

"You think having your pants slit is so fucking funny?"

A shriek pierces the room. Newell jumps out in front of me shaking his right leg and staring with horror at the white, hairy limb revealed between the flaps of what was once a pantleg. He literally dives into the crowd, his right buttock flashing.

"Jesus," Stevens says, ignoring the cries for more liquor.

At the front of the tent, Smith and the captain are conferring furiously. "Who's that captain, Stevens?" I grab him by the shoulder to get his attention.

"That's Howard, our new CO." Stevens laughs. "Man, he's getting an eyeful."

I feel a tug on my pants and look down as someone scoots away on all fours, a pair of scissors clasped in one hand. Newell and Gerty pounce out of the crowd in hot pursuit, brandishing their own scissors. I look down and find both my pantlegs slit. "It's the fucking major!" Stevens howls behind me and hurls himself over the bar.

"Who's got a pair of scissors?" I demand, grabbing the man next to me. He shakes his head violently. I reach around him and snitch a pair of scissors from an unsuspecting medic. Stevens jumps up in front of me, shirtless now and sweaty. He casts a wild eye around the room, then suddenly pounces on a hapless Davies. In one fluid motion, the blunt-nosed bandage scissors dive, then flash into view, their work done. Davies, astonished, watches the halves of his shirt glide down his arms. Before Stevens can flee, I attack his remaining pantleg.

The number of scissors that appear after the first assaults is frightening. The room gradually assumes the appearance of an ancient battleground with steel glinting in the smoky air. All around me, men collapse on the floor, their clothing in shreds but otherwise unscarred by the tools we use in the treatment room for the very same purpose.

From time to time among the writhing heap, I glimpse a grinning, maniacal Mendez, his uniform gone, hair plastered down his face, his skivvies—his last piece of clothing—already in tatters.

At some point, while I was still crawling about, I looked up and saw Morrisey at the door, his face frozen in amazement. "I tried to tell you you were missing a hell of a party . . . you sonuvabitch," I muttered to myself just as I slid under a pile of sweaty bodies and started snipping furiously at a random piece of cloth that had the ill-fortune to fall into my grasp. I also remember seeing Major Hargos teeter toward the door, a plastic glass balanced upside down on his head and liquor dripping from his hair, down around his ears.

Again I saw Morrisey, this time bent over and shaking hands with the new CO while Smith made some kind of introduction. ". . . keep up the good work. You're one of the best I've seen," I thought, remembering the night outside Smith's hooch with Stevens. Suckass! I concluded and scrambled off in pursuit of Stevens just in case he had any clothes left.

A while later, the two chairs were vacant and Morrisey was standing in the door, shirtless, a litter in his hand, a grin on his face as foolish as any I'd seen. We plunged through the darkness, around the hooches, through the trees, our laughter turning to tears, almost to hysteria as we stumbled and sometimes fell, but somehow managed to keep the major, giggling uncontrollably, aloft on his litter.

Then, in the harsh light of the treatment room, he suddenly sat up with a reflective, sober smile and surveyed us all, one by one. Quietly, he reached out and started to shake hands.

"My God, he is going!" someone said.

When I hit my cot, it was reeling; it tumbled over and over, and I knew, even as I heard myself giggle aloud, then laugh, that I would never sleep that well again.

I'm being dragged out of sleep, not by anyone or anything specific, because it's Sunday morning . . . still, there it is again, a deep, gut-wrenching dread. Something's happening. But the day remains shapeless; the only proof of my existence is tactile—the silky poncho liner across my chest and the coarse netting at my groping fingertips. The sun's blazing through the screen. Flies buzz languidly. What's there to fear?

Then I'm awake, running toward treatment.

The major's standing at the edge of the plantation, one foot in the road he must cross to reach the landing pad and the waiting helicopter with its dull brown enamel, red crosses, and black nose. Morrisey's here, and Brock, and Shelby, who looks totally disoriented. The major's dressed in his summer khakis; the rank on his lapel is gold now, not the nonreflective black of war. He's wearing his dress cap and clutching a Pan American flight bag. The smile on his face is one of immense pleasure, and, I suppose, relief. He's happy to be leaving the plantation, if not us. I can't blame him, but I feel a terrible sense of sorrow, of real loss. No one else's departure has affected me this deeply. I feel an unqualified admiration for Mendez without even knowing precisely what it is he's done.

"Just in time," he says, looking at me.

"What time is it?"

"Seven forty-five."

"That's all?" I've only slept three and a half hours—I'll never reclaim what I lost.

Major Hargos and Murphy wander toward the pad. They're wearing their flight suits—all business. The doors open and close.

"Hargos was ready an hour ago," Brock says.

"He's impatient. He's got someone to meet in Long Binh. Goodbye, Shel." Mendez reaches out and shakes hands with Shelby, then Brock, then me, and at last, Morrisey. He takes a long, hard look at Morrisey, claps a hand on his shoulder and smiles. "Don't let it get to you, Richie."

"Yes, sir." Morrisey has to shout.

Abruptly, Mendez turns and walks across the road, out to the landing pad. He removes his cap and lets his hair whip in the sunshine. He climbs into the helicopter and it flies away, rolling up on its side as it hammers around the distant edge of the plantation, out over the wire, out of sight.

"Some party," I say as Morrisey and I walk toward the mess hall. We lift layers of muck from the road with each step. The sky is cloudless, but the days always begin this way now, it seems.

"We're going to pay for it," he says.

"What do you mean?"

"Smith has the new CO convinced that what he saw in the club last night was normal."

"Awww, bullshit!"

Morrisey reaches up, pulls the door open and lets me go in. Jenkins is one of the three other people, including the cook, who have shown up for breakfast.

"I don't want to hear it, Morrisey!" he says as he kicks a chair out for his friend. Jenkins is good that way.

But Mendez is gone now, Navarra long gone . . . two months? His farewell was so poignant, many departures from the company are, but within a day or two, they're forgotten. It's a childhood Christmas all over: the intensifying anticipation as each man whittles down the days to a last evening. But when the next, the last day arrives, it's invariably anticlimactic.

One day Morrisey received a letter from Navarra and he showed it to me. There was something desperate about the letter, as though Navarra was romanticizing us, clinging to us. All he really said was that he missed us. How utterly incongruous for someone as ruthless as Navarra!

"Are you going to write back?" I asked.

"And tell him what the guys are doing while he's gone, O'Neill?"

We never heard from him again. Something in that letter made me think we wouldn't have, even if Morrisey had replied, and I wonder what that means? It's as though Navarra was returning one last time to a dream, and then awoke, leaving us behind.

*   *   *

"Te-enshup!"

All around me, men begin to shuffle into some semblance of attention. It has rained all night and the ground gives under our feet, rises up and clutches our boots. The sun pours in yellow streams through the leaves. It's morning formation.

Beyond the line of NCOs facing us is the NCO hooch, its flaps suspended on poles out over the stacks of canisters that form its protective wall. Off to my right, several hooch girls have gathered in front of Jenkins's tent to pick the lice out of one another's hair. Their boyish bodies are particularly unattractive when they're squatting. Buelen, in charge of the formation, stiffens and jerks his hand up in salute.

Captain Howard appears, throws a quick, saucy salute to the first sergeant, and pirouettes to confront us, his new charges. "At ease!" His voice has a slight nasal quality. The caduceus on his collar seems misplaced—he has the cloistered, intense bearing of an accountant's clerk.

"Gentlemen, as some of you may already know, I come from an infantry battalion." Howard pauses to let the significance of this sink in. "What most of you obviously don't know is that the life of an infantryman is rough and unenviable. He does not have hooch girls to shine his boots and change his bed, he does not have regular showers." He turns to Smith. "Hot showers isn't it, Sergeant Smith?"

Smith nods. "Some of the time, sir."

"Bullshit," someone whispers behind me. "Only the officers get hot . . ."

"Some of the time is more than enough!" Howard lets his gaze slowly roam the front line of the formation. My anger at Smith for his lie about the showers gives way to a barely suppressed urge to smile at this asshole.

"An infantryman gets shot at, gentlemen! It's a hard life, and it takes guts to do what they do. And you? I'm told there's a lot of grumbling in this company, a lot of disrespect, drugs, and a generally poor attitude for a medical unit.

"I've heard of units like this, maybe even seen something vaguely resembling it in the movies, but on second thought, I don't think so: nothing could be as disgraceful as your farewell party for my predecessor two nights ago. Nothing! I was sickened by it . . . and I will not be sickened like that again! This is not to show disrespect for Major Mendez. I'm sure he was a fine doctor, but I don't give a damn whether or not I'm admired or liked by you people! I will teach you respect.

"I have no patience, and will have no patience for complaints from you men. You have it soft. I'm going to make you into as tough a unit as I can, short of sending you to the field where maybe all of you belong. There's always some field medic out there who's put in six or seven months with his life on the line and deserves a rest; I'd welcome men like that in my unit! I'd willingly replace someone who just can't get enough frills. This is war, gentlemen, and I'm going to bring that home to you! If you want to stay in my unit, things will have to change."

Some men are always inclined to feel guilty. I feel them bow their heads under Howard's onslaught, but somehow I manage to stare back at the captain, a little timidly I must admit; I'm not sure I'll be able to hold out if the CO's eyes lock with mine. But there are others, like Jenks and Morrisey, who can be just as unflinching as Howard, and I take courage from this fact.

"Now for some rules. Everyone, and I mean everyone except officers and noncommissioned officers, will carry litters. I've been told that in the past there have been those who didn't want their beauty sleep interrupted. That changes as of this moment!"

What the hell's he talking about? This is horseshit! Where's he coming from? All around me I sense the same confusion. Maybe it's just a new man's assertion of authority—he can't be that ignorant. It'll go away.

"Anyone who tries to avoid carrying litters will immediately receive an Article fifteen. That's for beginners. You can also expect a transfer to an infantry battalion at the earliest opportunity."

Smith is looking straight ahead, motionless, the bill of his cap perfectly horizontal.

Howard goes on. "In the future, the enlisted men's and NCO club will be closed at 11 P.M. Under my command, the emphasis will be on performance, not on getting drunk and raucous. If another disgrace occurs like the one the other night, the club will either be torn down or placed completely under the control of the NCOs. This business of joint operation has no place in a well run military unit." He turns to Smith again. "You can remind me, Sergeant; one more disturbance and the NCOs assume full supervision."

"Yes, sir." Buelen's standing just behind Howard and it is he who should have been addressed. Howard realizes this breach of protocol, and turns to ask the first sergeant for his confirmation. Buelen mumbles his agreement.

"First Sergeant Buelen," the CO nods briefly in Buelen's direction, "and Sergeant Smith will be instituting a new system of inspections: there will be a general inspection for appearance once a week, inspection of hooches every other week. This won't be a sloppy unit, gentlemen! Those assigned to work in the treatment tent, I expect you to be exceptionally neat at all times."

"No sweat, Captain," someone whispers.

Buelen continues to look perturbed, as though everything he's hearing is as much news to him as to us.

"We have some new plans for the unit: we're going to improve it! We're going to increase our capacity and also the quality of our services. Sergeant Smith, as NCO in charge of the treatment area, will be overseeing much of this new program. In order to facilitate it, we'll be instituting evening work details for those who don't feel they can do a good job during the day.

"Once more, I don't want to hear a single complaint! You men are very fortunate. Now, you're going to work for that privilege. First Sergeant?"

Buelen moves forward, calls us to attention, then turns and salutes Howard. Buelen can't wear fatigues well—he's too big and his shirt bulges over his belt as though he's pregnant. Howard marches away.

The usual chatter and joking that mark dismissal and the official beginning of the workday are absent. In its place is a resentful, confused silence.

"What did we do to deserve that? Who's he trying to impress?" There's an uncharacteristic shrill note in Jenkins's query.

"You said yesterday you didn't want to hear it," Morrisey replies.

"I tell you, I'm not going to take this crap," Gerty says. "If it keeps up, I'll volunteer for the fucking field."

"Sure, Gerty."

"Fuck you, Morrisey! I didn't see him out at three this morning with the rest of us. He and the NCOs were the only ones not there. The major would have never treated us like that. 'Everyone carries litters except the noncommissioned officers.' Bullshit!"

"It's always been that way, Gerty. Mendez had no need to say it, that's all."

"Neither did Howard! And I'll tell you something else. I got a buddy in Howard's old unit. The bastard never left the battalion aid station—in other words, never left the plantation. To hear him talk, you'd think he was John Wayne. We got all his garbage. He never did anything except minor sickcall. I'll transfer before I take this shit."

"I'm going to talk to Howard," Morrisey says. "Smith's got him by the balls."

"Richie, it's not Smith. This guy's an asshole."

"You refuse to believe me, don't you, Jenkins?" Morrisey sounds angry.

Morrisey and Jenkins both dismiss Gerty's threat, but alone a few minutes later, I'm overwhelmed by the intimidation and guilt that the thought of transfer can produce: that I'll never be a man unless I confront what it is I fear, that someone will always have leverage over me. I wish I was a short-timer like Davies, and I wish this apprehension would go away.

And Morrisey does talk to Howard. Only Morrisey could do that and not be hesitant or self-effacing. He's reading a report on a man with boils. The man's pants are pulled down around his knees and he has huge abcesses on both thighs. They're as big around as softballs, and bright red.

Howard walks up to the table. "You're lucky you can still walk."

The soldier smiles gamely. "It's been difficult, sir."

"Shelby's patient, Morrisey?"

"Yes, sir."

Howard reaches for the report, reads it and hands it back. "Sir?"

"Yes, Morrisey?"

Morrisey looks right at him with a surprising lack of hostility. *He really doesn't blame this guy,* I'm thinking. *He's convinced it's Smith.* His eyes can't hide anything. "Sir, I think that was a little rough this morning."

"What was?"

A touch of color enter's Morrisey's cheeks. He's approaching his ninth month and he's still not tanned. "Your speech at formation, sir. This is a good unit. We've been working hard for a long time, working well, and we're still understaffed. What you saw the other night never happened before and probably wouldn't happen again."

"You're right about that! It won't happen while I'm in command. As to your feelings about this company, I can appreciate your position, but your information doesn't agree with what I've already been told. I do appreciate your concern, however. Brock and Shelby seem to think a lot of your work."

Morrisey blushes, but his look is one of embarrassment and anger.

"Is there anything else, Morrisey?"

"No, sir."

"Then I suggest you go back to your patient. Looks like we have quite a morning's sickcall before us." Howard smiles pleasantly with the first warmth I've seen him display.

You have yet to see what we're really about, I think; it was Brock on duty when last night's casualties came in. Morrisey returns to the man with the abcesses. He amazes me—he never seems to hesitate when he believes he's right. But now I remember the machinegunner and the lieutenant with the back of his head blown away. No, I can't understand Morrisey.

Morrisey's patient has fallen asleep, sitting up. It's damn hot in the tent. I look at his fatigues, stained brown and faded, slightly tattered, at a blotch of reddish clay on his tanned forehead. The hair is curly and brown, streaked by the sun. His shirt sleeves are rolled up, and he has a fancy watch on his left wrist. A watch is such an absurdity in this place.

When the soldier first entered the tent he looked like so many soldiers, grown men, strong and nonchalant; but in his sleep, he's a teenager again, the eighteen or nineteen years he probably is—the lines under his eyes, the harsh features softened. It's always a battle to stay awake in the army, and it's worse here in the moist heat where time means so much and moves ever more slowly.

There's a momentary lull in the war—this one lasts almost five days. More people seem to show up for sickcall and there are several accident victims. Accidents seem to increase when the war grows quiet, but no one's seriously injured and Captain Howard's not given an opportunity to prove his mettle as a doctor—"a surgeon" I'm told by Smith who doesn't seem to appreciate that such distinctions are meaningless in our kind of operation. Perhaps Smith's remark reflects what he's learned from Howard, Howard's ignorance as well as expectations.

The casualty that ends the lull is a Viet Cong soldier. Brock happens to be in the commo shack when the call comes in. He tells Dunn not to bother Howard and wanders over to treatment to take charge, convinced, I'm sure, that he's doing the CO a favor: he's been here too long to get excited about casualties. It's a cloudless afternoon following two days of almost constant rain and the sun glints fiercely off a small lake that's appeared to the left of the landing pad.

A speck becomes visible beyond the tower, and Morrisey and I head toward the pad. The treatment area is empty except for the three of us and whoever's on the ward. The lull has only vindicated Smith in Howard's eyes and everybody's being assigned work details. Smith has been allowed to launch the massive development scheme he's nurtured for so long.

Brock leans over the prisoner to adjust an inflatable splint on his left arm. The prisoner lies with his eyes closed, his dark hair puffing slightly in the breeze from a fan. The bullet, an M-16 slug, entered his arm near the shoulder and tumbled out just above the elbow, shattering the bone in the process.

The rear door opens and I look up to see an apparition in blue; a pair of dark eyes scowl at me over a surgeon's mask, a long gown sweeps down to the knees. The eyes turn quickly away and although I feel Howard's keen disappointment, I have to fight an impulse to laugh. He's wearing the only complete surgeon's outfit I've ever seen here. I can't imagine where he found it! I poke Morrisey lightly in the ribs with my elbow.

"Nothing's very sterile," Howard says as he rubs a finger on a table, then holds it close to his eyes. He lifts his nose slightly as though he's just extracted the finger from some-one's rectum. In his left hand, he holds a pair of surgical gloves.

Brock's absorbed with the prisoner and Morrisey's feigning some kind of assistance. Outside, a medivac ship rises from its revetment and clatters away.

"Dust-Off's been notified?" Brock asks.

"Yes, sir. They just went out to fuel up."

He nods and reaches for his cigar.

"Nothing's very sterile around here, Captain Brock."

"No, Grisholm. And if you think this is bad, wait for the dry season."

"I'm sure something can be done about it. Tell me, Brock, what kind of surgery do you perform here?" Howard has

166

walked behind his colleague, taking long, purposeful strides, hands locked behind his back.

Brock reaches for a towel, wipes his hands, and tosses it in the linen basket. "Like Juan told you before he left, tracheotomies and cut-downs—that's it. Juan and I trained Owen, Newell, and Morrisey here to do the cut-downs, if necessary. They also can suture. It takes a hell of a burden off us when we have mass casualties, or simply want to get a little sleep some nights."

Howard nods sagely. "I can't say I've seen much indication of such a need."

"I'll be in my hooch, Richie." Brock walks away from the table and down the aisle toward the door.

"He's just leaving the patient like this?"

"We've done everything we can, sir. We're waiting for Dust-Off," Morrisey replies.

"You a medic, too?" Howard demands of me, a trace of threat in his voice.

"Yes, sir, but A&D is my main duty." The field phone squawks and I walk up front to answer it.

"MI interrogation team wants to see the prisoner," Dunn says. "Should I hold that ship?"

"I doubt it, but let me check." Howard's bent over the prisoner, examining the splint. "Sir, the interrogation team wants to see the prisoner. Major Mendez always told them they couldn't interrogate prisoners here. Should I convey that message? I think they usually go on down to Tainan, the Vietnamese hospital."

"Do I look like Mendez?" He's removed the surgical mask.

"No, sir."

"Then the interrogation team can see the prisoner."

"Yes, sir." I turn to the receiver. "Hold that ship . . ."

"Wow, that's a roger."

How I envy commo operators at times like this—they don't have to see the results of what they've communicated.

"Sir," Morrisey says, "these guys from MI are a bunch of assholes! I don't think this is a good idea."

"If I want your advice, Specialist, I'll ask for it. They're trained, aren't they? You do your job and leave theirs to them, and in the future, show more respect—that's a problem in this company you didn't mention."

Morrisey goes over to the cabinet and starts shifting instruments, opening and closing doors. It's been a long time since I've seen him this agitated.

In no time at all, the jeep roars up in front; the two Vietnamese soldiers are all smiles. The American captain in the back seat grabs his cap when the vehicle jerks to a halt. The three of them clump into the tent and salute Captain Howard.

Howard returns the salute and points to the prisoner. "This is the man I believe you wish to see."

The ARVNs are efficient.

The advisor, clipboard in hand, remains a few feet away from the table beside Captain Howard. "We'll be having a change in policy," Howard says.

The prisoner's eyes are wide open. One interrogator jabs him in the chest with the tip of a ballpoint pen. The gestures are quick and hard, and the interrogator shouts the same word in Vietnamese, over and over.

When the prisoner replies, his tone is subdued.

The shouting continues for several minutes. Occasionally, the interrogator stops and walks over to the American advisor and confers briefly in English, whereupon the captain makes notations on the clipboard.

After a while, the other interrogator begins to examine the prisoner's arm through the transparent, plastic splint. With exaggerated care, he lifts the arm about two inches off the table. The prisoner rolls his head to one side and stares anxiously at the suspended splint.

The interrogator drops it. "Dau?" he asks softly.

The prisoner groans and turns his head away.

Howard's smiling foolishly, as though he doesn't know what else to do, or really how to react at all. The officer beside him watches the scene impassively.

The arm is dropped again from a little higher up.

Morrisey looks horror-stricken. I can feel my heart pounding.

The first interrogator brushes by me, trailing a sweet smell of cologne, and returns with a field phone. Field phones are battery operated. He attaches the lead wires to each of the prisoner's ears with small, toothed copper clips. It all looks so innocuous. He gives the handle a little twist. The phone whirrs.

The prisoner screams.

The second interrogator produces a pen, begins to jab the prisoner in the chest and shout in his face.

The phone is given a long crank.

I turn away and when I look back, Morrisey's in motion. The interrogator with the pen is pulling the prisoner's pants down while the other ARVN removes the clips from the ears.

Morrisey grabs the ARVN with the clips and whirls him around.

"WHAT ARE YOU DOING, SOLDIER!" the American advisor screams.

Morrisey has the ARVN by the upper arm and is squeezing as though he would crush the limb. He struggles to spit out his rage at Howard. "Goddammit, sir! We talk about the goddam French . . . what the hell do you think we're doing?" He shoves the ARVN against the wall and bursts out of the tent.

I find him at my desk, his forehead in his hands, but there's no time to say anything. Howard's right behind me.

"What the hell was the meaning of that, soldier?" Howard shouts.

Morrisey's savagery of a few moments ago has disappeared and his look is almost benign.

"Do you know we can obtain valuable information from that prisoner, and perhaps save American lives, soldier?" Howard demands.

"Did you, sir?"

Oh, God no, Morrisey! No one could miss the sarcasm.

"Morrisey, I don't like your attitude. I hope you observed that it was the South Vietnamese who were conducting that interview."

"Interview! Did you say 'interview,' sir?"

"How long have you been here, soldier?"

"Going on nine months, sir."

"Well, young man, you are about to get an Article fifteen. I've had all this kind of behavior I can stand!"

"Request a court-martial, sir."

"What?"

"I have the right to demand a court-martial instead of an Article fifteen, sir. I respectfully request a court-martial, sir."

"Where's that stated?" Howard asks doubtfully.

"The army regulations, sir. You can check in the orderly room."

"There are going to be some real changes around here," Howard mutters, and retreats.

Beyond the screen wall, there's another shriek. It's like a punch in the belly.

"You're very lucky, Morrisey," Smith says. Somehow his eyes look smaller in that smooth, square face. His fury shows, but it's reined. "Captain Howard, at my urging, decided to be lenient. I told him you've been under some strain. Someday, you'll appreciate how fortunate we are to have a man like him for CO."

It's early evening. Morrisey's on the bench in front of treatment, a book in one hand, a finger inserted between the pages to hold his place.

"Bullshit, Sergeant."

Smith recoils, just slightly. Morrisey is surprisingly tranquil, as though he's thought through his troubles and is free to face them. "You guys have been tearing the orderly room apart trying to find a way to hang me without a court-martial . . . you just didn't luck out."

"You'll go too far, Morrisey."

He studies Smith with nothing mocking or humorous in his appraisal. Abruptly, Smith walks away, the silence unbroken.

I started making insects. Before it was over I made about a dozen, some of which took over a week to finish. I built them out of copper wire I took from the books of field medical tags. I made flies, rhinoceros beetles, crickets, a spider. I'm not a reader the way Morrisey was. In idle moments you could always find him with an open book, sometimes in between helicopters if there was time; he would even read standing up, leaning against one of the treatment tables. Almost everyone came to respect that island of privacy he threw around himself.

I'm a slow reader, and if a book is serious, I reflect too long upon it. In our unit the effect could be devastating. I got bored with mysteries and thrillers: so often they were worse than fanciful, they were spurious. For me, books had to be realistic, but if they were, I couldn't handle them.

By accident almost, I began my first insect. I still have it; I gave the others away. I gave one to Shelby shortly before he went home—matters were pretty chaotic by that time and he seldom appeared in the daylight. Whenever he did, it was apparent that the marvelous control, his ability for incredible concentration, was gone. He would drop utensils and his hands would shake. Morrisey stayed close by when Shelby was on duty—I think Brock asked him to, but he would have in any case.

The insect I gave Shelby started with a mistake and became a creature with huge, lacy wings, ferocious eyes, and long, slender, fanglike appurtenances that flowed out of its mouth and dragged along the ground. I still don't know what possessed me to give it to him. I found myself in the doorway to his room with the creature cupped in my hands. I had applied acid to the copper and it had a lovely, green patina.

Shelby was bent over his desk with his back to me, supporting himself on his outstretched arms. His fingers were splayed, his head and hair drooped. Unaware of my presence, he stood like that for several minutes. Once or twice he groaned, the cry coming from deep within. The Circus Maximus lay empty except for the large piece of wood upon which many creatures had feasted and died. The centipedes were gone. I hoped he'd done what he said he was going to do and pickled them. The glass had been cracked and patched with adhesive tape.

I clasped the creature carefully behind its wings and knocked. Shelby jumped and whirled around, his eyes half-open, the dark pupils swimming slowly into focus. "Casualties?"

I shook my head. "I brought this to you as a farewell gift, sir."

"Ohhh, it's beautiful." He shuffled toward me, his eyes riveted on the copper figure. Gently, he folded both hands around it, and as I released it to his care, his eyes floated up to me. Here was a man over six feet tall, and I was looking down at him and I was scarcely six feet myself. "Thank you, thank you, thank you . . ."

But that was much later and everything had changed.

The first figure, my first creation, was a praying mantis. There were several living in my office, huge creatures that fed on the thousands of insects that swarmed around the lightbulb every night. I had spiders, too, but the spiders and I created a mutual nonaggression pact: if they didn't drop on me, I wouldn't sweep them out of the tent. Most of the time it worked.

Mantises fascinated me. I would watch them for hours as they swayed gently and studied their intended victims. The agile ferocity of those creatures with their ponderous bodies and long, delicate legs was marvelous. I began to understand Shelby's fascination with insects, especially the mantises and their mating habits. By that time, war for me had become feminine in its capriciousness.

Shortly after I started the first mantis, Brock walked in, looking for a report. "You making that?"

"Yes, sir."

"That's pretty damn good." He reached down, picked up the mantis and studied it under the light. "Trying to keep from going bananas, huh?"

The mantises were green, elegant, and I honored them among the other insects that obsessed me then: the Chinooks, Skycranes, LOHs and Hueys.

Now that first mantis sits poised on a window in my bedroom in the rivertown where the sun can play through old glass upon its soft green body. It's scarcely an object of curiosity anymore. It's a relic from a place that once existed, a bit of evidence that what occurred was not, in fact, a dream.

TWELVE

For a year I yearned to be where I am now, lying in a bed beside a woman. I wanted to press soft breasts in my face, push nipples against my eyes, to see minute glistening of sweat over a mouth and in underarms, to luxuriate in the moist smell and drench my face in sexual excretions. And in those fevered imaginings, I was not embarked upon an act of possession, but of absolution.

I've not known fulfillment of these fierce desires—not to-night or since I arrived home. I've emptied myself, maybe debased myself but I've not found what I sought. Now I'm afraid to move, to waken Casey, because then she'll move away from me and there will be nothing.

Suggestions were everywhere: the pinups—pneumatic, flaw-less creatures in color, and less flawless women in black and white who were correspondingly more interesting. Pinups proliferated in places like the club where they were associ-ated with male relaxation. In some cases, like the commo bunker (the old bunker before Smith fulfilled his dreams), they served as scenery, wallpaper. Only rarely did I see them in some superficially erotic sense. Even the films I saw with their pale white human figures and closeups of glistening members and stark, black hair, and (later) dogs and horses that became substitutes for men, were abstractions. But the films, shortlived as they were, were disturbing in a far more profound way than the cheesecake photographs: they touched the hidden sides of the eros of my imaginings, the eros of that war.

And there was Murphy's Christmas doll. He brought her to

sickcall on Christmas Day for a gynecological examination. She's a life-size inflatable woman one of the pilots brought back from R&R as a present—the deluxe model, white, complete with all apertures, head wig, merkin, and a sleazy cotton, polka-dot print dress.

Murphy's in the sickcall examination room with Brock. The doll lies on the table with her dress lifted up over her face. "I'm not going to touch her," Brock announces, causing Murphy to renew his entreaties.

Then Brock seems to relent, and touches the patient gingerly. "Well, if you're really afraid of getting something, I'll give her 1.5 million units of procaine penicillin in each cheek. How's that?"

Murphy seizes the doll and clasps her to his body. "You quack, sir! Charlatan! How dare you speak of a lady in that manner!"

Brock points the stub of his cigar at the creature jiggling in the pilot's arms. "I suppose I could run some tests if you want to leave her with me for the night."

"Ohhhh!" Murphy spins around and stomps out of the examining room, followed by several grinning compatriots.

Shelby, buzz-eyed, pokes his head out into the hall and shouts, "Murph! I'll give the shots! I'll be gentle."

Later, in my tent, I open the various small packages I've received during the past weeks. I've saved them all in order to have a Christmas Day. There are boxes of cookies, a couple of books, three fruit cakes—two of which are mouldy and the third to be given away because I can't stand fruit cake, a miniature Christmas tree with tiny lights, a box of teabags, and a taped "letter" from home.

The tape is awkward and obtrusive. I borrow Gittoni's recorder to listen to those voices that try to project a sense of nearness and familiarity, but there are thirteen thousand miles of total incomprehension between us, between this plantation and a place called home. The tape was obviously carefully orchestrated and I find that I have to fight back my emotions. I'm almost in tears, but they're tears of anger, sadness, self-pity—and I'm beginning to feel a self-indulgence I've tried assiduously to avoid. I vow to request only letters in the future.

There are two casualties in the afternoon, one of whom is a young GI with reddish hair who blew a Claymore mine, not realizing that the enemy had turned it around on him. He is

DOA. We remove the bottles of saline and discard them, then pull the blanket over the body and carry it to the morgue.

The other soldier has taken a piece of shrapnel the size of his fist through his thigh, demolishing the femur. Blood spreads rapidly beneath the leg when the tourniquet is removed. The soldier, displaying remarkable tenacity, has not gone into shock but has become hysterical, laughing and crying at the same time, then alternately, then together again. Several times, he tries to sit up and observe the hole. I manage to forget taped letters and Christmas for the time being.

Later I find Morrisey in my office. It's dark now and the helicopter has sailed out over the wire carrying a silent soldier with a ruined leg. Morrisey's absorbed in folding pieces of paper into narrow strips and stapling them together. "Why in hell are you making that?" I demand when I recognize the outlines of a skeleton.

He shrugs.

Twice I refill the stapler while he continues to fashion his life-size construction, the spine, the rib cage, the pelvis all emerging as if conjured by his fierce concentration. With strands of copper wire stripped from my books of field medical tags, he makes it three-dimensional. Only the skull remains flat, and on this he draws hollow features with a black marking pen. Except for the skull, the skeleton is a remarkable achievement. Carefully, he drapes it over his arm and starts for the door.

"What are you going to do with it?"

"I don't know. I didn't think that far ahead."

"Wait a minute, then!" I cut a piece of paper to resemble a conical hat with a fur base and pom-pom. I grab a red marking pen and color all but the fur lining, then, stapler in hand, attach the cap.

Morrisey holds the head aloft and admires it. "Brock ought to check this out. I'll put it in the treatment tent."

But I'm already dashing back, compelled by another inspiration.

With the skeleton flopped on one of the treatment tables, Newell attaches cotton to the pom-pom and fur base of the cap while I wire a field tag to one of the ribs. My effort is rewarded by that peculiar lopsided motion and ensuant grunt that pass for amusement as Newell reads the card.

It's the damnedest thing, Morrisey! I didn't hear any helicopter come in." Brock's approaching the rear of the tent.

Newell and I move quickly away from the table as the door squeaks open and Brock appears, followed by Morrisey, Shelby, then Howard.

"My God!" Brock exclaims as he spots the skeleton. He hurries to the table and picks up the identification tag. "S. Claus, civilian . . . Caucasian . . . I would never have guessed!" He places his stethoscope on one of the ribs, bends over and listens. Shelby wags his head from side to side as he tries to focus on the table where Brock is initiating a thorough physical examination.

"What happened to him, Morrisey? Here, hold the legs up above the knees, please." He pulls a rubber glove on his right hand in preparation for a digital rectal.

"Sleigh caught a rocket-propelled grenade."

"All the reindeer bought the farm, sir," I add.

"Villainous fiends!"

Shelby's eyes dilate briefly, the lids rise. "We could have done with some venison," he suggests, then chuckles softly to himself. His body twitches with his private amusement.

Our new commander seems puzzled. There's a taut smile on his lips as his gaze wanders from one to the other of us, seeking some sort of reassurance. Only Shelby betrays our intense pleasure, but he seems to frighten Howard and has no credibility.

"He's in bad shape, Morrisey. Call commo and get Hargos over here, ASAP. Tell him we've got a bad one," Brock orders.

I hear a muttered incantation and turn to find Shelby, his eyes riveted dangerously on a large beetle peeking back at him from a rafter. He hums a little tune:

> "Would my precious myriapods,
>   of the division Chilopoda,
> Delight in the sinewy flesh
>   of the Genus Rangifer-a?"

"What's with Shelby?" Newell whispers.

I shake my head.

"What the hell?" Hargos demands as he crashes through the front door in an unzipped flight suit, his helmet swinging in his hand. Murphy, another warrant officer, and a crewchief push in behind. Under his flight suit, Hargos is wearing his madras shorts and a purple T-shirt with a picture of Bugs Bunny on it.

Our own numbers have swollen as word of the skeleton travels through the company. Jenks is grinning. Even Howard looks decidedly more comfortable.

Brock points at the casualty.

"Murph!" Hargos roars, "we gotta fly this one south, priority!"

Instantly, an I.V. is inserted, a bottle of saline and a blanket appear, and the skeleton is covered. Several persons reach for the handles of the litter . . . and I wish Howard weren't around with his ingratiating, prim little smile, the same one he wore for the MI team.

I'm on the helicopter pad surrounded by a slightly boozy crowd and soft laughter. We watch the flashing light fade beyond the rubber trees. Gittoni joined us after an exasperating ten minutes on the radio convincing an irate operator at the surgical hospital that not only would they have to accept a civilian casualty on Christmas night, despite the regulation about civilians, but that there was an ETA of twenty minutes for the medivac and he'd best get some litter bearers out to meet it. "Merry Christmas, all you guys," Gittoni says as the first, invisible raindrops begin to pat on the earth around us.

Moments later, we're submerged in soft, hissing rain, and we're laughing again, everybody suddenly wishing everybody else a Merry Christmas, the amusement at some point becoming something else—a warmth, a heartfelt wish, relief and gratitude. No one had remembered the season's greeting.

Small, low sandbagged bunkers and semicircular nests dot the plantation among the endless symmetry of the rubber trees. Gradually they've assumed a forlorn appearance as they crumble under the rains. Breeding grounds for insects, they were here months before the massive influx of American troops occurred when the area, scene of small, insignificant skirmishes, was suddenly declared "strategic." Over a year later, we remain inside the plantation virtually hostage to the surrounding countryside.

As those silent sandbag relics disintegrate beneath downpours, we're enduring the whines and clanks of a huge bulldozer. It's been sent from the engineers at Smith's request to defy the very same force that is rotting the more modest remnants among the trees. Smith is challenging this will with the materials that were used in the first instance when security, not permanence or progress, was the only consideration.

Two deep, red slashes become part of the landscape: one for the new officer-patient bunker, the other for a new commo bunker. Trees crash to the earth and are pushed away to rot, making room for a third ward, a "rec center" in the company area next to the club, and for a new outdoor theater to replace the supposedly inadequate facilities under the huge arch of the motorpool maintenance tent.

Everything has been initiated in the name of "patient care." We're constantly reminded of this during the morning, noontime, and now occasional evening formations. Smith, like the CO, is seldom present on these occasions. First Sergeant Buelen and the other NCOs have been left to conduct the day to day inspections and to read the duty list prepared under Smith's supervision.

But as surely as the sun rises, the rains come and threaten to fill the excavations with water faster than the sun can drink it. We work urgently, trying to build and complete before we're thrown back and defeated by nature.

"Why couldn't he have waited for the dry season?" Morrisey asks. Frequently now, he's considered more of a crank than a complainer.

Even when one of the excavations does fill and Smith, with scarcely repressed fury, concedes defeat—announcing that the officer-patient bunker will have to wait for the dry season—it is only a set-back, a temporary loss of ground in a struggle whose outcome is never doubted. What can possibly withstand the material, manpower, skill, and above all, the very rightness, justness of the goals that Smith brings to the strife?

The completed communications bunker is a marvel of sorts, given the circumstances. Even Gittoni overcomes his initial skepticism, his loyalty to the crude box surrounded and heaped with sandbags that served so long as our commo shack.

The basic structure of the new bunker rises two feet above the ground so that with a combination cantilevered roof and circumventing, low sandbag wall, natural light can penetrate its depths without sacrificing security. But even the innovative use of natural light is not as impressive as the actual means of construction. Instead of simply covering a narrow trench with reinforced steel and sand bags, the usual method, Smith has somehow contrived to obtain timbers and planking, all new lumber, of incredible dimensions and quality, and with these has built a massive room, thirty feet long and fifteen wide, with a fourteen-foot ceiling. To crown this achievement, he has had perforated steel plate laid on the wooden roof beneath three feet of sandbags.

Several days are spent filling the surrounding trench by hand; the often liquid red mass slides off the shovels as fast as it's scooped up. The final results, however, are stunning, as all the inherent problems of construction vanish in the earth.

"Damn good thing they sandbagged that roof when they did," Morrisey remarks one evening, "before that bunker popped out of the ground like a rectangular balloon."

The bunker is of such monumental proportions that it swallows the banks of radios and the sparse, casual furniture and other odds and ends collected by many radio operators. Even the two bunks that Smith installs so that the radio operators can work as a team around the clock in the event of a "dire emergency" scarcely begin to fill that prodigious void. Hesitant questions such as "What did we have before but round-the-clock service?" or "What constitutes a dire emergency?" seem impertinent, and are, in fact, quelled. How did we get by with anything less? Morrisey, of course, remains impertinent, but to no avail.

Smith wins praise from the officers, and toward completion, even from the men who have labored with him, who have crawled antlike over the towering beams and have ultimately been startled by the creation that, through Smith's guidance, emerged under their very hands. Initially, some mud and water seeps up through cracks in the floor, but with the help of brooms and shovels, it soon disappears.

"Do you realize that all those timbers and planks were shipped from the States? It's all Douglas fir! Imagine the cost!" Morrisey exclaims, scarcely disguising his own reluctant admiration.

Inside the bunker, our voices are swallowed by the sheer, cathedral-like massiveness. Morrisey stares thoughtfully at the plank walls between the huge uprights, actually reaches out and strokes the smooth, untreated wood. I watch his hand glide back and forth. "Douglas fir is softwood—it rots."

"They stapled plastic around the outside walls," I say.

He laughs.

How was it Smith could slog around in that red goop, hammer, saw, oversee all at once, all in one apparent motion, be in that same mud doing the same things as everyone else, and still, even shirtless, look clean? When I say clean, not immaculate any longer, except by contrast with everyone else. The incredible white skin with the little red dots that were nascent moles and the few, dark chest hairs distinguished him immediately. He might get slightly sunburned around the neck and shoulders, but that was the only discoloration—never a tan, never a trace of bronze, no blemish from the sky and earth.

He could be in a hole one minute, up to his ears in filth, and in the next instant, beside me seeking information from the logs, or checking the wards and treatment tent, still shirtless perhaps, but clean. (For anything vaguely official, the shirt, most likely, would reappear.) Even his pants might still be creased, be free from all but the slightest trace of the mucky, smelly earth that had become our bane.

He was already compulsive by the time the commo bunker was completed, obsessed, everywhere at once it seemed, and behaving as though he were not only meeting the time limits of his tour there, but the Deadline defined by his very mortality, his Tour.

After an initial flurry of personally supervised harrassment that lasted three or four weeks, Howard became less conspicuous in the company area. Increasingly, he seemed to prefer the company of his fellow doctors in that one half of a tent they had designated as their club where they played bridge (less frequently with Hargos since Major Mendez's departure) and read paperbacks. Smith's name was always on his lips, however, and Smith himself invariably by his side when needed.

The long-sought reassertion of authority by the other NCOs, smarting under the isolation—both real and imagined—they had felt under the major's command, the significant increase in control they wielded over the minutiae of our day-to-day lives, didn't have the effect they expected. They, Buelen especially, seemed to fade farther into the background, to become more lost, more scorned and abused in the aggressive burst of development that was not of their making, not under their control.

Morrisey insisted even then that Smith was running the company, but it seemed inconceivable to the rest of us. Smith seemed so polite, deferential by nature, always willing to listen and help. Even his suppressed fury, the temper he refused to acknowledge, seemed fundamentally justified—as *though it were transcendant, dedicated to something much more important and idealistic than mere assertion of power.*

It was the autocratic, erratic Howard we feared and did our best to avoid.

Morrisey was alone in his perceptions: he would not concede the merit of Smith's goals, could not forgive the changes. He had idolized Mendez, who was no more than a ghost for the rest of us by then. His authority, moral and otherwise, ceased the day he walked, smiling, happy, out to Hargos's helicopter and flew away. That was the reality of the place. Morrisey should have known enough to admit it.

Several of us are ranged around a piece of plywood that Brock has nailed near the front door of the treatment tent. It's covered with color Polaroid photos of the more outrageous examples of venereal disease he's encountered. A sign at the top, lettered in script by Owen, reads: BROCK'S VD VISTA.

Brock points at a photograph of a venereal wart about the size of a silver dollar located just below a hairy navel. "This guy's a warrant officer—something to do with division supply. I never saw a wart like that before, so when I asked him if I could take a picture, he said, 'Sure, Doc. Just promise you won't tell my wife.' "

"Gerty's got a couple in the lab now," Owen chimes in.

"I know," Brock says, "but all they got is gonorrhea. Jesus, I get sick of this! If they'd let us clean up some of these girls, develop some kind of preventive program, I bet you we could eliminate ninety-nine percent of the problem at a fraction of what it's costing now. Short of that, short of a congressional act and the blessings of the DAR, if these dumb sonsuvbitches would just use a rubber, things would be a hell of a lot better! That's what I told this warrant officer— chewed his ass out, in fact, and you know what he said? 'It doesn't feel as good.' I told him to tell that to his wife."

The rear door squeaks and we find Smith holding it open for several men who shuffle into the room like a herd of wary sheep. "This is the treatment room," Smith pronounces as the ten men crowd around. Not one can remain still, however; all in factory-fresh fatigues, dark green and shiny, they scuff and scrape, turn their heads rapidly in our direction, then back to Smith.

Smith explains the function of the room, evokes images of tile and enamel, of only occasional splashes of human blood and garbage that skim off sanitized, stainless steel into the realm of happenstance. The amazement with which they encounter us, the continual glances back and forth between the sergeant's idealized presentation and our reality can only be a mirror to our own consternation. As one, we instinctively move backward toward that board, as though to cover some sin, some terrible childishness.

The rear door flies open again and Gerty barges in, head down, face beet red in an Irish rage. "Lookit this, goddammit, sir! I've had enough of this shit!" He storms past that startled congregation and thrusts a piece of glass toward us. He shakes it emphatically, and drops of whitish fluid fly off in all directions. "Lookit this shit, Captain Brock! I tell the fuckheads to squeeze a sample out on the slide and what do they do? They beat off on the fucking thing, that's what they do! I'm not doing another slide! I'm transferring to the field! I'm getting fucked for fair!" In midstride, Gerty whirls around and rages out.

Smith, close-mouthed, struggles perceptibly with himself, his anger reflected in the blink of an eye, the twitch of a cheek.

Brock mashes his hand against his face.

Smith, composed once more, drives the recruits in our direction. "I'd like you to meet our new men, Captain Brock, Captain Shelby . . ." But we've already met, all of us, their belligerence as blatant as our withering amazement. There are two pudgy black men and eight sunless whites, all shorn, the incredible strips of bare skin flowing, electric razor width, across where their sideburns once were, over their ears and down around the base of their scalps.

The recruits begin to shuffle again, then jerk themselves to the most rigid attention I've seen in months, yanking their hands up in salute.

"Pleased to meet you," Brock exclaims, and waves his hands downward in a futile attempt to cease this formal recognition of his rank. Shelby simply stares with his profound, electric concentration at a photograph of a bloated penis about two inches from his nose.

Two of the men are especially conspicuous; one, bearing a cryptic nametag "Nye," is very tall and skinny, almost half a head taller than Smith. He has gaunt, pale cheeks, butched hair, and the most hostile look I've ever seen.

The other, Gerhard, has a similar aggressive quality, but it's softened by the smugness of the well-fed. Gerhard has plump, fair skin that tans beautifully, giving him a sluttish sleekness that matches his brown, neatly-parted hair, pert nose, and a mouth that is too wide. But the eyes, beautiful cornflower blue eyes, betray him, betray the ease with which he could be provoked. Despite obvious tension between the two men, together they project an aura of incorruptibility over the remainder of the flock.

All are fixed in that horrifying salute.

"Sir," Morrisey mutters, "I think you have to return the salute."

"Saluting's not required in the treatment area, men," Smith interrupts with a scornful glance (or am I imagining that—Smith wouldn't do that!). The recruits gradually drop their hands.

Suddenly, Smith sees the photo gallery. Brock catches Smith's reaction and waves with a grand flourish at the board. "What do you think of that, Sergeant Smith?" he crows. "Gentlemen!" He bangs a table for emphasis and addresses the recruits. "There's venereal disease in Vietnam! In the ground, on the toilet seats . . . it's all around you! Beware! These," and again his arm sweeps out, "are but a few choice examples of what can befall you."

Shelby nods his head in agreement.

So Brock feels it, too, I'm thinking, and I smile as I overcome my surprise at his uncharacteristic histrionics. We move aside to let the new recruits press forward, drawn by their own outraged fascination. They move past us as though motion can only occur from physical, or near physical contact with each other, and they stare with horrible concentration at the VD Vista.

Brock isn't finished. "Sergeant Smith," he says when Smith is halfway out the front door, trailing the recruits.

Smith is alert at once. "Yes, sir?"

"Sergeant, I'd appreciate it if you wouldn't put me on the spot like that again."

"Sir, I didn't mean . . ."

"Thank you, Sergeant."

It doesn't end there. Afterward, Brock becomes contrite, rubs his hair as he often does when agitated, and stomps around a bit. "Christ, Shel, why did I let that piss me off? How was he to know that fucking bunch of weirdos was going to salute? Ahh, the crap he was feeding them—you'd think this was a fucking nursing home!"

Shelby moves within a hair's width of another photograph, his eyes roving the glistening paper. "These are pretty incredible shots . . ."

Brock looks at Morrisey and shakes his head. "I don't know what's wrong with me these days. I get mad as hell over nothing."

"Beautiful chancroids, Brock. Really beautiful."

A cry shatters the soft, humming stillness of the afternoon. We push through the door into the yard where Smith and his ten recruits, now joined by Howard, are again frozen. I follow their stares past the revetments toward the treeline and the barely visible structures of the air ambulance company.

"Rape! Ra-aape!"

Out of the trees and across the drainage ditch flies one of the crewchiefs wearing a yellow wig, blonde strands streaming. He hurtles across the road toward the helicopters. Clutched under his right arm, the head clasped like a football, is Murphy's doll, stark naked, jiggling violently with the motion of her abductor.

"Get that sonuvabitch! Kidnap!" his pursuers scream. Major Hargos and Murphy are in the lead.

Until this moment, neither Smith nor Howard have known about the doll. "What the hell?" Howard finally sputters.

Brock scratches an armpit and grins.

Hargos leaps through the air and tackles the abductor. The doll, Hargos, and the abductor vanish beneath a pile of bodies. There's the sound of an explosion.

Murphy, mud dripping from his face and chest, rises triumphant from the heap of men and waves a limp piece of flesh-colored rubber above his head. In his other hand, he clutches the blonde wig. He struts toward us, the undisputed victor before a delighted audience. The other men, extricating themselves, begin to scrape globs of mud from their limbs and clothing.

"This is disgraceful!" Howard mutters, but then Murphy, as though sensing his disapproval, appears majestically in front of him.

"Afternoon, Captain Howard, sir. Afternoon, Sergeant."

Smith, a bleak smile on his face, gives the warrant officer a curt nod.

Major Hargos ambles up, slaps Murphy's shoulders and causes bits of mud to fly. He steers him toward Brock. "Doc Brock! My man's woman here is in need of radical surgery."

Brock lights a cigar, waves the match in the direction of the treatment room, and at once the men from Dust-Off slog forward, past the new recruits they scarcely deign to notice. Their contempt for anyone who, in word or manner, might call their behavior into question is marvelous.

In the treatment room, Brock probes the remains with his cigar. The smell of melting vinyl fills the air.

Shelby gingerly sniffs the merkin.

There's a burst of laughter, and the guilty crewchief is catapulted into the room. "My first gang bang," he announces proudly.

THIRTEEN

"**A**n ambulance squad?" Morrisey asks. "Smith's formed an ambulance squad? To do what?"

"To answer all calls on base."

A smile creeps into his eyes, that warmth again, the incredible warmth of amusement or simple comprehension. Suddenly, he laughs outright. Jenkins has been standing beside him, bent over a copy of *The Stars and Stripes*, ostensibly reading.

"At most, we average one emergency call a week on base, but they don't know that at USARV headquarters, or division, or battalion, or wherever they assign personnel. It's a paper game—Smith's created a steady labor pool for his projects. Brilliant! A ten-man ambulance squad." Morrisey slaps the partition.

"They're the laziest bunch I've ever seen. Did you see them try to put that hooch up?"

Jenkins laughs. "That Lucius there was doing most of the work. The rest of them supervised."

"But they never complain," Morrisey says. "The lifers love them for that alone. Which one's Lucius?"

"The little short one with the Bible in his hand all the time."

"They don't come out of that tent now, except for meals and work. What are they doing in there?"

Jenkins shakes his head.

Gittoni enters my office and heads for the coffee urn. "I think Brock's clap board and Murphy's dolly scared the beejesus out of them," he says. "Did you hear? Howard told

186

Buelen to take over the club this morning. No more enlisted men behind the bar. Buster Wilbur's our new bartender."

"What's he doing? Still punishing us for Dust-Off's sins? That makes as much sense as that reprimand he gave Gerty."

"Gerty was shaken."

"Any more good news, Gittoni?"

"Nope."

I hold up an index finger. "Smith procured twenty-five gallons of paint so Milliken can paint the mess hall. Guess what color . . ."

"See you guys later," Morrisey says. Jenkins follows him out of the tent. Gittoni sits down at my desk and puts his feet on the top. He picks up a magazine and starts to thumb through it while he sips his coffee. I watch him for a moment, his absorption in the magazine, his sense of ease, even in these surroundings.

Gittoni's a favorite at Dust-Off, enjoys a popularity second only to that once commanded by Major Mendez. He reveres Hargos, the eminent flyer, and despite the difference in rank, a deep friendship has developed between the two men. A few of us have known for some time that Gittoni's been surreptitiously flying missions with Hargos, riding as a spare medic. I've heard he's even piloted helicopters under Hargos's supervision. It's hard not to be enamored of the machines and the easy fellowship of the men who fly them. I don't believe it's ever occurred to any of us that our air ambulance company might be different from others.

It must have been then that I began thinking seriously about a transfer to Dust-Off as a medic. There were at least two reasons: guilt and fear. Flying was attractive. I could do that, be more directly involved in combat, take risks, but do so without having to bear a weapon. That was beginning to seem important to me, not carrying a weapon. And nothing remained of my original relief, even pleasure with my assignment to the medical company. I felt only apprehension. I felt imprisoned in the plantation while all around me things, men, events mocked my paper war. The changes in the company, the streamlining, the new emphasis on patient comfort: it seemed logical and right. I wasn't passionately opposed to the changes as Morrisey was, but there was the apprehension—I still had half of my tour to complete. I especially envied Gittoni his friendship with the Dust-Off crew. He had a place to escape to, or so it seemed.

"How many casualties, Dunn?" Gittoni asks.

Dunn shakes his head. "The coordinates are almost in Cambodia." The pink and violet dials of the radios glow out from the darkness beyond the beam of a single, high-intensity lamp. The radio speaker crackles intermittently and quaking voices intrude on the silence, float on the shrill, internal whines of their wingless vessels, then click off.

A guard clumps down the ramp. "You guys up already? I wasn't going to wake you until we had an ETA."

"Shhh!" Dunn says and presses the earphones closer to his head. An excited voice wavers on the radio.

"They're taking fire," Gittoni says as he moves closer to the speaker. No one else moves.

"That crazy bastard's going in for the pickup!"

"Murph's just arrived . . . and there's a gunship out there."

Minutes go by. At first the voices bat constantly back and forth over the airwaves, then there's a sudden, prolonged grating noise in the background. Gittoni glances at us. "Minigun."

The pilot of the gunship calls Hargos who's lifting off:

"Murphy's going in, now," Dunn says.

There's another long silence. I listen to the bugs whirr against the screens high overhead. Gittoni checks his watch.

Suddenly the gunship pilot's calling Hargos again. Two, three times he calls but there's no answer, the call lightyears away, celestial, fantastic.

Gittoni stares at the speaker, scarcely breathing, his face ashen. The hush continues.

The speaker cracks. "We're inbound with four litter, three ambulatory," Hargos announces, his voice faint, chattering. "That'll be an ETA of about fifteen minutes."

Moments later, Murphy comes on with three litters and three more ambulatory. Dunn removes his headphones and looks at the guard. "Brock's on. Better wake Shelby, too."

I find that I've been leaning closer and closer to the radio. Gittoni's collapsed, motionless, in a chair. He looks pale and shrunken. I'm amazed that he's vulnerable too, that even his world might come apart. Then I become thoroughly disgusted with myself, my callousness, my blindness even after all I've seen.

In response to a distant noise, away beyond the tower and moonlit tangle, the conversation among the group of us gathered at the edge of the landing pad fades. Out of the darkness, the throbbing flows toward us with increasing intensity. I spot a tiny speck of red light to the northeast. It travels parallel to us for some distance, winking, a bit of flotsam in the night sky. It remains stationary for a moment, then begins to slowly dilate, the noise vibrating against us as it floods into the rubber trees. The light grows a belly, a silvered flash of plexiglass. Another light bursts on and washes the world beneath in a brilliant, white pool that skims toward us, a harsh, interplanetary device that subdues the moonlight as it glides over stark, gnarled shapes where there were once only gentle shadows. It flies upon us, blinds us as it blasts the earth.

A second red light appears, sweeps wide out of the no-where beyond the tower.

"What am I supposed to do, Dunn?" I shout above the rain. The receiver of the field phone is sweaty. "Yeah, I got the driver and one guard here. There's supposed to be three men on an ambulance! The other guard's down in the company . . . yeah."

"What's up?" Gerhard asks, leaning across the counter and rubbing his eyes. He's the driver on duty.

"Dunn, I can't leave the office empty! OK, you get the guard up here to cover for me . . . and Shelby's on duty. Yeah, OK, fuck you! So you know!" I slam the receiver down. "We got a casualty out by the north gate, Gerhard! You go warm up your ambulance. I'll wake the guard."

The ambulance splashes up to a small guard shack; the headlights isolate a cluster of white faces and squinting eyes. "Use your blackout lights!" a ponchoed MP yells. Beyond the north gate, out among the torrents that stream through our lights, several flashlights flicker. Highway 10 is invisible beyond the shack. Gerhard reaches past the steering wheel and twists the knobs into the blackout position.

I've never been to the north gate before—it's like another world. Who travels north? Out in the darkness ahead of us, Highway 10 wends its way toward Cambodia: a name like Jupiter, Saturn, a fix somewhere in the vast night, a reference point for creatures pinwheeling across the sky. I can't think of it as a refuge but as something nebulous, a place of menace, of screaming monkeys and eyes that watch from daylit shad-ows deeper than any night.

The guard sits between Gerhard and me in the doorway that

leads to the rear of the ambulance. A dull, red glow plays upon his shoulders. He yawns.

The MP bangs on my window and I lower it. I think of Johnny Mirrors, the MP I saw busting the soldier with the marijuana near The Yellow Peril months ago. I haven't seen him in a long, long time. I wonder if he's gone away . . . gone home. "Go through the gate and follow that guy wagging the flashlight!" the MP shouts. I raise the window, exclude the soggy world hammering on the roof.

We slosh and creak through row after row of concertina wire. Black jagged coils loom into our lights then vanish, an effusion of wreckage, of war, of wealth, treasure, human effort tumbling behind us. How can we ever retrieve it? We squander not only life and machines, but the very substance of the earth itself. The MP in front of us carries an M-16 as well as a flashlight; he seems in no hurry.

There has been no sense of urgency, not from the moment of the subdued ringing in my office, not in Dunn's voice, or even in the rousting of the guard and ambulance driver. I feel no urgency now, no sense of time. The pounding on the roof suddenly amplifies, quells even the clicks of the wiper blades. Out beyond the hood, the MP disappears, then reappears. Now I can see several more lights waving frantically.

A light shines in the cab and forces Gerhard to lift one hand to shield his eyes. The vehicle is clumsy, its steering stiff. "Turn those things away!" he shouts, but his frustration falls against the raised windows. Neither the guard nor I respond.

I knock the door open with my shoulder, descend into the mud, and am instantly soaked. We trudge toward the lights. The guard's behind me with a litter. Someone whispers, "Jesus, Doc . . ." I feel him grasp my sleeve, a soft, unsettling sensation like the bite of a toothless animal. I shiver and yank my arm away.

The flashlights part and reveal a man sprawled on the ground, partially covered by a poncho liner, the light camouflage colors now drenched black. A pallid face protrudes above the liner, the mouth slack; a trickle of blood glistens at the corner of the lips.

At the far end of the poncho liner there's a booted leg; the wide, unbloused pantleg hangs tramplike to the heel of the boot. Beside that lies the remains of another leg; a piece of the tibia blinks out from several field dressings that have been hastily wrapped around the few inches left below the knee. There is no trace of the fibula. The dressings, the pantleg above the wound, the ground beneath are scarlet.

I kneel in the mud. The wet earth clasps my knees, presses through my pants while I scoop gobs of bloody mucous from the man's mouth. "There a tourniquet on that leg?" I shout. Why do I shout?

"Just a rag tied hard . . . one on his arm, too."

I wipe the hair from my eyes. My fingers are pressed to the carotid artery, my ear to his mouth. "He's still alive."

The guard has been tearing the plastic wrapping off an artificial airway. I shake my head. "Wait."

I pull back the edge of the poncho liner and see a mutilated arm. What was he doing? I cradle his head in the crook of my right arm, slip my left arm under the good shoulder and start to lift.

There are lots of people around, a lot of soldiers. I know it, but I can't see them—only jiggling spots of light, Gerhard, the guard, the litter, the wounded man. No one makes a sound. A helicopter hammers out of the plantation. What am I doing here? Gerhard and the guard are taking their cues from me! I should be Morrisey, or Newell, Owen—not me. These guys are like cattle: they mill around, appalled and helpless in the face of their own slaughter. I feel the darkness part in front of me. The soft, red light of the ambulance yaws out of the rain as the ground sucks my boots.

"Let me take that, Doc."

A hand brushes across mine and I gladly relinquish one of the handles. The wounded man is heavy. I face a helmeted soldier across the litter as we slide it into the back of the ambulance. Grenade rings hang from the helmet. The litter's steel shoes screech on the floor.

"Doc, he's my friend."

I climb in after the litter. "Where was your medic when this happened?" The engine roars. I hear the thunk of Gerhard's door.

"You got him."

The door slams in my face. We're moving but for a moment I don't notice.

"Jon! I can't find a pulse!" The guard pleads with me.

"Put that airway in!"

He blows into the airway rhythmically, cinches the soldier's nostrils, then releases them. I am thousands of miles away as I straddle a man's body, ram the heels of my hand down into the chest. I saw the major do this—I've not seen it since. It's undignified. When we get this far, why bother? Is that what Howard thinks? The major was a believer. Gerhard's face appears briefly in the door. The ambulance lurches violently as it gains speed.

My hips strike the steel shelves on either side of me. One . . . two . . . three . . . four . . . five . . . I'm not doing anything—I can't be. There are only these palms and a convulsive, rubbery body beneath them. Who am I kidding? This has nothing to with something alive—this is not a human beneath me.

A rhythm has developed. I no longer concern myself with the guard, that burst of breath on the count of five. There was a moment when the doors were closing when I felt important, even proud. I was someone who could do something for someone else. They made me feel that way! Just one moment, then it was gone and I was isolated in the back of this vehicle. I am a fool. I'm helpless. I'm futile.

"Jesus, Gerhard!" I fling out a hand to keep my balance as the ambulance plunges into a deep puddle.

"I can't see!"

" . . . two . . . three . . . four . . ." I've had a couple of years of college. I'm not trained for this. The major was. I don't even want to be here. This life under me is not mine to bring back. "But I want to . . ." I whisper, never losing the rhythm, "if only so I'll never have to do it again." My arms, my body begin to ache. Where did I hear that if I stop before he's legally pronounced dead, I'll be guilty of manslaughter. No, no, this is a war! Manslaughter? No, that's artificial respiration—at a beach, maybe. It might conceivably go on for hours until a doctor shows. It's raining—this is no beach.

The sweat pours down my face, my back, trickles down my belly. I should be laughing! The bounce . . . was Murphy's doll like this? The heels of my palms ram into the chest. My God, I can't do this anymore.

The doors screech open; I feel the chill. I pump three more times and surrender the man to the waiting shadows. The soldier is dragged away from me into the darkness.

The burning, moist heat of my effort drains out of me. Bursts of color pop across my blindness. I press my back to the wall and feel the cool steel. It's still pouring; the water still splashes off the roof. Nothing's changed. I open my eyes and start to climb down from the ambulance. The door to the treatment tent swings open a few yards away and four men, a litter between them, are momentarily silhouetted. The door shuts and I can hear them splash by. I saw the poncho liner drawn up over the head.

When I enter the tent, I find a field tag on the stained, blue cloth of a table. Someone got the information. I pick the tag up, stare at it, at Morrisey's handwriting, then fold it and stuff it into my chest pocket. Someone's watching me.

It's Shelby. He's bent over a stainless steel bowl, washing his hands. "Quite a grandstand play, O'Neill." The voice sounds contemptuous but I can't comprehend the meaning. He waits an interminable time for me to reply. "You weren't qualified to do that," he says when I don't respond. His hands begin to tremble. He looks worn out, his eyes bloodshot.

"I know."

He's startled by that.

Suddenly Morrisey's between us, then next to me, a hand on my shoulder. "None of us were ever qualified for any of this . . . were we, sir?" Shelby's hands are violent now. I feel terribly sorry for him. I pull away from Morrisey, but he goes on. "We can only do our best, isn't that right, sir?"

"Morrisey, leave him alone, for Christ's sake!"

But Shelby doesn't hear me. He's nodding his head rapidly in abrupt, frantic little motions. "Yes, yes of course . . ."

I run from that room into the rain, and through the rain into my dingy office with its bug-spattered bulb lying face down on the desk where I left it over an hour ago. I pull the crumpled medical tag from my pocket, then mechanically reach under the counter and bring out some death certificates. I try to think about the dead man in the morgue, hoping it will be painful to think. I have no feelings at all. There are papers to type, and then I can grab some dry clothes, maybe some coffee.

I'm lonely! And often, so empty. All things, past events, feelings, knock around inside me and are without substance. My nerves have been destroyed. I no longer feel pain, and pain is substance.

"I've only ten, maybe fifteen years at most, probably less, before I'll die, or at least become immobile, God forbid," my grandfather once said to me (he's dead now—had only five years left), and it was almost a plea, a hint of the childhood, of the selfishness he had gradually relinquished over two

193

generations. These words, remembered now, are startling. To have seen the limits, the end so clearly, so resolutely . . . and to have accepted them.

I contrast him, his words, his age, with myself, with the fury I feel because I was forced to confront similar possibilities, similar impositions of time and chance, and was unable to accept them. Because I refused to believe I could die, scared as I was, even when death was all around me in the plantation, I failed as a man. How else can I understand it? What right did they have to make me confront something my very age made me reject? Neither youthful after a while, nor yet wise or even courageous, I abandoned myself to mindless luck.

The reality of death eluded me from the first. People died in the treatment tent, bags were deposited in the morgue to be unzipped, their contents scrutinized. Short of occasional, momentary revulsion, these were simple, unemotional events. There was no connection with the death of a relative or friend as I'd known it at home, the weeping in the graveyards, the whispering hearses, flowers, flags, dark, luminous caskets, pervasive mists or mocking sun, and the meat in the rubber bags. They sent them home in hermetically sealed steel boxes, and the living smuggled dope inside the same boxes; that was the reality—the dope, the callousness, the refusal to grasp what we were confronting, had in fact created. Death in any symbolic terms, in a manner that might allow knowledge, comprehension, respect, even glory for those brave enough to die, did not present itself. No matter what we might have thought before we arrived, by the time we left, few of us were certain of what or to whom we owed our allegiance. That is one thing I still know.

Not even Sylvester's fiery annihilation affected me as it should have. Should have—I was always aware of the imperative. His death was less a testament to mortality than our good intentions.

We do suppress things, or at least I do. I'm a creature of slow ingestion, someone who enters numbness, shock, rather than madness. But I'm also a creature of reason, an autocrat: there's the heart of my madness—my life never fits the facts . . . or is it the other way around? I'm an aberration. We all are. There's no Natural Law for me, no blind acceptance of the inevitable. Morrisey taught me that as well.

But I knew the smell of death before I saw my first dead man, knew it that first day on the helicopter pad with Major

Mendez standing in the trees with Brock, the dog sleeping at his feet; the smell permeated the air. Talk about instinct; I knew in an instant where we came from, what we truly were. I just couldn't accept it, that's all. But the smell was there, the heavy scent—sweet, pervasive, oppressive, glandular . . . a secretion. It was instinctively alluring, repugnant only on reflection.

The smell was my only conception of It; that state of nonbeing that sailed in and out over the barbed wire, past the tower with its two, ever-present silhouettes, that clung to the metal and vinyl interiors of the ships with their pilots, helmeted aliens who bobbed gently to the vibrations of their bizarre machines.

Just once, during the monsoons when the afternoon clouds had piled on one another in that fantastic, vertical assault until they seemed to reach the very top of the sky, my eyes were opened for an instant, and my feelings.

I was returning from battalion headquarters with Stevens. In front of us, in front of the jeep, was a massive wall of clouds, greenish as though reflected from the earth itself; behind us the sun blazed idly in an empty sky—a pale blue void, infinite, neutral vessel, guiltless although it harbored mechanical mutants, torrents, winds, flying menace.

We rounded a bend on the outskirts of the village. The road wound up a hill, its rich, red surface growing darker in the fading light. In a few minutes it would become a sea of stinking mud.

Over the crest of the hill we roared and almost collided with a monstrous gypsylike cart. It was painted brilliant colors, and its wooden wheels, back door and steps, rounded roof were peculiar intrusions on a world I might not have known well, but whose surprises and horrors seemed reasonably predictable by that time. Stevens swung out to pass.

A small pony with huge, black blinders labored between the traces, dwarfed by the cart. A bell dinged disconsolately with the animal's strained motions while the cart rocked from side to side through the deep ruts and holes, and the massive wheels sucked the earth up into the dwindling sunlight, then crushed it, over and over.

There were no reins to the pony, no driver on the massive seat behind which leather curtains had been drawn tightly shut. The pony plodded on, its bell ringing incessantly to warn of its approach toward a destination apparently known only to itself and whoever, or whatever, was hidden within the cart.

The jeep swept along the edge of the village, churning chickens in its wake. Its engine echoed against the stone tower, that relic of colonialism with its miniscule barricade of plastic Claymore mines bristling absurdly around its base. In the distance I could see the plantation perched on its hill, the trees brilliant green in a cascade of sun pouring through the clouds.

Alarmed by the sound of that pony's bell, I looked back, horrified, certain that the mammoth cart was upon us, the pony a mass of foam and flailing hooves, the eyes dilated, rolling blind in its face. There was nothing there, nothing except a road, the rooftops of a village and a tower. Raindrops splattered against the windshield.

I took a last glance over my shoulder. The cart was about to begin its descent into the village. I shivered as sheets of rain climbed over the hood and engulfed me.

FOURTEEN

One day the water in the puddles and drainage ditches vanishes, the bright green scum along the edges turns dark; the earth, the muck, splits and cracks, and discloses its pink innards to a fiery, victorious sun.

As the last vestiges of the monsoons fade, the smell of insecticide becomes more pervasive as tank trucks rumble down the roads. Bluish chemicals billow on the dry surface, spread low into the ditches and remaining puddles, in among the trees like a ground fog or morning mist. The smell lingers day after day and becomes one with the stench of oil, blood, refuse, burning excrement.

"Why don't you come in, O'Neill?" Morrisey asks from the cooler interior of the treatment tent.

I'm leaning against the sandbag wall that surrounds the tent, my arms on the dry top, my chin on my hands. "I kind of like it out here. Seen Lucius?"

"No. I thought he was supposed to be in the sickcall tent or his ambulance when he's on duty."

"Right. A wonderful job, huh?"

"How many emergency calls have they had since Smith set up the squad?"

"Only one, and I went on that. Their specialty is ferrying patients to the PX, standing by at the range, or with the engineers. Have you seen the inside of Lucius's ambulance?"

"I heard about it."

"He's got two crosses hanging in the cab, and a huge picture of Jesus. He even draped the partition between the cab and the back with purple satin."

"That's kind of hard to believe."

"It's true. All that's missing is stained glass windows."

I hear the rear door of the treatment tent open. "Richie?" someone calls in a languorous voice. I stand on my tiptoes and look inside. Sure enough, there's Lucius, Bible in hand.

Morrisey sighs. "Yes, Lucius?"

Lucius has withdrawn a huge red and white checked handkerchief and is mopping his face. The handkerchief drops and large, kindly eyes engulf Morrisey. "Have you been saved?" Lucius starts to raise the Bible and open it, the damp handkerchief still clutched in his hand.

Morrisey's dumbfounded.

"The ways of Jesus are powerful, Richie."

"Lucius, some other time, OK?"

"There's no time like the present, Richie. There's too little time."

"Lucius," he croaks. "I don't like to talk about religion, OK?"

"I understand these things, Richie. It's difficult for many people to . . ."

Morrisey slaps the table. "Don't start that shit on me!" His fury is as startling and unexpected to me as it is to Lucius.

"You don't need to swear."

"I really don't like to talk about these things." Morrisey's trying very hard to be patient. "It's private to me. Look, I'm sorry I swore."

"Lucius!"

'Who's that?"

"O'Neill. I got a call a while ago. You got a job with the engineers down at the waterpoint."

"But it's Sunday!" he complains. He makes no effort to leave.

"Yeah, and you're on duty! I called down to the orderly room for you twenty minutes ago because you didn't tell me where you were going."

"You didn't have to do that. It's Sunday."

"Take it up with Sergeant Smith. In the meantime, you got that call."

"He doesn't believe you," Morrisey says after the door shuts.

"He acts like that whether it's Sunday, Monday, or Tuesday. And it happens to be true."

"Thanks for telling him sooner, buddy."

The ambulance belches a sudden, large cloud of black smoke. Neither Morrisey nor I move for several minutes while we listen to the distant mechanized clatter of our war in the wake of Lucius's departure. I begin to feel an edge creep into my day, a restlessness that contradicts the world sunning itself around me. The feeling remains into the evening when Jenkins, Morrisey and I go to the club.

We've been talking about Lucius, listening to Jenkins's soft laughter as the conversation drifted into childhood recollections. Now Jenkins is talking about himself, reflecting on his growing up in the South; beneath the gentle self-mockery of a man who seems to have every confidence that he's risen above these experiences, there's a sense of pain.

At the bar, Buster Wilbur announces last call, his voice rasping from too many years of heavy smoking.

Jenks starts to tell us about his first job as a child of seven, mowing the lawn for a white woman, and about his mother's careful instructions to go to the *back* door and his total incomprehension as to why he should have to do this. In the midst of his story, we gradually become aware of undercurrents of rhythm, of a song at once suggestive and intense, rolling out of the darkness into the dimly lit club.

Everyone falls silent, even Wilbur, as the strains of a revival hymn permeate the company area. Incredibly, the music sounds live. Beneath the muted undulations, we can hear thumping feet and clapping hands. A tambourine and guitar roll into one with the ponderous, exorcising beat.

We wander to the back row of tents. Here and there among the dark hulks of the tree trunks, I can see the glow of cigarettes. A small crowd has gathered at the newest tent, that built by Smith's ambulance squad, but no one ventures too near; they maintain a discreet distance as though compelled to halt by the sheer force of their incredulity.

A shout rings from the lighted tent. "Yes, Jesus!" I recognize Nye's voice, harsh, insistent, belligerent even in praise. Ewald Nye's his full name, I think, suitable for a straight-backed prick.

Morrisey moves forward and draws the rest of us along. We look in the open door. Lucius is on his knees, head bowed. Nye towers over him, his gaunt, fierce face tilted back as he scowls toward the rafters. He clutches Lucius by the head and shakes it violently.

Lucius's back starts to quiver. The music stops. "Then

199

Jesus reached into the depth and pulled me from the water . . . from the jaws of Death himself,'' he moans, his entire body shaking.

"Amen!'' Gerhard whispers fervently from a nearby bunk where he sits guitar in hand, eyes closed, face glistening in the stark, electric light.

"Oh, the Lamb! The Lamb!'' Nye shouts.

"Ohhh,'' Lucius groans and slowly rises, both hands straight up in the air. He raises one foot, then the other, then begins to move with serpentine grace around the room. The thumping begins in earnest with the first bars of "Are You Washed in the Blood of the Lamb.''

"Are all of them in there?'' someone whispers.

"Yeah, all ten of them.''

"I don't fucking believe this,'' Morrisey says.

"You don't have to!'' a voice erupts loudly from the rear. "Lucius fell asleep in his ambulance at the waterpoint this afternoon,'' Gerty continues in his usual caustic vein, "with the emergency brake off. It rolled into the water hole.''

Jenkins chuckles.

"So,'' Morrisey demands, "how did he get out?''

"Anyone can see you're a sinner from way back, Morrisey,'' Gerty cackles with self-satisfaction. A ripple of laughter from the rest of the crowd encourages him. "You don't understand these things. If you'd allowed Lucius to save you this afternoon, instead of making him chase off to the waterpoint, none of this . . .''

"How the hell did you find out about that?'' Morrisey asks.

I can feel Jenkins shaking beside me.

"O'Neill, you sonuvabitch!''

"Don't feel bad, Morrisey. Lucius isn't blaming you. If he hadn't tried to save you, God might not have reached down and lifted him from the water.''

"Knock it off, Gerty! How did he get out of that hole?''

"The engineers, how else. One of them had to dive with a chain so they could hook him up and pull him out. That dumb shit was still kneeling in the front seat, praying like a bastard, when the ambulance came out of the water. They don't think he even tried to save himself. I wouldn't have thought an ambulance would have been that watertight.''

"Yessir, the Hand of the Lamb,'' I say.

Quiet, contemptuous laughter fills the darkness. Jenks is silent, however.

Inside the tent, the occupants begin to work themselves into a frenzy. Outside, the crowd becomes noisy and scornful.

Suddenly, I know Jenkins is gone. Back by the first row of hooches I find him sitting on the steps to his tent, Morrisey beside him. I sit down and in silence we listen to the hymn and the rising cacophony of the men outside.

The words of another song riding on the underlying rhythm of the revival hymn then in progress reaches us, shouted with apparent glee:

> Jesus loves me, this I know,
> Mighty, mighty fine for Jesus!
> He will wash me white as snow,
> Dirty, dirty job for Jesus!
> I am Jesus little lamb!
> Jesus Christ, how glad I am!
> Three cheers for Jesus,
> He's a damn, fine man!

Gradually, the singing, shouting, thumping dies away, superseded by the shriek of night creatures, that surge of invisible life, that incantation to victory through endurance in numbers.

Morrisey gets up and leaves Jenkins and me on the step making idle talk. After a while, I wander off to my tent. Inside it is dark. I undress in the darkness and roll under the netting.

I've finally closed my eyes and felt the first touch of sleep when the whine of a helicopter rips the night. "Shit!" I sit up. Someone in the tent's snoring, fortunate enough to have reached the sanctuary of sleep.

I stumble into the treatment room and switch on the lights. The scene reminds me of a railway station somewhere on the prairies, a whistlestop for the Limited. The room looks raw and harsh under the naked bulbs: the wooden tables, the blue, cloth-covered pads, the stainless steel pans and trays with their carefully wrapped bundles of sterile utensils, the hooks suspended from the open rafters above each table to hold the bags of blood, the red dirt that has been ground into the rough plank floor where no broom will ever penetrate. I walk down the center aisle of the long room and feel its expectancy tug ever so gently at my skin. The back door shuts behind me, snuffs the incandesence that for an instant flooded the darkness. The night greets me with no human sounds but my own.

I thread my way between the X ray and medical supply tents, curse once when I trip on the boardwalk. At last a dull glow from the depths of the communications bunker emerges from the gloom. I pause at the bottom of the ramp. Dunn's in his lawn chair with the earphones on. Morrisey, leaning against the table beside him, thumbs through a skin magazine. "What's happening?"

Dunn looks up with the arrogant appraisal with which he rewards any intruder below the rank of sergeant. His tone is equally uncivil, if melodramatic. "I don't know for sure," he says. "I think an armored unit's been ambushed, but you can't tell shit there's so much bellowing over the fucking air." He cups his earphones to his head. "And there's some other ship out there along with Major Hargos—it was there first. I don't know where it came from or what it is."

I sit down on one of the bunks to wait. I remember the time that Dunn shook the litter and Morrisey's response, and feel a keen sense of pleasure. My attention shifts to the wall behind the radios. The raunchier of the pinups have been removed on account of a recent inspection. Knowing Smith's present attitude, I'm sure they'll never go back up. Dunn doesn't have the guts to contradict Smith, mar his structural monument. Gittoni simply wouldn't give a damn.

My gaze rests on a glossy black and white photograph of a lanky brunette in a bikini, the only photo of a clothed woman. The picture has been relegated to the bottom layer of the display and is partially covered by more recent and explicit additions. A corner of the picture bears the inscription, "Love, Toni." I remember when she was selected by the military or some official body for promotion as the American dream girl for the boys in Vietnam. If she didn't catch on as a latter-day Veronica Lake or Marilyn Monroe, it wasn't her fault. She was overwhelmed by sheer numbers, rejected in favor of the countless women who displayed most or all their wares in the slicks at the PX newsstands and in the really hard-core photos available from the gooks. I recently saw an offer for twenty "all pose" shots of Toni in the back of one of the magazines. She's taken it all off and now is simply one more photographed hole. So much for a vision of clean, wholesome American girls—that special woman. You've got to believe it to want it, and nothing's special anymore—particularly not us. I suppose even the wogs are preferable to photographs.

There's too much clap around. A lot of it seems to be resistant to our drugs. I don't need that kind of permanent legacy.

A beetle swaggers out from beneath the radio table and disappears through a crack under Dunn's chair.

"Forty litterbearers!"

I don't understand—it can't be. We don't *have* forty litterbearers. Dunn yanks his earphones off and turns around. "Didn't you hear me? Forty litterbearers, goddammit!"

The radio crackles. A fluttering voice breaks in on our stunned silence.

"Morrisey!" Dunn hollers. "They're five minutes out!"

We run all the way: first to the officers' tents. We clatter through bamboo curtains, shine our lights at white faces behind hands, wait for murmured replies and hurry on.

My chest begins to hurt. I can hear Morrisey crash through the trees near by, can hear my blood pound. We stop at the top of the three rows of tents in the company area and holler. Our cry is met with silence. "Fuck this!" Morrisey exclaims, and plunges into the nearest tent and starts shouting. He yanks the light chains and bursts out the far door, leaving turmoil inside the tent. No one believes us.

"You're full of shit, O'Neill!" Gerty screams. "How are we gonna carry forty litters? How's any helicopter . . ." The door slams behind me. Morrisey grabs me by the shoulder.

"We're short!" he pants.

"Jesus . . ." is all I can say.

"C'mon, O'Neill!" He runs across the yard and up the steps of the NCO hooch.

"Hey, Morrisey!"

The door slams. "Forty litterbearers!" he hollers. I can hear him thumping down the hall, banging on the partitions of each room with the butt of a flashlight. "Outta the rack! C'mon! Let's move!"

"Goddammit, whaddaya doing in here?"

"Hey, you, Morrisey! We don't carry litters!"

"We haven't got enough men, Sarge! Let's go!"

Milliken scrabbles through a bamboo curtain right in front of me. "What the fuck?" I swing my light on him. "Turn that fucking thing off!"

I grin deliriously. "We're not kidding, Sarge!"

"They're due now!" Morrisey roars. His light bounces up and down the hall, catches white-faced rage and bewilderment. Lights pop on in the rooms. Smith runs down the hall yanking on his pants.

"This better be for real, Morrisey."

But he's gone, vanished out the side door. I turn, too, plunge down the stairs, in among the trees. All around me are sounds of running men.

Two brilliant beams of light sweep the trees, flick across the sickcall tent, the litter racks, on out across the road, the coarse grass, the landing pad, swing on around toward the berm where they emblaze the guard tower on the perimeter. I'm struck by a thundering blast of wind as I dash toward the dim outlines of a Chinook. It settles to the earth like a giant mantis; the lights die, fade from white to an orangeish rust, to darkness.

The crewchief, covered with grease and blood, stands at the cockpit end of the ship and stares at us as we pour up the ramp. As he guards the steps to the pilots, the two men who will get him out of this hell, his haughty, almost menacing air scarcely disguises a profound and bitter amazement. The wounded and dying are not supposed to be his cargo. Bodies, yes, but in discreet rubber bags.

The sweet, heavy odor of cooked flesh permeates the ship. Only two men are on stretchers, two blackened hulls on makeshift blanket and pole devices. I'm thinking, these two guys are drivers, they've got to be drivers of armored personnel carriers because they have no legs.

All around me, people kneel, lift agonized creatures, kick litters open, shout, and even cry. Lucius is immobilized by the sight of the scorched drivers. I yell, "Lucius! Help me lift this guy!" but he doesn't answer, doesn't move. His gaze remains fixed on those clear blue eyes peering through a black, blistered mask.

"Lucius!" I've knelt beside the driver, placed my stretcher beside the useless makeshift one. "God damn, you! Help me!"

Sweat pops out on Lucius's face as he kneels to help me transfer the dying man. We weave through the churning mass toward the door and the relative coolness, sanctuary of the dark.

Then it's four hours later, maybe an hour before daybreak, maybe less. I'm in the door of the treatment tent watching the revolving light of the last medivac ship as it disappears beyond the plantation, heads south with its load for an evacuation hospital. Not one of the almost fifty men on that Chinook remains.

Behind me, doors slam on the truck from Graves Registration, a leaden sound. There were five bodies in the morgue, eight more still at the NDP, but no one's going back out there tonight just to pick up rubber bags.

The Chinook is a memory now, an assault of sound and smell, of fantastic visions of blood, torn flesh, eyes—huge watery eyes, and insect motion. Brock, Howard, Shelby—they're all in the room behind me. Only the lifers have vanished, that infuriated, appalled group of awkward men, fled back to the desecrated sanctity of their rooms, to the shambles of Morrisey's wild, gleeful attack on privilege. I loved him for it.

The door creaks and Brock appears, wiping his hands with a towel, his T-shirt drenched with sweat. "That's it?"

"That's it."

"That's the worst I've ever seen."

When everyone's gone, when that room is once again what it was a few hours ago, a harshly lighted, empty station, when my eyes have roamed that place and assured me that everything's orderly and neat again, I turn the switch and banish the room and myself to the anonymity of night once more. My eyes still flare from the lights as I grope toward the motor pool. My hand touches cool steel. Lumps of mud fall away beneath the ambulance whose shape I only imagine.

" . . . then be risen with Christ, seek those things which are above . . ." The voice sounds muffled. "Set your affections on things above, not on things on the earth. For ye are dead . . ."

I yank the door open. The metal screeches. Chunks of dry dirt thud at my feet. The interior of the cab reeks of mildew, dingy water, and something acrid I can't identify. "Lucius, is that you?"

"Mortify therefore your members which are upon the earth: fornication, uncleanness, inordinate affection, evil concupiscence . . ."

"Hey, man! What are you doing?"

"For which thing's sake the wrath of God cometh on the children of disobedience."

My hand finds a sleeve. The cloth is soggy from work and

fear, the odor putrid. "C'mon, Lucius. Let's go to bed. We've had a hard day." I shake him gently and try to pull him from the cab.

He yanks free. "I'm reading! 'Where there is neither Greek nor Jew, circumcision nor uncircumcision, Barbarian, Scythian . . .' "

I reach into the darkness again, into that palpable, moist, human smell and clasp the arm more firmly. "C'mon, Lucius!"

" 'And all that dwell upon the earth shall worship Him, Whose names are not written in the book of life of the Lamb slain . . .' "

"Lucius, let's go to the hooch."

Slowly, his bulk begins to yield. I feel him stumble from the cab; something hard strikes my chest. It's a book, his Bible I assume. He stands, half-leaning against me; I feel his heat. He's breathing hard. My left hand finds his face, the skin hot and wet from crying, and he feels soft and pliant like something made of dough.

"I lost my place," he says. Hearing the flick of the pages, I suppress tears, the first I've known in so long. We're all cracking.

We begin to tread our way among the dim shadows of vehicles and oil barrels, then the rubber trees, toward Jenkins's tent.

FIFTEEN

Through Murphy, who had been conducting an unofficial courier service as far north as Cam Ranh Bay, Brock obtains several blue films to celebrate the grand opening of Smith's patient-officer bunker. We sit on the treatment tables, on the floor, in lawn chairs, down in the cavernous depths of this gleaming monument with its stainless steel cabinets, pristine blue paint, linoleum floor. The bunker's jammed with patients, Dust-Off personnel, our own men. The heat's already insufferable.

Brock hovers over the ancient projector, nurses it and the film, for the machine is also part of Murphy's service. Thick blue smoke from his cigar pours through the shaft of light that splits the bunker.

The films are silent, crudely made, but as someone mutters, at least the actors aren't gooks. The opening scene of the first film, *Naked Phantom*, shows a naked woman sitting on a couch in the middle of an otherwise empty room. Her legs are spread, the spike heels she's wearing point at the audience. She's playing with herself.

Suddenly a man in a black eye mask peeps stealthily through a crack in the door. A huge grin appears on his face when he spies the woman. He lifts his hands before his face and wiggles his fingers in anticipation. We roar with laughter.

With high, exaggerated steps, the man steals into the room, up behind the couch where the woman is masturbating furiously, oblivious of his presence. The man, already naked and still sporting a smile, flops a gigantic erection onto the back of the couch, next to the woman's head.

"Take it in the ear, lady!" someone shouts. The room erupts with laughter again, but this time there's an edge to it, a release of tension. That tension included me. I laugh at the catcalls and jibes, delighted with the relief they provide, but I'm also fascinated. Right in front of me, someone like myself, a human, is performing all kinds of sexual acts that I would love to perform—the film is like a reflection. I want to watch myself in a mirror, see myself do those things: the camera's letting me.

Thousands and thousands of frames later, still packed in the bunker, we watch without distinction or memory as bodies move, jiggle, bang together; white skin and enflamed sexual members contrast with dark hair, dark eyes, shoes—always spike heels—a wristwatch. But before the last film is over, my fascination and excitement die. I feel utterly desolate among sweaty, hot bodies like my own. Maybe it's this place, maybe the war, but I know that person on the screen is truly me, as much as it's anyone else, everyone else. I know I can act like that, any fool can.

"I left when they got to the donkeys," Morrisey says later. "That's all I could take. I was lucky to be at the back of the room."

I'm relieved to know someone else felt that way, but I'll never be able to tell him.

For if we were alone, isolated within ourselves, events isolated all of us. The pressure on someone like Morrisey who was very private by nature, must have been unbearable. At least my pride didn't run to that indomitable refusal to unburden myself on someone else and most of us made fragile attempts to establish communication. There was one topic we avoided, one that defied comprehension and comment and was at the center of all of our lives. It crippled the tentative gestures we made to each other with a sense of utter futility. Finally, all we could do was hope for a time and place where we could share anything, including the war; in our desperate fantasies, this is what home became. In the meantime, there were always the company dogs, the quiet, vague, one-sided conversations and the affection in return.

Major Mendez understood all of that. While minimizing as much as possible the peculiar harshness of our noncombat involvement, he, paradoxically, encouraged a closeness, a tacit recognition of the shared, if unspoken, problems. That understanding, that respect, disappeared when he left us.

208

I believe Morrisey was in more danger than the rest of us right from the beginning. I can imagine him being incredibly intimate friends with a woman, a good looking, intelligent woman ten or twelve years older than himself; he'd be impatient with those his own age. I would also expect such an affair to be impossibly torrid and pained. The pain is a certainty. Pain is what he conveyed by his very presence. Love would happen to him in a manner the rest of us could scarcely conceive, much less hope for. Yet, with the possible exception of Jenkins, and maybe Brock, I don't believe he was capable of deep male friendship. I don't think he'd ever known it. If Brock hadn't been an officer, or Morrisey an enlisted man, they might have become close. They thought so much alike—their attitudes seemed almost identical. If Morrisey had an extraordinary ability to say what was true despite the risk, to do what we all wished at one time or other we had the guts to do, it made him less real to us. He served a key function within the company, but he received little support from any of us; you can't make friends with someone who always made you feel your weaknesses.

His abstention from drugs was a perfect example: he was afraid of them, of the easy, chemically induced release of tension. He was afraid of the effects of something he could not do himself, or at least control. He turned his fear into a virtue—he was going to make himself survive. He was an anachronism, a relic from the days when men dug an acre of rocks for an acre of corn, forged separate covenants between themselves and God. I couldn't tell him then (because I didn't know—he would have to teach me) that this is a world for the malleable.

Several people hated him. They thought he was "stuck up," a phrase with peculiarly feminine and petulant overtones. They couldn't see he was a victim like the rest of us—he wouldn't show them. The drugs became a sore point.

For a long time, the only nonmedical stuff that I knew about was "Cambodia red." It was wonderful—a couple of good hits was all that was necessary. We bought it by the pound at the laterite pits. If we were lucky enough to avoid evening work details, or the other forms of harassment, we went to someone's hooch and smoked and listened to records —almost everyone did. The club was no longer a haven. After a while, Newell was always stoned. Some of the men routinely researched the Physician's Desk Reference *(located conveniently in my office) for counterindications suitable for new highs.*

One clue was the noise level. Within a month of Howard's arrival, the company had grown very quiet after supper, except for the sound of stereos. Maybe the lifers saw this as a sign of progress, renewed order, but it was really alien, nonhuman, unlike the old days when Navarra ran the club. Now the lifers would be down there listening to shit-kicking music and wondering why the revenues were so low. The only time we went there was in the late afternoon, or very early evening, before Annie was taken home.

It wasn't always easy doing litters stoned. Now and then, one of us would get pissed off. Also, sometimes if you were toting litters stoned, it could suddenly become real upsetting. It had a lot to do with your state of mind when you got high.

Owen was smoking a lot, too. He and Newell tried not to get blown away on the same night unless they made sure that Morrisey would cover for them so they wouldn't have to suture or do things like that. Morrisey didn't seem to mind, which upset some people, too. They thought it was hypocritical.

If you weren't stoned, what else was there to do? We still had a basketball team, but it was an obsession with those guys. Every nonworking moment, it seemed, they were practicing. They got so damn good, none of us could play with them anymore, so they set out to beat all the other teams in the plantation. They got so good, it became ridiculous— they didn't belong anywhere, least of all there. It's all they talked about, too. Major subjects of conversation: basketball and getting stoned. Safe.

One night we saw The Yellow Submarine. *We knew it was coming for almost two weeks, and we never got as hyped about another film. The majority of us, including the patients, were wiped out for the occasion. I remember laughing a lot. Next day, Morrisey said he thought it was boring, the animation crude, the storyline juvenile. What else could you expect from him? He could be an inflexible asshole.*

It was easy not to worry about anything except being sent to the field and the lifers finding your stash. They couldn't do anything to us unless they had the goods, and Anderson always warned us of impending raids. I remember a first sergeant coming into the treatment room one night with some poor company clerk who was tripping on acid. It had to be acid although I was surprised; it was the first I'd encountered in the plantation. God knows where he found it. His Top wanted us to verify medically that he was on drugs, do a blood test or something, so he could be court-martialed. Brock told him it couldn't be done. I know that first sergeant went out of there convinced it was a fucking conspiracy of drug addicts (Brock included. Good thing Shelby wasn't on duty.) All the lifers hated us, the insolent medical corps. They couldn't fuck with us because we had all the medicine, bandages, and knowledge. It was a draw between us and the MPs.

Shit-kicking music . . . Jesus, it was about that time division decided to perk up morale with a strip show down at the plantation's NCO-EM club, the same club where Morrisey and Newell spent their afternoons during the language school. A few local girls were hired to take it all off. Someone told me about it later: said there were almost a thousand GIs in the bleachers set up in the front yard facing the veranda. The girls had been stripping to country western music, probably the preference of some lifer at headquarters. When the third girl started her routine, somebody shouted, "Give us pussies with hair!"

A black guy up in the bleachers yelled back, "Give us anything besides this Texas shit music!"

From a silence in which the breeze sounded like a gale, a voice rang out, "What you calling shit, boy?"

We sewed up almost forty people before the night was over —they kept trickling in, trying to avoid the MPs. It was our first big riot in the plantation. There had been little incidents before, a lot of bad feeling about things like the blacks' domination of the jukebox at the club—you couldn't get close to it unless you could blend with that wall of eyeballs surrounding it. For a long time, a lot of white soldiers didn't say anything, afraid of being branded as prejudiced.

(Someone else said that the brawl was a hell of an improvement over a bunch of slope strippers you couldn't even get close enough to fuck. I had to laugh at that one.)

I'm sorry Casey wanted to do dope tonight. I didn't mean to blow. I just didn't want it—I haven't smoked in almost three months. Jesus, but I did a lot of it then!

Buelen shuffles his feet, shakes his shoulders up and down, and blows the whistle. "Let's dress it up, dress it up!"

There are two lines in the formation. Morrisey yawns beside me, straightens his cap with his free hand.

"Attention!"

The two lines shuffle a bit, then assume a stance of relative rigidity. Sergeant Smith moves forward, up beside Buelen. He starts reading the roll, but stops when Stevens answers with "Yo!"

"Stevens?" he repeats, very patiently.

"Here, Sergeant."

Smith completes the roll call and steps back. Buelen glances swiftly from left to right and glares at someone in the front row. "At ease! Stevens, why are you wearing sunglasses? Sun hurt your eyes?"

Stevens is in the shade with the morning sun at his back.

Smith, holding his clipboard, looks spiffy. He seems to be putting on weight. Big-boned to begin with, he looks sleeker somehow. I believe he's even beginning to tan, the awful whiteness is fading brown. He gazes at Stevens with apparent calm.

"It's the heat, Top. Sunglasses keep me cool." Laughter ripples through the formation.

"Maybe a little time in Long Binh Jail will cool you off! Maybe you want to talk to the CO."

"Don't know what you're talking about, Top."

"Sure, Stevens. You'd best watch yourself, you and those other addicts. Why don't you just take those sunglasses off?"

"Nothing in the ARs about it, First Sergeant."

"What's that around your neck?"

"Beads."

"Yeah? Where are your dogtags?"

"They're here, too, Sarge." Stevens pulls the front of his shirt out and looks down inside. No one moves.

"I wanta see' em, Stevens."

Stevens yanks something out. A splash of chrome glints in the sun, then tumbles down the front of his shirt. I've seen it before: no dogtags flash like that. It's a miniature hand with the middle finger raised. "Whooops . . . !" Stevens fumbles madly inside his shirt and pulls out something else. I hear dogtags jangle.

Smith has just read the morning duty roster. Buelen starts to mumble some announcements. "Per order of the commanding officer, there will be no reading by personnel while at their duty stations or during duty hours at all." Buelen looks up over the tops of his too-small glasses and scans the formation. "That understood?"

Sure we understand it—most of us do. There's only one person, really, for whom that order was created.

Smith steps forward. Slowly, he appraises us. "It really looks bad when someone comes for treatment and finds the medical personnel lounging around reading. You have plenty of time for that in the evenings, after duty hours. You can look alive when you're on duty. There are always little chores to be done, picking up the work area, policing the yard, something like that. And if you can't find enough to do, we'll be happy to find it for you. I'll tell you now, and Captain Howard feels this very keenly, we're going to be paying a lot closer attention to the neatness of work areas. That's all I have, First Sergeant."

Buelen starts to dismiss us when Smith interrupts.

"O'Neill. The CO wants to see you in the orderly room after formation."

"I don't like problems, O'Neill," Howard says. "A good commander shouldn't have this kind of problem to deal with. A well-run, well-disciplined unit should almost take care of itself."

"Yes, sir."

"Sergeant Smith has spoken very highly of you, of your work. I'll tell you, he was more than just a little surprised at this."

At what? I can't imagine what I've done.

"And I have had no major problems with you, and I don't want any to begin now."

"What's this all about, sir?"

"What do you mean, 'What's this all about?' "

"What have I done, sir?"

"You haven't written home in two months! That's what you've done, or not done . . . this is what you've done!" He reaches over and snatches a piece of paper off the top of a pile that has been stacked and squared on his desk. "A letter from your parents wanting to know if something's happened to you!"

"Nothing's happened to me, sir."

"Don't be flip, soldier! Obviously nothing's happened to you, so why haven't you written?" He puts the letter back on the stack and aligns it with the pile with an index finger and thumb. The motion is surprisingly delicate.

What can I tell him? That I didn't have the time? I was too busy? He would love that, I bet, love the vindication. I get the feeling he loves a bad lie. Tell him the truth? That would be worse because it would be consigned automatically, and with a vengeance, to the former category. He would wonder what makes me think I'm suffering. And I have no answer for that.

"Look at me, soldier! I have more important things to do than let you waste my time while you daydream."

"Yes, sir. No explanation, sir. I guess I just haven't gotten around to it."

The contempt fades. His attention returns to the paper in his hand, the one he was reading when I entered. "I get another letter like that, and you get disciplinary action. Now go and write home, now! I want you back here in thirty minutes with a sealed, addressed envelope."

"Yes, sir." I come to attention and salute, but he doesn't look up.

I don't call you, you call me. You write me, but don't expect me to answer. Don't expect anything of me anymore. What was it Morrisey said he told his parents? Something like, if you don't hear, don't worry—it's a good sign. You'll hear if something happens.

The letter was brief: "I'm sorry," I wrote. "It's very hard to say anything sometimes. The only thing that has really happened to me is your letter to the CO. Please don't do that again. Please write—I appreciate your letters. I will write when I can. Please don't worry."

And why did I have to lie? I had half a dozen of their letters on the shelf of my locker—and maybe two of them had been opened, and maybe I had read half of what was written in those two. (And I left them all behind to rot, a huge stack of them.) They were chatty testaments of someone's love and they made me feel terrible. They still do. I didn't feel worthy, and not writing made me feel worse, but also free.

There's no logical reason why I couldn't have written. I would have felt miserable if the letters had stopped coming, even if, automatically by then, I shoved them on that shelf and tried to forget them. I always lined up at the orderly room with that gut expectancy and received another one.

Not that there wasn't plenty of other potential misery to come from that confrontation with Howard. The same way the key phrase in my letter home was, "Please don't do that again." Howard's key phrase was "disciplinary action." Maybe my imagination was wild, but that string of words terrified me . . . and probably always will. The longer I've been in the army, the worse it has become. And it isn't simply visualizing the worst of what might happen to me, but the fear that if I once let go and let my feelings out, I won't be able to stop until the worst they can do to me will be happening because I was able to imagine it too vividly at the beginning. One-way hysteria you might call it, and the military certainly knows how to take care of that.

I saw my first stockade during the fifth day of my induction. We were being bussed from the reception center to our basic training company. A black DI with a Smokey hat yanked down to his moustache was draped between the posts at the head of the aisle, and no one was saying shit. I was staring out the window when I saw the big sign over the gate of the post stockade: "Obedience to the Law is Freedom." No! I thought, that's fear, the beginning of hysteria. Right then I thought that, and then, "Arbeit Macht Frei." I thought that, too!

Behind the double wire fences with their steel posts were barracks and wooden guard towers. The towers were wooden boxes on top of trussed legs and their roofs sloped shedlike in one direction. There were searchlights in the towers, and multipaned windows. Everything was painted mustard yellow and faded.

When we pulled off the street and roared between two-storey barracks identical to those in the stockade, the feeling of oppression became almost unbearable. No matter what, I believe that was the most awful moment I'll spend in the Army. From time to time in the following weeks, they made threats about the stockade, but they didn't need to.

And LBJ—Long Binh Jail—was even worse. It squatted near the four lane blacktop in Long Binh, within range of traffic and life. A jewel in its own right, constructed not of wire and steel posts, but of sandbags piled twenty feet high, maybe higher, and God knows how deep, forming impenetrable walls that were capped with barbed wire and guard towers—a true, sunblasted monument.

As Brown, one of our mechanics in the motorpool, said,

"The guards have shotguns and real machineguns. It's like a prison: I wasn't expecting that."

I am the stenographer at Brown's court-martial. I'm embarrassed because I'm curious, and also because the entire proceeding's a joke. And I find myself thinking, this wouldn't be happening if Mendez were here! I'm a requirement, not a functioning necessity. It's apparent from the beginning that no one except Brown gives a damn what I write down. Brown asked Smith for me, for my services because I'm in A&D, I can type, and I've always given him a few minutes whenever he's wandered by. He's worried about his rights. He wants a clear, legible, typewritten record.

I like Brown, the little I've seen of him. He's a wiseass sometimes, but he's honest and speaks his mind. I always know where I stand with him. I felt sorry when he went nuts one night, got a little drunk, and emptied his M–16 into the air between the third and fourth row of tents. No one was hurt except the lifers who were scared out of their wits. They immediately collected all the M–16s in the company and locked them in the supply tent. The lifers have a very elaborate plan for our defense in case of emergencies, but Brown threw this very fundamental kink in it: we no longer possess our rifles.

The MPs came and took Brown. It was dark and all the NCOs were jumpy. Brown was very quiet by then, probably feeling like a damn fool. He's from somewhere in the Arkansas–Texas area.

The NCOs, weapons clinking, nervously searched the darkness with their flashlights; the beams seized each flash of a lighter or a match. Just about everyone in the company was standing around among the rubber trees, or sitting on the bunkers and steps of the tents, smoking and watching. Jenkins asked Buelen if he could talk to Brown, but both Buelen and Smith refused. They're afraid of Jenkins, of any doctoring of the head: *psychology.*

"All right you men! All of you back to your hooches!" Milliken bellowed. Nobody moved. *Mendez wouldn't have allowed any of that, either.*

The MPs arrived in a jeep. We caught a glimpse of blue helmets and white stripes behind the glare of the headlights. Buelen mumbled to one of them for a long time; the MP nodded occasionally in response but never spoke. I couldn't see their faces. All I could see was a flash of something silver, like glasses, hanging from the breast pocket of one of them. The jeep went off with Brown.

Brown was very subdued when he returned four days later for his court-martial. He went about his duties in the company under the direct supervision of Buelen and didn't speak to anyone—but he never did talk much. Two hours before the courtmartial, Smith came into the A&D office and asked me to be Brown's stenographer. Jerk that I am, I couldn't refuse.

We rode together in a jeep over to division headquarters and went into a little wooden building that contained a long table on a low platform against one wall, some chairs behind the table, a couple of flags on either side, four chairs at floor level facing the platform, and a small table for me.

The officers act as though I'm not here, but Brown wants me here. It's nothing he says so much as the way he's acting. He has a lawyer from the base JAG office, a captain who seems singularly unconcerned. The proceedings are monotonous. I can't write fast enough to put down everything, or even a fraction of it, and I don't know what I should be putting down, or what I should do with it. No one has told me anything and they don't even seem to be saying anything of importance.

In thirty minutes it's all over and Brown's going back to LBJ. He's a private now. There are no other members of our company present, not even Buelen or Smith who pressed charges. Brown tells me to beat it when the trial is over, but I sit down on a bench outside the building and wait with him and his guard for the rest of his escort.

"It's an awful place," he says in that flat, nasal voice of his. His face is badly acne-scarred and his cheekbones protrude garishly. "I'd be afraid of dying there. It's a nigger pen."

I remain silent.

"They're all niggers, most of them . . ." Brown and Jenkins get along. I think about this. Jenkins must know how Brown feels, but maybe he knows something else.

"Guards, too?"

"Nah. They're like me, man, only stupid as shit. Hell, they probably come from the same town, and I guess I ain't so smart after all. I'm just a white nigger to them."

"What's it like in there?"

"They put me in a CONNEX them four days."

I'm incredulous. I think of our one CONNEX, the mysterious, square steel box next to the morgue that I've never seen opened.

"Nah, it's true," he says, reading the question in my eyes. "They put barred doors on them, some slits, and put them down in this long ditch so they face each other, tops just level with the ground. I want to piss, I got to be nice: just about got to beg them guards. Got a cot and a blanket in it—that's all." He laughs, without humor. "Scared shitless when I hit that gate, man. Whoooo, boy."

He has torn up a piece of paper and rolled the bits into tiny balls that he now catapults aimlessly with a finger and thumb. "When I first got there, made me take off all my clothes. Guy tells me when you're there full time, they give you all the thorazine you want. All you want. I'm gonna need me all I can get, I suppose. Lot of feeling in that place. Guy says the niggers are always talking about "rabbit soup"— that's "white rabbit soup." If you're white, you're afraid to go to sleep and all that shit."

He is saying this matter-of-factly. I can see him forty or fifty years from now sitting on a bench somewhere, squinting into the sun, his face sunbrowned, crinkled and cracked: unflappable, the scars too deep.

A jeep careens around the corner. Johnny Mirrors is riding shotgun. So he hasn't gone home! Why should I feel surprised? A guy like that would be comfortable anywhere. As always, with those mirrored glasses on, I can't tell where he's looking: he seems to be looking everywhere at once. Brown shuffles to his feet, then stands erect, waiting for them to come to him. "Thanks, buddy."

"I didn't do anything!" I feel terrible.

They cuff him, and with a soft push, start him toward the vehicle.

It's just a helicopter out there on the pad, idling, contributing to a sense of isolation and unreality. Suddenly, two men burst out of its turbulence with a litter between them. A short woman with a flat, stricken face, fluttering blouse and pants, runs along beside. One of her hands fights the strands of hair that whip into her eyes, the other clutches the side of the litter. On the litter is a mound of yellow and black silk, black hair, and a single, clawlike hand swinging over the edge.

The girl is rent from her shattered forehead to her vulva; the yellow and black clothing, only partially intact, forms webbed, silken strands across the jagged flesh. I look at her genitals, at a few black hairs that curl among the blood like snakes rising from the smooth, barren flesh of her youth, and again at that scarlet gorge that streaks away to the partially opened, unfocused eyes; the whites roll upward. She gurgles. Bright blood bulges between her ruined lips and down her chin.

Brock, pale, more ruffled than usual, presses two fingers to her throat under the questioning gaze of her mother, then reaches down and jerks the blankets up over the head in a reluctant, haphazard manner. He looks at Howard who has displayed a curious impatience, almost anger, since the arrival of the girl, as though what has happened was not only to be expected, assumed, but was especially annoying in its embarrassing implications.

Hargos has left his copilot and idling machine to come in and witness what should be the conclusion. The rest of us wait for the inevitable, deserved intrusion of grief—an occurrence rare and alien, dreaded because it's a reminder of the pain we so carefully shun.

And then it happens: the shriek, the awaited realization.

"What do you normally do with civilian bodies?" Howard demands, looking at no one as he vents his impatience, the verification of events as he anticipated them. The now hysterical woman stands a foot or two away from the table, arms by her sides, not daring, it seems, to approach her child.

"Well?"

"Sergeant Thieu's on the way, sir. It takes him a while," I reply in a hoarse voice. There are red and blue appliqued flowers, small ones, on the cuff of the girl's shirt, an extraordinary touch of ornamentation. Moments ago, I discovered myself unconsciously rubbing them between my thumb and index finger.

"Well, do something with her, dammit! Get her outside, do anything—she's driving me batty!"

Owen retreats to the cabinet and starts to clean up. This leaves Newell closest to the mother, the once meticulous, if grumpy Newell whose eyes seem bloodshot much of the time now, who's given to spells of such intense lassitude that he's virtually unable to function. The woman begins to hyperventilate. Newell fumbles in her direction, places his oversized hands on her shoulders and turns her to face him. Her hysteria subsides into sobs and she buries her face in her hands. Newell keeps holding her, almost at arm's length, in his rigid, tentative way.

I'm angry with myself, angry because I resented her shrieks and because Newell did what he did, what we all should have done.

Hargos steps forward and assaults Howard in furious tones. "You know, goddammit Grisholm, she was struck by the blade of an earthmover? You know that?"

"Yes, Major."

"That sonuvabitch had to be doing at least forty miles per hour. He just didn't want to move two feet for her! She was walking with her mother on Highway 10, holding her hand! How does that grab you?"

Howard doesn't answer.

"Well, I'm telling you something! That vehicle and that driver are right up the road at the engineers. You'd better do something about it!" I've never seen Hargos angry before, much less shaking. "What are you going to do about it?"

Howard starts to regain control, his natural appearance of disdain. "I'm in command here, Major Hargos."

"You bet your ass, Captain Howard!" Hargos turns and storms out of the tent. Through the screen, I watch him walk toward his helicopter, the helmet swings jauntily in his hand, but there's a pronounced sag to his shoulders.

"I'll call the engineers for you, Grisholm," Brock says, and goes to commo to make the call directly.

Somewhere down the road I hear the gnatlike sound of Thieu's motorbike. Moments after Thieu arrives, a blue pickup truck from Pacific Architects and Engineers rattles into the grove. The driver's an American, a chubby man with bright red skin. He climbs down and approaches Howard in the doorway of the tent. Thieu's inside with the mother and the body. There's been an unnatural silence since he came. I feel as though I'm dreaming, observing through a wall of glass.

I scarcely notice the second man in the truck until he passes in front of me, pushes around Howard into the treatment room. This man is Vietnamese. He's young, and like the driver of the truck, is wearing neat slacks and a clean white shirt with an assortment of pens and pencils in a plastic case in the pocket.

"Who's that?" Howard snaps.

"The girl's brother," the American from P.A.&E. says just as Smith walks around the corner of the tent and spots him.

"Lester!"

"Mel?"

They shake hands and move away toward the ward where their conversation becomes quite animated, even jovial.

"What the hell do you do in a case like this?" Brock mutters when he returns from commo. Surely he doesn't expect an answer.

"I wish there was something I *could* do," Howard ventures.

"Well, if it's any help, the engineers had a rig answering the description between here and the laterite pits a while ago. They're sending the driver down with a Lieutenant Cornish."

At this moment, the door squeaks and the woman appears. With an arm around her shoulder, her son escorts her slowly to the edge of the porch. Thieu's holding the door, not looking at anything it seems. They step to the ground. The son, his face inscrutable, looks toward his companion from P.A.&E.. The American catches the glance and brings his conversation with Smith to a halt.

"Is there anything I can do, Nguyen?" he asks, his voice sharp and unreal, too loud. He makes no movement toward the Vietnamese, merely turns his head.

The Vietnamese ignores the question and whispers to his mother as he guides her to the bench.

The American blinks, then resumes his chat with Smith in a lower, more respectful tone. His perfunctory manner conveys a sense, even belief in the inevitability of what's occurred. Why haven't I been able to achieve that?

Thieu stands to my left, watches with the rest of us. He deliberately walked past Howard and came over beside me. I felt that deliberateness, and I'm feeling his anguish now. "Where Morrisey?" he whispers.

"He's off. He was on duty for the last twenty-four hours."

Thieu nods. The jungle hat with its brim curled on two sides like a cowboy's, the creased fatigues with the Bausch and Lomb sunglasses dangling from the left pocket, the tight pants—all of which normally conspire to make him look ludicrous, too young for any war—can't hide the bleakness I see now, and an inescapable sense of his real age.

Lieutenant Cornish is in his early twenties, deeply tanned and scrawny. The driver of the earthmover is a large, equally tanned soldier of perhaps eighteen or nineteen. The two of them are beside their jeep, conferring with Howard. The driver, sweating fiercely, follows Howard's every motion, nods in agreement at almost every word, and suggests by his fervent gestures an eagerness to convey absolute innocence. Lieutenant Cornish stares at us with the unimpassioned, weathered eyes of a person accustomed to long hours in the sun.

Howard puts his hands on his hips and confronts the driver again, confronts a shaking head. Our commander scratches his head, then turns abruptly.

The brother of the dead girl watches the lieutenant and the driver climb back in the jeep and speed away. As Howard approaches, the eyes of the Vietnamese challenge him, but he passes by without a glance and walks over to the American civilian. I see the anger rise in the brother's face; gradually he becomes unaware of his mother, of his hand on her quivering shoulders, of anything but Howard talking to his employer.

The man from P.A.& E. excuses himself. He draws near, reaches out and places a thick hand on a sharp, hard shoulder. "Nguyen."

The hand is shaken off.

The American looks at the mother for a moment, then begins to speak rapidly in Vietnamese. The brother's response is instantaneous, a question, judging by the tone and his employer's response. The American shrugs.

The brother turns his back and buries his face in his hands. Later, when he turns again to us, his face is tearless, his pain unassailable.

"We just made another enemy," I whisper, sensing Brock next to me.

"And he's going to be a lot worse than most," is the reply.

"What the hell could I do, Brock? The driver denied everything," Howard protests as the pickup truck with its three occupants disappears.

Shelby's turned up in shorts and sandals. He watches the conversation, as is his custom; his eyes move from person to person with a convulsive intensity all their own. He's been sunning himself, baking his thin, wired body; he reeks of suntan lotion.

Brock doesn't answer.

"Well, what about the girl?" Howard asks.

"Graves is coming to get the body, sir," I reply. "Thieu's made arrangements from there."

Howard glances ruefully at Thieu, then walks away. He's not obese, but misshapen, clumsy.

SIXTEEN

Kostek lives in front of fans. He is always smoking dope or guzzling beer, ensconced in a lawn chair like a pasha while two fans blow on him. He sweats like a pig. Despite a ready, if sarcastic smile, something about his deportment and his cynicism commands respect: he is a person of incredible cunning.

He arrived in the ambulance that took Davies to the airstrip. One minute, Davies—skinny, a bit gawky in clean fatigues and new cap, pathetic after all—was hefting his huge new Samsonite suitcase into the back of the ambulance, and a short while later, there was Kostek, his piggish face pressed against the glass of the passenger window. His face was pink and moist from the heat, his shirt black where it squished against the seat. He climbed down and looked around.

A heavy-set person, muscular, Kostek held his cap in his hand and wiped his face with his sleeve. He was apparently not the kind to be bothered by base rules about headgear, unlike Nye, his driver, the last person who would have told him about any flexibility in the rules. I could see no indication that Kostek had worn his cap for some time. Nye's cap is never off, not even during work details. He can be standing on a pile of laterite, filling sandbags, dirt-stained and stinking, but his cap will still be perched on top of his head like some symbol of defiance against the Babylon in which he's found himself. They all wear their caps, all the members of the God Squad, except for Lucius who's another memory now, flown out of here, sent home on Jenkins's and the division psychiatrist's recommendation.

"You got many assholes like this guy?" Kostek asked, untroubled by the fact Nye was still within hearing. There was a wide grin on his face that became wider still as he sensed my surprise and discomfort. He started to laugh, one quiet, nasal burst, then two more.

"We live in pretty close conditions, man," I replied evenly. His back was to the sun, deliberately it seemed, and I felt my face contort as I squinted against the light.

"I'm assigning Kostek to A&D, O'Neill," Smith announced the next morning. I looked up from some lab slips and met his gaze. I noticed his face had tanned dark and that a second chin was developing. At one time Smith might have sought my approval about assigning a new person, or at least gone through the motions.

Kostek immediately grasped the onus of the coffee urn in the A&D office. I had bartered for it with a man from a supply company and since then routinely provided the coffee, sugar, canned milk, cups. It stands on the table in the corner of the office. It is a service I once wanted to provide until gradually it became an expectation, and more recently a demand on behalf of our officers if I failed to have a fresh pot brewed when they wanted it. I've grown to hate it, as has Kostek.

One night, Kostek started brewing the next morning's coffee at 10 P.M. He ran the coffee through the same grounds four times during the night, and even stayed awake to help me with sickcall just so he could see the results.

I don't know how they figured it out. All the consternation and complaints that morning were directed at me. They never said a word to Kostek, and they've never asked him to brew coffee since, or hassled him in any way about it, or for that matter asked any other favor of him. Now he brews coffee only when he wants it.

Because of this, I've had to knuckle under to the officers' demands. And I feel Kostek laughing at me, even if his appraisal is silent, or even if he isn't there. I hate that urn all the more because of his victory.

But none of it matters any more, not the urn, not Kostek, not Smith—I have my own plans now. For the moment I actually need Kostek, I'm reflecting as I walk across the narrow bridge that leads from the road into Dust-Off's company area and Major Hargos's quarters.

Hargos lives in a small wooden building with a peaked metal roof, almost an exact miniature of the mess hall with its louvres and screened walls. One half, his private quarters, contains a cot, a locker, chair and desk. Beyond a partition with a solid wooden door is Dust-Off's orderly room. Inside, there's a steel desk, an old Underwood typewriter, two steel chairs, a lamp, and an overhead fan with rust-flecked blades.

After knocking several times, I peer in through the screens. I can almost hear the heat drum on the metal roof. I go around to the opposite end of the building and discover the major at his desk, feet propped on the blotter, reading *Playboy*. I'm sure he heard the knocking, but it would be like him to ignore it.

Hargos, just shy of thirty, displays the calm, matter-of-factness of a man who's flown a long time, flown well, and always survived. He is halfway through his third tour.

I tap lightly on the door.

"Come in." Hargos keeps his feet on the desk, turns his head to look at me. The room is neat. A fan whirrs on the desk. Two of the year's better looking Playmates, the same two Navarra once gave prominence on the marquee above the bar, adorn one wall. On the desk is a photograph, framed in mouldy leather, of a pretty woman with a baby. I cast a quick look under the cot for signs of the legendary python. Nothing's there.

"What is it?" Hargos is obviously puzzled by my interest in his bunk. The blue eyes are observant, almost belligerent. He's wearing a faded pair of shorts. His flight suit hangs from a nail beside his cot, his helmet's on his pillow.

"Sir, I want to transfer to your unit as a medic."

He studies me.

I swallow. "I believe I'm qualified, sir. I want to fly and it's the only way I can do it." I'm sweating but manage to resist wiping my face.

"You talk to Captain Howard about this?" Hargos speaks quietly, the contentious quality gone now.

"No, sir. I wanted to be sure it was OK with you."

"You want to fly . . . that's all?"

"No, sir. I feel useless. I want to do something—to be of help."

He nods. "I have no objections."

Captain Howard's playing rummy at the table in the officers' club. Brock's reading a book. Howard glances at his cards and says, "You want to fly . . ."

"Yes, sir."

"That's asinine!"

"Sir?"

"I said that's asinine! You understand English, Specialist O'Neill?"

"Yes, sir." I can hear men shouting beyond the next row of tents—there's no urgency. It's like a summer evening. I waited until now, hoping it would be a better time.

"Well, what else do you want?"

"Sir, I want to transfer to Dust-Off."

"I told you that was asinine! What more do you need to know?"

"Sir, this means a lot to me. Major Hargos said it would be OK."

"Is Major Hargos your commanding officer?"

"No, sir."

"You want medals? Little baubles? Your Combat Medic's Badge?"

I hesitate for a moment, then say it, ashamed at the hypocrisy as soon as the words spill out of my mouth. "Sir, you advocated your belief that we needed combat experience. Well, I believe you. I'm asking permission to get it." I blush fiercely at my lie.

He rewards me with a slight, contemptuous smile. "That's very good. If you want to transfer to the field—I believe that's the way I originally put it—I'll let you go any time. Otherwise, you can stay here where we need you."

"Flying, my ass, Grisholm!" Brock says. "O'Neill here doesn't want to fly. He wants absolution."

The CO looks puzzled. "What do you mean?"

"O'Neill knows what I mean, don't you, Jon?"

I bite my lip so hard I taste blood.

"Well, whatever you mean, Brock, he isn't going to get it! Transfer denied, O'Neill!"

"That's final, sir?"

He leans forward and cups his hands. "What do I have to do or say to convince you?"

"Yes, sir. Thank you, sir." You fucking arrogant bastard, I'm thinking.

I'm overwhelmed by a feeling of wretchedness as I think of the months ahead. I remember Brown, LBJ, that farce of a court-martial, his misguided appreciation. I wonder if he's still there, facing each new day in that blazing pit, crying for thorazine.

And I feel regret for what might have been a passionate commitment to something more than survival. If it wasn't anything more, so what? And there's an intimation of something else now. Feral, trailing a scent of fear, it's an element of the miserable land around me and of the mechanical insects that prey upon it. Somehow, everything's affected by this danger: the pressure to submit, to become part of it. There's a smell of desire, a heavy repulsive odor of ruin and the need to feast upon it. I need protection—I've always needed it.

I stand in the wash of a departing helicopter. The ship's shadow flits across the earth as the helicopter floats higher, effortlessly scales the tower, the rubber trees, the barbed confines of the plantation to become a receding vision of freedom. The image I retain of the ship's medic, two fingers frozen in a casual wave, sears me.

To experience torture, something must occur at the level of consciousness—and so began my torture with Howard's refusal, although ironically, at first I felt relieved! There's no other way to describe my feelings once he said no. I slept like a rock that night. It was that total submission to someone else, the feeling I was being taken care of and had no cares; someone had lifted all the responsibility from me, no matter how.

It couldn't last. It lasted that one night.

Minutes after I'd been refused, I threw a tantrum, primarily for Morrisey's benefit, and, I suppose, to fight the sense of relief that overcame me. I slammed a fist against the door-jamb of the treatment tent and shouted things that were terribly true: that I was sick of feeling guilty, of feeling that the closer I got to the stinking war, the guiltier I was, that I was guilty because I wasn't dying, that I would be damned if I killed or didn't, was killed or wasn't.

"Brock was right," Morrisey said, unimpressed. "Even the smug bastards who make you feel like a coward because you haven't done what they've done—and even those who don't feel that way and don't mean to make you feel it: once the bullets aren't coming at them anymore, they're going to have to deal with it just like us."

In what was my most honest statement that day, I said, "I wish I could believe that . . . I'd feel a lot better."

I wish I could now. If I could, I wouldn't be here, I wouldn't be on the verge of breaking down and crying for, God knows, the nth time since I climbed into this attic simply to screw a girl. Not even that can be simple anymore. Why shouldn't I like myself? Is death better? I don't want to die and I never did. Neither did anyone else.

Kostek found out, somehow. How did I manage to forget that? He was the worst, worse than Howard, Brock, or Morrisey. He saw it all in me. And he laughed.

He was in the A&D office the next morning, logging sick-call, facing that endless line with a ferocious, even savage efficiency. That was the thing about Kostek: he didn't look as though he should be intelligent. His brains seemed to be at war with everything else about him. He turned the moment I entered. "You were going to screw me royally, huh, O'Neill? Leave me alone with this fucking job while you tore up the skies on missions of mercy. Face it, O'Neill, you're chicken-shit like the rest of us!" He laughed and turned back to the log and his work. From that day on, I always felt vaguely beholden to him, and he never did a thing for me. Even now, there's little comfort in knowing I wasn't alone.

Smith was OK about it. I'm sure he was pissed, but by the time he came into the office a couple of days later and stood rummaging through the log, then quite bluntly confronted me with it, he had already dealt with it in his own mind. He let me ramble on, let me release some incredible frustrations, and managed somehow to contain his temper, to not take it personally.

Then he told me I'd be flying to a leprosarium, part of a public relations tour organized by USARV in conjunction with the division surgeon. Two members of the division surgeon's party had canceled and Gerhard and I were to take their places. We were to be at division by 1300 hours and in anticipation of my protest (I didn't even know what a leprosarium was) I was to consider it an order. "You need a break," Smith said.

The noise of the Chinook reverberates through its shell, subdues the chatter of a pair of nurses, two colonels, several doctors and high-ranking medics. Beneath nets, a refrigerator—a gleaming white porcelain and stainless steel obelisk—rises amidst assorted cartons and wooden crates that fill the aisle separating the long webbed benches where we sit.

Gerhard and I boarded with the division surgeon at that same piece of tarmac where Sylvester and his slide were annihilated. As we boarded, we were scrutinized as though we had feelers dangling from our foreheads. Was it our association with the plantation, I wonder, a remote embodiment of The War itself to these other passengers? At least they separated Gerhard and me.

It's one o'clock in the afternoon on a scorching day, and assuming that Gerhard rose with the rest of us at 6:30 A.M., he's miraculously dry. There's not a trace of sweat on his face or his crisp, spotless fatigues. If he wasn't such a damn spaniel, he'd be just like Smith. I could put on clean fatigues every damned hour and someone would still have to shred them off my back when I changed. I feel ugly in army clothes.

Beyond a round window beside my head, mile after mile of obliteration rolls away beneath the belly of our ship. Tread marks make circular patterns on the raw land below, convey a lingering sense of violence. I'm entranced. It's like the tracks of mechanical hounds—tanks, Rome plows, armored personnel carriers—tearing round and round, wrenching every living speck from its hold on the earth as they seek the enemy. Only scarred land and frenzied tracks remain . . . *and you never heard anyone say they failed, not McNamara, or Johnson, or Westmoreland—not even now. They count victory. They count everything, I suppose, even tread marks on some wretched piece of land. If there's enough of anything, then you have to be winning something if you just take the time and total it up. So what if it's a numbers game? But I knew . . . I knew when I saw those marks that they, the machines, had failed to destroy the enemy they most savagely sought: darkness itself. If we win, I thought, all Vietnam will look like this, and they'll still come for us in the darkness.*

We're lower, skimming the ground. The blackened hulks of trees and shrubs, defoliated skeletons, become rich and green; palm trees sail in our downdraft, bright flowers wave.

"Look at that!" someone across the aisle exclaims. "My God, it's beautiful!"

I'm stunned by the scene below me, amazed by a vision, not of this country as I've come to know it, but of a small remnant of a peaceful Indochina. The crewchief stands beside the door to the cockpit and shows mild contempt for our fascination. I guess he sees this day after day and feels he knows the irrelevant for what it is.

Down the ramp and into the sun we walk. Waist high grass engulfs us as it sweeps away beneath the roaring blades toward a shore of high, green bushes. A rusty bicycle piloted by a spindly, white-haired apparition suddenly careens through a gap in the bushes and wobbles across the small meadow. Several Vietnamese in khaki pants and colored sports shirts pursue the vehicle. The cyclist slides off the seat and jams his heels into the ground a few feet from us. The Vietnamese bunch up behind him.

There's a shout. The division surgeon and the other colonel have taken command of the unloading of the medical supplies and the electric refrigerator. In this garden setting, their exertions seem moronic. I climb into the shadows of the transport's belly just as the netting comes off the cargo.

All of us face the strange man holding the bicycle. An old man, a priest, he jingles the bell on the handlebars, then lets the bike fall and walks up to the colonels. He shakes their hands, smiles, thanks them profusely in French accented English for their trouble in coming, and asks them in the same breath if they wouldn't, please, move the material to that shed? He indicates a large, tall structure with no walls and a metal roof.

I'm amazed by the officers' capitulation to the priest's gregariousness; promptly, and with much bustle, they do his bidding. The priest smiles, the Vietnamese smile, and both colonels assume positions of intense supervision.

With the supplies removed to the shed, we find ourselves in the presence of the priest once again. I feel foolish in front of this ingenuous cleric, and I can sense that the others feel the same way as they shift and stir like uneasy schoolchildren. He turns from the colonels, lifts his red face, flings his arms wide as though to encompass us all, and shouts, "Welcome!" A marvelous grin curls out from under his hooked, veinous nose.

I become aware of the steel of the weapon in my hand, for we've all come armed as though, indeed, we might be prepared to fight. I feel like a jerk.

The priest says to the colonels, "Please, I will have to ask you to leave your arms while I guide you through the colony. There is a perfectly safe room in one of the buildings down the road where no one will bother them."

"Well, Father, I don't . . ."

The smile remains. The helicopter's gone. "Please, I understand, but if you insist, so must the VC."

The priest, pushing his bicycle between the two colonels, leads us along a red, dusty lane. The colonels dwarf him.

They bend to listen as he waves his free hand frantically and points here and there in a dizzy continuum.

Behind the hedges that wall the lane I catch glimpses of huge, exotic flowers, small paths, lush gardens. Rambling bungalows lie buried in shade. Everywhere, floating in the hush of this verdant island, are men and women, and whether they are at work, or convalescing, they invariably greet us with friendly smiles and waves. There is not a sign of subservience or embarrassment.

"I thought this was supposed to be a leper colony," a medic beside me remarks. "I expected to see people lying around rotting."

The colony is phenomenally neat and orderly. It puts the Vietnamese facilities beyond its confines to shame, and the American facilities as well. The plantation, my plantation, once a retreat from the bleakness of the bases farther south, now seems grim.

As I walk down the lane toward the heart of the leprosarium, I feel elated for the first time in months. I sense a world around me, feel the warmth of sunshine, the blueness of the sky, conditions that have existed in varying degrees since I arrived in this country, but which have only been footnotes to my growing sense of oppression. Now I discover I'm aware of the beauty of land once again. I feel free to breathe the air, and this feeling makes me want to return the gift. If I could only work here, I might stay here forever, bury myself the way this kind old man has.

"How many VC live here, Father?" The question is facetious, but it jars nonetheless.

The priest glances at the colonel who asked the question, a man from Long Binh, then bursts into shrill laughter, a laughter that seems to flow too easily. "Oh, none in the leprosarium, Colonel, but many, many within the colony's no-strike zone."

"No-strike zone?" The colonel looks uneasy. "You're joking, of course, but how large an area is it?"

"I'm not joking, Colonel," the priest replies, then works out some arithmetic on his fingers. "Six hundred acres I think you say."

"No fighting inside it?"

"None . . . but of course the VC will come tonight and take at least half of what you have brought us." That high-pitched laughter again. "The more useful half, of course."

"Yes, yes . . ." The colonels glance at each other, then purse their lips into small, indulgent smiles.

"Representatives of the Sixth Infantry were here last week," the priest continues. "They brought wonderful supplies. Do you know Colonel Jackson?"

"No, no, can't say that I do."

"Ah, he might have been a lieutenant colonel, what you say . . ."

"That might account for it, Father."

"There is a significant difference?"

"There certainly is, Father." The tone is paternal. The thought that the priest might already know the difference obviously never registers, and why it occurs to me I can't say, but I suddenly feel compelled to watch the priest more closely.

"Well, Lieutenant Colonel Jackson brought us a radio set, a marvelous machine, in case of emergency so we can reach help. But we need more batteries. He was unable to find many."

"Yes, we might be able to help you on that score."

"And that is certainly a wonderful refrigerator you brought us today, but we have petrol for only two hours of electricity a day and all of that is used in our operation room . . . would you like to see the operation room?"

His question is greeted with enthusiasm.

"And if you could find a larger generator than the one we have, and maybe more petrol, we could use the operation room more. We might even be able to run the refrigerator.

"The Viet Minh prepared here for some of their first operations in the South almost two decades ago." The priest stands on tiptoe and points over a cluster of bushes and brambles. A slight breeze raises his hair in light, snowy wisps. All I can see in the clearing is a scarred, rectangular piece of concrete protruding above the weeds.

"That's fascinating, Father." The colonel who speaks, the same one who's been doing most of the talking for the two officers, scans the clearing while he professes a deep interest in the history of the country. "I make it a point to learn as much as possible about every country to which I'm assigned," he explains, speaking in low tones.

"Everything except the language, Colonel?" the priest says in the same conspiratorial manner. At once, however, he begins to laugh, that hysterical, childlike laugh.

Profoundly disturbed, I glance around, but if anyone else has had a similar reaction, I find no indication of it.

"Those were intellectuals who left that clearing to begin a revolution, Colonel, as I'm sure you have read."

"Communist inspired, Father."

"Of course." And there it is again, the irony . . . but the priest's face is expressionless. He excuses himself and rejoins the rest of us, leads us farther along the lane that seems to bisect the colony before it winds into deep, shaded jungle. We pass a huge plantation house and stop at a long, low barn. Next to the barn several pigs, huge creatures, slosh about in a wooden pen. The priest points them out with tremendous pride.

From the pig pen we move on to the chicken yards; the priest names the colony's accomplishments, displays them to an audience enraptured not so much by what he and his lepers have done, but by the fact that he's able to find such satisfaction in the midst of this war.

Everywhere we go, the priest introduces the residents, nurses, the old men in khaki shorts who tend the barns and sheds, by name and accomplishment. There is no indication of his personal assessment of them: that they're alive and useful, and happy to be so, is all that seems to matter.

Unlike the enlisted men and doctors—the latter have disappeared to examine patients on the wards—the colonels are growing restless. The more talkative of the two now discovers the shell of a small chapel rising from the dense underbrush; the remnants of a rose window graces its facade. "What happened to the church, Father?"

Enjoyment vanishes from the priest's face. "It was burned."

"By the Viet Minh?"

"No, the French. Before my time."

"And when was that?"

"I came here in 1957. This was a ruined plantation then, not yet a colony."

"Why don't you rebuild the church, Father? The walls look sound. The window could be beautiful."

"I find the window pretentious. The Gothic Age was some seven centuries late in arriving in Indochina, Colonel. Besides, we have a nice chapel in one of our new buildings."

The colonel chuckles good-naturedly. "Your political allegiances seem to have mellowed, Father. Tell me, have you ever been back to France since then?"

"Belgium. No."

I look back up the road toward the plantation house and watch the silhouette of a bird sail across a small mowing. It shrieks into the emptiness of the afternoon.

The priest breaks into his hysterical laugh and grabs Gerhard by the arm. "But I must show you our breadfruit trees!" He claps his hands, delighted as though by a conjurer's trick; his eyes sparkle. He yanks a beaming Gerhard away along the dusty lane.

Once again, we plunge into easy chatter . . . but are stunned when we enter the small operating room a few minutes later. "God!" someone whispers. The room is cleaner by far than any medical facility I've seen in this country. Two large lights hang over an adjustable, stainless steel table. The walls and floor are tiled. There's a plaque on the side of the operating table that reads, "Gift of St. Andrew's Parish, Liverpool."

There's another plaque outside the building, also in English: "Constructed with funds raised by the Heilige Geist Lutheran Church, Nordlingen, Germany." The building is brand new. A one-story structure of block and concrete with a covered patio connecting the infirmary with the new chapel and wards, it was built entirely by the residents of the colony.

I sit down on one of the benches on the patio and regard the lushness of the colony and surrounding jungle. I feel a poignant peacefulness, an immunity from the war. I can almost hear my mind thinking again, am almost prepared to let feelings surface.

The priest must be on the brink of madness. He has to be to have made his way this far through such a maze of burgeoning pressures and contradictions. This incredible quietude he's created for others must be cannibalizing his own. Never before have I been able to truly grasp altruism in a human dimension. By contrast, our own efforts seem monstrous.

The roar of descending helicopters intrudes on and destroys the late afternoon. They've sent two slicks to fetch us, ordered two ships to cross miles of ruin to this oasis and reclaim us. The colonels are eager to go.

We've taken our weapons from the small storage room and started back up the lane. This time, the priest walks with us —the doctors, nurses and medics—and lets the colonels hurry ahead. One of the doctors asks the priest if some of us can return on a regular basis, a Medcap basis, and thereby assure the colony of more staff and supplies.

I hold my breath and wait for the reply we all must desire.

"We would certainly appreciate the supplies, Captain, and cannot thank you enough for what you have brought us today . . . truly." The refusal is emphatic. The priest claps his hands, smiles, and stops at the break in the hedge while we file through.

My ship begins to rise, smoothly like an elevator. I look down from the open door at the swirling grass, then the top of the hedge and the roofs of the buildings as they begin to emerge among the trees. We swing on our axis, lower our nose, and thunder across the lush vegetation. A last green bush sweeps by. Now there's only blackened, treaded ground.

Far below, I glimpse the priest waving. I'm overcome by a feeling that something I never knew was within my grasp is slipping away. And worse, the priest has reawakened a yearning in me to do something, to be of good use.

Far away to the northeast, the colony is a speck of green in a burned out land. Our shadow lingers behind as we pinwheel toward a giant evening sun.

For days afterwards, I thought about the leprosarium. I had an awful time making the transition back to the rubber plantation. There were casualties all night the night I returned, and when, finally, I flopped on my cot in the grey, pre-dawn of Sunday, it was with a sense of futility and emptiness. Many of those who got better went back to fight, but I'd never know who they were. So many disappeared beneath a red light flicking through the darkness south to the huge, humming evacuation hospitals.

There were a few bodies to dispose of that night, and a few injured civilians destined not even to become jottings in a ledger, but simply to be gotten rid of. They all went south, too, packed under the same red light to be deposited in utter bewilderment at Tainan, their hospital. Once there, they faced journeys of several days on foot to get back up country to wherever they came from, assuming they weren't so badly injured that they had to risk the medical treatment.

I talked to Morrisey at great length about the leprosarium, found myself spewing a profusion of thoughts, feelings, sentiments, random and confused. He would sit in my office and listen; I believe he actually understood my turmoil. Often he

236

left (for I talked to him many times those first few days) in a reflective mood.

Gerhard's getting on my nerves. Every day he shows up to gush about the colony, making me almost regret that I went. Sometimes, now, I even hesitate to talk to Morrisey for fear I'm afflicting him in a similar manner.

The attraction in my office is a small table on top of which is a crusty sugar container, paper cups and tongue depressers, and my scourge, the chrome tank of black, oily liquid. Morrisey's standing at the table, pouring himself a cup of coffee. I'm in my chair, leaning back against the screened wall. I've been feeling lethargic for a couple of days. I have no inclination, despite a wish to be awake, to move enough to light a cigarette.

A hand slaps the counter. "O'Neill! Guess what? I wrote my ma and told her all about the Father and his work."

I focus on Gerhard, on the hostile blue eyes over a friendly smile on a too-wide, froglike mouth. I make some incoherent response.

"You know, Jon, back home those pigs could win a prize!"

"Yeah, you've said that before."

"Well, when I wrote Ma, I suggested she could get the Ladies Guild of our church to send clothing and maybe money. I told Dad they need a decent generator."

"That's nice, Gerhard," Morrisey interrupts. "Tell me, did you stay home on Saturday nights and play cards with Mom and Dad?"

Gerhard's eyes flicker. "We don't play cards, Morrisey. In our faith, it's a sin."

"Oh, I didn't realize."

Gerhard turns abruptly to me. "You know, Jon, I heard the enemy took more than half of the supplies we took to the Father—the very night we left!"

"That surprises you? The priest himself said he expected it."

"I know he said that, Jon, you're right, but I don't think he meant it. You know we sometimes say things like that to ward off what we hope won't happen. I think he hoped the enemy would see the colony's need."

"Oh, bullshit, Gerhard!" Morrisey says. He churns the contents of his cup with a depresser. I'm surprised at his impatience. Gerhard isn't worth this.

"You weren't there, Morrisey. O'Neill will tell you, as a

237

man of faith, the Father had to believe otherwise or he wouldn't have the strength to keep on going.''

''I don't agree,'' I say quietly, beginning to enjoy my role, whatever it is: onlooker, mediator, or instigator—I'm not sure, yet. The sudden edge to Gerhard's voice, the look of momentary bafflement are my reward. I'm thinking, I really don't like this guy.

''Haven't you got any faith? Don't you believe in something?'' he demands of Morrisey. ''If you did, you'd know what I was talking about.''

''How do you know what I believe?'' Morrisey's genuinely angry. I can feel it. He's deliberately let himself into this.

''I know. There are lots of people like you around—doubters, atheists, whatever you are, Morrisey. I'm not saying you're necessarily wrong.''

''No? Did it ever occur to you that maybe because you believe one way, you're blind to the possibility that someone else can still have faith and expect the fucking gooks to take his damn medical supplies?''

''Everyone to his own belief, Morrisey. You can believe he did expect it and I'll believe—and of course I was there so I might know just a bit more—that he didn't.''

They're like a couple of male dogs who've met by accident, and there's no one around except me—and they're no longer aware of me. They seem intent only on finding a graceful way to go back the way they've come. But I feel that giddiness, that impulse to smile, even laugh, that is raw anticipation. I bow my head and avoid looking at either of them. Do I hear them breathing?

''It was a beautiful experience for both of us, wasn't it, Jon?'' Gerhard's voice is slightly shrill now. ''I felt so clean afterwards, like there was work to be done and I could be of real help.''

My God, he felt it, too!

''I talked to Captain Howard about arranging another trip out there, to bring more supplies to the priest, and maybe help him a bit. Dust-Off might take us. We wouldn't bring any guns, of course, so the enemy wouldn't mind.''

Speak, Morrisey! Say something . . .

''I told Captain Howard what a beautiful place it was.''

I bet you whispered it right in his asshole.

''He said he'd look into it.''

''Gerhard,'' Morrisey says at last, ''maybe I wasn't there,

but from what I understand, he wants our supplies, not us. You're dreaming.''

There's a look of momentary consternation, but when Gerhard confronts Morrisey again it's with a knowing, confident, even pitying countenance. ''You can't possibly understand, can you? That priest is a man of faith. His job is to take care of those lepers. He needs aid, and that means more than supplies. Just think of yourself! A person with your experience and skills could do marvelous things in that situation.''

Morrisey winces. ''Gerhard, what about Charlie crawling around out there in the bushes? Are you suggesting they're just going to stand around while we flood that poor, beleaguered priest with salvation? Or maybe you feel that if they created problems, they might have to be eliminated?''

Until Gerhard made that remark about feeling ''clean,'' I was enjoying myself. I was marvelously aloof . . . but not now. I tip forward in my chair and clap my hands on my knees. ''Jesus, man! Can't you see we're his enemy, too? We'd tear that place apart giving him peace! I knew it the day we were there!''

''That operating room,'' Morrisey quietly suggests. ''You think he just works on lepers in there?''

The question doesn't register with either Gerhard or me.

''Well, c'mon, Gerhard! Do you?'' Caught up in the logic of the question and my emotions, I begin to press Gerhard although I'm not sure what the import really is . . . some kind of alarm's going off. ''You saw the lepers! They were phenomenally well cared for. I didn't see any demanding immediate surgery. Hell, one of the doctors said that afterwards! And you heard him! If someone hadn't told you that was a leper colony, would you have known?''

''But they might need it later . . .''

This room is too small, too close now for whatever's developing. I'm not sure who the antagonist is, and who should run. ''The VC need it all the time,'' Morrisey says. ''Gerhard, you can't tell me that if they're taking half the medical supplies, they're not claiming equal time in the operating room. Or more. That's a damn fine hospital right under their noses. It's clean, it's in a no-fire zone. O'Neill says the place is immaculate! It beats the hell out of a tunnel, and it won't get bombed.''

Gerhard shrinks away from the counter. ''Who would perform the operations?'' he demands.

"The priest—the nuns . . . who else?"

Yes, who else? I wonder, because this hadn't occurred to me. This is the bottom line. Leave it to Morrisey.

"You're crazy!"

"Why, Gerhard? Why do you say that?" Morrisey reaches down, picks up his cup and sips at it. Here he is, suddenly in full control, the emotion gone, speaking as though he were conducting a seminar. And now I'm like Gerhard, waiting, wanting, dreading to know what's next. It's like the morning the admiral came for his son in that spectral white helicopter, and Morrisey knew immediately, implicitly what it was all about. "I'll tell you why, Gerhard. How can he refuse? He lives among them. If he didn't cooperate, they'd blow the shit out of the place. They're quite capable of that. It's really that simple."

I exhale. For a moment I feel profound relief because of this explanation, because of something he didn't say, some conclusion he didn't make.

Gerhard relaxes, too, but his eyes are unrelenting. "I'm sorry. You're entitled to your own view, but it seems cynical to me, warped."

Morrisey shrugs. He doesn't care anymore. It doesn't matter to him that this little turd will go away as smug as ever, will never admit that his little dream (if not my little dream) has been blown to hell.

"Well, I'm sure he's grateful for what supplies he has left." Gerhard backs away from the counter a second time and starts for the door. There's more than bitterness in his voice—I can feel it.

"Yeah, Gerhard!" I call, almost shout! "Sure he's grateful for things like a fucking refrigerator that runs on 110 volts! That poor bastard doesn't even have gas for power—even if he could produce 110!"

Gerhard turns and stares at me. It's ours, now.

A detail comes into the yard behind me, between my screen wall and the treatment tent. I listen to Buster Wilbur mumble orders.

"You working in here, Morrisey?" It's Wilbur. He's breathing hard. His home is generally behind the club's bar now, where he studiously cleans glasses and graces all customers with his wide-eyed, dull-witted stare.

"Yes, Sarge," Morrisey says pleasantly.

"With a cup of coffee, huh?"

"You're very observant, Sergeant."

"Someday, Morrisey, I'm going to get your ass. I'm going to get you on the sandbags."

"You do that, Sarge."

Wilbur snorts and backs away from the screen. Gerhard and I continue to watch each other, the sergeant's antagonism merely feeding our own. "Hey, Jon!" someone in the yard cries.

"Yeah!" I shout back, irritated by an additional intrusion that threatens the intensity that I now actively welcome . . . nurture. How long have I been here? How long has this been building? I wouldn't dream of stopping it now.

"Hey, Kostek says the lifers got a new hooch girl and Buster's got two fifths of Seagrams for lubrication! Going to be a busy day in the orderly room!" A burst of laughter from the men in the detail accompanies this announcement.

"Get to work, Stevens!" Wilbur shouts from some distance away.

I can't stop. "Maybe I haven't got your kind of faith, Gerhard, but at least I got more pride than to kiss Smith's ass so I can take a helicopter ride out of here within a few weeks of my arrival."

A curtain separates my office from the hall. Gerhard yanks it aside. His other hand's balled into a loose fist. Why does he remind me of a peaches and cream slut? "And while I'm at it, Gerhard, I want you to know I'm sick of this masochistic Christian bullshit! Whether you want to admit it or not, we made that priest manipulate us for whatever he could get, because he's a havenot. You can't accept the fact that he told us to fuck off when we tried to climb in the sack with him, too, can you? That's what that was all about. And you, with your letters to your Ma and Pa and the Ladies Guild and all that crap—you're still trying to fuck him!" God, I can scarcely stand to look at him anymore! "It's bad enough that I have to be party to that, but what I dread is what's going to happen when you wake up from your pretty little dream about charity, saving people. I don't want to be around. You're going to want to blow the shit out of everything, like the self-righteous prig you are! It's going to be like getting kicked in the nuts, Gerhard . . . can you imagine that?" Was I shouting?

"Go to hell!"

"Harsh words, missionary . . ."

Gerhard almost tears the curtain off its wire when he charges out the door.

"Whatever happened to the guy who spent five days dutifully taking lessons in Vietnamese so he could learn one word he already knew?" Morrisey's still here.

Now it's out of me. "Jesus, what have I done?" I groan. Morrisey starts toward me.

"Don't touch me! Just get the hell out of here!"

He's only inches away and I can hear him breathe, can smell him, can smell the heat, the sweat, the sour uniform, and I know I'm smelling myself, too, smelling something I'm coming to hate. "I mean it, Morrisey. Don't touch me!"

The eyes, those inky eyes roam my face, not hurt or angry, but questioning, even kind. I look down as the blood pours up my neck. "Get out! *You* did this . . ."

I never hear him leave; I only hear the blood pound in my ears. When I look up, he's gone and I'm alone in a sun-drenched cubicle that reeks of hot canvas and foul humans. Why did I do that? Why did I hurt him, too? What is this war inside me? I'm tired of being judged, of justifying myself daily. And the priest, his feigned and real madness, the irony and contempt he hid behind his shrill laughter . . . he must be in collusion with the enemy! He probably planned to give them those supplies. What enemy? Why am I thinking this?

I stare at the log on the counter, at the battered edges of the cloth binding, at the stained white paper with its insane, illogical detail, its total lack of reality. I look beyond the counter, through the far screen wall into the linear exactitude of the trunks of the rubber trees that proceed in perfect perspective, then become luminous green shade. I've less than half a year to go . . . half a year of this.

Someone's crying for litterbearers, eight of them. That's four litters—the mathematics are easy. I grab a book of medical tags and stuff them in a side pocket.

SEVENTEEN

"**A** new patient's bunker, a new commo bunker, a new ward, a new officers' tent, a brand new movie screen with a shelter from the rain, and now this . . ."

"You forgot the mess hall with its new, baby-blue coat of paint," I enumerate.

No one laughs. No one's in a laughing mood. We've been up since first light being diddled by the NCOs and their latest obsession: security. At the moment, we're lined up in four groups of ten, side by side along the entire front of the treatment area. We're preparing for our third assault on the perimeter just because of a fucking satchel charge in someone else's company.

They found the charge in a hooch in one of the infantry companies down the road, so Buelen claimed with a fine display of emotion at yesterday's noon formation.

Satchel charges are homemade bombs, "weapons of terror" an instructor once told us, often constructed with plastic explosives or hand grenades. For reasons of transport, they are designed to be disguised and hidden. It's implied that satchel charges are essentially unfair and immoral, like the Viet Cong who dress in peasant garb instead of distinctive uniforms like a self-respecting army.

"What did it look like, Top?" Stevens asked (we were still standing in formation).

"Well . . ." Buelen began, and we waited.

"Like a briefcase? If we're going to watch out for them, we got to know what they look like."

"That's right. Look for a briefcase, or maybe a package."

"Will it tick?" Kostek asked.

"How about it, Top? Do the gooks wear trenchcoats when they leave satchel charges?"

A whistle shrieks. "Forward!" Smith yells. We start to clump unenthusiastically toward the tower. The straps of our M–16s clink, background for the pants, grunts, and curses that punctuate our forward movement. In front of us trots our squad leader, Nye, Smith's choice for excellence, I suppose. I'm beginning to despise that skinny frame with its bony shoulders.

The whistle blows again. We fall on our stomachs, our rifles in front of us, and start to scramble through the stinking dust. "I hate that sonuvabitch," I groan.

"Relax," Morrisey says. "You could be down there with the rest of the God Squad—they're loving this shit!"

Nye's walking now, not lying down like the rest of us. He holds his left arm out and hooks the forearm up parallel to his body. Every few steps he pauses for us to catch up, gives the forearm a quick thrust toward the tower and marches off again, leaving us cursing . . . pompous incompetent!

"You know," Gerty gasps as he pulls himself up and brushes the front of his shirt.

"Run! Run!" Buelen screams from the other end of the line. "You come up running!"

"Fuck you!"

" . . . as I was saying, this just might work," Gerty continues—we're trotting now, "because the goddam gooks would be laughing so hard if they ever did try to come across the wire."

"Down!" someone cries as the whistle blows.

"You're falling behind! You're falling behind!" Smith shouts.

"You're falling behind," Milliken growls behind us. "C'mon there! You Gerty, Morrisey! Get your asses in gear!"

"Jesus, the God Squad's halfway to the perimeter already! Do you see that?"

The sun feels hot on my back now; I can feel the earth lift and float around me, dig at my belly, my thighs, make mud of my sweat.

"Up! Up!"

"Why doesn't he eat that whistle?"

"Sergeant Smith! Can you wait a minute?" Nye shouts and waves his hands frantically.

244

Smith walks along, or rather, down the line for it's no longer anywhere near parallel to the treeline, but has veered off at an acute angle.

"Sergeant, I'd like a moment to demonstrate to these men the proper technique for moving forward."

Smith, clipboard in hand, shiny whistle around his neck, surveys us one by one: me, Morrisey, Stevens, Gerty, Owens, Jenkins, Newell, Kostek. "What's the matter with you men? You've caused nothing but trouble this morning. Someday the VC might be coming at you, right over the wire, and you'll be glad you had this drill. Now pay attention to what Nye has to show you."

Brock and Shelby are watching the spectacle from the treatment tent. I realize I'm as much an observer as a participant, the automatic weapon slung against my back as credible as a waterpistol or a cap gun; in no way can I conceive of it as something that will shoot real bullets at a rate of 800 rounds a minute. Furthermore, I don't care. Why wasn't this done months ago when the war was busier, when it strode furiously up and down beyond that tower and hurled torn remnants over that same wire at us?

Nye stares at us with bleak aggression. He turns his back to us and trots away. His body bounces up and down, springless; the rifle does the same, parallel to the ground.

Suddenly the knees begin to buckle, the body falls forward, the rifle swings over Nye's head in a high arc, then hurls outward and pulls him into the earth. Astonished, we watch him squiggle away with incredible speed like a snake or two-legged dog.

Now he's up. His face and hair are covered with dust. The harsh eyes glare from a red mask. He turns his back to us again, displays his lean tautness as he wanders out through the ragged brush. A quick thrust of his forearm beckons us.

The whistle shrieks. Reluctantly, slowly, I let myself fall to the earth. I lie there, paralyzed by my misgivings, and inhale that smell like garbage, feel the heat suck the juices from the withered ground and me. Tough brown grass forms jagged hallways of light and shade before my eyes. A cricket the size of my fist tumbles into view, freezes a moment, then hobbles around a stalk of grass.

"Up! Up! Up!"

I pull myself to my knees and watch the distant antics of Gerhard's squad. Morrisey's beside me, his rifle still slung. I look at the rest of them—Gerty, Stevens, Kostek—and they're all looking at me with disbelief, even amusement. None of them dropped!

"Fuck this shit!" Gerty announces and starts to walk toward the perimeter. Morrisey follows, and soon we're all ambling through the scrub. Far out ahead, Nye marches on, his eyes on paradise.

The whistle tweets. "Down! Down!" We keep on walking.

"Hey you, over there! Down on your bellies!" We stay on our feet. Morrisey's a short-timer, Jenkins is very short, Stevens has a few days less than I have, Owens, Newell—everyone's short except Kostek, who's outrageous. I have over five months left—that's short, but barely. I can still be sent out there where the war is. I didn't learn any Vietnamese at that damn school! What will I learn on my belly?

The next time the whistle blows and the other squads fall, I fall down and start to crawl, to grovel, tears in my eyes. I dread their stares as their footsteps crash ahead, away from me—I'll never catch up.

Brown was in LBJ that day, two weeks into that steaming compound, probably screaming for thorazine . . . and I was on my belly, pissing my pants. I scrambled uselessly with a weapon that took twenty minutes to be issued because, even with this sudden, belated terror of being overrun, the lifers still would not trust us to keep our own weapons again—not after Brown tore up the night with tracers. So we had to wait in line to sign for our weapons and ammunition while the imaginary little men in conical hats swept gleefully past the tower headed for our strategic supplies of penicillin.

The guards on the tower were real, the silhouettes that is, because soon we were able to see that they were real people. By then their diligence was no longer directed beyond the plantation; their amazed faces gaped down on us as we slugged through the brush. We were halted only by the unexpected appearance of six coils of concertina wire and trip flares separating us from the tower and the outer perimeter. While we stood there sweaty, swatting indiscriminately at everything that climbed over us, Smith yelled, "Just practicing!" to the guards, by way of explanation, his hands pressed victoriously on his hips. In his pleasure, the mutiny in our squad was apparently forgotten.

* * *

":It's no good," Morrisey says.

"What isn't?"

"I once thought Mendez, or someone like him, could have carried us through—I was wrong."

Jenkins is tilted back in his chair. As usual, he acts as though he might be dozing when in fact he's listening carefully. So far he's said nothing.

I feel compelled to answer Morrisey's pessimism. "All that matters is that we get out of here—get home, Morrisey. It's pretty much of a given: there's not too much chance of our being killed, or even wounded, so it's just a matter of putting up with it a few more months, then getting on a plane and flying home. It'll all be behind us, then. You just got to hang on." I glance at Jenkins for support, but his eyes are still closed. Am I really trying to convince Morrisey, or myself?

One of Morrisey's legs is slung over the arm of a grey office chair. The suspended leg swings now and then, convulsively as though by a jolt of electricity. "I was a shitty math student, O'Neill. Same with physics. I used to wonder if I'd ever get out of high school, not to mention college, because of math and science requirements. I was always being told that there were 'givens' and if I'd just accept them, I could understand the rest. But, oh no, I had to question centuries of conjecture, I had to understand why the givens had evolved their own empirical truth.

"I could feel the teachers cringe when I asked 'Why?' maybe because it was so apparent to them. Maybe they thought I was just trying to make trouble. I don't know. It wasn't impertinence—I was really confused. I didn't understand then and I still don't, although I gradually learned not to ask for explanations. I've never been able to think that way."

"So what are you saying?"

"Look, I have no guarantee I'll be on that plane in two months, or whatever it is. Neither do you. I don't even keep a short-timer's calendar. Why taunt myself? I know I'm here now, that I survived yesterday. Every new day, each passing moment brings its own reaffirmation . . . and, O'Neill, it won't 'all be behind us' like you said. We're accumulating baggage. Sure, I can hope I'll be on that plane, but I can't allow myself too much of that: I can't sacrifice what I am today to the hope I'll be out of here tomorrow. It's like believing in eternal life: you can duck a lot of reality, cause a lot of pain by focusing only on paradise. Mistakes don't go away.

Later I say to Jenkins, "He's a lot worse now. It's been downhill ever since that shit with the MI team and the prisoner." I look at the chair where Morrisey sat, at the vinyl seat still depressed.

"You're right," Jenkins says. "He spent an hour in here yesterday fuming about no one getting up for litters except a few of us old-timers. I told him he couldn't take it all on. I think he's been fucked up by that rule about reading."

"He's still reading."

"Sure, but he's paranoid about it. He's always got to look over his shoulder—he can't afford any mistakes with Smith and Howard. He's gone too far."

"That's an understatement. That litter thing is pretty bad, you know. Some of them have started turning the lights back off after the guards come through. The God Squad did it the other night."

"That wouldn't have happened with Mendez."

"How can you say that? Not even Morrisey buys that anymore."

"He contradicts himself all over the place! He was saying something about the past being meaningless the other day, and you just heard what he said about 'baggage.' "

"It's hard not to be depressed by him."

Jenkins lets the chair creak forward. "Did you finally write home?"

"What choice did I have?"

Jenkins laughs and stands up, a gradual unravelling.

"It was short," I insist. Jenkins leans against the doorjamb and watches me. "You've got only a month!" I exclaim as I suddenly remember and feel a lurch in my guts. I can't look at him, feeling this way.

"Yes, sir," he says, quite cheerfully. "I've been here fourteen months, and I get out of the army the day I hit San Francisco . . . and, I'm keeping a short-timer's calendar, despite Morrisey."

"I'll be a real short-timer when Morrisey leaves. I'll have less than 120 days. At least they won't be able to bother me after that."

"You're not going to extend?" Jenkins asks.

"No way. I'm not going to risk the field now—I couldn't handle it."

*　　*　　*

The ten men in black, enemy soldiers, are sitting on the bench in front of treatment, their hands tied behind their backs. None of them is injured.

"Why the hell did they leave them here?" Morrisey asks, watching the helicopter shimmer in and out of focus.

"That isn't the question," Brock replies. He spits out a piece of cigar wrapping. "What the hell are we going to do with them?"

"We could ask Dust-Off to airmail them from a thousand feet or so," Dunn says and laughs at his own cleverness. He stands in front of the prisoners and rakes them with his eyes, one by one.

"Souvenir hunting, Dunn? Why don't you just give one of them a ride on a litter?"

Dunn's jowls fall. "Up yours, Morrisey."

Buelen arrives, a .45 automatic pistol in hand, followed by Milliken, Smith, and Wilbur. Wilbur's wearing a flak jacket and helmet; an M–16 is cradled on his forearm. Buelen bends down and checks the knots that secure the prisoners' wrists. His face turns crimson with the exertion.

"Where are they going to run away to, Top?" Gerty asks. "The airstrip? As a matter of fact, there is a plane leaving in about fifteen minutes."

"Hell, if they'll just hang on a few minutes, Nye can give them a ride home in his ambulance."

"   . . . and convert them in the process . . ."

"   . . . and shoot them if they don't."

"Amen."

The prisoners are wearing peasant garb and sandals made from the carcasses of old tires. The long, tubular sacks of rice that hung from their shoulders have been removed and are being enthusiastically examined by the NCOs. Only Smith remains aloof. I'm struck again by how he's changed. He really believes what he's doing is right . . . and why should that surprise me?

The atmosphere is very relaxed with the exception of the lifers who are so busy posturing that they haven't realized no one else is particularly concerned. The prisoners bear a striking resemblance to those stereotypes caricatured during our training, except that they look younger and do not seem menacing. They're not behaving as I'd expect them to; they don't seem truculent or dejected—their heads don't hang down. Can they, of all people, be naive, unaware of what awaits them? They chat quietly among themselves and often lapse into periods of silence when they look around with unabashed curiosity. They obviously sense the impotence of the NCOs despite all the fuss and muttering, and they don't seem afraid of the rest of us: they shouldn't be. They've got a lot more to be afraid of. Morrisey can tell them. For the moment, however, we are complete strangers, unwillingly thrown together, who simply don't know what to do with each other.

Where did they come from? From vast, deep plantations where their saffron-skinned faces appear and vanish like faint, elusive blooms? From blasted, torn foliage, from pits in a ruptured earth, from intense, explosive silences? From the barrenness of Miss Lahn's dispensary? They're like fabled creatures—how on earth do they survive? What a strange sense of peace has fallen over us as we all wait for Thieu to arrive, and eventually the MI team, but they can't know about them, not the way we do. They shouldn't be so relaxed.

I can't judge ages. These men look no older than the young ARVNs I see so often. I hear Thieu's scooter pop down the road. The timing's off and the machine backfires furiously.

He's not wearing his jungle hat today; his sunglasses are pushed up on his forehead. He leans the scooter against a tree near the road and says hello to several of us individually as he walks toward the bench. He smiles and flips a salute to Brock, who grins and waves back.

"Hey, Thieu!" Buelen calls. "Can you talk to these guys?"

The faces of the prisoners have been without expression since Thieu's arrival. They've been regarding him carefully, his scooter, his clothes, his casual relation with us.

Thieu does not posture or swagger but addresses the prisoners as a group in a subdued voice. One of the men, the one I judge to be the oldest, replies briefly. Thieu turns to Buelen. "What you want to know, First Sergeant?"

Buelen quickly looks to Smith, who shrugs. Everyone is watching. "Jesus, I don't know!" Buelen blusters as his color rises. "Ask them their ages!"

Thieu speaks rapidly. All of the prisoners break into smiles and start to talk at once. After two or three minutes of easy chatter, Thieu looks at the first sergeant. "Top," he says and begins to point as he speaks, "that one be seventeen, that one twenty-six, that one twenty-two, he thirty, he nineteen, that one also nineteen, that one twenty, that one twenty-three, that one twenty-five, him twenty-two."

"Very good, Thieu. Jesus, where's the MI team?" Buelen glances over his shoulder, studiously avoiding the grins of the crowd. Even Smith is smiling.

Dunn walks up to Buelen and asks permission to take a pair of sandals from one of the prisoners. Relieved by the distraction, Buelen waves a hand magnanimously. "Sure, go ahead! Take all of them for all I care."

Dunn kneels and yanks the sandals from the feet of a startled prisoner. *What was it—only a day or two earlier when he helped himself to a belt from a dying enemy soldier? Morrisey caught him at it, caught him as he rolled the man over in the process of removing it, the man still conscious, if only barely so. He told Dunn he ought to have some goddam respect for a dying man, but when we carried him to the helicopter a short time later, two bottles of saline glinting on each side of him like rockets, the belt was missing. Morrisey saw it, too.*

"What the hell do you think you're doing, Dunn?" Morrisey asks now.

The radio operator stands, the sandals in one hand. "Top gave me permission. You heard him!"

Brock puffs on his cigar and watches Morrisey. The blood rushes to Morrisey's face. "Going to put on a show for the folks back home, Dunn? Snatched those sandals from a VC who jumped out of the bushes at you with a four-foot machete?"

"Careful, Morrisey," Smith says.

"Going to go home the big hero? With all your souvenirs?"

"Morrisey! I'm warning you! Dunn has the first sergeant's permission."

"That makes it right, Sergeant?"

Buelen's furious. "You hold your tongue or I'll slap you with an Article fifteen."

Morrisey makes no effort to disguise his contempt. The rest of us wait for the finale . . . Suddenly Jenkins pushes through and drops a hand on Morrisey's shoulder. "Hey, Richie."

Morrisey exhales slowly. I can see his sudden, profound realization of what's been happening and was about to happen. I'm disappointed—I think most of us are. It was so close, he's never been that close before. I shouldn't feel this way.

"Sorry, Top," he says softly, but as clearly as though he were shouting. "It wasn't you that made me angry."

"That temper's going to get you in big trouble some day."

"First Sergeant!" Thieu calls. He's been speaking with one of the prisoners. "This man need go to bathroom."

Buelen hesitates, then points at me. "You, O'Neill. Take this man out into the trees."

"Good God, Top! I may be a medic . . ." My eyes are drawn to the ropes that bind the prisoner's hands.

The prisoner is the first to understand my hesitation, and grins. Suddenly everyone, including Top and Morrisey, is laughing.

Buelen hands me his pistol. "It's your problem, O'Neill. Know how to handle this thing? For Chrissake, don't prove it on me!" He backs up in mock terror, then chuckles. Obligingly, everyone smiles.

This is absurd, I think, as I motion the prisoner toward some dense growth beyond the sickcall tent. I stuff the pistol in my belt and follow the man in black. I can feel the sun and the knowledge that everyone's watching. "Fuck it!" I mutter aloud. This causes the prisoner to turn and stare anxiously at me. I've already withdrawn a small penknife, and I begin to saw through the cord around his wrists. The effort is curiously intimate. Once my hand touches his and I'm surprised by the warmth of that touch, surprised at my own surprise.

The prisoner relaxes, smiles. I don't. I point at a clump of bushes. The pistol feels heavy, ridiculously heavy in my belt. I look away, set my gaze on a pottery bowl at the base of a rubber tree, the bowl cracked, half hidden by coarse grass. It's been at least three years since these trees were last tapped. I glance once at the prisoner, then turn away and let him finish.

When we come back, the prisoner walking quietly beside me, hands free, Buelen starts to speak but decides not to. The look on my face must have restrained him. I hand him the .45 without comment, then move away to stand between Jenkins and Morrisey.

"Here's the MI team!" Wilbur announces almost gaily, as a jeep roars into the grove. The two ARVN interrogators are in the front seat, the American captain as usual in the back, gripping his cap.

An open two-and-a-half ton truck stops beside the road. Two MPs are in the cab; two more stand in the back grasping a steel roof support. All of them are armed. One of the MPs in back doesn't move when the others begin to climb down, but studies us through flashing, silvered glasses. His face is without expression. It's a long time since I've seen Johnny Mirrors . . . and there's an odd thrill, even pleasure in this recognition, this familiarity.

"Somebody tie that prisoner's wrists!" Buelen shouts. "Don't give him a chance to escape!" Johnny Mirrors is looking directly at me—I can feel it although the mirrored surfaces reveal nothing.

The prisoners suddenly look tense under the bland scrutiny of the two interrogators. They are loaded in the back of the truck. Johnny Mirrors has turned his back to point his rifle at the enemy. It could be worse for them, I suppose; they could be thirteen thousand miles from home.

Smith accosts Morrisey at the door to the treatment tent. "What's bugging you?"

Morrisey mumbles something glib about Vietnam and starts to enter the room.

"You wait a minute! I haven't finished talking to you! You were out of order a few minutes ago."

Morrisey's still pissed—strung out. "I know, Sarge, and I agreed."

"If you were out in the field, maybe you'd feel a little differently about Dunn. Good thing Captain Howard wasn't here."

"Captain Howard spent most of his time in the infantry right here in the plantation in a snug little battalion aid station. As for being in the field, I suppose I might feel differently, but I hope I wouldn't. In any case, I'm not there . . . and neither is Dunn."

The initial reaction to the threat is very quiet. Four or five months ago, the result would have been immediate vocal outrage, but then four or five months ago, it would have been unthinkable. And what makes it worse is that it began as rumor, deliberately, I'm sure. And just because Milliken, or Buelen, or Smith *allegedly* told someone that it was going to happen shouldn't make it true. But, because of the nature of this place, the possibility of its being true is better than good: we've come to expect disaster.

Despite all of Smith's activities, his development schemes and tidying-up, a listlessness is pervading the company. It's reflected in the resentment against nighttime cries for litter-bearers, the dire mutterings and simple apathy the guards encounter as they turn the lights on in the hooches and shake this person and that. More and more, the noise of stereos surrounds us as we cluster in small groups in various hooches and listen to someone else voice our antagonism.

It's obvious now that even the NCOs are aware of the change, or are at least aware of the increased use of drugs, but these perceptions have not been graced by any intelligent means of solving the problem. And it is a problem.

It's a problem for me now as I stand in this darkening tent and watch four men who have yet to become aware of my presence. I wait for an excuse to talk to them, to share this latest trouble, the latest rumor which should be troubling us all, but I also wonder if it's really worth the bother, if I shouldn't sit down with them and forget it.

The saccharine, cloying smell of incense glides over me like a shroud. Soft, hip chatter from the base radio station issues from somewhere beyond the luminous blue dial behind Owen's head. Four fans aimed at the center of the room purr with steady contentment. Stevens giggles suddenly for no apparent reason and lapses into silence. Gerty has the roach.

"Heyyyy, Jon!" Stevens waves from the depths of his lawn chair. The rest turn and stare at me like a flock of owls.

"For Christ's sake, knock, O'Neill!" Newell scowls at me. He's been scowling constantly, seems perpetually irritable. Several times he has arrived in the treatment tent stoned, a practice he once scrupulously avoided. I wonder if he's only stoned. The degree of his self-absorption, his lack of awareness at these times is unusual, not like someone on a regular high. If he's suddenly spoken to, his head turns ponderously in the direction of the voice. His eyes, bloodshot and without focus, drag along in a reluctant, rolling pursuit, scarcely discover the source of the intrusion before they move on, then stop and drift back. On such occasions, we quietly herd him to one side while Morrisey or Owen assumes the additional burden. And he's been lucky . . . none of the doctors or NCOs seem aware of his strange behavior.

"Do you think there's really going to be a levy?" I ask.

"Ahhh, shit!" Gerty says. "How many rumors have you heard since you got here?"

"I know, but Anderson says battalion's going to levy ten

of us to the field before the month is over . . . we're over strength, Smith told him.''

''Well fuck'em! I'm not a goddam medic so they can't send me anyway.''

''Me and Newell are ninety-one Cs—they sure as hell aren't going to send us,'' Owen says. ''Besides, we're short.''

''Why the fuck are they telling us now?'' Stevens asks. ''Why don't they just do it instead of fucking with our minds for weeks.''

''That's what Morrisey said.'' Our eyes meet. We both have enough time remaining.

''Good thing *he's* short!'' Newell grunts. Despite myself, I laugh with the rest of them.

''C'mon, Jon!'' Stevens says, his face suddenly lapsing into a smile. ''Sit down! They're not sending us anywhere tonight.''

It's almost dark in the tent. Why do I have to feel ambivalent, like a coward?

''Where's Morrisey?''

''On duty.''

Newell laughs. ''Good fucking thing . . .'cause I ain't for shit!''

''Reading a fucking book, I suppose,'' Stevens says.

''Yeah, the lifers won't bother him at this time of night.''

''He never leaves the company anymore.''

''Nope. He's afraid he's going to blow his cool, or something.''

Stevens lights a candle, leans over a crate that serves as a table, and rolls a joint. He does a very professional job, thumbs and fingers moving mechanically.

''Well, when was the last Medcap?'' Owen asks.

''Weeks ago,'' Stevens says. ''I drove.''

''He didn't go on that one. I heard he refused. He doesn't even go to the PX anymore if he can help it. He's always asking me to get stuff for him.''

''Fucking lifers! They're doing this deliberately!'' Stevens swears with sudden fury.

EIGHTEEN

"**H**i!" the soldier says, a smile on his handsome, tanned face. He's wearing blue pajamas, sitting on a cot in the old ward. Magazines are scattered on the floor beside him.

"Hi. When did you get here?"

"About two hours ago."

"Funny, I didn't know about it. Did anyone come and get your name and unit—that sort of stuff?"

"Yes. A kind of chunky guy."

"Kostek."

"That's him. I'm Sam Hardaker."

I sit down on an empty cot. The canvas and wood frame creak under the sudden weight. "What's the problem, Sam?"

"Got a fever. Captain Brock thinks I may have malaria. They're doing a blood test now . . . it might take a while. What do they do if I have it?"

"Evacuate you to one of the surgical hospitals. Wrap you in ice blankets. It's all pretty routine. How are you feeling now?"

"Not bad. A little woozy—nothing much." He touches his forehead.

"Where are you from?"

"The First and Fourth. I'm a mortarman."

"Hey, I know a guy in Alpha Company."

"That's my company!"

I don't remember what I came through the ward to do, but it couldn't have been that important. Suddenly, none of it seems that important—all the hurry. I could count on one hand the times I've stopped in the wards and talked to a patient. A couple of the other patients are sleeping, some are reading. There's a hushed, calm feeling in the tent. Sam and I talk quietly. I like him. He seems direct and unscathed, gentle. Some people must be like that, I think: able to survive any cataclysm and remain at peace with just being alive. He's been in Vietnam as long as I have. We discover that we came on the same plane. There seems to be so much distance between now and back then, far more distance than time would indicate, and yet I feel as though I've gone nowhere. I tell Sam that. He seems to understand.

I look down at my watch. "Damn! Hey, man, I've got five minutes left to get chow. Want to play cards after supper?"

"Sure."

"I'll see you in a little while."

I'm the last one in the mess hall. There's no line at the steam tables, only a couple of cooks in greasy white who gape listlessly over the containers of food. I grab a tray and shove it along the stainless steel rack. "You damn near missed it, O'Neill," Milliken growls.

The cooks dump waxed beans, mashed potatoes, and some kind of slimy meat on my tray. "Want another spoonful?" the cook over the mash potatoes asks.

"No extras!" Milliken says.

"You didn't have to bother, Sergeant."

The mess hall is empty when I leave. I wander into the ward and stop at the orderly's desk. "Got a deck of cards?"

"Sure, Jon, but they can't leave the ward."

"That's no problem. I'm playing with Hardaker."

"Who?"

"Sam Hardaker." I point down the aisle toward his cot, but the cot is empty, the blanket folded at one end as though no one's been there at all.

"Where the hell is he?"

"Who do you mean, Jon?"

"The guy they were waiting on the malaria smear . . . I didn't hear any helicopter take off."

"He died, Jon."

"Sure, so did my great grandmother."

"Hey, I'm not kidding!" The orderly stands up behind the desk, his distress obvious.

"People don't die of malaria like that! Cut the shit! I was just talking to him thirty minutes ago. He was fine! We're going to play cards."

"It was cerebral malaria. His temp went to 112 in about five minutes. He's in the morgue."

I shake my head. Why's this fucking orderly being so goddam insistent?

"Hey, Jon?"

I shake my head again, then drop the cards on the desk and walk down the aisle to the door. There's no one in the A&D office. I walk a few feet farther, past the sickcall tent where I can see the morgue. Kostek is standing in front, wiping his face. A book of field tags dangles from the other hand. He wipes his mouth with the back of his hand, almost like he's washing himself, I'm thinking. He sees me. "Jesus, where were you?" He sounds pissed. "They had to come get me for this! You're supposed to be on duty!"

"Sorry."

"That all you can fucking say, 'Sorry?' Here's the information—you can do the death certificates. Graves'll be here in a couple of minutes. And I don't want to be bothered again!" He looks at me. "What's your fucking trouble, O'Neill?"

Kostek's stoned. He always gets like this when he's stoned and is interrupted. He doesn't mean anything by it.

No one ever means anything by it.

Night comes and I can't sleep. Finally, I lie down on an examination table behind my office, but there are no thoughts and no sleep either. I shut my eyes.

. . . and can't remember falling to sleep until I wake up to find the entire tent shaking. For an instant I'm terrified as I listen to instruments and bottles clink quietly on waves of distant thunder. I feel the table, the earth itself crumbling away beneath me when, miles away, the bombs from the B-52s cease and the world becomes quiet. In the first light of morning I watch the silhouettes of insects on the screen wall beside me, feel cold sweat on my forehead, feel the skin of my body, my stomach, my groin, my thighs shrouded in clammy, day-old clothing. A cricket begins to chirp in the dark recesses beneath the tent. In the dawn chill, I flop over on my belly and pull my arms in beneath my chest. My eyes close and I plunge into a bottomless void.

"Hey, O'Neill!" Someone's shaking me. There's a high whine in the distance, coming toward me. Where the fuck am I? I sit up. A few feet away from me, through the screens, the treatment tent basks like a huge vessel in golden sunlight. "You awake?"

"Yeah . . ."

"Gotta hustle, man!" The guard disappears through the curtain.

The helicopter roars down on the pad. I barge out of the room after the guard.

Inside the ship are a young girl, an older woman, and still another woman whose face is partially hidden behind her huge belly. The girl is about ten, eleven at most. I shiver in the still-cold dawn but she seems oblivious of anything but this raw, fresh world with the gale from the helicopter whipping her hair and thin blouse, and the flashing sunlight against which she shields her eyes. As we walk toward the treatment tent, I feel awkward and lean toward her, as though to protect her, but her eyes are wide and happy. She smiles with the delight of discovery—this is a place that never existed for her before.

Something presses my hand, tries to cling to it. Startled, I realize that her hand is seeking mine, wanting to hold it. I feel her vibrancy, her thrill, and above all, her trust. She has absolute faith in me, in us. She's alive and happy to be alive. She has no knowledge of death.

I can't remember such instantaneous happiness, such total delight and need. I hover near her while she absorbs the next events: Brock's examination of her mother's belly with a stethoscope, the counting of contractions, her mother's pain that somehow conveys no fear, the strapping of her mother's legs in the hope she can make it to Tainan. I offer my hand as we start back to the ship; the girl seizes it with that incredible confidence and joy.

And three hours later my shirt feels waterlogged and smells as sour as my disposition's become. It's Monday sickcall, the worst, and a long time before noon. Kostek's gone on a Medcap.

Smith squeezes past the endless line into my office with an X ray request slip in his hand. "This wasn't filled out properly, O'Neill."

I turn from a Vietnamese soldier who has just moved up in line. "What's wrong? That's the way we've always done it. They do it like that in treatment."

"This isn't treatment, remember? Over here, you're supposed to complete all the information requested, even on the slips from treatment. New SOP."

"I see. How the hell was I supposed to know that?"

"Don't start sounding off, O'Neill! I just got finished with Morrisey, because they're going to have to do it, too, from now on. That was meant as a service to you. So I'm telling you now!"

"Lookit, Sarge . . ." I wave a hand behind my head. "I'm up to my ears . . . can't this wait? And why the hell did Kostek get allowed to go on a Medcap on a fucking Monday? The worst day! I've been on duty almost twenty-four hours."

"I'm getting a little tired of the bitching around here! Kostek put that request in over a week ago, and these forms should have been filled in properly right along!"

"You want it all filled in?" I ask in a quieter voice, taking the slip. Morrisey must have done a job on him.

He nods. "Like that."

I don't so much hear as feel Smith leave. I drop his completed slip beside the log and return to the ARVN, who snaps to attention and salutes me. A boyish grin spreads across the smooth, round face beneath the jungle hat. I've been here long enough now to know that the smile doesn't mean amusement, isn't proof of the man's puerile charm, but simply a reflection of uneasiness. Simply . . . hah! He hands me a note from Thieu.

As I study the delicate handwriting, I'm well beyond the point of feeling sympathy for this man's ignorance of our military protocol. The soldier is a friend of Thieu's, thus undoubtedly the source of some potential, or realized favor. He needs some shots.

I yawn and point at the bench a few feet away. I haven't spoken a word since Smith left. The men on the already crowded bench make room for the ARVN. He sits down, looks cautiously about, and smiles briefly at each of his neighbors.

A black hand places a lab slip on the counter. I look up into a pair of purple-tinted granny glasses. Lovely beads dangle around the American infantryman's neck, shimmer against his moist, dark skin. I logged this man a while ago and he's back with confirmation of what we both knew.

"The man says I got to come here before I get my shots."

I reach for a book of field medical cards which are used for reporting venereal diseases as well as tagging the wounded and dead. I place a card on the open log book and start to fill in the soldier's name. "This your first dose?"

"No."

260

I turn the card over. "Where did you get it this time?"

"What you got to know that for?"

I force myself to meet the soldier's tinted, rectangular gaze. Don't start acting like a snot, I think, like Davies. Why get upset? "Look, we keep a record of the places where you guys pick it up, so if we see too much of a problem in one area, we can report it to the division surgeon and he can take some kind of corrective action, OK?"

I hate to look through colored glasses, I hate the advantage it gives the person wearing them. "Dong Nai Bridge." The lips move, thick, ribbed, with a deep cleft in the top lip.

I start to fill in the card. "Christ, they must have a plum out there," I say conversationally, thinking I don't want to be like Davies. "We've had two guys from the engineers already, since yesterday."

"Hey, why don't you can the lecture."

"If it bothers you that much, OK." I bend over the card. When I reach the section for race, I write "*N*" for Negroid.

The soldier points at the N. "Put AA there, man."

"AA? What the hell is that?"

"Afro-American."

We're interrupted by an approaching helicopter. I look out the front of the tent, over the line of sickcall patients that stretches almost to the treatment tent. The ship churns in as a dozen men run toward it. Conversation inside and outside the tent ceases.

"What's going on?" the soldier asks.

"Six bodies—the remains of a firefight last night." Stevens and Morrisey have teamed up with the crewchief. They drag the bodies out of the Huey and stagger the few feet with each bag to the stretchers. The rubber bags are wet, gleaming in the sun. From here I can feel their bulkiness, smell the pungent hint of decay. I'm going to have to open each one of them.

"Fucking gooks!" the soldier beside me says.

The train of litters passes the sickcall tent on the way to the morgue. An almost physical strain moves from man to man along the waiting line. Those who have been sleeping on the bench waken, turn slowly as the procession goes by.

"Hey," I say to the black infantryman, "I've got to do death certificates on those men, so will you please take my word? I'd just as soon put 'AA' in that space—it really makes no difference to me—only they're going to keep sending that card back until I change it to 'N.' I have no control over the way they want things done."

"That 'N' means nigger." The soldier punches the tip of his index finger on the mark I entered in the space.

I smell the acrid, alien odor of his body, something I never noticed with Jenks . . . Fighting for control, I meet that comic purple gaze. "If that 'N' means 'nigger' to you," I say very carefully as I feel my way through the thought, not daring now to make a mistake, "what do you think the 'ARVN' I put down for him stands for?" I point at the Vietnamese soldier who promptly responds with a smile.

The black soldier turns and looks at the Vietnamese. The ARVN stands up and salutes. Soft, short laughter undulates along the line.

"Well, what do you think it means? 'Fucking gook?' "

The black soldier picks up the medical tag and carefully tears it to pieces. He gathers the remnants, raises then opens his hand, and lets the contents twirl to the floor. "I'll get my shots some other place."

"You do that!"

He pushes away toward the door. When I see him next, he's walking stiffly through the grove, his medical records twisted in his hand.

A field medic from down the road enters the office and helps himself to coffee. "Giving you a rough time, Jon?"

"This job sucks. How are you doing?"

"Fine! My buddy Ernie got himself this gorgeous gook gal in Vung Tau a couple of weeks ago—brought home some pictures."

"And a dose, I suppose."

He laughs. "Hell, no. She was clean. Ernie took some penicillin with him and dosed her for two days before he screwed her. He had to rough it with blow jobs for a while."

"That's too bad."

He laughs again, a dry sound. His look is hard and vaguely wary. He's not pleasant when he's drunk, or so I've been told. I've been drinking with him only once. "Yeah, Ernie said she was the best gook gal he ever screwed. Her cunt and her armpits weren't shaved. Black hair everywhere. He could put his nose in one, his cock in the other."

"They're putting Preludin on the dangerous drug list," I say.

"No kidding? Just diet pills?"

"Nope. All amphetamines. Preludin's been banned in Sweden, or so I've heard."

"How are my boys going to do guard duty?"

"Yeah."

"Price is bound to go up."

"Were you paying Davies?"

He's silent.

I ask the next man in line to wait a minute, and take the medic over behind the original ward to the drug supply tent. The druggist knows him because he obtains his field supplies here. "He needs some Preludin."

"Jesus, O'Neill, they've gotten strict on that stuff."

"I know. I thought maybe the two of you might talk it over." I start back along the boardwalk.

A few minutes later I hear a tapping on the screen. I look around. The medic is standing in the sunshine, all sweat and smiles. "Thanks, buddy." He pats his chest pocket. "What do I owe you?"

"Nothing."

That one time he and I went drinking, he had to show me pictures of his wife. We were in his hooch. "She didn't want me to forget her," he explained as he took the photographs from his foot locker. There was a suggestion of apology, even embarrassment in his voice. He sat down in front of me and slowly handed me several colored polaroid pictures, then reached for his can of beer. His eyes scrutinized me carefully, waiting for something, challenging me.

It was impossible not to show my astonishment when my eyes rested on the top picture. I understood then that there was something else in his look: puzzlement, even anxiety.

The woman in the photograph was young, in her late teens or very early twenties. Her hair hung long, her eyes gleamed pink in the light of the flash, and she was naked. She was good looking, her body young and firm—and already I was worried about what to say since the customary remarks one makes when presented with family pictures were out of the question.

There were several frontal views of her, sitting with her legs apart, standing, lifting her breasts with her hands, looking like every woman I'd seen in Brock's blue films and in the skin mags. There was even one of her going down on her husband.

"How in hell did you take this one?" I asked and turned the self-portrait to my companion.

He looked at the picture and blushed. "I used a broom."

I roared.

For a moment he stared at me, the wariness pronounced, and then a smile crept onto his face. Soon warm tears of laughter flowed freely; when one of us would lapse the other would produce fresh gales. Gradually, the hilarity became unrelated to the original cause, became something deeper and more painful. At last we left the hooch, arm in arm, exhausted, seeking more liquor.

And by morning, the previous evening's hilarity was relentlessly suppressed as I thought of the pictures, the pretty woman, and with a soft ache in my loins wondered with whom she was making it while her husband died nightly in the rustling darkness. He was a fine medic—I heard more than one of his men say that, but she could never know. Not that it would have mattered. That isn't how the world works, I mean The World, too.

It was around that time Brock put up his short-timer's calendar. (Like me, he had about five months left.) His calendar consisted of a crude, mimeographed drawing of Lucy and Charlie Brown. Lucy was bent over, exposing her ass, while Charlie, sweat flying from his face, inserted a monstrous penis. The figures had been segmented into 180 numbered parts, each one to be blocked out with every passing day. The last day, number one, was the head of the penis. "Oh, good grief!" was the caption.

NINETEEN

*W*hen dusk overcame the land, it was as though someone had closed a huge valve; the roar and surge of the highway trickled into silence becoming isolated pools of motion revealed here and there by the incautious winking of a light, and then darkness.

Only in the sky was something approaching life ever-present as strange, invisible ships blasted and clattered through the night, their passage traced by flecks of red and green, flashing red, sudden brilliant beams of white that burst upon the sable land for an instant or two and vanished. Streams of explosive orange and red crashed from sky to an ingestive, smoky earth; flares fell away into obscurity.

It was lovely. The most spectacular fireworks display couldn't begin to convey the reality, or the waste. Sitting on the bench in front of treatment, gazing between the silhouetted trunks of the rubber trees, time and again I wondered at the primeval fear compelling us to strip this land, to tear at the secretive depths of its jungles.

I saw Puff (the Magic Dragon) only once, a dream weapon for a dream war. It came and spewed its flame upon the earth. It roared in cumbrous, ponderous motions about the sky; the blaze of its miniguns, the thunder of its propellor engines ripped the humid darkness. And once, in the glow of a flare, I caught a glimpse of the huge, winged beast as it slipped through orange clouds of its own making. It vanished into the night and moments later flames roared out of nowhere, down upon our world, and exploded in stone, earth, wood. How could a stream of tracers, solid red, literally thousands *of bullets a minute, ever luck upon something so minute as a man?*

It was night, precious night, and we sat on the bench and watched thousands upon thousands of dollars, watched a glowing treasure flow out of its smelter to be swallowed by the earth while Cobras and Hueys flitted, darted, clattered overhead, the frenetic issue of that winged creature. There was no related pain or misery; we sat there, smoked cigarettes and dope, drank beer, and watched a wondrous spectacle with no more impact than a mugging on the twenty-one inch screen. It was beautiful.

"Kostek's going to do a siren."

"A what?"

Gittoni gestures to me to follow and disappears out the door of the hooch. He's carrying his lawn chair. "Kill the lights when you come!" he calls back.

Across the way I can see the lifers seated around their table. I'm prepared for this scene of domestic tranquility, but not for the crowd outside the hooch. Within moments I've collided with several chairs and their contents. "Jesus, man!" someone whispers.

I call quietly for Gittoni.

"Over here, O'Neill," Gerty hisses.

No sooner have I settled into my chair when away in the distance, from the direction of division, a siren begins to wail. "That's incoming!" I cry aloud as I start out of my chair. A hand grabs my arm and forces me back down.

"That's Kostek . . . over behind the supply tent."

For several moments the siren hovers at its peak, then drops to a low growl. Immediately, it begins to rise again.

Inside the NCO hooch, there's instant chaos. Chairs fall as the lifers scramble down the hall to their rooms. We can see the vacant table and scattered chairs. Locker doors clank, lights flick on, then off. Suddenly, the hall explodes with men in helmets and flak jackets. Rifles clink. Buelen snatches the light chain over the table.

The screen door slams repeatedly and boots thud on the steps that lead down into the NCO bunker. The siren pierces the night again.

"Shit!" Buelen mumbles. We hear him clump back up the stairs, hear the hooch door slap.

"Yeah, don't forget that bottle, lifer!" Stevens calls softly. Smells of marijuana and beer eddy around me. The minutes go by. There's a sudden burst of light and a face appears, cupped behind a hand that shelters a cigarette lighter, then everything's dark again. In this thick blackness I feel an insane urge to laugh, the way I did as a child playing hide and seek. I cover my mouth.

"Hey! This is a red alert! Get into your bunkers!" Milliken's hoarse voice rings out.

No one moves.

"Who's that out there?" Buelen demands.

Nobody replies.

Someone starts whistling, the sound like a descending rocket.

"Incoming!"

"Oh, mercy! Oh, oh!" Gerty squeaks.

"Medic!"

A prolonged hush settles on the bunker. Finally we hear the clink of weapons again, scuffing feet as the NCOs begin to emerge. A flashlight sweeps over us but is quickly extinguished. The lights in the NCO hooch pop on. We watch them mill around their table. Wilbur bends over and picks up a fallen chair.

"Sandwich time, lifers!"

"Yeah, eatta bun!"

They start to remove their headgear. When the helmets come off, it's embarrassing, the baldness in some instances, the greasiness of the hair in others, the signs of ineffectual, mediocre men posing as soldiers.

Smith, however, stands with his back to the table and faces the darkness and us, his face in shadow, his thoughts impenetrable. Before we have to learn those thoughts, we fold our chairs and wander away to our tents.

"Just got here; got a three-day standdown," the infantryman, or "grunt" says. His fatigues, normally a faded green, are reddish brown and filthy, as are his helmet, face, and boots. Several grenade pins dangle from the webbing on his helmet. From where I'm sitting in the back of the ambulance, I can read "Short!", "96 days!", "F.T.A.," "Peace," "Make Love, Not War," these slogans written on the camouflage cover with a ballpoint pen. His rifle lies on the floor; surface rust spots the barrel, and the stock is chipped and taped in one place. Whether it's from naivete or inexperience, I'm always a little startled, even horrified by a weapon in such condition, as though weapons above all (unlike everything else) are sacrosanct, cannot age or deteriorate with use, but must always convey pristine efficiency equal to the sleek technology that records their results. "My battalion got the pennant this month," the man explains to Morrisey, who's riding shotgun.

"Incentive program," Morrisey replies and raises a grim smile on the soldier's face.

"Tell me, Morrisey!" Stevens hollers over the whine of the motor as he downshifts onto Highway 10, "what the hell got you to leave the company?"

"The weather. It's such a lovely day for a drive."

"The club, Stevens! You're going to drop us off at division on the way back," I shout, pressing my head into the cab over the infantryman's shoulder.

"Nice of you to invite me!" Stevens says.

"You're invited." I settle back into the depths of the ambulance, my back to the wall, and watch the trees, the steel air control tower, the blue, dust-tinged sky flow past the rear windows. Jenkins engineered this trip to get Morrisey out—he's going to meet us at the division EM club. He's more worried about Morrisey, although I don't know why so much now; Morrisey's been very quiet since that last outburst with Smith, has kept to himself more than ever, has, if anything, seemed more cautious. I'm sure that all he wants is to get through the remaining weeks, few weeks for him, and get home. (It's always worse at the end, just like the beginning for some: enough people have come and gone—I know the signs.)

My thoughts have been on home more frequently. It's the company, what's happening to it. I want things to be alright for just a little longer—then I won't give a shit. I write now, about once every two weeks—enough to keep Howard off my back and to encourage the daily arrival of letters, that sensation of receiving something tangible from the World regardless of what it is and whether I read it or not.

Morrisey holds the door for the grunt and me while he stares intently in the direction of the PX building. From where I am, halfway into the cab, I can't determine the source of his interest.

"Look, man," he says, and grabs the grunt by his sleeve. "Why don't you let me or one of the other guys get your cigarettes?"

The grunt rubs his face with the back of his wrist. "Hey, you guys have been real nice, giving me a lift and all that, but

I'm not so tired I can't walk down there and get my own cigs."

The grunt ambles down the path toward the twin doors of the low, one-storey building. Several men burst out through the doors of the PX, their arms full of bags. Three uniformed men stand just off the path about fifty feet away from me and watch the flow of people. Suddenly I focus on the three men as the grunt approaches them.

Morrisey starts past me, down the path at a cautious gait.

The infantryman walks right past the three men, a lieutenant colonel, a first sergeant, and a master sergeant. I don't think he even noticed them. They've been talking idly among themselves, but the first sergeant looks out of the corner of his eyes and runs his gaze over the grunt. "Soldier!" He hails the grunt, but not loudly. The infantryman continues toward the building.

"Soldier!"

The grunt stops and looks back. "Sarge?"

"Don't you believe in saluting an officer? Are you deaf? Come here, soldier!" The sergeant moves away from his companions, closer to the path. Others leaving the PX look away.

The grunt stands still while the first sergeant walks slowly around him and checks his hair, his uniform, even the inscriptions on his helmet; and I remember battalion, almost half a year ago now, another colonel and a sergeant major, Stevens skipping away among the hooches with his pack of cigarettes that weren't cigarettes, leaving me prey.

"What's your unit, soldier?"

The grunt tells him.

"I want you to get a shave, and a haircut, and a shower, and a goddam clean uniform."

"Sarge, I just came in from the field—I'd like to get some cigarettes."

The first sergeant's voice grows quiet and soothing. "Sure, that's just fine . . . but you run along and do those other things first, and then you can buy your cigarettes."

The grunt's back stiffens slightly. He looks straight at the sergeant as his right hand, pressed to his thigh, makes a slow, circular motion. Suddenly he looks old, older than the men he's confronting. As I watch him, I feel callow. Reluctantly, he turns and starts back toward us, the face softening into the nineteen- or twenty-year-old he is, once was.

"Soldier!" It's the master sergeant.

The grunt's head droops as he stares at the ground, bites his lip, and turns back.

"How long have you been in this man's army?"

"One year, three months, Sergeant." I have to strain to hear the reply.

"Well, now, in all that time did anyone ever teach you to salute an officer?"

"Yes, Sergeant."

"Do you consider the colonel here an officer?"

The grunt looks startled, then stiffens into a salute. "Sorry, sir. I guess I didn't see you."

The lieutenant colonel returns the salute. "What's your unit, soldier?"

The grunt repeats the information.

"Take that down, First Sergeant!" The lieutenant colonel points pistollike at the sergeant, but his milky eyes never leave the infantryman. "If you ever want to come to this PX again, soldier, you will look and act like a real soldier of the United States Army! That means you will have a proper haircut and uniform!"

Once again the grunt turns and starts for the ambulance, but now Morrisey has planted himself in the middle of the path. He reaches out and stops the grunt. "What kind of cigarettes do you want?"

"Don't bother!"

"What kind do you want?" His voice is loud, too loud.

The grunt mutters something and Morrisey starts down the path. He walks right by the three career men and neatly salutes the lieutenant colonel. He receives a hesitant salute in return. The combined stares of the three men follow him into the PX.

Several minutes pass, much too long a time for a single purchase. The doors open occasionally and someone wanders out to pass under the scrutiny of the three lifers, but it's as though they're waiting, too, and their inspections seem cursory.

The doors open and a group of men jostle each other into the sunlight, laughing, calling back to the Vietnamese sales girls. Morrisey's among them. They're almost even with the lifers. One by one, the men begin to salute.

"Soldier!" The grunt tenses beside me. The cluster of men shuffle to a stop.

"Hey, you!"

Morrisey slowly swings to face the three men . . . the first sergeant seems to be looking directly at him.

"You!"

Morrisey starts to open his mouth but the man next to him speaks first. "Me, Sarge?"

"Who the hell else would I be talking to? When did you have your last haircut?"

Morrisey shrinks slightly, turns and continues up the path.

"Jesus, how do you stand it?" The grunt is incredulous.

The ambulance grinds back up the highway toward division headquarters. "I don't," Morrisey says. "That's the first time I've been in there in three months. Why don't we forget the club, O'Neill?"

"Jenks is waiting."

"He'll get over it."

"Sorry I got you into that," the grunt says.

"Hell, man, that wasn't your doing."

They tried to blame Stevens, to say he precipitated it. I thought it was hilarious. I was in the motorpool when he drove in, the side of the ambulance peeled back all the way from the driver's door to the taillight like the top of a sardine can. The rolled metal jiggled and squeaked as the vehicle lurched through the holes and ruts of the driveway. Stevens jumped from the cab, grinning from ear to ear (probably still stoned—he must have been when it happened: no one could have controlled it otherwise), and casually announced to the motor pool sergeant who had signed for all the equipment, that they had been sideswiped by an earthmover on the way back from the village, but that "everyone was OK, just fine."

"Everyone" included Brock and Nye. Brock climbed down from the cab, shook his head and muttered, "damndest thing I ever saw," then stumped off in the direction of his hooch and a stiff drink.

Buster Wilbur was standing right behind the motor pool sergeant. He laughed uproariously like the rest of us, convinced, I'm sure (like the rest of us) that what we were seeing was the funniest thing that had happened in a long, long time. Suddenly he was on the ground, holding his jaw; blood oozed from his mouth. The motor pool sergeant towered over him, both fists clenched, and called him a "goddam fool!" before he stormed away. So it was getting to them, too . . .

Nothing happened to the motor pool sergeant, nothing at

all, and that was worse—he had to live in silence with Smith, with Smith's special silence and all the scorn and contempt and revulsion that implied. It was awful. He was immediately an outcast, increasingly morose as he drank himself sick at the club almost every night, and bored anyone stupid enough to listen with the problems of the new army. Annie avoided him like the plague; she obviously dreaded those moments when they might be left alone and she would have no excuse not to listen.

Smith ran the company—nobody doubted it by then. It seemed as though no one cared anymore, except Smith. He could have the company as long as he left us alone.

He didn't. Two days after the incident with the ambulance, he announced (through his mouthpiece, First Sergeant Buelen) who was going to the field—who the ten would be. And we all stood in formation that morning, frozen in silence, and momentarily hated everyone around us, our friends, our companions, anyone who might not be going when we might be. It had been that way on a more subtle basis ever since the rumor started—but I don't think too many understood it: the peevishness, the increased ill humor and mutual distrust.

Nine of those called out of formation (to pack and leave for their respective infantry units within the hour) were new personnel, people who had arrived within the past month and a half, people we didn't really know yet. Kostek stayed with us —A&D, the paper war, was critical. Stevens was tenth. He didn't say anything to anybody from the moment his name was read (and it was read last) until he climbed into the back of a three-quarter-ton truck. I watched the truck drive away, watched it disappear down the tunnel of rubber trees toward the middle of the plantation, Highway 10 and the infantry battalions beyond, watched him stare back at us with a bleak, uncomprehending look.

There was talk—very briefly. "She's getting fucked," Kostek says. "You guys are like a bunch of kiddies with a virgin queen. I tell you, when a woman looks that good, she's getting her eyes fucked out on a regular basis, and loving it."

"Why don't you shove it, Kostek?" Gerty snaps. Except for our voices, the only clue that we exist at all is an occasional glow of a cigarette. There are the usual smells of overripe foliage and marijuana. "I get goddam sick of listening to you shit on everything! What's it like, Kostek, to get up every morning certain that everything sucks just as bad as it did the day before?''

For once there's no response, no cocksure laughter. For just this instant, I see clearly that Kostek needs us, just as we usually find his dark wisdom irrefutable. He's infectious in a perverse way—at least I find understanding of sorts in his eyes. This is the only time I've heard him challenged.

We're a desultory group—it's hard to be cheerful after what happened to Stevens. He's a felt presence as we lie sprawled on the sandbags of a bunker, our thoughts and feelings as black as the night that's fallen around us. Grass isn't always a pleasure. But we still have Annie, and not even Kostek can assail her. So we don't know much about her private life. She's an ARVN whatever that means, and she lives with a maimed, twelve-year-old sister. What we see is sufficient indication of the tone of her life, if not the details. That's all the truth we need.

I slide down to the ground.

''Where the hell are you going, O'Neill?'' Kostek demands.

''The day was bad enough before you had to open your mouth,'' I reply. ''I need some fresh air.'' As I trudge away toward the club feeling the dead silence behind me, I feel bad. I kicked Kostek when he was down, emboldened by someone else's courage.

It's been weeks since I've been in the club after dark. Nowadays we congregate elsewhere, isolate ourselves in cliques from the lifers and a chance meeting with anyone else we might not want to encounter. Except for three patients at one of the tables and Morrisey at the bar, the club is empty. Wilbur's wiping glasses.

Annie gathers a light sweater and a purse from behind the beer cooler, then moves back up the bar to wait beside Morrisey until Buelen comes to take her home. Six months ago, this room would have been jammed on a Saturday night. The stereo is silent.

''Hi,'' I say as I climb onto a stool.

Morrisey looks up, Annie smiles.

''Whaddaya want to drink, O'Neill?'' Wilbur asks.

''A Bud, Sarge.''

He snatches a can from the cooler, yanks a towel off his shoulder, briskly wipes the bar in front of me, then places the can on a napkin.

''Service, huh, Sarge?'' I find the extravagance of the

napkin and all of Wilbur's fawning gestures revolting, but I should know that my sarcasm's too subtle for him.

"Yeah, try to do our best," he pants as he throws the towel back onto his shoulder. Despite numerous ceiling fans and a wall fan at the end of the bar, sweat pours down his face. Encouraged by my silence, he leans toward me. "That was too bad about Stevens. I was really sorry to see him go."

"That a fact, Sergeant?" My voice is even, but louder. I discover that I've focused on a lump of pale skin drooping beneath one of his eyes. I feel the people in the room watching me, but I really don't give a hit.

"Sure. Stevens was a nice guy, just . . ."

" . . . lacked proper respect, right, Sarge?"

He looks up, wary. "Yeah, I'd say so." He doesn't wait for me to say anything else, but hurries down the bar. I watch him scoop some ice and pour himself a glass of water. Very righteous gesture, Wilbur, you asskissing sonuvabitch. I look the other way, at Annie and Morrisey, talking now, their faces almost touching. There's a radiance about Annie, a softening of her features that's new. Ordinarily, I've thought of her as pretty, but when she's like she is now, she's lovely. It's this quality about her that elicited Kostek's remark. We've all noticed.

Morrisey, however, looks thinner, his stark features even more drawn. He's becoming erratic, as though he has too much on his mind. He doesn't seem at all relaxed, or happy, in contrast to Annie, but they seem mutually unaware of each other's state. They're really attached, really friends, I think, but not the way Kostek said, because if it were, Morrisey would be just like her—any of us would. The brief envy I feel, have always felt for Morrisey's friendship with her, fades. Such a friendship is a product of age. Morrisey's older, the two of them together seem much older than the rest of us at this moment, older even than the officers, the NCOs, the entire war. I've never considered this war as young and somehow savagely naive before, but I suppose it is.

"How about another drink, Sarge?" Morrisey says.

"That six drinks tonight!" Annie scolds as Wilbur pours some gin into a fresh glass. She looks at me and winks. "Richie re-upping for twenty," she says and flashes a warm smile.

I laugh. "You're right, Annie. He's showing all the signs." Her concern seems superficial. Nothing can phase her these days, it seems. It's wonderful to see someone happy. Whatever the cause is, I'm sure we're all part of it, and that, too, is gratifying, even precious in my state of mind.

"The division surgeon," Buelen mumbles, his cap leaning to one side of his head, "has issued the following directive about the use of drugs . . ." He reaches in his shirt pocket, withdraws his glasses, slips them on, then gropes in the opposite pocket for a piece of paper which he carefully unfolds and begins to read. "Drug use within this division is on the increase!" He stops and looks around significantly. "It is my duty to remind all personnel that the inhalation, ingestion, or taking of drugs by any other means without a proper prescription is illegal and punishable under the Uniform Code of Military Justice. Punishment can entail loss of rank, fines, and imprisonment.

"Due to the alarming increase during the past few months, I am instructing all commanders and all commissioned and noncommissioned personnel to be on the lookout for illegal drug use: its effects on the morale of military units can be devastating. I am also encouraging all enlisted personnel to feel free to report suspected drug abuse and/or sales to their immediate superiors. The conduct of this war and its outcome could be at stake!

"Signs of heavy drug use include the following:" Buelen raises his voice. "bloodshot eyes; frequent, unexplained fatigue; the continual wearing of sunglasses; the wearing of beads . . ."

Hoots and catcalls greet these pronouncements. Buelen stops reading as Smith rushes up. His fury explodes as he yells, "Alright you men! That's ENOUGH!"

There's an immediate, amazed silence punctuated only by Kostek's laughter. He's right in front of me, wearing sunglasses. We all gawk at Smith, scarcely believing it was he who shouted.

"You men will listen to First Sergeant Buelen, and to this directive." He's become more subdued, conscious of our surprise as well as the extent of his anger. "Go ahead, First Sergeant."

Buelen begins to read again. His voice quickly slips into a dull monotone, but we aren't listening to him anyhow—we're still watching Smith. As I look at him, I feel anger—for what he is and what he's done. I think I know now what he's done, and what he stands for, and I know I'm not alone, that the silence among us has taken a new direction. It's become impossible for Smith, legs apart, hands behind his back, to continue to face us. He finally turns away and starts to talk to Milliken, tries to act as though business must go on, as though nothing has happened.

"Any questions?" Buelen asks.

"Say, Sarge?"

"What is it, Kostek?"

"The division surgeon left something out."

"Yeah?"

"It takes away your sex drive, Top! So if there's anyone around here not getting laid on a regular bas . . ."

"All right, Kostek!" Smith breaks off his conversation and watches Kostek closely.

"No dope in the NCO hooch, that's for sure!" someone down the line shouts.

"Kostek, front and center!" Smith marches back beside Buelen and points an accusing finger.

Kostek flamboyantly stamps forward a few paces, pivots to the left, stamps to the center of the formation, pivots again, twice stamps his feet in place, then comes to attention, his chin raised twenty degrees from the horizontal.

"This isn't the goddam English Army," Buelen snarls.

"I suppose we could always have another levy, First Sergeant," Smith says. "I'm sure the commander would be only too happy."

But the threat doesn't work the way he intends. His audacity is incredible. Who would help him with his precious projects, in any case?

Smith begins a slow turn around Kostek. "First Sergeant, this man needs a haircut. Note that, please."

Buelen fumbles with his shirt pocket, finds a spiral notebook, and absently records the information. He seems as absorbed as the rest of us, not by Kostek's predicament, but by Smith's personal intervention.

Smith looks down the front of Kostek's shirt, open two buttons at the throat. "Are those beads, Kostek?"

"Yes, Sergeant."

The sun spotlights Kostek and Smith, and a bewildered Buelen. Behind them, beyond the NCO hooch, Jenni rolls on her back while one of her brothers nips at her legs and throat. No sounds of this frolic reach us. Black smoke billows over

276

the rows of tents: papasan burning the shit. The hooch girls squat in a cluster in front of Jenkins's hooch while they communally shine boots and fold clothes, the pink, yellow, blue pastel blouses meager adornments for boyish frames and sinewy feet.

"Where are your dogtags?"

"I've got'em, Sergeant."

"Let me see the tags, Kostek." Smith puts out his hand but does not touch Kostek. Everyone is conscious of the ARs at moments like this.

Kostek lifts the chain over his head and hands the tags to Smith. He examines them and hands them back.

"First Sergeant Buelen," Smith says. "I think we'll have a complete haircut inspection. Anyone in need of a haircut must have obtained one by 1700 hours, or face extra duty."

"Now, Sergeant Smith?"

"Now, First Sergeant!"

Slowly, the other NCOs begin to walk up and down the ranks while Smith and Buelen look on. For once I don't feel sullen: I feel outraged, a good, sure, hateful feeling. And Milliken and Wilbur, and the other COs convey something other than the usual hostility, almost as though they're apologetic. None of this will last—it can't.

It didn't—just long enough for me to make a damn fool of myself. Smith had the lifers under control by evening chow; all of them stood outside the door like a welcoming committee, checked our hair and inevitably passed it—knowing they would have to, but already having a new wrinkle in mind, that being an old one that had lain dormant for a while: namely what constituted the "corner" of one's upper lip, the limit defined by the army regulations for the length of a moustache.

"Jesus!" Gittoni laughs, a refreshing sound. "Everyone with a moustache got nailed on that one."

"It's fucking horseshit!" Morrisey storms as he scowls at the results of his "trim" in a hand-held mirror. He twists the glass one way, then the other.

"Gerty's talking about going to the investigator general," I remark hopefully.

"Yeah, when have you heard that before? He was going to the field, too, once upon a time."

I haven't shaved yet—formation's in twenty minutes. Morrisey looks ridiculous with his moustache trimmed vertically to the corners of his upper lip instead of horizontally. The result is an incredibly puny brush. He glares at me. "You going like that?"

"No. I'm going to trim the damn thing. I may as well cut it off for what it'll be worth. Heil!"

Morrisey winces.

I reach into my locker. I'm feeling skittish now. On impulse, I know exactly what I'm going to do. I actually begin to whistle as I walk through the company area to the twin fifty-five gallon drums and wash basin, my ditty bag bumping against my leg.

I burst around the corner of the tent as the last whistle dies and discover everyone in the formation—Morrisey, Jenkins, everyone except the God Squad—is wearing sunglasses! They're all wearing beads as well!

But now they've heard me, have turned and discovered me. Although I can't see their eyes for the sunglasses, I can see the sag of their mouths, the slow horrified dawning on Buelen's face, hear it in the laughter that erupts.

"What the hell do you think you're doing, O'Neill?" Buelen says as I slip into line. "You go shave that off!"

"Nothing in the ARs about half a moustache, Top!" I manage to reply, not only with clarity, but with some forcefulness.

"O'Neill, you look idiotic!" Smith says. He shakes his head and grins.

I wore it for a week, I made myself, though I did feel like an idiot. I know it galled them, galled the hell out of them, and even Smith's good humor about it disappeared rapidly. There was nothing they could do. "You want to look like a jerk?" Smith asked a day or two later, still trying to convey that original nonchalance, but the question was more than rhetorical—it was meant to cut, so I had him, too.

It was Morrisey who got to me, however, not intentionally —he just did. (The use of sunglasses fell off some, but not the beads. Even Morrisey admitted he liked them—he had a very classy set. I don't know where he found them but he apparently spent an entire afternoon scrounging them up.) No, it was in his attitude. Maybe, in a way, I shaved off half my moustache to prove something not only to myself, but to him. I think I probably did. But the minute I saw him looking at me, laughing with the rest, I knew it was the wrong way. It didn't have the force, the power of something he would do himself,

*the forethought. In that instant, I felt like a child, and when-
ever I met Morrisey during that week, I felt that way. I still
do; even now I blush thinking about it.*

I don't think he knew he had that effect on me.

Certainly I'm bitching. I don't like to bitch, to complain, I
don't like to stay up all night with human rubble, I don't like
this heat, I don't like the smell of this place, and I don't like
Smith coming in and announcing that I'm going to have to
type the goddam monthly report, the score card, because
that's the way battalion likes it now. "Sarge, I've been up all
night! So was Kostek. At least he's getting some sleep."

"I know, I know, and I'm sorry about that, but this is
going to have to be typed today. Sergeant Wilbur and I are
leaving first thing tomorrow for battalion and I want it ready."
He drops the report on my desk.

"It *is* ready!" I protest.

"I told you, it's not typed, O'Neill."

"Kostek did that report. It's his first, and his handwriting's
neat. That's the only reason I ever typed them—my handwriting's so damn bad! Anyway, the orderly room can type it
if you want it typed." I pick up the report and flop it on the
counter. "How the hell am I supposed to run sickcall and do
this?"

"Get Kostek up if you have to! We've got more than
enough to do in the orderly room."

"Bullshit!"

"What did you say?"

"You heard me, Sergeant. I got plenty to do without that,
and all you people down there had your beauty sleep last
night."

"What's going on around here?" Smith sounds genuinely
surprised. "Do you know, O'Neill, that I personally intervened on your behalf when that levy came down, saw to it that
you weren't sent to the field?"

There it is again! And I'm speechless as I stare at that
smooth face with its double chin and violently compressed
jaw.

"Is he supposed to be appreciative, Sergeant?"

Both of us turn, startled. Morrisey's at the counter, not
three feet from Smith, a hand pressed on the oilcloth. It's
Smith's turn to be at a loss for words.

"I think that sort of attitude stinks, Sergeant Smith. I think the way you people played with the morale of this company, with our very lives—and don't tell me you didn't do it deliberately—stinks! And I think your trying to use it now, for gratitude, stinks!''

The color rises in Smith's face. ''Morrisey . . .''

''Don't make any threats, Sergeant. I'd be only too happy to repeat what I just said to the IG.''

After a moment, Smith walks out the door. I watch him cross the yard and disappear. The screen door to the ward shuts behind him as the first jeeps begin to arrive, the battalion aid stations' vehicles with sickcall patients.

And you felt embarrassed! Moments before you couldn't speak for anger, outrage, or whatever it was, and you felt apologetic! Without another peep, you went and woke Kostek, and typed a nice little report which you handed to Smith (made sure it was Smith you handed it to, so he would know it). A few hours later you received that anticipated, yearned-for "Thank you," which meant you were forgiven, which meant you wouldn't have to be angry because he wasn't angry at you anymore, which meant you wouldn't have to deal with those feelings again, at least that day; you wouldn't have to confront someone who didn't like you . . . oh, God!

The first time I was aware Morrisey was gone all night was shortly after that clash with Smith. A couple of litters came in late, but Owen took them, so no one noticed. He was at formation the next morning. It was as though nothing unusual had happened. He grinned at me once. He looked surprisingly calm and steady, maybe a little tired.

TWENTY

"*L*ike compassion," Morrisey said. "You don't show compassion—I mean you can be OK, nice, but not compassionate—not really, because when you do that, you're doing something to yourself: you're sticking holes in a dam and if all the feelings pour out, you'll go nuts."

"That's bullshit," I said. "You're contradicting yourself again. I've watched you too much; you're compassionate."

"You don't understand," he said. He turned abruptly and walked away. I knew his feelings, yet I didn't know. We couldn't allow that, he was right. There was no room for that kind of understanding there. What he did was forever his own.

On the first really warm spring day after I'd come home, the towpath beside the canal in my river town was still muddy from the rain. Jack and I walked along the canal and looked down into the back yards. Jack had a can of beer in his hand, but for some time he hadn't seemed aware of it. In one of the yards some children were swinging on swings, shouting the way kids do. We'd talked some about the weather, the canal, but after the yard with the children, Jack became silent.

A car bumped over a bridge up ahead. Across the canal there were overgrown tangled scrub woods and grape vines, weeping willows with a soft, green hue, sycamore trees.

Jack was quiet for a long time. I turned, finally, and saw him bite his lip. He glanced at me for an instant, then looked away, but I had already seen his eyes, the redness, the tears seeping over the lids. "What I did . . ." he murmured, and laughed that nervous, shrill laugh.

281

He began to cry. I wanted to reach out and put an arm around him. If this had been the plantation, my arm would already have been around him, hugging him . . . but this was home where we could be judged and misunderstood.

I watched him fight to control himself while I fought my own feelings, my own tears and guilt and inadequacy. How could I relate to whatever he'd done? But at some level I would have known it and might have related to it. Would he have believed me? My words would have rung hollow, false, self-justifying . . . at least to myself, maybe to both of us.

And there are times when events don't seem quite real—something's wrong with the setting, with a place one knows so well that anything out of the normal discolors it, makes it seem wrong. Like waking from a deep, feverish sleep and finding the sun pouring into the room when it had been raining when you dozed off; even when your feet touch the floor, you're not sure of the reality of it, of anything. Death might be like that. Hargos had a mission. Somewhere the war had crackled to life and there was blood, and pain, and smells, but everything was cast in browns and golds—it still is. I don't know the reality yet, because I can't feel it. Everything's discolored, even my memories. It was the smoke.

I had lain on a floor in the dark for over an hour, listening to a faint siren, then the dull thumps of incoming rockets creeping across the plantation. I just rolled out of my sleep onto the floor, covered my head and waited. It didn't occur to me to go to the bunker. There were snarls of miniguns, the hammer of helicopters, bangs of cannon, and the persistent, patient thumps of the rockets . . . and then an awful roar and fire over the trees. It went on all night, the fire. We watched the brilliant glow and the curling bellies of smoke. A flame would rise and lick the bellies and subside. For a time there was a wind and the black, limber trees swayed.

Darkness melted away. A pale sun crept up through huge billows of oily stink that drifted higher and higher in a windless, empty sky. Late in the afternoon a breeze came and pushed the smoke down over the plantation, immersing the trees, treatment tent, and helicopter pad in kaleidoscopic hues of brown and gold like a river bottom as the remnants of thousands of gallons of fuel floated off into Cambodia.

Hargos's ship turns and hangs in that brown-gold sky, brown itself, the black jet orifice shimmering on its whale back. It hesitates a moment longer, then we're listening to its dying echoes.

"I feel like I got colored glasses on, man," I say. "I'd like to take the fucking things off!"

Morrisey only nods his head.

Jenkins wanders up in sneakers, a pair of cutoff fatigue pants, a headband. He has a basketball tucked under one arm. The sweat gleams on his face and body like oil. Within moments, he's joined by Brock, similarly attired, but still breathing hard. It's two or three minutes before anyone speaks, and then Morrisey breaks the silence. "Who called you guys?"

"No one."

"This damn day seems weird," Brock says and after a few minutes, walks into the empty treatment room to claim his shirt and pack of cigars. By the time he returns, we've been joined by several patients from the ward.

Diagonally across the road, beyond the revetments and remaining helicopters, two of the Dust-Off men are throwing a softball. The ghostly sphere sails back and forth.

The breeze has shifted. The smoke drifts lazily northeastward, now lightening, then darkening the landscape, the tower, the berm at the edge of our cul de sac. Above us the sky is crystal blue. Shadows have slipped out of the plantation and over the helicopters; the high tips of the canted blades are bathed in golden light.

The field phone whirrs on the porch of the treatment tent. Morrisey goes in to answer it just as the two men at Dust-Off drop their ball and run toward their quarters.

"What?" Morrisey yells. He shouts the question again. "OK, Gittoni, listen to me man, just hang on. I'll be right over." He drops the receiver. Helicopters start to crank up behind us. Morrisey points at me. "Go get Dunn, quick! They shot down Hargos."

Gerty's across the road when I come back, standing beneath a helicopter and heaving bags of blood up into the open doorway, into the hands of the crewchief. I watch the ship float in its absurd, illogical manner, the earth beneath it churning for yards around as Gerty, his eyes protected by his arms, heaves the bags of blood. They could break a tail rotor, I'm thinking. There's so much haste . . .

"Do you smell something burning?" The smell's immediate, close by, unrelated to those distant clouds sweeping across the berm.

Morrisey's grabbed a handle at the front of the litter. Owen's beside him, Jenks beside me. No one answers me. We're running from Murphy's ship to the treatment room, trying to feel our way over the ground. We can't see Hargos, fallen like an alien from the sky, entombed in his flight suit, a blanket pulled up to his chest, a bag of blood held aloft on each side by two more medics.

A large crowd greets us in front of the treatment tent, the entrance looms, the thump of our boots on the wooden floor echoes our insane, frightened urgency. Hargos twists his head and groans as we swing the litter onto the table. Three other litters are brought in behind us, followed by a mob of Dust-Off personnel. Smith tries to keep them out. Furiously, Murphy shoves him aside.

A stethoscope hangs from Brock's neck, down his bare chest. Hargos is dead before the instrument can chill his skin. Then Brock is astraddle his friend, his knees on the table. Curly blonde hair bristles under Brock's hands. How long has it been since I've seen this, even done it, this violent affirmation? How long since it mattered? Hargos's body jerks ludicrously with each sharp pump on his chest.

I can still smell something burning.

Brock has climbed off the body to face the confused anger of the men from Dust-Off. He speaks to them softly, fighting to control his own voice.

Owen's holding the major's helmet. Murphy reaches out and snatches it away. He storms outdoors into the dusk, but then he seems to droop as he stares out across the empty revetments, past his idle ship.

Beyond Murphy, far off below the thinning clouds of smoke, far off in the deepening blue of the evening sky, a flashing red light appears: another helicopter inbound with the casualties from Hargos's aborted mission.

Brock turns back to the table to determine the exact cause of death, but only after I've played the bureaucratic worm and nagged him. Howard, Shelby, and everyone else not waiting on the landing pad, concentrate on the remaining crew members . . . but I've already told Kostek to call Graves, to tell them we have at least four bodies.

I'm at the foot of the table, an open book of tags and a pen ready. I wish I didn't have to be here at all, didn't have to translate the dead man in front of me to paper.

With more than characteristic deliberation, Brock twists

Hargos up on his side to examine his back. Slowly, with detachment, he scans the pallid flesh. A faint puff of smoke rises from the blanket at Hargos's feet, *its* feet, for whatever it is, it is no longer Hargos. I reach for a corner of the blanket, and I yank it away. I see smoldering, charred chunks of boots; the legs just above the ankles are blackened and popped like burnt hotdogs.

I sat in the darkness on my cot, tried to conjure the moment of Major Hargos's death and couldn't. I sat, forehead in hand, and listened to the uncontrolled grief of Gittoni and knew that it was pain beyond my reach, but felt somehow it ought not to be. I felt incredibly sad for the radio operator.

Never again will time be linear for me, for linear time suggests progression, progress, future, hope. Instead it has become, will be, and was a random collection of exclamations, miniprogressions that led nowhere except forever back into the mind of the beholder.

Time is circular, eddying, retrograde, and even, from a distance, static. How can I believe anything else, for here I am in the future confronting it all over again?

At first there was talk of transfer: Dust-Off had lost four men. But even while the rumors grew, while a shattered Gittoni functioned as a radio operator in the most aimless fashion, a new helicopter sailed in. Instead of alighting for a moment, then buzzing away, it flies into the one empty revetment and settles to the ground. The front door of this strange Huey opens and a thin, dark-haired man emerges, his helmet cradled smartly in one arm. Followed by three crewmen, he starts to walk across the coarse, open ground toward the road and mess hall, toward the buildings of the air ambulance company as though he owns the place.

Suddenly Murphy appears among the trees, followed by several other members of his unit, all of them looking like wild-eyed savages. "Get that fucking machine out of there!" Murphy hollers.

The dark-haired man halts. "What did you say?"

"Who the fuck do you think you are?"

"I'm Major Newman, your new commanding officer. You must be Warrant Officer Murphy."

"You bet your ass, sir! Now get out of here! We haven't got a commander!" The other pilots, medics, crewchiefs continue to gather silently behind Murphy.

"You have a job to do, Murphy," Newman calls.

"We've been doing our job!"

The three men behind Newman are watching him as intently as the group by the trees. He hesitates a moment, then marches the remaining distance, across the little bridge and directly up to the warrant officer.

Murphy glares at him, suddenly looks down at his shorts, rubs his unshaven face, and finally salutes his new commanding officer.

The unshaven faces vanished and a certain, grim competence pervaded the air ambulance unit in the manner of their leader, Major Newman, an unemotional, humorless man. "A fucking marvelous flyer," I once overheard Murphy telling somebody, but there was bitterness in his appraisal.

I never found a cheerful Gittoni at his tape recorder again; I never found him at the recorder at all after that, as though he was afraid of his own voice.

Changes in people aren't always noticeable here, changes that would scream at you if you were anyplace else. Whatever patterns and habits we have seem so distorted or exaggerated. It's just that every day you get stretched a little tighter and become that much different. If for every day someone I knew died, even if I watched all of them die, it wouldn't register after a while, not so I would notice.

"I'm sick of this!" I blurt out.

Morrisey's squatting a couple of feet away from me, but seems much closer: everything in this tent is compressed, not by space but by feel, and especially smell. The canvas smells rank. He doesn't answer me.

"Why did you stay?"

He shakes his head. He's watching my right hand pull the zipper. Sometimes zippers glide like ice. This one grates. Sometimes I feel a fierce, perverse pride in this . . . this turning over of rocks. But why has Morrisey stayed? What possesses him? He's never done it before. The others who stay are predictable: it's like a fix, a recognition of some obscene truth. That isn't Morrisey's way.

The head is turned to one side, the thick, reddish beard pallid and moist like some fungus against the chalky skin. The mouth is frozen open. The shirt's saturated with blood as I lift it away from the chest. I push the other half of the shirt away and there's a hole almost a foot in diameter all the way through the body where the stomach and solar plexus once were.

"I don't see any tags—he's gotta be American, but look at that beard!"

Brock is looking over my shoulder. Morrisey, still squatting, stares at the head with a disturbing intensity.

"Know the guy, Morrisey?" My voice sounds shrill.

"I think so."

I reach over and shake him gently. "Hey . . ."

"Let me help!" He thrusts his hands in the bag, burying his face behind his shoulder so I can't see his eyes. He rips at the sodden clothes. His hands glide like serpents over the body, plunge into the moist darkness at either side, grope, glide dangerously near that orifice that's become sticky with congealing fluids and tissue.

"Morrisey!" Brock grabs him hard by his shoulders.

"Here!" He yanks a crumpled wad of paper out from under the far side of the body and tenders it, dripping. Then he stands up and lunges out of the tent.

Brock kneels beside me; together we decipher the smeared, wet field tag. "Edward Charles Mathias, E-6, MACV, Cau, DOA, RPG lower chest, stomach."

I try to feel something other than the recognition of a name. I feel nothing. "At least they got a good medic—did most of my work for me," I say as Brock lets me take the card from his hand. "That's pretty unusual."

Brock observes the wound thoughtfully.

"Is this your diagnosis, sir?" I push the tag toward him. He looks distractedly at the card, then back at the wound.

"Get me a flashlight, Jon. There's one on my desk."

I feel lightheaded walking down the road from the morgue to the officers' quarters. The sun seems too bright, the red of the road too pale, the world around me—the trunks of the rubber trees, the whitish, sandy earth, the deep brown canvas of the tents—too vivid.

"I want to turn him up on his side." Brock examines the wound with his flashlight, then grabs the far shoulder as I grasp the man's hip, and together we pull. The bag wants to move with him. Clinching the dead man's pants in my right hand, I reach over the body and push the bag back down; it falls away like a large, deflated balloon. Brock arches over the corpse, examines the wound from behind, then shines the light into the bag.

"Hold it." He takes the body's weight against the inside of his arm as he reaches down inside. His hand rises above the body, into the light. He lifts his elbow and the body twists back down into the bag. I let go of the hips.

Pinched between Brock's thumb and index finger is a tiny, steel dart, like a nail with a cylindrical cup at one end. "I didn't think a rocket-propelled grenade made that hole." He plays the flashlight over the black object, unaware, it seems, of his hand gleaming crimson. "I want you to call CID and tell them I'd like to see them, and then get ahold of Captain Howard and tell him the same thing."

"CID?"

"The Criminal Investigation Division."

"I know."

He stares at me, amazed. "You don't understand?"

"No, sir . . ."

Over a half hour passes after I phone CID, and by this time, Morrisey's come back. We hear a truck drive up in front of the sickcall tent and I expect to see the Military Police. I've never dealt with the CID and I'm looking for a jeepload of officialdom, maybe even Johnny Mirrors. On the door of this truck, however, on a yellow square, is the silhouette of a wolf's head. There are two men in the vehicle. One wears a baseball cap and a pressed uniform. The other, the driver, is wearing a helmet and has the dust of the countryside all over his fatigues.

The man with the baseball cap barges into my office. I see the sword on his shoulder patch, the emblem of MACV, and then the second man pushes in. The first thing I note about the man in the helmet, a master sergeant, are the goggles draped around his neck. He grins, a sudden, pristine flash. "Hey, sport! You guys been patching up any gooks gored by a waterbuffalo, lately?" He grins again, a humorless, automatic gesture. A sudden memory grips me of bleak-eyed men and a young Vietnamese girl whose own appearance and baleful look are far more naked and desolate than theirs, who is the vortex of all their gut emotions.

"You've been promoted," I say feebly.

"Yeah!" The grin again. He glances down at his collar. "Yeah, some time ago. Say, sport, you didn't get a body in here, maybe an hour back?"

"A sergeant name of Mathias?" the man from MACV, a lieutenant, interjects.

"Yes, sir."

"Well, I'd kinda like to pick up his personal effects, see that the body's taken care of."

"I haven't finished the death certificates." I jerk my thumb at the typewriter.

"Good! We can wait and take those with us."

Panicked, I look at Morrisey. "You'd better call Brock, Jon."

I reach for the field phone. "Yeah?" Dunn says.

"What's going on, Specialist?" the lieutenant demands.

"We're waiting for a cause of death, sir." Morrisey replies. "The medical officer . . ."

"He was hit by an RPG!" the sergeant snaps. "Any fucking idiot can see that!"

"The medical officer's waiting for the CID before he makes a final determination, sir. He's on his way over here."

The sergeant starts to open his mouth, but the lieutenant puts a hand out. "What's this about the CID, Specialist?"

"Captain Brock will explain, sir."

"No, goddammit, you will!"

"Sir, he found a flechette . . ."

"You sons of bitches wouldn't know the difference between a flechette and a baseball bat!"

"Robbie!" The lieutenant clamps a hand on the sergeant's shoulder, restraining the tank commander as he moves toward Morrisey.

"You're telling us, Specialist," the lieutenant continues, trying to control his voice, "that the medical officer has called in the CID? He thinks Mathias was murdered?"

"Yes, sir. He was shot at point-blank range. The hole's too clean for anything else."

The sergeant whirls on the lieutenant. "You think my unit's fucked up now, you wait 'till they hear this bullshit! His own fucking gooks probably did it to him! The dumb fuck going around and playing hero all the time, trying to get them to do the same!"

"His ARVNs don't have tanks, Robbie, and you know what your guys thought of him."

"What kind of outfit do you think I run?" The sergeant's livid. "I'll have your ass, buddy!" he shouts at Morrisey and charges through the curtain.

"Jesus!" The lieutenant rushes out after the sergeant. "Robbie!"

"Here's Brock," Morrisey says calmly. The doctor and two other men in neat fatigues have intercepted the lieutenant and the sergeant.

"Who are those guys?"

"That's CID. They don't wear any rank," Morrisey says with a hint of satisfaction, "so no one can talk down to them."

Of course it didn't end there either, any more than Morrisey's great myth of Eddie Mathias. A jeep pulled off the road in front of the treatment tent the next day, and stopped. There were three ARVNs in the vehicle, and a woman in black pants and a black shirt. The woman climbs out of the jeep, walks quickly around in front of it and hurries toward us. "Can I help you?" Howard asks. I wouldn't call her pretty, but she's not bad looking. She has long, dark hair and seems young and lithe, even skinny, except for her belly—she's pregnant. She's barefoot and her feet look petite, nice.

"I'm looking for my husband, Captain," she says in English.

"Yes?"

"Sergeant Eddie Mathias." Her girlish voice seems misplaced.

"Who . . . Do you know anything about this, O'Neill?"

"The thing with CID, sir." Why do I try to whisper?

"Speak up! You mean that sergeant yesterday?"

"Yes, sir."

Howard turns to the woman again and studies her, the bare feet, fat belly; his lips turn down slightly. "I'm sorry, Miss, but he was killed."

"I know." Her eyes have never left Howard. "I would like his body."

"Why that's impossible! He's an American!"

"He was also my husband."

"I'm sorry, but that body's on its way home, or will be when the investigation's complete. There's nothing I can do for you." He leaves me to face those steady, dark eyes.

"I'd like to do something, ma'am." I shake my head helplessly. Why doesn't she cry? Not a tear, not a goddam thing! Just those eyes . . . and then Morrisey is here, his hand on my arm.

"Let's go over to commo," he says, "and see if we can get MACV." That simple, that logical, but excruciating! And so she walks behind Morrisey while he leads the way around the first ward and along the boardwalk to the gaping entrance to commo. Her feet make little slapping sounds as she scurries to keep up.

It took a while, but she finally cracked. *I saw her lips tremble as she blurted a quick "Thank you," and rushed up the ramp, out of the bunker. Morrisey had tried for three hours. He called everyone. He got passed from person to person, and I could see his agitation increase, hear the growing anger in his voice, the exasperation and disbelief; and sense his embarrassment toward her. "No one seems to be able to tell me anything," he told her at last.*

Later, on our way to chow I suddenly became furious. "What was that shit about the 'Dragon Lady incarnate' of Southeast Asia? 'Educated in Paris!' She was just another scrawny hooch girl. So she could speak English."

"O'Neill, you don't know what you're saying."

"All that shit about Mathias."

"I believe it more than I ever did. He loved her—you could see it in her! That's why he was so goddam good."

"Morrisey, you said it yourself! He had nowhere else to go."

"I was wrong." Then he turned around and walked back toward the treatment area, past the last revetment, and I knew he was crying. I could tell by the way he walked and had his hand clapped on the back of his neck and was rubbing at it frantically, distractedly.

TWENTY-ONE

Whenever there are casualties, it seems as though there's an audience in the yard in front of treatment: ward patients, sickcall patients, personnel from the field units, chaplains . . . there's always a group of people there, especially in the daytime. Their faces reflect all degrees of fascination, anxiety, bitterness as they watch the gored and dying rock gently by along a well-trodden path from a mechanical bird to a wooden table. And there's something more keen in their absorption if we run with a litter.

Men run with litters with a special intensity: their faces flush, they sweat profusely and concentrate on the approaching door to the treatment room and the release of their burden. It's as though they're in more danger than the person they're carrying, as though speed aggravates fear. I often wonder if I look that way when I run—I'm sure I do. There's always the creak of canvas and wood, the heavy breathing, the special urgency that is also avoidance, release. One shouldn't take time to contemplate.

But we run with litters less often since Mendez's departure. I can feel the difference, the lack of concern: everyone can who served under the major. At times we talk about it. Other times it is a more nebulous awareness. Brock's slightly plodding qualities, his deliberateness complemented the major's decisiveness, a decisiveness that often verged on impatience, if not outright recklessness. Under Howard, Brock's skills seem diminished and infuriating. Surely he feels it, too, if only as an unspoken pressure, an erosion of confidence.

Murphy and his crew and their commander Newman leave

one day, are reassigned farther south in the Long Binh area where there isn't much war and no one will have to worry about them just let them finish their time and go. Maybe they're burned out, but they've been so good. Of course, no one says that, not in so many words, but we all know that's what it's all about. Newman couldn't handle it—probably no one could. They need time for grief, but who's got time for that?

One day there's a horrendous racket and through the billowing dust we see several strange medivac ships without the familiar slogans; they hover and twist and finally settle some distance beyond the pad. They crouch there, rotors idling, sun flashing off the plexiglass while the ships in the revetments, our ships, whine into a mutual crescendo. One by one they lift out from between their steel walls, float over the pad, dip their noses and clatter away. Just like that—gone, all the men we've known for so long. We'll probably never see them again.

Soon enough, the strange ships are in place and their occupants walking across the barren ground toward us. They are new and fresh and smiling. They shake hands and assure us of quality service. Smith and Howard seem pleased, full of smiles, while the rest of us stand around and indulge reluctantly in the gladhanding, unable to overcome a profound skepticism. Brock reflects our feelings in his polite but noncommital response to the new CO's introduction. They are so damn excited—their unit, the 653rd Air Ambulance, has just been formed. They just can't wait.

"Look at this," Morrisey says a while later as we treat three litter patients, the first in several days, the result of the new Dust-Off's first mission. One of the crewchiefs is waiting outside the tent, I guess to escort the litter back to his ship, he's so antsy.

"What is it?" At first, all I see is the sallow face of the GI. His eyes are closed and there's a two- or three-day stubble on his cheeks. My glance wanders to his chest, exposed where the shirt has been cut open.

"This!" Morrisey shakes a piece of paper that seems to be attached to the soldier's shirt. On closer inspection, I see it's a business card. On it is a primitive engraving of a helicopter with a large red cross on its door, and the inscription: "Glad to have you aboard! You are the result of another daring rescue by the 653rd Air Ambulance—'Dust-Off!'"

Morrisey yanks the card off its button, stuffs it in one of his pockets, and continues his work.

I don't know what he did with that card, but it was the last one I ever saw.

We were devastated by the loss of Murphy's group. A few nights after their departure, I took one of the chaplains aside. I ask if I can speak to him outside when he's through. Commo has standing orders to notify them of casualties. I've watched this particular man a long time—he calls me by my first name—and choose him because he is the most direct, least frivolous of the lot. Although he's a career officer, a lieutenant colonel, he seems genuinely compassionate and disinclined to make the fool assertions many chaplains do in the face of mortal agony.

I've never seen him angry until now, and even now, don't so much see as feel his intolerance as I desperately try to explain that our company is thoroughly demoralized, our performance getting worse and worse, sooner or later something terrible is going to happen . . .

The chaplain crushes his cigarette between his fingers, releasing a stream of sparks, then flicks it away. "I don't know what you're talking about. This is a fine unit!"

"Not now, sir. Not since Major Mendez."

"Captain Howard is a fine man—he's doing a fine job. Just look at the difference in this place since he took command!" By this time there is such scorn in his voice that I give up. "You haven't any problems," he continues in that savage tone, "compared to what those men out there have."

He doesn't have to point. I know the direction . . . even in the dark.

I'm sitting at a table in The Yellow Peril. All around me, among the tables and stony faces of other GIs, girls flow in brilliant dresses split to their thighs, the grace of their movement belied by the coarseness of their voices.

Across from me, a GI tries to slip his hand into the crotch of the girl on his lap. From where I'm watching, fixedly and unabashedly, it seems like it ought to be a piece of cake. Her left leg is exposed all the way up and he's already moved his hand inside the leg. I feel myself leer with anticipation, and take another slug of beer. I'm better than halfway through my sixth bottle of "33."

Suddenly the girl claps her hand over her privates and

successfully blocks the invasion. "Hey, you number ten, honey," the GI mutters, using his free hand to try to remove the obstacle.

"I not be number ten! You crazee American!" I can't pull my eyes from that beautifully shaped bare leg. It has an existence of its own for me now, without relevance to any other part of her body except the slender foot, encased in a delicate and very high-heeled red satin shoe. I have a maniacal urge to crawl over and lick that leg, from the foot up, to bite it and nibble it. I giggle at this thought, then bury my face in my arms and watch red and gold streaks shoot through the darkness of my eyes.

When I look up, the girl is struggling to her feet. "C'mon, baby, you fuck?" the GI pleads. He almost falls out of his chair in his effort to cling to her.

"No! You bad shit!" She clatters off in a big huff and yaks for a couple of minutes with a fat, ugly woman, the proprietor of the place. When her tirade subsides, the fat woman says a few words. Obediently, the girl marches off to a distant corner of the room and a new customer.

"Nice try, buddy," I say to the frustrated GI, and raise my hand to give a sympathetic wave. "I could have eaten that myself."

"Go fuck yourself, asshole!" He lunges among the tables for the door.

I pick up the brown bottle and stare at the black panther on the label. Made by the French, bottled in Vietnam—there has to be some irony there, but it's going to have to wait. I can feel an awful headache approaching.

There's a crash of cymbals behind me, a rolling of drums. The band has returned. Immediately all other sounds are buried in a jarring rendition of *If You're Going to San Francisco*. Some idiot's singing the words, no mouthing them; damn gooks probably don't even know what the words mean, much less know what San Francisco really is . . . goddam ignorant little bastards . . . San Francisco. I've only been there once, but the name is special—hell, this song is special. It's lousy, but the tune makes me teary. Awful circumstances to go there, to Oakland across the Bay. I could see the lights of the city until that last night when they closed the warehouse doors and locked us in. It was vibrant—you could feel it even in the lights. And the airport; not dirt-bitten and blown out like this place. Who are they fucking kidding playing those songs? They couldn't begin to imagine what San Francisco's like, much less the whole United States! They'd be overwhelmed, blinded by it all!

"Hey!" A hand claps my shoulder. "Did that little fucker come back in here?"

Kostek swims into focus, his face all sweaty, his fatigues black and gooey with sweat. "Christ, you wouldn't know if your own mother was here, O'Neill!" he says with disgust. "That was a fucking hundred dollar Seiko that little peckerhead stole."

I manage a grin. "No luck, huh?"

"I'm going to look out back."

"Yeah." I stare at the band, at their high-heeled boots, bellbottom pants, lace shirts, caps; the colored lights flash and glitter off the glossy guitars, the steel strings, the drums. "You guys think you're pretty hot shit," I whisper to myself.

"What's your name, sweetheart?" someone says nearby.

"My name Number Fourteen."

"Number Fourteen! What kinda fuckedup name is that?"

I look around and see a soldier press his head against a girl's breasts, lock his hands behind her and turn his face sideways the way a kid does with a large teddy bear. The girl glances around the room from her perch on the soldier's lap. Suddenly she laughs, a bright, ugly slash of thin lips and teeth, and with both hands, pushes the soldier's head away. "Hey! What you do, GI? You buy me drink!"

"Yeah, yeah," he mutters, and reaching into a hip pocket, brings out a wallet crammed with flimsy paper money.

"Hey, GI! You rich! You buy me many drink!"

"Yeah, sure."

My headache has mushroomed. The weight of my head's unbearable.

The din of the room subsides and I can feel people looking at the door. I already know what it is, but eventually I turn, too, and stare at the MP standing there like some goddam Nazi, holding the beads apart.

· The caterwauling from the band increases in volume. After a minute, the MP backs out into the street. I watch the ceiling roll slowly around a fan vibrating gently on its axis. Sharp pains burst across my temples and I lean forward again.

"He got away," Kostek wheezes and wipes his forehead on his sleeve. "Let's get out of here."

I stagger to my feet and follow his flushed neck and

dripping hair to the beads. A blast of heat and light strike me when I push through the curtain. An old woman squats against the tin sides of a stall a little way up the street. I watch her float in and out of focus. A box full of cheap, metal toys is spread on the ground in front of her.

"C'mon, O'Neill!"

We cross the street and start to walk between the main flow of people and the stalls. Kostek walks faster, impatient to get out of this place. A few steps past the old lady, he stops and I have to grab him with my hand to avoid a collision.

"Hey, mamasan! You boom boom?" He laughs his dry laugh as the old woman looks up from under her shroud.

Someone tugs at my arm. I look down. There's some kid. "Hey, GI! Girls be best at Blue Baby Bar."

"Screw kid!" I push him away. "Kostek! What the hell are you doing? Let's get out of here!"

"Mamasan, I'd sure like to take you home to give my father's pigs something to fuck." He laughs again. He squats down in front of the toys and picks up a duck with huge feet and a mouth that clacks open and shut. He winds it up and lets it waddle through the dust, the mouth clack clacking. Once more he laughs. The old woman watches him warily. She's incredibly ugly, the remains of her teeth stained with betel nut.

"None of them smile unless you put something in their sweaty little palms." Kostek reaches into his chest pocket and pulls out a wad of piasters. "You want, mamasan?" He slowly extends his hand until the money almost touches her face. The duck jiggles to a stop a few inches from one of his boots. It's a yellow duck with a blue coat and big red buttons all painted in glossy enamel.

The woman eyes the money. Gradually a palsied claw emerges from the folds of her dress. She doesn't smile despite the fact that Kostek's encouraging her with a huge smile of his own.

He snatches the money out of reach. "No grin, no gin, mamasan!"

Several people have stopped to watch Kostek. My gaze strays up into that infinite, burning blue sky. "Ohhhh . . . Kostek, for Christ's sake, let's get out of here." I bend down and grab his sleeve, feel his clammy shirt.

"Awww, fuck these gooks, anyhow!" Kostek crumples the money and flings it to the ground. His boot descends on the duck and flattens it. Children dart from everywhere, dive at my feet as they scramble for the money. With surprising alacrity, the old woman leaps among them, shrieking. Someone kicks her box and the toys go flying. I reel backwards, almost fall, catch myself and turn around. Way ahead of me, in the jostle of people, is Kostek. I stumble after him.

Highway 10 is deserted. When we crossed the culvert there were no children at the dike laughing, swimming, only the water, a deep red, almost scarlet in the dying day. I'm with Morrisey and Brock. We huddle beside the ambulance on the causeway at the far edge of the hamlet. Ahead of us is the bridge with its sandbagged guard hut, behind us the thatched huts, but they all seem empty, abandoned. There's a hole, a horizontal slit in the sandbags. I stare at it intently, into it, waiting for something to move, to peer around the edge and suddenly point death at me. Where all the armored personnel carriers once were, the tanks, where that yellow flag with its fanged wolf hung, where the eyes of that girl pierced and knew us, there's only a lone personnel carrier, tipped slightly up on one side, one of its tracks torn off and lying rusted on the ground. The huge, toothed nakedness of the unburdened sprocket is terrifying.

Morrisey says something to Captain Brock. I can touch him with my hand. I do. I reach out and let my fingers slide down his shirt sleeve, but his voice is far away and muffled. There is such a stillness.

"What did you say?" I say. Morrisey doesn't move. His head is rigid like a statue's, the chiseled cheekbones, the sunken hollows beneath, the dark curly hair and sable eyes. We're only three people. I call again, shout, and Brock turns. He looks jaundiced and bleak. It's too soon for him to look like that. I feel a chill slide down my back and slowly look over my shoulder but the hamlet's empty.

We walk through the grass along the top of the dikes, walk away from the causeway and the highway; the moist grass tugs at my waist and legs, grates over my bare arms like cat tongues. I look back but I can't see the ambulance anymore. "A hundred men were killed here," Morrisey says. I look down at my feet for signs of blood, then out into the motionless water for the carcass of the buffalo. We're by ourselves, now; Brock's gone. The sky flames around us, but the earth is dark, the shadows deeper, more secretive. I look out across the dikes.

Morrisey gets down on his hands and knees and crawls through the grass. Cautiously, he reaches a hand over the bank. "Let's catch frogs," he whispers. My eyes are suddenly where his hand is, mesmerized by an enormous, beautiful frog with brilliant yellow eyes. The creature's at least a foot long, and I'm afraid to touch the glistening, lime-colored skin. "It won't bite," Morrisey assures me as I gingerly place my fingers on the soft, gooey back. The water is inky black but I see fish in it.

Morrisey's urgently calling from somewhere. "There's trout here!" I scream back. My face is down the bank, inches from the surface of the water where the trout swim, silver gray, speckled red, yellow, traces of blue . . . now they're monstrous, gigantic, and growing bigger, becoming brilliant red with gaping mouths of teeth. A satiny blue green fin breaks the water. The spines of the fin rise high above the webbing like spikes as my knees begin to slide down the bank . . . Swirls beneath me, the water churns . . . flashes of incandescent green . . .

. . . I'm suddenly awake, sweating, propped against the headboard, the pillow at the small of my back like a rock . . . what a terrible dream! The moon is shining into the room. Casey's asleep with her back to me. I clench my head with my hands. I didn't realize I'd fallen asleep! I can still see the fish.

Someone starts to pound on the front door. I lift my head, stiffen. The pounding reverberates through the house. Casey rolls over on her back, props herself up on her elbows. The hammering echoes again beneath us. I don't want to move. "Your roommate going to answer it?"

"She could sleep through a bomb."

The knocks become more urgent. Casey gets up. "Wait . . ." Naked, like her, I step out of the moonlight into the dark, touching her occasionally so I know she's still there.

We're down in the kitchen. The pounding is very loud. "How can anyone sleep through that?" I wonder and glance toward her roommate's door. Casey's silhouette passes in front of me, heading toward the front door. There are windows on each side of the door, and through them I can see the shadows of the porch and sycamore trees in the yard below. The door shakes violently with each blow.

I'm across the room now, beside her, to her right. My bare arm touches her hand once—I feel the warmth . . . but something's wrong! I start for one of the windows to look and see who's at the door, but Casey grabs the knob.

"No!" I lunge for her shoulder, but she twists the knob and pulls the door open. "No!" I scream as a huge silhouette of a man swings to face me, arms stretched out stiff in front of him, and rams a revolver in my face . . . "NO! Ohhh, Jesus . . . God, nooo . . ."

"Jon! Jon . . ."

"I didn't see that one coming! Oh, God, I didn't see it coming. I didn't see it . . ." My hands are mashed in my eyes. She's sprawled on top of me. Her hands tear at mine, try to pull them away. Something hot and moist flows down my fingers . . . it's my tears, and hers. She's crying.

"Are you alright?" she whispers frantically. She pulls at my wrists, slowly draws my hands away and presses her face against mine. "Are you OK?"

I should have known! "That's the worst dream I've ever had," I whisper, not to her so much as to the darkness, to me, to my lingering disbelief. How can I be alive? My body is soaked, the sheets beneath me are soaked, her body is almost too hot, stifling. She wipes my forehead with her hand, strokes it over and over, brushes the hair back, and I can see, almost feel her study me, her eyes inches from my own: the worry, the concern. She shouldn't be looking at me, not like that. "It's fine . . . I'll be alright." Suddenly my body shakes convulsively and I bury my face between her breasts. The heat of her body melts my tears, suffocates me in liquid flesh. Her hands clench my back with incredible strength and urgency.

"Ohhh," she groans in my ear and presses her lips softly against the lobe. Then she begins to talk, the sound muted as through a door for she's speaking against my neck now, still lying half on top of me although my head is free. My arms are around her, squeezing her. She talks about someone she knows who went to Vietnam (trying to communicate with me!), only she says "Nam," this someone a doorgunner, "Is that right, a doorgunner? Or something like that. He said he sat and shot 'Cong from the air, hundreds of them, he said, and when he would tell me this, I'd see his eyes, and they'd be watching me, and they weren't like his voice, disturbed really, you know—upset—but were just watching me like he wanted

*to see how I was reacting; like I think he felt he was supposed
to feel guilty and all that, be upset, but his eyes showed me he
wasn't—he was enjoying it, enjoying watching me, but more,
kind of glowing like he really wished he was still doing it. I
mean, like he'd really gotten into it. It must be terrible to get
into killing people . . . what an awful thing to do to someone,
to send them to someplace like 'Nam and get them to like
killing. Did they do that to you?'' She shakes her head.
''Jimmy, he's the doorgunner, I've known him all my life,
and he just wasn't the same.''*

*I've begun to struggle with her now, struggle against that
word ''Nam,'' or ''THE 'NAM'' with all its macho implications. I fight her cheap talk and sympathy, try to pull away,
but the harder I struggle, the tighter she holds me, thinking
that's what I want. She kisses the top of my head, mashes
herself against me.*

*I slam my palms into her ribs and sneer, ''Do you feel
guilty about what's happening there? Do you know what's
happening? Do you feel ashamed because you never killed
anyone, or risked getting killed?''*

*I hear myself gulp air, the prolonged hurt of her quietness,
and at last a tentative, pained, ''Don't hate me . . . I can't
stand it. I can't stand anger and hate like that.'' Her voice
betrays no awareness of the depth of my disdain, is instead
reflective and small, but when I don't reply, when I lie there
steaming, poised like some predator waiting for her to blun-
der again, she adds (still cautiously, even with confusion),
''No, why should I feel guilt? I didn't do anything. I was
never there.'' She touches me gingerly with her fingers.
''What's wrong? If you didn't kill anyone, that's wonderful.''*

*''No! No, goddammit, it isn't! It's a curse, a curse just like
it would have been the other way.'' My arms are across my
face. I shake my head, roll it back and forth and cry, ''Why
are you making me like this! Why are you making me bury
this?'' and then shout, shout ''What fucking right did you
have to cripple me!'' She flings herself over me again, blankets me; her hands reach around my body, try to cradle me
once more, and I relapse into soft tears and isolation . . .*

*Suddenly, instantly, I'm aware of our bodies pressing against
each other; one of her nipples touches one of mine, the soft
hair between her legs brushes my thigh. As I realize this, and
know her realization of this, I begin to grow, get hard. She*

rolls off me, moves quickly away. I feel the bed sag as she sits up. Neither of us speak. She moves slightly and the bed jiggles.

My hand finds one of her breasts, slides down over the hardening nipple, but she remains motionless, fighting it. "Please," I say and roll up on my side.

"Oh, God no," she says. "You're OK now."

"I never said I wasn't." My hand starts to move down her belly.

She shudders. "Maybe, if you're having trouble, you'd better go back to your house."

"No," I respond carefully, gently. "I want to be here." My hand is on her thigh now. I look up at the soft whiteness of her.

"Look! I told you earlier, I've got to go to work." She's angry again, but there's something else, something that is making her shrill. "You've ruined my night!"

"Please."

"Why can't you just get out of here?"

And then my hands, both of my hands, are against her shoulders and I'm on my knees, forcing her down. I get an arm around her and pull her toward me, then fall on top of her and press my lips against hers, force them apart. For an instant she responds, then tries to writhe away. I roll her over, force her down on her belly. She whines softly, then goes limp, no longer fights me as I enter her, no longer moves except as my motions force her body to move on the soft bed. A quiet, rhythmic creak pervades the room. My ears are filled with wet sounds and I push harder, rise to a squatting position, then to my toes so I can thrust even harder, ram myself against her, through her, beyond her . . .

I collapse upon her moist back and lie there gasping. Still she doesn't move. Only when I roll off does she move away, turn her back to me. I watch her whiteness for a long time, the sudden ascent of her thighs and buttocks. She lies very still. I reach out with my hand and place it on the soft, fleshy mound, but there's no reaction. I can scarcely feel her breathe. At last, I remove my hand, draw it into myself and listen again. The bed starts shaking gently, almost imperceptibly. I think I hear her moan, the sound muffled, very faint. She's crying, but not because of that . . . surely not! Hell, she's been fucked countless times before me . . . so why's she crying? Christ, does she really think I wanted to hear her telling me that shit?

"Do you?" I demand loudly, and grabbing her by the shoulders, shake her.

She curls into a ball like a caterpillar. *"Please,"* she whispers.

"Oh, God!" I flop back and wait for her to move. She doesn't. I know I'm going to have to piss in a few minutes, feel my way through the attic and down the stairs to the john. The insides of my thighs, my belly are wet with semen; it feels clammy. I hear a whistle way up the valley but several minutes go by and no train comes. What's changed? Why do I feel so much more desolate now, more than ever tonight? Why is she killing me with this silence? *"Casey?"*

I start to say I'm sorry . . . but about what? Where would I begin even if it meant anything? Why should I be apologizing, justifying myself again, always justifying myself, justifying . . . the words never leave my lips.

The silence in the room is more oppressive than the heat and still she waits, futilely now.

I get up, start to grope for my pants, change my mind and head into the darkness without them. So what if her roommate sees me?

I reach the bottom step. The moon's coming in through the windows over the sink. The windows face the road. A car speeds by as my feet touch the cool linoleum floor. Through the archway that separates the kitchen from the rest of the downstairs, I can see the living room just as I saw it in my dream, and the front door with the two, dimly lit windows on each side. It is several moments before I can turn away and walk across the kitchen into the bathroom. I can feel that lovely, cool freedom against the bottom of my feet. I don't shut the door. After a brief, initial mortification at the loudness of my urinating, I become defiant. I don't care if Casey's roommate hears.

Casey's sleeping when I return, her breaths deep and rhythmic. Despite the heat, she's wrapped a sheet around her body and curled herself up away from my half of the bed, as close to the edge as she can be.

I lie on my back again and listen to the woman beside me sleep. I hear another whistle. This time it comes from the south, down river below the house. Soon I hear the grinding of the multiple locomotives echo the half mile across the *river. The noise grows louder, much louder than it has ever sounded and then the engines pass, trailing screeching box-cars that clatter through with a hollow sound, empties headed north.*

TWENTY-TWO

"**W**hy you so quiet?" Annie asks and impulsively places a small hand on top of Morrisey's. I've been watching her hover in his vicinity, feeling her want to relent, to touch him as she has finally done. He looks up from his book and places his free hand over hers. He's been reading the same book for two weeks—it looks as though he's scarcely turned a page. Suddenly she pulls her hand away and hobbles down the bar toward a group of customers.

The parachutes have been removed from the ceiling of the club, and only bare rafters support four fans and the brown canvas. The bar's been moved to the back of the tent; the marquee and the Playmates are gone. The tables are covered with gold flake, candy-apple and candy-blue oilcloth, the walls with day-glo landscapes in plastic frames, just like the mess hall, and all the other mess halls in this goddamned country.

Wilbur comes in, grunting behind two cases of soda pop. He sets the cases down on a table, then leans on the table and wipes the moisture from his very red face. I recently heard Brock predict that Wilbur's confronting an imminent coronary.

"Where were you at evening formation?" Wilbur demands of Morrisey.

"Had a couple of casualties."

"You guys don't do shit up there—maybe twenty, thirty minutes a day."

"And what are you doing, Sergeant? Building yourself a little matchstick paradise? Why don't you stop up sometime and stick your nose in? You might learn something worthwhile . . . but maybe that's asking too much.''

Wilbur yells, "Annie, put this pop in the cooler, hey, girl?''

Annie clops over to the table and with surprising ease tears the top of the first case open.

"You know, we got that battalion inspection tomorrow, Morrisey!''

"How could I forget, Sergeant?''

Which is true. We've spent the past two weeks getting ready for this inspection, our battalion commander's first visit up country. Smith, Buelen, and the other lifers can scarcely contain themselves. You'd think the Pope was coming. No one knows what Howard thinks—we scarcely see him anymore except for disciplinary reasons and in the treatment tent.

A new NCO bunker has been built for the occasion, not unlike the grand commo bunker, and the recreation tent has been completed, including snooker and pingpong tables. The butt cans in all the hooches, wards, and recreation areas have been given a fresh coat of red paint. Signs in both English and Vietnamese have proliferated: "No Smoking—CẤM HÚT THUỐC!'' and "No Parking—CẤM DẬU'' in front of the treatment tent and wards; "Exit—LỐI RA'' over every conceivable egress; "Danger—NGUY HIỂM!'' on the road leading to the helicopter pad and in front of the auxiliary generators; "Quiet—YÊN LẶNG!'' in front of the wards.

"This is war?'' I asked Gerty the other day.

"It certainly is. The lifers' whores and visiting Viet Cong got to find their way around.''

Twin posts appeared miracuously like sentinels at the edge of the road facing the helicopter pad, defining the width of the culvert over which we cross with our burdens from the ships, and back again with the remnants. Their slender shapes rose like young rubber trees, fully fourteen feet in the air. Yesterday, the God Squad with Nye in the lead and Smith in command, marched up to the posts like a Chinese dragon bearing a huge, arched sign and two ladders. Now, with the sign in place, I can stand at the door to the sickcall tent and look straight out under its arch, across the dirt road, out the tarred passage to the landing pad, and beyond to where the tower rises and shimmers in the sun. The sign says, in foot-high letters: "DOCTOR BRAVO—CARE FOR OUR FIGHTING FORCES.''

I am still marvelling at this advertisement when the battalion commander, the colonel who nailed me when I delivered my first monthly report so long ago, arrives. I hear the shrill announcement of a helicopter and dust crashes into the trees. I crank the field phone.

"Nope," Gittoni replies. "It's only that asshole colonel from battalion."

"Great! Of course he had to come during sickcall." Standing beside the coffee pot, feeling the scratchy coolness around my ears and neck (we've been subjected to endless haircut and moustache inspections during the past several days), I watch Howard and Smith flock with the other lifers to the open door of the ship. They shuffle and primp, then salute. But that wiry-haired, effete shithead of a colonel, along with his sergeant major and snotty captain, scramble out with extraordinary haste. Suddenly Smith's gesticulating wildly, hollering for litterbearers.

"Why the hell don't they grab their own litter?" someone asks.

"Good question!" The field phone buzzes.

"Dust-Off wants that ship off the pad. It's in the fucking way!"

"You tell 'em!" I drop the receiver into its cradle. Owen and Gerhard rush up to the helicopter door. Owen drops a litter and frantically kicks at the struts with the back of his boot. Then they lift someone out of the helicopter, someone in fatigues wearing a helmet. I can't see any dressings on the patient, no signs of blood.

"What the *hell* are they doing?" Jenkins asks.

Owen and Gerhard start to walk in with the litter, but both the colonel and Howard begin shouting at them. Startled, Owen looks back at the two officers who shout angrily at him again. The two medics start to run with the litter, run hard toward that welcoming arch. The colonel runs alongside, a hand clasping the canvas possessively beside the man whose head rolls from side to side. The rest of them, Howard, the sergeant major, everyone trots absurdly behind. It's really quite funny.

"That poor fucker!" Morrisey says a while later, unable to keep a grin off his face. He stirs his cup of coffee. "They actually ran with him!"

"Yeah, so I noticed." The soldier had a compound fracture of his left leg, and has been evacuated. I'm logging the information from the field tag.

"He and a buddy were driving a track along Highway 10," Morrisey says, "somewhere south of the village when they spotted some good looking broad out in a rice paddy . . . no, I'm serious!" he protests in response to my laughter. "He told me himself. So they were watching the broad and the track went into a ditch and tipped over, crushing his leg. His buddy got thrown clear and had already dug him out by the time the colonel came flying over in his helicopter. A fucking doctor, mind you, and the dumb ass just shoves the fucker in the helicopter and brings him here—no splint, no first aid at all! Then he had Owen and Gerhard run with the litter."

Brock barges through the curtain, stomps over and looks at the log. "Where did Howard send that guy?"

"It's right here, sir. The Eighty-fifth."

"Call 'em! Tell them to get rid of the guy—send him to Cam Ranh, the DMZ, Hanoi, anywhere, just lose him! Get him the hell out of there and don't leave any record."

"I can't do that, sir."

"Well, by God, I can! Get them on the phone." Brock turns to face a quizzical Morrisey as I reach for the phone. "That fuckhead of a colonel is putting himself in for a Silver Star! Says he landed under 'hostile conditions,' performed emergency medical treatment and withdrew with the patient. I knew it! I smelled it a mile off!"

"Not a word, O'Neill!" Brock cautions, pointing at me. "He went to the Eighty-fifth and that's all you know, no matter what."

"Yes, sir." I'm grinning.

The colonel's inspection lasted scarcely half an hour after we shipped the soldier. He zipped through the company, was effusive in his praise, then dashed back under the archway and out to his helicopter. He and his entourage hurried right under that sign and not a one noticed something new on it:

DOCTOR BRAVO—
CARE FOR OUR FIGHTING
FORCES

The Dead and Dying

But Smith glanced up on his return from the pad. The sign disappeared within the hour and reappeared in its original form three days later, shielded in plexiglass.

The calls from battalion started late that same afternoon. "Do you have a record of a Spec five Lawrence, Martin C., Company A, etc., etc., compound fracture left leg?"

"Yes . . . our records indicate he was evacuated to the Eighty-fifth Evacuation Hospital."

"They have no record of him there. Will you please check again?"

The calls continued for almost two weeks. Twice Smith came in and pored over the log himself, obviously annoyed, but never saying why. Exasperated, he resorted to nit-picking criticisms of my office, my work, the coffee. No Specialist Lawrence, no confirmation, no medal.

"Where's Morrisey?" Smith asks when he spies the unused, neatly made cot. It's three in the morning and I've been awakened by the routine clatter and bang of locker doors, muttered curses and grousing that signals a raid. We knew it was going to occur before supper. If the raid isn't alarming, Smith's manner is. Suddenly the satisfaction of watching the lifers make fools of themselves as they rummage through our belongings fades before the puzzled but keen, almost pleased look that's come over Smith as he scrutinizes my face.

"I don't know, Sergeant," I answer truthfully, but not without some nervousness, which only convinces him I'm lying. "Maybe he's up at treatment."

"There haven't been any casualties in at least two days." Smith would know that.

"Sergeant Smith!" Wilbur exclaims and backs his head out of Gittoni's locker. In triumph, he holds up a half-empty miniature bottle of Seagrams. Smith looks at the prize with a faint smile.

"That yours, Gittoni?"

"Yes, Sarge. A Christmas gift from my girl. I'd completely forgotten about it."

Wilbur says, "Only noncommissioned officers of grade E-5, hard stripe, and above are allowed to . . ."

"Put it back, Sergeant Wilbur." Smith turns to me again. "Can't you do better than that, O'Neill?"

"Sarge, I really don't know."

"Sergeant Smith! Sergeant Smith!" Buelen crashes into the tent with a large plastic bag. "Must be two pounds of it!"

Every eye is riveted on the bag, obviously someone's stash.

"Where did you find it, First Sergeant?"

"Johnson found it under the front steps of the cooks' tent."

"Who does it belong to?"

"No one knows. They say they don't know how it got there. Should I bring them all over to the orderly room?"

"I wouldn't bother, First Sergeant. Just keep the marijuana. It is marijuana, isn't it?"

"I think so. They said it was. Anyhow, what would it be doing under the steps if it wasn't?" He looks around the room, taking in all the smiles.

"We'll give it to Papasan to burn tomorrow, First Sergeant Buelen. By the way, you haven't seen Morrisey, have you?"

"No! You don't think this belongs to him?"

"No, of course not." Smith drops his hand briefly on Buelen's shoulder. "You've done an excellent job."

"Where were you?" I demand later as Morrisey sits down on his bunk and begins to remove his boots. They're badly scuffed and dusty. He pulls a second pair out from under the cot where the hooch girl left them, then looks up at me with dark, haggard eyes. There are lines and heavy pouches beneath them. "Smith found out you weren't here! He's gunning for you."

Outside the tent, the first whistle blows for morning formation. Soon bits of conversation filter in through the screens as men pass on their way to the area in front of the NCO hooch. "So what? He's been gunning for me for a long time." Morrisey seems distracted, slightly troubled, even sorrowful. His lack of concern about Smith seems genuine.

"Well, look, man! You can't expect me to cover your ass."

"I don't."

I start for the door.

"Thanks, Jon," he says. He sounds very tired. "I really appreciate your concern, but don't worry about it." He stares at the floor, then pushes himself to his feet and follows me out.

Buelen went home a week later, retired out of the army. He just went home—had Anderson drive him to the airstrip so he could fly down to that plain with its bleak concentration of tin-roofed buildings inside barbed wire where battalion was

located—the colonel, the sergeant major—and where he was
processed on down to Long Binh and the 90th Replacement
Center with orders for home. He was gone. There was no
farewell party in the club, no muddled but tolerant Buelen
who once threw his arms around Navarra on the latter's final
night with us: only a subservient, aging man with a lot of
veins showing in his nose. We scarcely gave a shit by the time
he left.

And battalion, upon his early re-enlistment, promoted
Smith, with an extended tour, to E–8, First Sergeant.

I'm on the veranda at the base EM club sitting at a metal
table with a striped umbrella over it; the umbrellas are something new. There are even rumors that our battalion is going
to move its headquarters here. Highway 10 is now paved
halfway up from the plain.

The EM Club is the only place Morrisey will go outside the
company area, at least during the day, and he will come here
only with Jenkins and me, and only if we have a ride. He's
absolutely paranoid about MPs, officers, and harrassment in
general.

I notice Morrisey's hands. They're on the table on each
side of a can of beer, trembling. His attention's been caught
by something in the yard and he's unaware of his hands,
unaware that I've nudged Jenkins.

Jenkins reaches out and covers the hands with his own. This
startles Morrisey. "When did this shit begin?" Jenkins asks.

"What?" Morrisey clasps the beer can.

"The hands, Richie."

He bows his head, then slowly looks up. "I don't know
what I'm doing anymore, Jenks."

"You never did . . . none of us do, except O'Neill who
came over here to learn Vietnamese."

Morrisey grins, but it's mechanical. "I don't know what
I'm doing here anymore. It's never been delightful, but there
was once some kind of reason, or purpose. Not the war, not
that. Just other things, like being a good medic."

"Richie, one month more! Keep a calendar now. It'll help
you to hold on. You've got to relax."

"Yeah, relax." He says it with a terrible bitterness. "You
have only a few days left, Jenks! Smith got that promotion. I
relax once and he'll nail me."

"Look, in a little more than a month, you're going to be

wondering why it all seemed so urgent, so bad. You're going to be going home.''

I think it was that same day, in the evening, when we saw the freedom bird. The DC-8 must have flown off course, because we'd never seen one near the plantation before, and never would again. But there it was, out beyond our tiny, familiar world—the tower, the helicopters, the dust and wire —floating through the hazy sun, huge, its meaning unmistakable.

It was dream white with gold and blue stripes, one of the charter services' birds. It absolutely dwarfed everything, not only in the sky, but on the ground as well. It seemed as big as a space ship from another, bigger world. Soon it would be going back there with a bellyful of happy veterans. It seemed to fill the sky with a misty presence as it drifted slowly past on its descent into Bien Hoa.

Men ran from everywhere, the motor pool, the wards, the orderly room, to stand under the eaves of our rubber plantation and gaze at this eclipse of our war, a vision that consumed us with a longing at once poignant and specious.

I'm thinking how I hate the lack of seasons, how even my body, accustomed to a seasonal clock, hates it, how I miss the acrid smell of late autumn, that special sweat of exhaustion, of decaying pores and greasy rot awaiting the snow. I'm so sick of the heat.

They arrive shortly after noon, escorted by two MPs. Morrisey's going through the log, looking for the disposition of one of the sickcall patients when an MP appears on the other side of the counter and jerks a thumb toward the door. "They walked from Saigon."

"That's nice," Morrisey says. "Who?"

We follow the MP. The new arrivals are a woman with black hair and neat clothes despite several days on the road, a chubby baby in diapers cradled on her arm, and an old man, white-haired and spindly. The old man's grubby pants and tattered shirt are covered with a film of dust. All three of them stare at us while the MP wanders off to his jeep.

"Hey!" I yell as the jeep jerks alive. "What are we supposed to do with them?" For answer, I receive a brief wave.

I make no attempt to hide my consternation, my profound conviction that we've been suckered. This is going to be another one of those damn occasions . . .

Morrisey has said nothing.

I can feel the woman assess me, my feelings. Her look is one of concern, but not for me—for something that might be explained on a scraggly piece of paper she's holding out.

In a fragile hand is the peculiar compilation of information that I've long since recognized to be a request: 18 May, TaNang, husband, followed by a name. "No keep wounded," I explain. "Tainan? You try Tainan?"

When I say the name of the Vietnamese hospital, the woman nods, then points at the paper and shakes her head. This one's not dumb, I decide. I won't escape easily. I look at the scrap of paper again, gesture for them to wait as I retreat to my office where the dusty, scarcely blemished Vietnamese casualty ledger is under the counter. I flop it open. The soldier's name is one of six listed on the clean, white page, one of three for that particular day. The preceding entries were for a week prior. I reach for the field phone and ring commo. "Get ahold of Thieu. We need him."

"Roger that."

"Well?" Morrisey asks. He's seated the Vietnamese on the bench that Smith recently installed to the left of the door, having slathered it first with the abundant baby-blue paint. The heads of the Vietnamese, even the child, are turned, their eyes fixed on me. I avoid their gaze and maintain my composure. "I had to put in a call for Thieu."

"Lovely. Why don't we get them something to drink, Kool-Aid or something from the ward. They've had a long walk to learn that."

"Why don't you get it? I've got to wait for commo in case they find Thieu." At least Morrisey doesn't laugh outright. I should know better, and I do . . . but now, at least, I can turn my back and escape those searching looks for a few minutes.

The Vietnamese never move from the bench. They don't follow me inside. They seem to know Morrisey's coming back—such docile acceptance!

Thieu doesn't come. Just before evening chow, commo calls back and with characteristic terseness, suggests that the interpreter's probably out dunning his whores. The woman and child, the old man still haven't moved, except to drink what Morrisey brought them, haven't even gotten up to go to the bathroom or anything human like that. "What am I going to do, Morrisey? Lookit the time."

"Call the CO. See if he's got any ideas."

Howard suggests that I should notify Thieu. He says that is what an intelligent person might do instead of wasting his commander's time.

"I did that, sir, about four hours ago. They couldn't find him."

"Then wait some more. Maybe he'll show up."

"We've got curfew to think about, sir."

"Well, for Chrissakes, we can't keep them here!"

I place my hand over the receiver and whisper "No shit!" for Morrisey's benefit.

Finally Howard suggests that I get a pass into the compound and take the Vietnamese to the interpreter.

"And what then, sir?"

"What then?"

"Where are we going to put them?"

"I told you we can't keep them here!"

"I know that, sir."

"Well, I don't care what you do with them! Take them to the village . . . to Miss Lahn's . . . anything. Just get them the hell out of here."

It's been a light afternoon. Only two helicopters flew in and the child, his head resting on his mother's shoulder, hair lufting in the sudden wind, slept through it all. The woman and old man watched impassively as the procession of stretchers wound toward the plantation. Everywhere I went, for whatever purpose, I felt their eyes follow me.

I'm still fuming at Howard when Morrisey comes over and takes the dead receiver from me and calls the mess hall. "I'm bringing three Vietnamese over for chow, Sergeant Milliken."

He waits patiently. I can hear a faint squawking over the phone and he gives me a wink. "Nope, Sarge, don't bother sending any trays. These people need to sit down somewhere where it's cool. They've been on the road for days and are probably starved. Yeah, all the way from Saigon. Yes, Sergeant, I know it's against company policy but they need some comfort . . . Yes, yes, we're taking them out of here right after chow, O'Neill and I . . . No, if we do it now, we won't get anything to eat. We have to go all the way to the village. We'll be right over." He drops the receiver and grins. "Milliken is bullshit!"

"Morrisey, you know we ain't supposed to serve gook civilians in here," Milliken mutters as Morrisey and I file through the line. He wouldn't permit the old man and woman to go through the line, but had trays taken to a table at the back corner of the mess hall. The Vietnamese workers in the wash house were aghast as we led the three civilians into the dining area, and so were the occupants of the mess hall.

The old man and the woman have eaten the meat and peas, but only poked at the mashed potatoes and gobs of ersatz gravy. The meal passes in silence.

One thing has changed, though. The Vietnamese no longer look to me for their cue, haven't since we left the treatment area, and the realization is less a relief than I might have expected. I'm embarrassed and a little ashamed . . . I gave something away.

"Someone must have pissed you off," Jenkins says clamping a hand on Morrisey's shoulder on his way out of the mess hall. Morrisey grins and rises from the table. The family rises with him, scarcely noticing me.

They are waiting for me in the ambulance in front of the sickcall tent when I wander over from the mess hall. I was hoping they would be gone. Morrisey drums the steering wheel as I climb into the passenger seat, then slaps the vehicle into gear before I can shut the door.

We seem to be moving backward in time as we approach the civilian compound next to the GI recreation area. Just down the highway is the air control tower and the firehouse. Johnny Mirrors is at the gate near where, seven months ago I first saw Mathias and the three-quarter ton truck with the Vietnamese flags over the headlights. Only in this manner do I comprehend time and motion. Morrisey swings the ambulance off Highway 10 and we rumble up to the gate. Another MP who's on duty with Johnny Mirrors scowls at us as we approach. A line of civilians returning from work are filing through the gate, their I.D.s being checked by two additional MPs.

"What do you want?" the scowling MP demands as he saunters up to the driver's window and peeks inside.

Without bothering to reply, Morrisey hands him the pass we had to obtain from division headquarters. Mirrors moves up behind his partner and reads the pass. "Looks OK," he says.

"I want to see both of you coming back out of there," the scowling one says as he reluctantly waves us through the gate.

"How's it going, Doc?" Mirrors asks as Morrisey puts the

ambulance in gear. Startled, I turn to see if he's addressing me, but the question is directed to Morrisey.

"Fine," is the noncommittal answer.

"You know him?" I ask.

"Seen him around . . . now check this out, O'Neill." The ambulance enters the hamlet, rolls down an incline into the thicket of trees. The brakes squeak intermittently as we pause to let pedestrians and cyclists move aside. Among the bushes and trees, I glimpse huts made of poles and thatch, of masonry and tile, and suddenly we thump and bang into a world I've never seen before, a place of serpentine lanes, deep shade, of children laughing, playing, crying, being kids, of adults who watch us silently and without visible hostility. I'm carried back to that day at the leprosarium, and farther back to a time I never knew in this land, a quieter, more secretive era before the American war with its seas of regulation buildings, stripped, defoliated land, mounds of machinery. Morrisey stops and leans out the window. "Hey, boysan!"

A boy of nine or ten, wearing a military jungle hat, large khaki shorts, and nothing else jumps onto the running board and hangs onto the window frame with both hands. Morrisey quickly removes his arm from the window and lets his hand drop into the safer depths of the cab where his wristwatch is out of reach.

"You find Sergeant Thieu?" Morrisey asks.

"Ah, Sahgint Thieu! Sahgint Thieu!" and with a vigorous nod of his head, the boy lets go with one hand and points straight ahead. The vehicle lurches forward along the deeply rutted, dusty road through an array of fowl and urchins. We turn up one lane, then down another. The boy steadfastly points the way, sometimes directly across Morrisey's windshield. He smiles and waves to friends, enjoys himself immensely. It's hard to believe such a verdant maze exists here, so close to the Blue Baby Bar and the Yellow Peril and the airstrip with its thundering planes.

The trees and underbrush fall away, and sprawled across a knoll in front of us like a dream is a huge, one-storey building, its walls bathed gold in the evening light. A vast, ballustraded veranda spans the front. The entire face of the building is lined with louvered French doors. Several of these are open and from within the deep, interior shadows, their glass counterparts glint dimly. A wide, dirt drive sweeps across the clearing, across the front of the veranda, and back around an elaborate, defunct fountain.

Morrisey stops the ambulance in front of some wide steps. "I get!" the boy shouts, and jumps off the running board and scampers across the veranda. He disappears through one of the many doors.

"He's going to want money for this, Morrisey."

"Fuck him!"

"What did this used to be?" I wonder aloud, primarily to change the subject. The harshness of his reply disturbed me.

"An estate. A Frenchman who owned a part of this and a couple of small plantations farther north." Morrisey absently drums his fingers on the steering wheel, totally unaware of the surprise his knowledgeable answer has produced. "The place is a warren. Must be fifty families living in there, a lot of them behind blanket walls. Thieu's got his own pair of rooms, though."

"You've been here before?"

"I've heard about it."

I'm aware of people now. A few were on the veranda when we drove up, and a couple of children were clambering over the fountain, but now I feel their presence at the windows of the building. I feel the tension caused by our arrival. "It's as though it's been desecrated."

"Is that what you feel?" Morrisey asks with faint curiosity, and looks at the building anew.

"Don't you?"

"I don't know what I think anymore. It's like what you told me about the priest and the chapel with the rose window, except there's some terrible melancholy I feel when I think what this once represented. I guess your priest would feel that we can't afford such luxuries."

Before I can answer, I spot two birds sailing over the low, tiled roof. A soft, melodious cry floats back as they disappear. "Did you see that?"

"What?"

"A couple of birds. I didn't think any lived in the plantation." The house is vaguely V-shaped, but with no point. The longest part of the building is where the point should be. Beyond the distant wing are high brambles, concertina wire, a machinegun tower, and finally, glimpsed through occasional openings in the foliage, the ruins of the jungle stripped to make our defense perimeter.

I've almost forgotten why we're here, our passengers in the back of the ambulance, when Thieu emerges from a door with the boy. Morrisey climbs down from the cab and walks around the front of the vehicle. Thieu smiles in recognition. "Hey, Morrisee!" He gives a small wave, then spots me. "O'Neill!"

"Why you come?" he asks Morrisey. He's dressed in fatigue pants and a white T-shirt.

"For Christ's sake, Thieu, we've been trying to get you all afternoon!" I exclaim, shoving my door open. The interpreter looks surprised.

"Hey, O'Neill!" Morrisey puts his hand up. "Relax."

And why are you so damn circumspect, I wonder.

"Thieu, in the back of the ambulance we got a woman, her kid, and an old man—her father-in-law, I think. They walked all the way from Saigon looking for her husband. He was one of those bodies brought in a few days ago, remember? Someone's got to tell them what's going on. Also, they can't stay in the company." Thieu's look is bland, without emotion. "They can't stay here, can they?"

"No. Division no like."

"Then how about riding out to Miss Lahn's with us?"

"Oh, wow." His look of skepticism reflects my feelings precisely.

So we've creaked back through the gate, past the scowl of the MP and the inscrutability of Johnny Mirrors, and we're churning down along the airstrip. Thieu's fully dressed, sitting between us on the floor. He leans against the closed door separating us from the back of the ambulance where the three civilians jostle around. At the South checkpoint, we're reminded that we have only an hour before the gates are closed and locked for the night.

We roar along Highway 10, virtually empty at this time of evening, past the shattered graves, the dense, darkening foliage of the abandoned rice paddies. Morrisey has the vehicle floored. We careen off the highway in front of the tower and bang through the market place, Morrisey using the horn liberally to clear our way. To my left, up a narrow street, are the rotten gates to the old French compound with its swarm of native inhabitants. Morrisey downshifts, whips the wheel. We blast through the blue gates into the small courtyard and screech to a stop at the infirmary. Thieu grins at Morrisey's performance. "You drive like fucking madman!"

"I don't want to spend the night here, Thieu." Morrisey shoves his shoulder against the door and scrambles to the ground. Miss Lahn appears at the top of the steps, stands in that huge, open doorway clasping her hands. Under the massive, three-storey building with its iron grates and feeling of implacable, vast solitude, she seems brittle in her white dress. The shadow of the courtyard wall behind us glides up the reddened walls of the infirmary. "Tell her, Thieu," Morrisey says, and holds the door for the interpreter.

Miss Lahn's long, dark hair seems slightly disheveled as though we've awakened her from a nap, and as I look down for that gnawed Oxford, I find instead very beautiful, delicately formed bare feet. They are breathtaking, and so, for a moment, is she, as I let my gaze wander upwards and absorb that sleepy, youthful anxiety.

Then she speaks, loudly, angrily, in response to a quiet statement by Thieu. Neither Morrisey nor I can understand what's been said, but we don't need any explanation. She stamps her foot and her face colors when Thieu says something else.

"No!" she says, changing to English. "No can stay here— no got room!"

"Looks like you've got plenty of room, Miss Lahn," Morrisey begins as he moves around her into the building.

"You keep!"

"We can't. S.O.P. No civilians in the American part of the plantation."

"I got S.O.P., too!"

The panelled doors on both sides of the main room are open, those on the left disclosing the metal cabinet—Miss Lahn's symbol of authority—and those on the right two hospital beds and spotless, pressed sheets. "Hell, you can put them in here, Miss Lahn," Morrisey suggests as he walks over and leans into the room. "These beds don't even look slept on."

"I just clean hospital today. People you bring be poor . . . cost money to clean sheet."

I reach the back of the ambulance just as Thieu yanks the handle down. The steel door screeches open. Inside, the woman and her baby and the old man are huddled on one of the benches. Their faces are frozen. Thieu speaks briefly in Vietnamese.

While we watch the two adults, their mouths fall open,

their faces contort, and the first wail of grief escapes. The baby starts to cry.

("It doesn't bother them that much," Howard, in a moment of unsolicited advice, had said two or three hours earlier. "They're used to it.")

Now Thieu says, "I tell them he dead, Morrisey. I also say they stay here with Lahn. You right. That be dead man father."

The wailing increases. I'm suddenly irritated by this lugubrious bellowing and the frail echoes of the child. I didn't want this! I didn't ask for it! And Thieu, that callous bastard!

Who am I to say callous? How long have I been here now? How else can one survive?

Morrisey and I lift the old man from the ambulance and carry him up the stairs. His face is red and tear-streaked. I don't think he weighs more than eighty pounds. It's a miracle he walked from Saigon. The woman, her crying baby on one arm, is in front of us. When we reach the top we stand him up and she helps him into the large room. Miss Lahn seeks somehow to block their entrance without actually touching them.

Sleep was simply darkness that year, but there were living dreams. That empty, vast-roomed building was one, with its little metal cabinet downstairs where the shadows of bars flowed out upon the floor on the sunlight, with its ethereal caretaker, fastidious, immaculately dressed in crisp white, only that chewed shoe suggesting the possibility of a facade, of shame and hidden neglect beneath her starched surface.

TWENTY-THREE

Not since the days of Mendez has there been a night like this—not that I can remember. We're jammed. The tables, the aisles, the yard are filled with American casualties. Flashlights wag among the rubber trees, seeking a path toward pale flesh, the fantasy of night blood. For the new ones in the company, it's an electrifying event, a source of amazement that casualties could ever be like this . . . and of course, among those of us who remember, there's a perverse, smug satisfaction: we're the veterans. It does feel good, this particular chaos, this sense of mad purpose.

Howard's not quick the way Mendez was, doesn't possess that almost unerring ability to perceive and select the worst cases for priority treatment, triage. And those of us who were around then are not as good anymore. We've lost the edge. So, if anything, a bad situation is becoming worse than it need be. Some of us are aware of the problem, but the sheer exultation of involvement, of reflex work, as clumsy as it might be, suppresses all other concerns.

Brock stumps through the bedlam with his usual, if excessive care. He's looking more harrassed, however, feeling more pressure because Howard's a problem and everything's started to stack up. Brock's done at least three cut-downs in the past twenty minutes or so, a remarkable undertaking for a man as deliberate as he. He hasn't stayed in one place long enough to see the unconscious men carried out, bloodbags on their chests, between their legs. He can't possibly have a sense of progress, no sense of conquering this human tide. At one point he drops his cigar, steps on it, and doesn't light another—this is unusual.

Shelby's trying to keep up, but he's been working on the same patient for ages. Somehow, Brock manages to concern himself with Shelby's problem. "That one going south, Shel?"

"Yeah, yeah," Shelby mutters, the response scarcely audible as he tries to concentrate on his work, a cut-down. His hands are trembling.

"Jesus, Shel, let me give you a hand! They got another ship going out now . . . this guy should be out there."

"Yeah, priority," Shelby says, "priority." He shuffles aside as Brock slips in, quickly inserts the intravenous and ties off the vein. Brock moves on, leaves the rest to Shelby and Newell, who's hardly in better condition.

"Where's Grisholm?" Brock asks. His hands spread the hair around a patient's head wound. He bends close to the area and examines a jagged hole. "This one goes to the Eighty-fifth, priority, O'Neill."

"Yes, sir."

Brock raises his head and looks around. "Where the hell is he?" The groans, the yells and cries, the shouts for instruments and blood nearly drown his words.

"Out in the yard, Captain Brock," Gerty says from the next table.

Another ship tears out of the darkness and illuminates the front of the tent. "Is that ship empty?" Brock shouts to Kostek, who's by the phone. "I hope," he adds under his breath.

"No, sir!"

Brock's examining a bullet wound in a corporal's arm when four men crash in with a litter. I can see the head of a soldier; the lower part of his face is torn and smashed. A plastic airway juts from the bloody pulp of the mouth, and it rolls from side to side.

"Down here!" Brock yells. He indicates the table. "Take this other man outside." The litter with the corporal is lifted off and trundled down the aisle.

I write furiously, taking information about the new casualty from a soggy tag wired to a buttonhole. A light has been drawn up and the plastic airway removed. Morrisey has already cut the shirt open and discovered another large wound in the stomach.

"Two I.V.s, Morrisey, and wrap the stomach wound. Get me a trach set, Gerhard."

Gerhard disappears. It seems forever before he returns with the blue, cloth-wrapped package. Brock snatches it. "Eight litterbearers!" someone hollers as another brilliant, howling beam of light flashes across the tent.

"What have you got?"

I turn. It's Howard. He peers over my shoulder, studies the wounded man with infuriating detachment.

"Take those new arrivals, will you, Grisholm?" Brock's hands have begun to shake in the taut, rubber gloves as he spreads the incision to accept the sleeve for the tracheotomy tube. Blood bubbles in the incision as the man exhales. Morrisey adjusts the flow of blood from the first bag while Gerhard desperately tries to raise a vein in the other arm. Watching Gerhard, I'm reminded of myself that first day. But that was my first day . . .

And my war hadn't turned to paper and rubber bags.

Two men arrive at the front door with a litter. "Not in here!" Kostek shouts. "There's no goddam room!" The lead litterbearer looks flustered. Brock's entire body is trembling.

"Jesus Christ!" He flaps one gloved hand to shake off the excess blood. "Where's the goddam tube, Morrisey?"

"Right beside you, sir, next to your left elbow . . . on the tray."

"Oh yeah . . . Jesus. Why doesn't Grisholm get his ass in gear!" Brock's hands shake violently as he tries to insert the curved tube. The soldier emits a low, growling sound through the sleeve. "Damn!" Brock mutters, still struggling with the tube.

"Gerhard, come over here. I'll take that arm." Morrisey moves around the table, up beside Brock. "Give me a hand, O'Neill."

I stuff the book of tags in my pocket.

"What's this damn thing lodging against?" Brock pulls the tube out of the sleeve—blood skims off the stainless steel. He tries to re-insert it, twice misses the hole, almost completely the second time.

"Sir, can I help?" Morrisey says.

Brock pushes the tube into the sleeve again, almost rams it in in his frustration. Sweat streams down his face. I think of the missing cigar and concentrate on the soldier's arm, on the blood from the second bag dripping through the tube into the vein. My guts contract fiercely; a bitter taste fills my mouth.

Time—no it isn't time, but motion—becomes suspended. We become a still, a single frame, frozen except for the minute drip of the red liquid, the curses of the doctor, and the strange hollow sounds from the tracheotomy sleeve.

"Oh, God!" This time it's a plea—quick, final. Something metallic clatters on the floor. Brock moves away from the table, his gloved hands dripping blood. The tracheotomy tube lies on the floor, the dust around it turning muddy. A rasping sound escapes the sleeve in the soldier's neck, followed by blood and bubbles, then the head rolls to one side, eyes wide in a stare.

"He threw it down," Gerhard whispers.

Morrisey catches up with Brock at the back of the tent, slaps an arm around him and guides him back to another table, another wounded man.

"You should have seen him," Morrisey says later. He looks across the aisle into my dim reading light bleeding green through the mosquito net. ". . . and that asshole, Howard, that fucking jerk! 'What's the matter? Not going to let a few casualties get to you, now?' The guy's crushed, O'Neill . . .

"And that goddam little turd, Gerhard! You watch him flap his mouth, that self-righteous . . . I'll kill the sonuvabitch!"

"Jenks knows about it. I told him."

"Brock was trying to write a letter to his wife—you imagine that? Trying to tell her what he'd done. He was crying when I left, bent over the remains of that letter. He'd shredded it."

I push myself off my cot, walk to the door and open it. The warm, moist blackness enfolds me. I let the door slide out of my grip and feel my way through the trees, *through the high grass and the brush that smells acrid and clings to my pantlegs. I squint in the sun and feel an intense desire just to lie down and sleep. Sleep is gentle. Sumac climbs the embankment in front of me, towers over me. Among the dense trunks of trees and dry, wispy grass I can make out an occasional rail of brown steel lying flat on the earth.*

I push through the brush, out onto the top of the embankment, stop, bend over and rub my hand along the rail at my feet. The ties are rotten, light brown and punky. Large, flat pieces of rusted steel peel away under my hand. I rub it

324

several times, my eyes pressed in close upon the section I'm stroking. Soon, I've peeled a chunk several inches deep out of the rail.

I walk down the ties between the rails while the sun burns overhead in a sky of no blue I've ever seen. Ahead, I hear a deep rumble. Around a sharp, right-angled bend, I find two diesel locomotives, back to back, vibrating in their own shimmering heat. Their black paint has blistered away in large areas and the exposed metal is corroded. A ventilating door is wide open and I push against it, try to close it, but it won't move. The metal's very hot. Beyond the door, along the catwalk, is the cab, its windshield shattered. I hear a whistle among the trees where the tracks curve away out of sight. I want to leave, to run, but I can't move . . .

I'm on my belly. I hear the whistle again, this time outside my dreams. I roll over on my back. There's faint, gray light at the window above me. Casey is still wrapped in the sheet. I look at her, inches away, but she's utterly unreachable now. No signs of physical damage, no gobs of blood and pallid, torn flesh, no sweet smell, but she's as surely dead to me . . . only here I feel a sadness, something verging on remorse, and this is new.

What was it? A week later? No more, certainly. Morrisey, no one, said a word about it but we all knew, sensed it immediately. It was one of those things you couldn't talk about. It's strange how you don't recognize the symbolic power of something until it's taken away, turns up missing. Smith removed the VD Vista, Brock's VD Vista, just walked in and took it down (so I was told). Nothing appeared to take its place.

If nothing else could do it, that should have told us, should have confirmed it all.

"Can I talk to you a minute, Morrisey?"

Morrisey's putting wrapped utensils, trach kits, cut-down kits, that sort of thing—all fresh from the autoclave—in the cabinet. He looks over his shoulder at Wilbur. "Sure, Sarge. What is it?"

I've just entered the tent. My hand's on the door; instinctively I let it shut. Sergeant Wilbur hasn't heard me.

"We've been talking it over . . ."

"Talking what over, Sarge, and who's 'we?' " Morrisey asks.

"The CO, Sergeant Smith . . . First Sergeant Smith, even

325

Captain Shelby.'' Wilbur shuffles uneasily. ''We all feel that maybe you should take a sedative . . . tranquilizer, try to calm you down. Your tour's almost over! We don't want nothing to happen.''

''What?''

''Librium. Shelby will prescribe it.'' Wilbur starts to move back. ''We're only trying to help.'' He raises his hands slightly, as though to protect himself.

''Goddam, I don't believe it! I don't need your fucking help! What kind of stooge are you, Sergeant? *Whose* stooge?'' Morrisey seems to grow, to rear above Wilbur who circles slowly around him, about to bolt for the door and the security of the NCO hooch.

Just as suddenly, Morrisey relaxes, stares at the hound eyes of the dumpy little sergeant with the bad heart—Wilbur's already wheezing. He shakes his head. ''Sarge,'' he says gently, ''this is my body, my head. You guys can't have them. I'm not going to zonk myself into passivity—I'm not going to do that to myself!''

Wilbur nods his head rapidly and starts down the aisle.

''Sarge!'' Morrisey shouts at the hapless man. ''Don't do their dirty work! Tell Smith he ought to have guts enough to talk to me directly!''

''I only wanted to help.''

''Yeah, I understand. We could all use tranquilizers, couldn't we, O'Neill?'' Morrisey grins, but Wilbur's gone, uninterested in my reply.

I shrug noncommittally. ''Maybe they have a point,'' I suggest.

''You mean I should take tranquilizers?''

''Why blow it all?'' I am discussing it rationally, so I believe, weighing the pros and cons—and I even allow myself to think he is, too. Then I catch the sarcasm. He's furious.

''O'Neill, I'm going to make it out of here just fine!'' he explodes.

''Why don't you tell Jenks about this? See what he says.''

''Where the hell do you get off making that kind of suggestion?''

''OK, I'm sorry . . . no, I'm not! I was only trying to help.''

Morrisey flashes a smile, but it's not warm or appreciative; it's frightening.

326

I really don't think Jenkins could have acknowledged how serious it was, not by then. He wouldn't have been able to. Jenks was counting the hours before he could leave that place forever. There was no room for anything else.

"Morrisey, goddammit! That sonuvabitch Smith, that fucking bastard actually accused *me* of inciting that grenade! *Inciting it,* he said, like I'm some damn firebrand!" Jenks's mortification and rage are incredible. Sitting on his cot, dressed only in pants and a pair of rubber sandals, he's trying to control himself with an almost pathetic fury. His hands are balled into fists. Periodically he plunges them in his eyes, then yanks them across his cheeks, wiping the tears.

I heard the grenade go over the tent—the clink of the falling handle was unmistakable. It was the third such incident in a week, so I hardly glanced at the roof before I went back to the letter I was writing. A minute or two later, the shouts and curses of the enraged NCOs filtered through the front of my hooch. Even then, I didn't have to get up to know what was happening; the hissing grenade projected lurid images of red, green, purple, yellow smoke around the lighted doors and screens.

It was the other cry that brought me to my feet, caused me to drop the box of stationery on the floor, because it was none other than Jenkins, the person who never raised his voice.

" . . . *inciting* the brothers to rebel! *Militant* he called me! Just another militant black leading others into trouble! Lord, Morrisey! I was right here, we were all right here in full view the whole damn time! How dumb does he think I am?"

Morrisey's sitting on a large, wooden crate that Jenks has packed with his accumulated possessions to send home. Oddly enough, he's smiling.

"What are you smirking at!" Jenkins demands. "That bastard reduced me! Made me some kind of . . ."

"Nigger."

"Yes!"

"Amazing what an instinct he's got for it, isn't it?"

Jenkins doesn't look the least speculative. "Yeah, I know," he says, "I see it now, the fucking bastard!" He's slowly gaining control. "What the hell *are* you grinning at?"

"It wasn't the racial slur, Jenks. He outsmarted you. That's what's got your ass!"

"I don't know who's worse, Morrisey," Jenkins allows after a long pause, "you or Smith."

Morrisey roars.

I begin to laugh and even Jenks cracks a smile. "He hasn't gotten you yet, Morrisey."

"Not yet."

"Two days to go before I leave." Jenkins shakes his head, marvelling. "Lord, he must hate you!"

Morrisey bursts into fresh laughter, but it's relief now, a desperate relief as though he's sure at last that he hasn't been going crazy . . .

And Jenks is going home.

The three of us hitch a ride to the airstrip in the water truck on its afternoon run. The roofless cab is jammed. I'm squeezed between Morrisey and the driver who's battling a reluctant gearshift. He slams his palm against the handle and the lever flies back against my knee. The truck lurches. "Sorry, man," he says, easing himself back onto the seat.

Shadows of leaves fly over the hood, over us as we rumble down the corridor toward a splotch of dazzling sunshine that is the airstrip.

Jenks is pressed against the door, his arm hanging down outside. He holds a TWA flightbag on his knees. "I can't believe it!" he announces, and I can feel his exhilaration, that grip on the insides that means freedom, going home, getting the fuck out of here.

Morrisey laughs. "I feel like an old man, Jenks. Worn out. You're making me feel older." There's no humor left when he falls silent.

Jenkins stares rigidly ahead as though he's forcing himself not to look at his friend. "Hang in there, Richie. Just days, now."

"Yeah."

Jenkins wanders over to the manifest hut and gets himself on the next plane, then rejoins us by the truck. There are several men lounging on the benches around the hut. One man is sleeping, his helmet off, head propped against his pack. An M-16 rests against his thigh and the bench on which he's sprawled. His face looks gentle.

Jenkins leans against the truck and glances frequently toward the airstrip. Our conversation becomes aimless. Suddenly I don't want to be here. Just let him go!

A fat-bellied plane drifts soundlessly out of the sky. Its tires screech on the runway. The plane roars into life as its engines reverse. It wobbles off the runway, its mouth whines open, and Jenkins moves out into the sunshine along with the soldiers bound for down-country bases.

The plane climbs higher and higher, then veers off into the brilliant emptiness of the sky. We start back to the truck, a deuce-and-a-half with a 500 gallon tank on it. "How many days do you have left, Morrisey?" the driver asks.

"Less than a month."

"Lucky bastard! I've got ten months to go."

My God, what a lifetime, I think. I'll have 100 days when Morrisey leaves. The driver pushes a button and the diesel bursts alive. Billows of dust drift away behind the truck as we bounce along Highway 10 toward the South checkpoint and the waterpoint. The sky is like a transparent blue dome, a barrier that surrounds the hilltop through which the sun blazes. The driver pulls a pair of sunglasses down off the top of his head and covers his eyes. "You and Jenkins pretty good friends, huh?"

Morrisey mutters something vaguely affirmative.

"Yeah, the black guys in our company are OK, not like some of the shitheads in these other outfits."

Eight trucks are in line in front of us. The drivers sit in their cabs and doze or read magazines or chat with whoever's currently pouring water from the wood-framed tower. On our left is the waterhole where Lucius, long departed Lucius, was totally immersed—and Saved.

Our driver has climbed down and sauntered a few trucks forward to visit. Morrisey pulls his cap down and starts to doze. His face relaxes into a look of uncommon serenity; small drops of perspiration glide down his cheek.

The trucks begin to fire up, jarring him momentarily. Our driver returns, moves the truck ahead, then disappears. Morrisey is asleep seconds after the door slams.

There's a continuous stream of military and Vietnamese civilian traffic at the checkpoint; trucks, cars, pedestrians, motorbikes, lambros, all pour into the base, and out, heading home. I hear the faint gabble of oriental voices, the putt-putting of scooters, an occasional shout from one of the MPs, somnolent sounds of a hot, late afternoon. In a few hours, the coils of concertina wire will be strung across the road, the gates will be shut, and a new day of war will begin.

I wasn't going to take an R&R, and then I changed my mind . . . suddenly it seemed very necessary. But it was also another reminder of the clock that wasn't a clock, stepping out as I did from one set of images into another, then back again, to find the first altered, changed, like Morrisey—the relative calm that existed when I left, shattered. He was, if anything, more strained. The situation had deteriorated for all of us, as I was to discover immediately. Morrisey had no intellectual peers left—no one to humor him, no one who was not somehow intimidated by him. I was never his peer in that way, Jenkins was gone, and Brock might just as well have been, for he had isolated himself from everything but his work—and even that he performed with a truculence that all too clearly revealed his wrecked confidence.

But first I had to take that vacation. That vacation from a war . . . I boarded a Pan American 707 and flew across the South China Sea, north to Hong Kong, where I bought a conservative summerjacket, slacks, a summer suit, read the morning English papers while the Star Ferries plied the water beyond my terrace in Kowloon. And I bought a woman—I'd never done that before. I did it for only one night, then returned to my English papers (with news of a distant war), my wanderings through the city, my train trip to the Chinese border.

I wrote home about Hong Kong, wrote to the place where the first buds of spring would be appearing on the mountains. The letters were long (the hotel provided a typewriter at my request), or seemed that way. When I looked at them again at home, looking I suppose to recapture a moment, I was surprised by their brevity and insignificance. They seemed curiously devoid of any intimation of a return to something other than the comforts of home. Actually, as I wrote them, it was as though I was talking to myself, saying "Look, this is me! This is really quite nice!"

Yet I was haunted. Going to bed late, rising early, I dreaded the loss of a single moment of the day. The second morning, the morning after my whore had quietly closed the door behind her and disappeared in the pre-dawn city, I awoke late, bewildered. It was almost noon, the sun was high and the murmurings of Kowloon rose the fifteen stories to my balcony and fluttered through the curtains, filling me with panic, morbid fear that time had run out. I had to remind myself that I still had two mornings left.

That was the day I took the train to the Chinese border,

became enthralled with the beauty of an Orient at peace. I
needed to feel the pulse of people absorbed in living.

A constant din filters through the screen doors, a composite of the roar of traffic, whine of engines, clatter of helicopters, the ceaseless thunder of jets, military and civilian, leaving Tan Son Nhut. An airman is perched on a stool behind a counter at the far end of the manifest room, reading a skin magazine. Despite the noise, I have this terrible feeling that we are the last two living men.

A blackboard on the wall has some times below "arrivals," but none entered below "departures." The same numbers were on the board when I entered the room almost four hours ago, when I left behind me, forever I assume, the blue quonset huts, hedges, manicured lawns, flowers, trees that comprise the living quarters for the airmen, and through which I passed on my return from the R&R Center. It was the final frame on something totally absurd, compelling, jewel-like in its vividness. I stepped into this room and immediately felt comfortable—quite a contrast to seven, almost eight months ago and that early morning ride through Bien Hoa.

The room was packed at first, but everyone else has left, most on a plane for Da Nang, three others on a Huey down into the Delta.

The airman looks up from his magazine. "Hey, buddy, can you turn on that fan?"

I stand up, lean across the back of my bench and yank a chain dangling from a stainless steel floor fan. I sit back down and wait, feel the sweat drip down my face, fight the sleepiness of boredom. The airman wanders into the clamor of the outside world. When he returns a few minutes later, he calls me. "They're going your way," he says as he holds the door open and points in the direction of a Huey slick idling on the concrete.

The open doors of the helicopter tilt forward; hazy buildings, fighter planes with cockpits glinting in the sun begin to drift by. Coils of wire and fence fall away below us and the door frame on my left rolls downward toward the crammed streets and byways of Saigon where streams of human and vehicular traffic flow without the slightest awareness of me. Rivers meet then snake away together into the Delta, away to the horizon where the water sparkles without color. We fly over the Saigon River, our shadow following us over the brown water; the land becomes intermittently green and lush, then blackened, stripped streaks of raw earth. Some kind of factory belches red smoke into the brilliant haze. High tension lines march across the open, flat land.

We follow railroad tracks for several miles, but they cease abruptly at a small village station. Scores of people mill around some passenger cars. Beyond the village, the tracks become brown and overgrown as they snake across a scarred world, transverse rusted trestles.

I watch Long Binh approach between the helmets of the pilots. From here the metal roofs, the fences, the wire and guard towers, the clouds of oily, black smoke pouring into the sky above the wasteland where a jungle once teemed, the ordered military symmetry, conjure a vision of Europe a quarter of a century ago. A century . . . a quarter of a century once seemed like a long, long time.

The helicopter descends smoothly, rapidly, skims over waves of corrugated sheet metal and drops into an area about the size of a football field that was not even visible from the air. The landing area is surrounded on three sides by barracks, revetments, and a hospital. At the far end is a fence and on our side of it a road that winds up and down through raw gullies toward a distant hill. Over the hill march the desolate, tract development outlines of more barracks and offices, and a naked jungle of wires and utility poles. A jeep bangs along the road hurling a cloud of dust, disappears in one of the gullies, then pops back into view.

We're in the air again, heading up country now with two officers, obviously new arrivals; their fresh green duffel bags are planted on the floor in front of our shared seat. They gaze at me good-naturedly after buckling themselves in, but I turn away and lose myself in the outside world. In the distance I see the plain, the metal roofs, the towers of the base where battalion's located.

We cross Highway 10. Our shadow darts among vehicles barrelling in minute obscurity through small villages, between rice paddies and ruptured, open land.

Away from the highway on rough, secondary roads, I can see occasional vehicles, usually military. The tracks of ROME plows, of tanks and APCs wind through and around gutted buildings and hamlets deserted as a matter of policy, I'm sure, but cast now in the middle of a defoliated nowhere. Only the ancestral shrines that appear intermittently still suggest some creative human will.

Beneath our belly sail helicopters, spotter planes, all measure and kind of flying creatures. I feel like a fish in crystal waters watching other fish swim soundlessly over the bottom of the sea.

"Where's my goddam dog? Where's Jenni?" I've just crashed through the front door of the treatment tent, painted blue in my absence and emblazoned with a huge, red cross on a white square.

Smith and Wilbur are rummaging under one of the tables; they seem to be making an inventory of supplies. Smith looks over his shoulder, then smiles. "How was your R&R, O'Neill?"

"My R&R? Where's my dog? I just heard you had her taken away!"

The smile vanishes. Smith stands up. "Now wait a minute, buster! You don't come roaring in here accusing anyone of taking your dog!"

"The hell I don't!" I yell right back. "That was my dog! I saved her life!"

"That dog was unauthorized! Base regulations state two dogs per company and you know it, O'Neill!" He's shouting now. "And you calm down this instant, young man, before I have you go to the commander!"

"Screw this unauthorized shit, Sergeant! She was a living thing, a pet!" I can hear myself scream. Everyone within a mile must hear me.

"The CO ordered the dog population reduced to conform with regulations. I warned you men! There were too many mutts around here . . . always scaring the civilian workers."

"Fuck the civilian workers! You goddam had my dog killed!"

"I did not! I won't stand for this kind of behavior!"

Two hands grab my shoulders. I try to jerk away, but then someone's speaking beside me. "Tell him what you had done with them, Sergeant Smith."

"I didn't have anything to do with them, Morrisey."

"Don't hide behind Captain Howard, First Sergeant."

"Soldier! I've got Sergeant Wilbur here as a witness." Smith puffs up.

"Tell O'Neill here how you had sergeants Wilbur and Milliken gather them all up except Mamma and Pappa, put them in an ambulance and take them to the base vet."

"That little bitch bit me, too," Wilbur mutters.

"Good! I hope you die of fucking rabies!" I bellow.

Morrisey shakes me. "Get him out of here!" He shoves me into the grasp of a couple of bystanders. "See what you've done, Sergeant Smith? The fruit of your leadership." His voice is low and explosive.

"Morrisey, you're meddling!"

I'm dragged backwards, out that flaming blue door with its flaming cross and all the flaming assholes who ever wanted it put there . . . and then I'm released. I stand there, motionless, with no energy left at all. For a long time I have no sense of where I am. There's just this pain . . . When I move, it's to a bench in front of the sickcall tent where I sit down and feel people stare and hesitate to come close to me.

TWENTY-FOUR

They changed the Military Payment Certificates, our paper money, at least three times while I was there. During these "secret" changes, the Vietnamese scrambled around making deals with their American friends to exchange their personal hoards for the new money, usually at a percentage. The Vietnamese weren't supposed to have any MPCs. The changes were secret in the hope that the black market might be severely curtailed, if not wiped out, and the native economy thus instantly stabilized. MPCs were redeemable at face value for dollars upon leaving Vietnam. They were paper gold, very valuable because everyone knew that the piaster, the native currency, was wildly inflated. It was all a game. One day we'd be carrying wallets full of red, blue, yellow money with pictures of airplanes on it, the next day, purple, green, and orange money with pictures of submarines and other ships on it . . . and so would the Vietnamese. It was a joke, like so many things there.

"Is Morrisey there?" a faint, native voice asks on the phone. It's eight thirty in the morning.

"Who's this, Thieu?"

"Yes . . ."

"Hey, Morrisey's not around now, Thieu. He's on some kind of call down at the South checkpoint—some kind of accident."

"When he be back?" There's a note of distress.

"Shit, man, I don't know."

There's silence at the other end of the line. "You still

there, Thieu? Look, I've got sickcall. Can you call back later?"

"O'Neill. They having MPC change."

"Is that right?" I should be surprised at learning this from a Vietnamese, particularly Thieu? "Thieu, that's strange. I haven't heard a damn thing about it. When is it supposed to happen?"

"Nine o'clock."

"No shit!"

There's another pause. "You help me, O'Neill?"

I'm instantly wary. "How?"

"We not get warned. Got lots of money to change." A suggestion of panic accompanies this declaration.

"Where are you, Thieu?" I'm stalling, trying to give myself time.

"Hamlet. Locked in. They not let us out. I give you ten percent."

He is panicked. "I don't want anything for it, Thieu, but I can do a little. How much do you have?"

I have to strain to hear his reply. "Five thousand dollar."

"What?"

"Five thousand!"

"No way, Thieu! I can't do that—they'd spot it immediately! That's more than I've made all year. No, I don't want twenty percent, either."

"What's he got, O'Neill?" a voice says. I turn and discover Kostek with a cup of coffee in his hand. "That Thieu?"

"Yeah. You hear anything about an MPC change?"

"They're setting up in the orderly room right now."

I clap my hand over the receiver. "I don't fucking believe it! It's the first time they ever succeeded in keeping it secret since I've been here!"

Kostek's eyes dart from me to the receiver. "What's he got?"

"Five grand."

"Give me that phone!" He snatches it and speaks into the receiver behind a cupped hand, as is his habit. "Thieu, this is Kostek. What's the deal?"

He listens intently while I watch. The patients at the counter are also engrossed, everyone momentarily forgetting our reasons for being here. "Yeah, I can round some guys up . . . but it'll have to be thirty percent, OK? Hey, Thieu, it's no easy thing, not on this short notice. Any of us have too much and they'll get suspicious. Thirty percent . . . OK? Now where can we get it through the fence?''

Kostek drops the receiver and starts for the door. ''You cover, O'Neill. I got to get some guys rounded up.''

''He's actually giving you thirty percent?''

''Fuck thirty percent!'' Suddenly, there's nothing but a rustling blue curtain in front of me. Kostek's disappeared.

''Name?'' I say to the next patient. It's not my problem, I tell myself, over and over.

The news of Kostek's coup spreads throughout the company, but the degree of Morrisey's distress is surprising. ''You let him do it!'' he says to me accusingly.

''Hey, man, that's Thieu's problem. Thieves among thieves. And what the hell do you care?''

''You don't know what this means, O'Neill! That wasn't just Thieu's money. It belonged to the owners of the bars and all the other shit. That's the hoard for the entire hamlet! They're fucked now! That stuff's like gold to them . . . and that's the end of Thieu. God knows who will end up running the place.''

''Where are you coming from, Morrisey? What's all this shit! Were you going to change all the money for him?''

He backs away. ''No . . . no, I couldn't have done anything for him except a little.''

''Which is just where I came in! I told him I'd do a little at no charge. And anyway, what difference does it make whether it becomes valueless in his hands, or is stolen here? Either way, he loses.'' I wipe my face on my sleeve.

''You're wrong. It's a lot worse that it was stolen. The rest can blame Thieu now.''

It takes us both a few moments to calm down. Behind me, the sickcall line snakes out the door and well into the yard. Everyone showed up after the change and it's turned into a beaut of a day. The phone rings.

''Is Kostek there?'' I recognize Thieu's voice.

''No, he's not.''

''He get money, O'Neill?''

''Jesus, I don't know.'' I lie and feel miserable.

''Can you check?'' He sounds desperate.

''Thieu, I got sickcall! You'll have to call back later.'' I hang up and avoid Morrisey's eyes.

''That was Thieu?''

''Yeah, he wanted Kostek.''.

Kostek barges into the room, flushed, sweaty, beaming. He chuckles to himself.

"Hey, Kostek," I say over my shoulder. "Thieu just called."

"Fuck him!"

"Yeah, well you tell him. I don't want to be bothered."

"Kostek, did you guys keep all that money?"

"What if we did, Morrisey?"

"You're screwing those people."

"That little gook's screwed us in ways we'll never know . . . and the same for those bitches who run the bars. What are you, the whores' White Knight?"

"Give them their money, Kostek! Thirty percent's nothing to sneeze at."

"Fuck yourself, Morrisey!" He shoves between us to the desk and sits down just as the phone rings. He snatches the receiver. "Yes? . . . yeah, well, if you want your money, come and get it!" He slams the instrument down. "That little bastard wouldn't dare go to the CO. It would finish him."

"You already have, Kostek," Morrisey says quietly and leaves the room. Kostek watches him through the screen with a suggestion of anxiety I've not seen before.

It's a scorching afternoon. Even with the fans going, the inside of the treatment room's sweltering. Morrisey's examining shrapnel wounds in an ARVN's ass. I go over to him and whisper, "Thieu's in the orderly room. He arrived about half an hour ago asking for Howard."

Morrisey grabs a towel, wipes his face, then pulls me across the room. "You're sure of that?" he says, studying me carefully.

"I was getting my mail when he came."

"Jesus!" He flings the towel onto a table and walks back to the ARVN who's on his belly, pants down around his knees, obviously feeling ridiculous.

"Have we got anybody in this tent who can open a goddam suture kit?" Brock barks. He's holding an X ray in front of one of the surgical lamps and glaring at Newell who has been unsuccessfully trying to undo a suture kit ever since I entered the tent. A GI is sitting on a table nearby, pressing a wad of gauze against his shoulder and looking with annoyance at the doctor.

Newell continues to fumble tremulously with the tape on the suture kit, oblivious of Brock's growing anger. A second

GI, a litter patient, his arm in an inflatable splint, dozes as he waits for the first helicopter south.

Brock drops the X ray on a table and watches Newell's futile efforts. "Jesus, why can't I have a 91-C who isn't a vegetable!" Suddenly, he marches across the room and pushes Newell aside. The utensils fall out of their wrapping and clatter to the floor. Confused, Newell stumbles backward with the empty blue cloth. He regains his balance and tries to focus on Brock.

"Damn dope-head!" Brock grumbles.

Morrisey grabs Newell and points at one of the new medics. "Come here, man! Newell, you're going back to your tent."

"No goddam way for an officer . . ." Newell sputters.

"Take him," Morrisey orders. "And find someone to sit with him, even if you have to do it yourself."

Brock's retrieved another suture kit from the cabinet. The litter patient's awake, his head to one side, watching. The GI with the shoulder wound is making no attempt to hide his disgust. Brock's hands tremble as he unwraps the kit. He seems puffy in the face. There are deep lines beneath his eyes and the tangled mass of hair looks shabby. He told me the other day he'd given up smoking—it seemed important to him.

"Why don't you let me take care of this man, sir," Morrisey says.

"I'm getting goddam sick of all these drugs, Morrisey!"

"Yes, sir."

"I mean it! That Newell's a vegetable! I can't protect him anymore. I can't be responsible."

"Yes, sir."

Brock starts for the back door. "The X ray on that guy's OK. Got a laceration to his right shoulder, but I can't see any metal. A few sutures ought to take care of it . . . and that ARVN's got shrapnel in his back as well as his ass. You need me, I'll be in my tent." The door closes.

The ARVN looks frightened.

Morrisey pulls the surgical lamp over and tells the GI to lie down on his left side. He lifts the gauze from the shoulder and examines the cut closely—it's more of a tear. The blood seeps into the crystal light beneath his probe.

"Am I going to get out of here alive?" the soldier asks sarcastically.

339

"You will if you don't move."

"Hey, no shit, man! This is nothing. I can get fixed up at my battalion."

"Stop worrying!" Morrisey flicks a used sponge into a nearby trash can, scarcely repressing his anger.

The new medic rushes into the tent. "I got a guy," he says breathlessly.

"Good," Morrisey snaps. "Now why don't you go to work on that ARVN." He's concentrating on the GI's wound. A few moments pass, and then he turns his head to find the new man still behind him. "Well?"

"I think maybe I should get one of the doctors . . ."

"No. You do it yourself! You'll be OK—you've been doing fine."

Morrisey's started to suture the wound when the GI speaks again. "Glad I'm not a gook."

Kostek, Gerhard, Anderson—the company clerk, Dunn . . . there were two or three others at least, but I don't remember their names. What difference does it make now? But it was enjoyable to see Kostek sweat for some reason other than the heat. Those piggy eyes of his were scared—he smelled of fear. Everyone got fined and busted a grade. Thieu got his money back but lost his job as interpreter, lost the possibility of any work for the Americans on the base. Naturally, Howard saw to that. There were rumors that the ARVN command was going to pack him off to an infantry battalion. He was ruined, and so, I discovered, was something else . . .

"Maybe you no need Thieu," Annie says matter-of-factly, but not hopefully. She's no Miss Lahn, no little girl, but it's upsetting to hear her speak now with a voice that is at once soft and dying. That isn't the Annie we foster. Annie's standing outside the back door, behind the bar. I look at the bright sun on her orange *ao dai*, and on the matching headband. She seems worlds away from this empty, silent room. I didn't intend not to be heard when I came through the front door —none of this is intentional!

"I tried something else," Morrisey says to her. "I tried going to the MP directly. He said he'd do it but he tripled the price."

"He want more money?"

"It's not that simple. I've been paying with outdated penicillin. He wants a case each time, outdated or not, or I don't get through the fence."

There's a long silence. "I just can't see you anymore," he says at last. His voice doesn't sound natural. She remains quiet as she waits for him to finish, waits for them both to fully comprehend what's being said. Finally, he reaches out and touches her lightly on her cheek. "It isn't just the cost —I haven't got that kind of money, sure—but it's the penicillin, the whole bit with Thieu and that fucking MP—the MP in particular. He makes me feel like shit. He asked who I was seeing, where you live. The price went up when I didn't tell him. God . . ." His voice breaks and he hesitates.

"Richie."

"Annie, this is the last goddam thing in the world I want." It's as though there's an invisible barrier between them. I can almost see them lean against it, wanting to let go. I'm ashamed now, humiliated at my intrusion. A welter of other feelings surge inside me including anger—anger at Morrisey, and at Annie.

"It's OK, Richie. You go home soon."

He groans.

Suddenly she laughs.

"It isn't funny!"

"I know . . . I know. I not laughing at you. Americans win war," she adds and turns away from him.

"I don't think so."

"But you winning! New highway, not much shooting here now, more soldier. You tell me it change, too!"

He shakes his head. Those marvelous eyes devour her, and then she's against him and he's stroking her long, dark hair.

I'm nauseous.

I let them find me. He looks awful—absolutely drained.

And hours later, exhausted by the emotions and talk, and then by a silence that neither Morrisey nor I seems able to break, I feel smothered by knowledge I didn't want. I can't stand to be here much longer . . .

"Going to go to Howard?" Morrisey asks. There's no anxiety attached to the question—simple curiosity. I don't think he really cares at all.

"Now why the fuck do you think I'd do something like that?"

"Because you're upset."

"I'm not that kind of turd, Morrisey!"

"So how did I betray you, O'Neill? That's what you think, isn't it?"

I don't answer. I don't move a muscle.

"So I bought my way into her—I bribed your 'Johnny Mirrors' with a little help from Thieu. I left my duties. I risked letting someone die because I was taking care of my own needs, and hers. Is that it?"

When I still don't reply, he says, "I'm not Mathias. I can't stay in this fucking country! God damn you, O'Neill! What do you want from me—you and all the other bastards in this place?"

"I didn't think I wanted anything."

"That's bullshit! Absolute bullshit, you sonuvabitch! You thought I was above corruption, didn't you? That *I* thought I was above corruption!" He's almost laughing, a hideous, bitter distortion. "I could do no wrong."

"I didn't say that." My voice sounds harsh and strange.

"You didn't have to."

"Well, I should have known better."

"I'm not Mathias!" he storms. "I'm not trapped here! I don't have to stay! I'm not going to die here!"

I get up and leave the tent, feeling proud of myself for a moment, proud that I can be righteous as I crash past his anguished face with my name on his lips. *But the pain wasn't for me or anything I did, damn fool that I am! It was grief for what he was and wasn't, regardless of me or anyone else.*

But I felt a lot of revulsion, too. He told me about Annie's sister with her one leg and arm, lying on the other side of a wall in that mansion where Thieu and God knows how many others lived, where the coughing, crying, and endless stirrings of all those people, their unseen presence choked off anything romantic and beautiful—only he didn't say that, didn't think it. It wasn't just rutting to him. I guess if he wanted her that bad, he could have found beauty anywhere.

He said her sister had the most beautiful face he'd ever seen and that he could feel her eyes even in the darkness, that it made him impotent sometimes and Annie didn't understand. What he felt then wasn't the sister's knowledge and fear of his ability to take Annie away, but her recognition of his own inevitable departure.

His talking about Annie and her sister. I couldn't look at Annie the same way again, not after that . . . The way she held him. She was just another gook, like all the rest of them.

TWENTY-FIVE

It was awful after I came back from R&R. I mean, with everything else, there had to be casualties, too. Maybe without them, it would have been different . . . but how can I say that? We got the work done but we bickered incessantly among ourselves, crabbed about who wasn't showing up for litters, who was getting stuck with all the work details, who was getting a chance to sleep, argued about something all the time. So much for our outstanding unit! Fuck that smug, sonuvabitch of a chaplain! He would never have admitted the truth even if he knew.

Morrisey was in rough shape, and so much worse after that business with Annie. He tried going back to the club a day or two later, taking up his old seat, his old habit of reading and being there, as though nothing had happened . . . like all he'd given her was a pair of earrings. Annie tried, too—for two or three days, but then she became distant, at first only with him, then with all of us. It was as though her sister was right. Suddenly Annie knew that Morrisey would be gone forever, that there had been no hope with him, and, by extension, any of us—that everything was an enticing, terrible dream.

Morrisey was miserable after that. He didn't say much to anyone, no more than he had to. He and Smith had a couple of arguments—real beauties. Like everyone else, Smith was on edge, beginning to sense, maybe, that things had slipped out of his grasp. He found fault with everything and everybody. At one point, Morrisey told him to get off his back, that he had bitched things up enough, a remark so close to outright

*insubordination that I was afraid Morrisey would lose what
frantic control he had left.*

*More than a few of us had begun to think that when
Morrisey went home, things might get better, if for no other
reason than Smith might calm down. Smith was obviously
convinced that Morrisey was the source of his problems, his
failure. To have tolerated Morrisey's outspokenness as long
as he had was a fundamental mistake. At least once during
those last days, Smith deliberately provoked the anger, hoping,
I suppose, to be given the excuse he needed. Predictably,
however, he lost command of his emotions and became his
own victim.*

*Smith had no business doing what he did to that company.
It was no different from cutting off ears. I understand that
now.*

"Did you know about that ARVN body?" Smith asks. He's
called me to the commo bunker directly before morning
formation.

"No, Sergeant."

"Well why don't you?"

"I must have been asleep, Sergeant. I've had four hours
sleep in the last three days!" Just like that I'm popping off! I
look away from him for a moment and collect myself. "I
think Morrisey told me there was something coming in but
that he'd take care of it."

"Where's Morrisey now?"

"Gone to bed, Sarge. He was up all night."

"I want him up here, ASAP!"

"Please, Sergeant . . . none of us has had much sleep."

"What's the matter, O'Neill? Go get him!"

At the top of the ramp leading out of the commo bunker, I
submit unwillingly to a yawn; this mundane need, like the
early, brilliant sunshine, contradicts my irritation and a deeper
anxiety. Dunn and Smith converse urgently in the sepulchral
room below. Their voices echo up the long, wooden passage-
way. I pass Gittoni, heading for the bunker and work. He
waves without enthusiasm.

I find Morrisey in the latrine, laboring, while Papasan
bangs and thumps the other tubs impatiently as he waits for
him to finish. Smoke curls around the wooden edifice.

"Hey, Richie."

He looks out the screen, over the top louver. "Hey, Jon.

What's up?'' His voice sounds strained suggesting not only fatigue, but a reluctance, even fear of what my answer might be.

"Did they bring an ARVN body in last night?"

"Oh, Christ!" He claps a hand against his forehead. "I forgot all about it! There were four ambulatories that came in at the same time. It was all I could do to patch them up and get them the hell out of here. I'm sorry. That's an awful thing to have to deal with—it must stink by now."

"Hey, I don't care. It's Smith. He wants to see you."

"Look! I completely forgot about it!"

"I know, man, but Smith wants to see you. He's in the commo bunker."

"I need him like I need a hole in the head." The door opens and Morrisey steps to the ground. He's shaking.

"Relax, Richie!" I cry as a dreadful excitement seizes me. "It's nothing!" But I know the lie even if I don't hear it.

"The hell it's nothing! I'm sick of his shit! Of everything he's done to us! Where the fuck was he last night when we were busting our asses?" He pushes me aside and charges off.

"Richie!" I catch up with him and grab his sleeve, only to have him tear it away. His eyes seem glazed as though the rage he has suppressed so long has gripped him at last, is guiding him. He's not unaware of it—he's decided to submit, to acquiesce.

I can hear his feet pound on the ramp as I plunge into the dim light behind him and then into the cathedral depths of the bunker where the sun streams from high windows. When I overtake him, he's glaring down the room at Dunn, who's seated in his lawn chair.

Off to one side, Smith suddenly becomes alert. With his sleekness he reminds me of a corpulent, cynical monk.

. . . and it's as though I'm in a car again, a child on the rear seat looking up at the windows, and the world is being driven past me. All I can see are the tops of the telephone poles and the wires that rise and fall, sail by with the world while I lie suspended in space.

My hand reaches out, touches a damp shirt. "Tell him, Richie!" I shout. "We're tired! Explain . . ." But he's looking at Dunn, not Smith.

"You really fucked up this time, Morrisey," Dunn says and scowls. Another voice simultaneously assaults Morrisey, challenges the taut figure with his fists balled by his side.

But he doesn't hear the second voice.

"It stinks like hell!" Dunn goes on. "Why didn't you call Graves?"

"Stop sucking ass, you bastard!"

"You watch that goddam tongue, Morrisey!" Smith screams. His face contorts, turns red with restrained fury.

Morrisey whirls to his right and I begin to yell. I hear myself yell.

Smith is on the floor. I watch his hands jerk wildly, then his face—his eyes seem huge. That's Morrisey on top. Those are his hands around Smith's throat, but I don't move . . . not through this silence. I'm loving it. Smith is dying.

Smith's hands slap the floor convulsively. I want to laugh, and laugh, and . . .

"Sweet Jesus, Morrisey!" Someone hurtles past me and lands on Morrisey, shatters my silence, my acceptance. The noise is real, the scream, everything is real all of a sudden. It's Gittoni. I didn't see him!

"Oh, Jesus," Gittoni yells as he locks Morrisey's neck in the crook of an arm and tries to yank him loose. Smith's face has turned blue; Gittoni's face is wet, streaming. "Jesus, Morrisey, you stupid bastard! Let go! You've killed him."

He stands in front of the orderly room, hands cuffed behind his back, looking pale and shabby, his fatigue shirt torn open to his belt. The yard's full of jeeps, military policemen, and CID officials.

An MP stands on either side of Morrisey. A third, standing behind him, wears mirrored sunglasses that flash in the sun like unearthly eyes. In front of the steps of the orderly room, a small crowd surrounds Captain Howard and a silver-haired man in jungle fatigues with no rank on his collar. I watch from the NCO bunker, watch a dazed friend. Something propels me forward. I watch from the NCO bunker, watch a dazed friend. Something propels me forward.

"You! O'Neill!" Howard shouts. "Stay away from that man!"

I hear the soft progress of my boots on the dusty ground, feel the hot blood rush to my ears. "Morrisey . . . ."

"Soldier!" An MP unsnaps his holster. A radio squawks in one of the jeeps.

Suddenly Morrisey's eyes are focused on me. He's seeing me! His lips move.

"What?" I move more quickly, knowing that I must hear.

"Tell my family what happened!" he cries.

"Morrisey!"

"Tell them I didn't want to die here . . . I hate this fucking place!"

"Yes, goddammit, I will! But don't leave! Goddam you, you sonuvabitch! You can't go away, you can't leave!" Hands seize my arms and pull me back. I lurch forward, kick my feet and strike something hard. Someone groans close to my ear.

"Get that prisoner out of here!"

Morrisey's head turns briefly with a slight twisting of his mouth. Then he's yanked away, out of my sight and more hands are on me. My back strikes a sandbag and I'm pinned. I stare at watery blues and greens in the canopy above me, listen to the grunts of my captors, feel and smell their sweat and mine, listen to Howard holler to have me brought into the orderly room. There's the gunning of a jeep engine, and then the sound fades quickly down the road toward Highway 10.

How many times I wondered what he saw in me, why he included me? It's as though he made some judgment, some decision about me that very first day in front of the helicopter when I stood immobilized and appalled. Maybe he thought I could learn outrage, too, learn to speak my mind. What did he see in me? He wasn't usually wrong, as it turned out—except about me, my timidity, or fear, or whatever it is. Cowardice? I wish I'd never met him.

I started a letter to them, his parents, started to do what he wanted . . . it's still around someplace, unfinished. They couldn't understand, even if I could explain. Why did he saddle me with it?

Smith looked old when I last saw him. His body lay on the bunker floor, the face pale, unnaturally still, flaccid in the sunlight. He was on his back staring fatuously at the ceiling; his mouth hung open with an uncharacteristic slackness. His uniform still looked immaculate though, untouched, unwrinkled despite what had happened. It just looked too large for the shriveled corpse that had come to inhabit it.

When Howard busted me that same morning, right down to private, I stared unabashedly at him, never flinched, and hated the bastard. It was the most pure and positive feeling I've ever had.

*   *   *

It should be a lovely day, I mean the moon shone all night, but its grey beyond the small windows above the sink, and the road glistens. Casey's wearing a blue dress that ends six inches above her knees and a pair of brown suede shoes with crepe soles—no socks or stockings. Her skin seems much too white. Automatically, I look for varicose veins.

A few minutes ago I watched her dress, something I found curiously moving. She pulled on her panties first; the soft hair disappeared within that bright yellow slash of nylon. Then she slipped a bra up under her breasts. The nipples were very prominent. As she leaned forward slightly and reached behind her back to hook the bra, she seemed distracted. The possibility that I had possessed her in any fashion seemed implausible. I was sprawled on the bed with nothing on, and she kept insisting that I get dressed but wouldn't look directly at me.

She's exasperated, but more with herself than me, I imagine, for having allowed my presence in the first place. She's trying to disguise her vexation by banging the cupboard doors, slamming the icebox. She manages to offer me an orange, but I refuse. She takes one out for herself.

"You didn't sleep much," she says.

"I'm used to it."

"Don't you go to work?" she asks with something just short of desperation.

"No, not today. Some kind of federal holiday."

"No war today. The army's got a day off."

"Something like that." Actually, I don't consider the army work. Driving to the base through Trenton, stopping at Dunkin' Donuts on the east side of the city, then going on out, under the Turnpike and into the dying farmlands with the ratty houses and Land for Sale signs isn't work—it's a matter of endurance. There's a back road I take sometimes. It winds through countryside where the land is still well-tended, the houses old but cared for. Remnants.

"Look! Have you got everything of yours from upstairs?"

"Yes." The idea of going back into that silent attic by myself is devastating. If there were anything still up there, I'd leave it rather than climb those steps alone.

"I've got to be going."

"Can I come see you again tonight?"

She's quartering the orange, her movements brisk. She doesn't falter. "No. I have a guy I see pretty regularly, OK? I got a date with him tonight."

I find myself thinking of the body beneath her blue dress. I don't like her particularly, but maybe she's alright. For a while there, in the car last night, I could have liked her . . . but I need her. I want to tear her clothes off and put myself inside her again. "Tomorrow night?"

"No!" She shakes her head.

"How about next week sometime?"

"Look, I'm going to be late for work . . . it was nice, OK?"

"You don't have to lie."

She snaps out the light. It looks as though it might rain again any minute. She's waiting at the front door, holding it open.

It's cool outside when I step onto the porch. She grabs a raincoat, pulls the door shut, turns the key, says goodbye, and walks out to her car, an older model Chevrolet. She starts it up and drives away without looking at me again.

I feel bereft, but there's no reason. I've lost no one. I knew it would be this way. It's been like this for months now—any leave-taking by someone else, or by me. Going away. I grab the corner post of the porch and look down into the front yard at a wilted badminton net.

(It really started the day I left for Vietnam, almost a year and a half ago. I pushed open the door of the waiting room and stepped into the blazing sunlight. The pavement deflected the heat and smelled of oil and fuel. In the distance I glimpsed the hazy line of green of early fall woods, and beyond them, fields and tobacco barns.

The last of the passengers were climbing the steps when I started out. I walked the two hundred or so feet alone, my shoulders aching with the tension of not turning around. The terminal glass was a huge, dark eye at my back. The steel rail of the stairway was hot. At the top, a stewardess stood with her hand on the door.

I had never seen my father cry before.

I relented as the plane started to roll, but if they were at the windows, I didn't see them, and when I heard their voices again, on the phone some ten hours later, they had no reality—they were gone.)

I dislike flying commercial now, flying by jet plane. It's a melancholy experience, especially at night because there's no sensation of flying, only floating, watching the lights of San Francisco, or New York, or some other city (but maybe only

*a farmhouse on the prairies) drift into sight then spread like
an alluring, cancerous growth. Or places slide away behind,
become shrunken and remote, something missed . . .*

*And this anger that's inside me, just below the surface. It's
no more than the ability, power if you will, to project instantly all events to their logical, if not always actual,
conclusion: violence-brutal, savage violence. At the slightest
provocation, I can see people as they will be if they're not
careful. Not as they think they are, or wish to be.*

*"And I saw one of his heads as it were, wounded to death;
and his deadly wound was healed . . ." Listen to me! I once
laughed at Lucius and all his rantings.*

*It starts to rain. I climb into my car as large drops tap on
the roof. Within moments, it's pouring. I drive through one of
the small river villages. It feels empty in the early morning, a
world of greys and greens as sheets of rain sweep across the
highway, the yards, and through the trees. I glimpse an
occasional splash of white, someone's home, old and secure,
a revolutionary ghost that is like a yearning, like autumn in
this most seemingly durable of places. A relic. Maybe a small
fire crackles in a fireplace. Or maybe the hearth is cold
because everyone's gone to work and only a trace of old
wood smoke lingers.*

*I'm crying. There's no reason. I wipe my eyes with my
arm, then shift gears. The car crashes through puddle after
puddle. I am sitting* in the rear of the jeep when the rains
come. All day the clouds have been laboring in the sky while
the shattered land sweltered beneath. In midafternoon they
break.

Our escort, another jeep with a machinegun mounted on it,
quickly disappears in the streams of water that tear at the red
ground. We're only a few minutes from the village. In less
than sixty days, I'll be going home—a PFC, the same rank I
was when I arrived almost a year ago, when Morrisey was
here, and Jenkins, Navarra, Mendez . . . Smith.

Dim hulks of jungle roll past, the dreary monotony broken
once by the ruin of a temple with thick, white walls. I can
hear helicopters flying overhead, but can't see them.

With a clatter of boards, the jeep crosses a wooden bridge.
There's a guard hut at the far end of the bridge constructed of
green sandbags and surrounded by coils of barbed wire. A
sodden Vietnamese flag dangles from a pole on top of the
hut. An ARVN soldier leaning in the doorway flashes us the

peace sign as we go by. Kostek, riding shotgun, gives him the finger.

The ruined jungle marches out of the rain again and follows the road, its tree trunks strewn as though ripped from the ground and hurled by enraged gods. I'm viewing the remains of chemicals and cannon feasts: scraps left from the defoliants and the steady, inevitable shellings that begin at the plantation every night. The earth and what fragile life it sustains has been devoured.

The village creeps into view, humbled by the density of the sky and the miracle of its own survival. A few wood huts with Coca-Cola aluminum siding are scattered along the roadside. More peace signs, many smiles, the shanties suddenly punctuated by more substantial housing, the village dispensary with its blue gates and aura of vacant menace, windows in the village without glass, louvers over doors, overhanging roofs and tiled floors; the buildings spill their human contents into the street.

Someone shouts, "Hey, GI!" A girl mounts a motor-scooter and drives out from underneath a stall. She's wearing a white silk top and black trousers. The scooter swings in behind the jeep. As the rain pours down my face, rolls over my lips and drenches me, the girl on the scooter seems to become unclothed.

Incredulous, I watch the wet silk top turn transparent. The color of her skin, her breasts, the darker brown of her nipples emerge. Fighting the mud behind the jeep, the girl smiles when she spots my concentration.

I can't stop looking at her. I see her laugh and begin to laugh myself, yanking my hat off and twisting it in my hands as the rain flows through my hair.

We pass the ARVN compound, the stone tower, the concertina wire, the Claymore mines, and swing onto Highway 10. The girl still splashes in our wake, still laughs in the downpour. Gradually, she begins to fall behind; then I see her pull off the road. She waves and turns back toward the village.

I grab the tops of the front seats. "Take me back!" I yell at my companions. They look at each other, the driver shrugs, and Kostek laughs uproariously. He's been stoned all day. The jeep turns around.

She's almost to the market place when we catch up with her. She glances over her shoulder, sees me, and leans her head back. Her long black hair hangs down in a sodden tangle, and beads of water flow over her smooth, uplifted face. A fleck of gold pegged to an earlobe glints among the plastered strands of hair.

The rain begins to subside as we follow the scooter into the market, around the fountain and up the side street into the ARVN compound. The center of the compound is a sea of mud bordered by two rows of long, one-storey barracks that have been partitioned into individual apartments. The gates to the compound have sagged in the muck. Mobs of children pick their way among trucks, scooters, and litter. Women hang from the windows and squat on the verandas that front the buildings, raising their own cackle. The long lines of sandbags piled waist-high in rather shoddy fashion along the length of the verandas are broken by dark, narrow doorways.

The girl leans her scooter against a veranda and waits for me. Ignoring Kostek's and the driver's taunts, I jump over the side of the jeep and feel my boots sink in the mud. As I approach the veranda, I pass an ARVN soldier. He salutes me.

He's much smaller than I am. His fatigue pants look like leotards, the M–16 in his hand like a toy. I ignore the salute and slosh on.

The girl places a cool hand in mine as I enter the room. In the dim interior I can just make out a table and two small children with large, round eyes. Gradually, I see cooking utensils heaped on the floor, others in ammunition boxes fastened to the wall. Several mats and some pillows are scattered about. A curtain, suspended from a piece of rope, is pushed back against one wall. The curtain serves as a partition for a small area that contains a solitary army cot and some fatigues hanging from hooks.

I'm bewildered.

The girl, sensing this, tugs gently at my hand, leads me around the table and down some wooden steps into a bunker. Cool air with a smell of mildew engulfs me as I'm led into the darkness. I hear her fumble, then there's light from a single bulb hanging by its wire. She turns and faces me, leans back against some crates. My soggy clothes press against my groin. I cease to notice the stench of the bunker.

I want to take off all my clothes and stand free before her. The girl remains silent as she watches me kneel and untie my boots, then begin to unbutton my shirt. And I do feel free as I stand naked in this bunker and feel the rough planks of the floor beneath my feet, the mud oozing up under my weight, creeping about my toes, the painful buoyancy of my erection.

I reach under her blouse for her breasts and fasten my mouth to one of the nipples. She moves away, slides out of her pants and pushes herself up on one of the crates. I'm still bent over slightly, looking down, but now at the head of my penis against a hairless vulva. I feel sick with revulsion, fearing some awful, ugly incurable disease.

She grabs my penis with both her hands, squeezes it, presses it against the lips, shakes it from side to side until suddenly I slide in, am pulled in as she clamps her legs around me with astounding strength and violence. Crossing her feet over my buttocks, she starts to jerk upward against me. I don't know where I am anymore . . . everything's unreal: her hairless organ, the brownish lips eating my whiteness, swallowing, devouring, then releasing it, sucking at it.

I collapse forward and catch the earthen wall behind her with the flat of my hands while she grinds, jerks, and stares dispassionately at me. I flood her. It's involuntary, for I no longer wish it, but it rises slowly, then pours out of me. No sooner have I begun than she slides away and pulls her pants up, leaving me spanning the crate with my hands against the wall.

My head aches savagely as I remain in this position for several moments, dribbling onto the floor. Finally, I push myself upright. My clothing looks like a deflated corpse. The girl waits at the bottom of the steps and gazes at my naked white body as I dress, her face inscrutable and older.

I'm mashing my hat back onto my head when she speaks. "That no freebee."

Without comment, I pull out my wallet and hand her two thousand piasters, the going price—everybody knows it— then numbly start up the stairs behind her. Someone in the room overhead shouts in Vietnamese. The black, swathed hips inches from my face sway to a stop. The woman snaps a reply.

I see a pair of army boots behind the table when my eyes come level with the floor. Seized by panic, I remember I've left my weapon in the jeep. I'm trapped! Breathing rapidly, I try to control my confusion. Maybe I can barge through like a football player.

But by now I've reached the top step and find myself

looking down at an ARVN soldier. He yells something at the woman. She shouts back and waves the piasters in her husband's face. He reaches for the money but she snatches it away and proceeds to drown him in a torrent of verbal abuse.

The ARVN slowly shrinks under the woman's onslaught until he can bear no more. I'm standing at the top of the stairs, motionless, clearheaded now, and unafraid. He pulls out a chair, sits down at the table with his two silent children, and buries his face in his arms.

I see now that the woman is twenty, or thirty, or forty years old—I can't tell. She keeps shrieking at the ARVN.

At the doorway, I tense for a moment because her husband's probably armed . . . but then I know nothing will happen. I step out onto the veranda into bright sunshine. The sky is a deep blue, cloudless, the glare blinding. My two companions are waiting in the jeep.

Kostek laughs that soft, mocking staccato laugh . . . soon they're both laughing, shaking their heads and laughing.

About the Author

Rob Riggan, a medic in Vietnam in the late sixties, wrote FREE FIRE ZONE because "the war wouldn't go away. I set out to put my life together again by the only means I had that I felt I might trust." Riggan now lives with his wife in western Massachusetts, in a small town where he is a part-time policeman and tax assessor. He is at work on a new novel.